THE PILOT

DISCOVER OTHER TITLES BY SUSAN STOKER

Delta Force Guardians Series

Rescuing Brinley (September 2026)
Rescuing Cypress (January 2027)
Rescuing Talia (February 2027)
Rescuing Amber (May 2027)
Rescuing Kisha (July 2027)
Rescuing Heidi (November 2027)
Rescuing Juniper (March 2028)
Rescuing Kristin (May 2028)

Rescue Angels Series

Keeping Laryn
Keeping Amanda
Keeping Zita
Keeping Penny
Keeping Kara
Keeping Jennifer (November 2026)

Alpha Cove Series

The Soldier
The Sailor
The Pilot
The Guardsman (March 2027)

Game of Chance Series

The Protector
The Royal

PRAISE FOR SUSAN STOKER

"I will read anything Susan Stoker puts out . . . because I know it's going to be amazing!"

—Riley Edwards, *USA Today* bestselling author

"Susan Stoker never fails to pull me out of a reading slump. With heat, action, and suspense, she weaves an incredible tale that sucks me in and doesn't let go."

—Jessica Prince, *USA Today* bestselling author

"One thing I love about Susan Stoker's books is that she knows how to deliver a perfect HEA while still making sure the villain gets what he/she deserves!"

—T.M. Frazier, *New York Times* bestselling author

"Susan Stoker's characters come alive on the page!"

—Elle James, *New York Times* bestselling author

"When you pick up a Susan Stoker book, you know exactly what you're going to get . . . a hot alpha hero and a smart, sassy heroine. I can't get enough!"

—Jessica Hawkins, *USA Today* bestselling author

"Suspenseful storytelling with characters you want as friends!"

—Meli Raine, *USA Today* bestselling author

"Susan Stoker knows what women want. A hot hero who needs to save a damsel in distress . . . even if she can save herself."

—CD Reiss, *New York Times* bestselling author

The Hero

The Lumberjack

Ace Security Series

Claiming Grace

Claiming Alexis

Claiming Bailey

Claiming Felicity

Claiming Sarah

Mountain Mercenaries Series

Defending Allye

Defending Chloe

Defending Morgan

Defending Harlow

Defending Everly

Defending Zara

Defending Raven

Silverstone Series

Trusting Skylar

Trusting Taylor

Trusting Molly

Trusting Cassidy

SEAL of Protection: Alliance Series

Protecting Remi

Protecting Wren

Protecting Josie

Protecting Maggie

Protecting Addison

Protecting Kelli

Protecting Bree

The Refuge Series

Deserving Alaska

Deserving Henley

Deserving Reese

Deserving Cora

Deserving Lara

Deserving Maisy

Deserving Ryleigh

SEAL Team Hawaii Series

Finding Elodie

Finding Lexie

Finding Kenna

Finding Monica

Finding Carly

Finding Ashlyn

Finding Jodelle

Eagle Point Search & Rescue Series

Searching for Lilly

Searching for Elsie

Searching for Bristol

Searching for Caryn

Searching for Finley

Searching for Heather

Searching for Khloe

Delta Force Heroes Series

Rescuing Rayne

Rescuing Aimee (novella)

Rescuing Emily
Rescuing Harley
Marrying Emily (novella)
Rescuing Kassie
Rescuing Bryn
Rescuing Casey
Rescuing Sadie (novella)
Rescuing Wendy
Rescuing Mary
Rescuing Macie
Rescuing Annie

Badge of Honor: Texas Heroes Series

Justice for Mackenzie
Justice for Mickie
Justice for Corrie
Justice for Laine (novella)
Shelter for Elizabeth
Justice for Boone
Shelter for Adeline
Shelter for Sophie
Justice for Erin
Justice for Milena
Shelter for Blythe
Justice for Hope
Shelter for Quinn
Shelter for Koren
Shelter for Penelope

Delta Team Two Series

Shielding Gillian
Shielding Kinley
Shielding Aspen

Shielding Jayme (novella)
Shielding Riley
Shielding Devyn
Shielding Ember
Shielding Sierra

SEAL of Protection Series

Protecting Caroline
Protecting Alabama
Protecting Fiona
Marrying Caroline (novella)
Protecting Summer
Protecting Cheyenne
Protecting Jessyka
Protecting Julie (novella)
Protecting Melody
Protecting the Future
Protecting Kiera (novella)
Protecting Alabama's Kids (novella)
Protecting Dakota
Protecting Tex

SEAL of Protection: Legacy Series

Securing Caite
Securing Brenae (novella)
Securing Sidney
Securing Piper
Securing Zoey
Securing Avery
Securing Kalee
Securing Jane (novella)

THE PILOT

SUSAN STOKER

Montlake

This is a work of fiction. Names, characters, organizations, places, events, and incidents are either products of the author's imagination or are used fictitiously. Otherwise, any resemblance to actual persons, living or dead, is purely coincidental.

Published by Montlake, Seattle

www.apub.com

EU product safety contact:
Amazon Media EU S. à r.l.
38, avenue John F. Kennedy, L-1855 Luxembourg
amazonpublishing-gpsr@amazon.com

ISBN-13: 9781662527333 (paperback)
ISBN-13: 9781662527326 (digital)

Cover design by Hang Le
Cover image: © FTAPE LIMITED; © JHON CLAUD / Shutterstock

Printed in the United States of America

THE PILOT

Chapter One

Harper stared blankly at the Walmart store at the other end of the parking lot. She was parked all the way in the back of the lot, under a light to be safe. Her adrenaline was still coursing through her body after the fight with her dad earlier in the evening.

She wasn't even sure *how* the argument had started. All she knew was that she'd needed some space. Needed to get away. And her dad had the audacity to order her to leave . . . which was fine with her, since she was already halfway out the door.

Sighing, Harper closed her eyes and rested her head on the seat behind her. How had she ended up this way? In high school, she was part of the popular crowd, smart and with a ton of friends.

Well . . . she'd *thought* they were friends. The girls she'd grown up with, who she'd thought would stay in touch forever, seemed to disappear entirely a few months after graduation. Sure, they'd gone their separate ways, but Harper honestly hadn't thought that would matter.

She'd moved to New York City, ready to take on the world. She'd had aspirations of getting into modeling, which was ridiculous. She wasn't nearly skinny enough, liked sweets a bit too much, and while she was five foot ten, plenty tall enough to be a model, she was told she didn't have the "right look." Whatever that meant.

But Harper was stubborn, like her dad, and she'd refused to give up. She worked crappy jobs that barely paid the bills while attempting to get the one big break that would make her famous.

What a joke.

All moving to the city had ever gotten her was heartache.

Except for Kash.

Her boy was literally the only reason she was still breathing today. There were plenty of times when she'd wanted to give up. To throw herself in front of a subway train and end it all. But her little boy would have had no one. So she kept going, even when she wanted to quit, because of Kash.

She loved that kid more than she'd ever thought possible. He was a bright spot in her otherwise bleak life. Every time she lost a job—the buses were running behind and she was fired for being late one too many times, a boss thought she owed him sex just for hiring her, or the hours didn't work out with Kash's schedule—she'd think about moving back to Maine, putting her pride aside and asking for help. But she always seemed to find another job right when she was at her lowest.

Except for that last time.

She'd lost their apartment, as shitty as it was, because she had no money for rent. She'd gone to a few shelters, but having Kash with her made things a little more tricky. And none of them really felt safe.

Then one night, when she and Kash were sleeping in her car—again—she'd heard his little stomach growling, because she didn't have money to get them anything for dinner. And Harper was done.

She'd put her pride aside and asked her dad if she could move home.

Harper had known it would be difficult. Part of the reason she'd left home at eighteen was because of her dad. He was strict and judgmental. Never seemed to approve of anything she said or did.

When she'd called home and told him that he was going to be a grandparent, instead of being overjoyed, her dad had asked about the father. When she'd admitted that he wasn't in the picture, he'd harrumphed and told her not to expect any monetary help. She'd made the decision to have a baby out of wedlock, so she was on her own as far as raising that child went.

It was a blow, but nothing she hadn't expected.

She was now thirty-eight years old, almost thirty-nine, but there were times she felt as if she were eighty. Harper couldn't think of anything she'd done in her life that was special. She was a failure at pretty much everything, except for her son.

And now here she was. Sitting in a Walmart parking lot in her hometown after storming out of her dad's house in a snit.

Sighing, she opened her eyes and stared into space. Being here in the dark reminded her a little too much of those nights in the city, when she and Kash had found a dark corner of a free parking area to sleep. Was she really any better off now than she was then? Harper wasn't sure.

Maybe her son would be better off without her around. Her dad could raise him. He'd have a warm and safe place to lay his head every night, and he wouldn't have to be embarrassed that his mother worked an entry-level job in retail.

But the thought of leaving Kash at the mercy of her father's influence made her lip curl.

That was the very subject of the argument that had sent her running.

Kash had come home from school so proud that he'd been chosen to be part of the robotics club. Apparently it was a pretty competitive thing, and while robots weren't his first love, he enjoyed tinkering with them enough to want to join.

Her dad had actually *laughed*. Told Kash he would've been better off trying to join some sort of sport . . . even though Kash didn't have any interest in sports. He backed off some after that, but when Kash went up to bed, he started in again. Telling Harper that her son was going to be a laughingstock. That he was going to be picked on. That he'd be bullied because he was such a *nerd*.

Harper saw red. She might allow him to bad-mouth *her*, but she wasn't going to sit by and let her father tear Kash to pieces.

She'd lit into him, claiming he was a judgmental jerk and warning him to leave her son alone.

That had been enough for him to turn his judgment on *her*. Expressing his disappointment in how she'd turned out. Saying he'd expected so much more.

The last straw was when he'd said her mom would feel the same way.

It was a low blow, and Harper was done. She'd stormed away before she could say something she'd *really* regret.

To save face, her dad yelled at her to get out when she was already halfway to the door. It was typical Victor. Always determined to have the last word.

With nowhere to go, she'd ended up in the parking lot of her workplace. Where she felt as if she spent most of her time these days. She'd missed out on too much of Kash's life. Before she knew it, he'd be graduating and moving on. She'd already missed his amazing performance at the crate race at Lobster Fest because she was working.

Her boy was growing up, and Harper both hated that and was as proud of him as she could be.

Pressing her lips together, she decided everything that was shit in her life was karma doing her thing. Harper was well aware that she hadn't been a nice person when she was in high school. For no reason at all, she'd thought she was better than most of the kids in her class. And when her so-called friends started bullying some of their classmates, she went right along with the pack. Back then, it was more important for her to fit in than to do the right thing.

Those thoughts led Harper to think about Lincoln Young.

She'd been particularly horrible to him. A total bitch. A classic mean girl. And she had no clue how to make it right now. Or if she even *could* after all this time.

Linc had been a scrawny kid back then. Which didn't make it right that she and her friends picked on him every chance they got. And having a kid like Kash made her actions back then seem so much worse . . . because he reminded her so much of the boy Linc used to be. Smart, lost in his own head, obsessed with all things nerdy.

But the man Linc grew into was someone to be admired. She'd heard the stories of his career as a fighter pilot in the Air Force. How he was literally an American hero. It made her treatment of him when they were kids all the more painful. She wasn't the same person she was back then, but she wasn't sure how to change the perception Linc, and everyone else, seemed to have of her.

The truth was, she liked Linc. Was grateful to him and his family for embracing Kash the way they had. She knew about the fort in the woods that used to belong to the Young boys, the one that Kash had taken over. She wasn't upset about it in the least . . . not like her dad would be. He disliked the Young family and did his best to discourage Kash from spending time with them, to no avail.

Kash loved Evelyn Young. She was the grandmother he'd never had. After a misunderstanding about the kind of person she was—thanks to his very own grandfather—hanging out at Lobster Cove, the Youngs' property, was one of Kash's favorite things to do after school. Mostly because of the cookies he got from Ms. Evelyn . . . but also because he got to see Linc.

Harper's mind went back to the man she'd so badly wronged when they were teenagers. He was so good with Kash. Had taken him under his wing, so to speak. Been a mentor to him. Encouraging him, supporting him, and her son had a huge case of hero worship . . . not that she could blame him.

She wished moving into the small house on the Lobster Cove property had worked out. It would've been a huge break. Her dad was making her pay rent to live with him, which she honestly didn't have a problem with . . . but she was barely making ends meet. She was managing, but living at Lobster Cove would've helped her actually *save* money. Evelyn had only planned to charge her two hundred bucks a month. Which was ridiculously low, but Harper wouldn't have complained.

That opportunity had fallen through when unexpected repairs had to be made to the small house. Unfortunate . . . especially considering her dad had been even *more* impossible ever since she'd told him that she and Kash were moving to his neighbor's property.

It was as if he considered it a personal attack against him, which it wasn't. Harper would literally move into the heart of enemy territory if it meant improving Kash's life. At this point, her life was all about her son. His needs. His wants. What she wanted didn't matter.

Although Harper had no idea *what* she wanted. She'd been on autopilot for so long, struggling to keep her head above water, that she hadn't been able to stop and think about what she hoped to get out of life.

Motherhood hadn't been something she'd aspired to. Kash wasn't planned, but she wasn't sorry she'd chosen to have him. She didn't even want to think about where she might be today if he hadn't come along twelve years ago. Probably dead in a gutter in New York City.

With that depressing thought swirling through her brain, Harper didn't even see the car pull up behind her and cut its lights. She was so lost in her head, she also didn't hear the car door shut or see the man walking up to the driver's side of her older-model minivan.

So when he rapped on her window with his knuckles, she jumped about ten feet and let out a girly little screech in fright.

When she turned her head, Harper saw the very man she couldn't get out of her head, slowly backing away with his hands up as if to show he was no threat.

Her heart beating a hundred miles an hour, Harper frowned. What was Linc doing here? How did he know where she was? Was he driving by and just happened to see her car? Her face flamed. The store wasn't open. So there was no good reason for her car to be sitting in the lot.

Karma, that bitch, was still hard at work. Making Harper pay for the way she'd treated this man all those years ago. Making sure he saw her at her worst, time and time again.

Frowning, Harper disengaged the locks and cracked her door open—she didn't have the engine running, to save on gas, so she couldn't roll down the automatic windows. "What's wrong?" she asked Linc. "Is it Kash? Is he okay?"

She both hated and loved that her son had such a good relationship with Linc. That he felt comfortable enough to text him whenever the mood struck.

"He's worried about you," Linc said simply.

Harper closed her eyes for a beat. Of *course* her son had overheard her arguing with her dad. Of *course* he'd been worried. Her son had taken on the role of protector as well as he could at such a young age.

"I told him I'd check on you."

"Well, you've checked on me. I'm fine," Harper said, her words sounding sharper than she meant them to. This man brought out her defensiveness faster than anyone she knew. Well . . . maybe other than her dad.

In response, Linc stared at her for a beat, then walked around the front of her minivan to the passenger side. He climbed inside as if he had every right and sat, slamming the door behind him. He turned in the seat so he could see her better and simply stared without saying a word.

"What are you doing?" she asked.

"Checking on you," he told her.

Harper sighed. Fucking karma. How long was she going to have to pay for the horrible way she'd treated this man? Wasn't her life turning to shit while he'd *literally* soared to great heights enough?

Apparently not.

It felt as if every time she turned around, he was witnessing her humiliation.

"I'm fine, Linc," she said, letting her head drop back on the seat behind her. Her head felt way too heavy to hold upright. She was exhausted. Mentally and physically.

"You don't look fine," he countered.

Harper let out an unamused huff. "Well, I am. I just needed a break from my dad. He's kinda difficult. I'll go back before Kash gets up for school. I work in the morning anyway, so I need to shower and change."

Linc nodded. "Your dad is . . . he's a lot."

Harper turned her head where it rested on the seat and snorted as she said, "Yeah."

"I'm sorry things didn't work out with the house on Lobster Cove."

Harper shrugged. She was sorry too, but there wasn't anything anyone could do about it.

"You planning on living in your car again?" Linc asked, in that blunt way he had.

Harper blinked. "What? No!" She hated that he knew she and Kash had lived in their car at one point, but the gossip network was alive and well in Rockville. And since he and Kash had gotten so close, she wasn't surprised her son had told him about that time in their lives. Just another humiliation this man was privy to when it came to her personal business.

"Look, I'm sorry Kash overheard my dad and me fighting. I'm sorry if he thought I might have left the house for good to live in my car. I'm sorry he contacted you in the middle of the night, and I'm sorry you felt the need to come all the way out here to find me. If you get out, I'll go home now. Will that make you happy?"

"It's not about what will make *me* happy, Harper," Linc said, almost gently. "It's about you. And your boy." He studied her for a long moment. "You know I bought a house when I moved here. It needs a ton of work. It's drafty, smells a little funky, and it's probably not the most comfortable place in the world. But I do have hot water—the water heater was one of the first things I replaced—and the roof is good, thanks to my brothers helping me put a new one on recently. There are also more bedrooms than I know what to do with . . . You and Kash could come live with me.

"There's a bus stop on my street," he hurried to add, almost as if rushing to get the words out now. "I've seen kids standing out there in the mornings, so Kash can still get to school easily. I'll stay out of your way. I'm at Lobster Cove a lot anyway, and when I'm home, I'm usually working. I recently finished one of the two main bedrooms in the house, the one on the first floor, which I'd planned to move into. You and Kash can have the entire second floor to yourselves. I won't bother you, Harper."

She stared at the man sitting next to her in disbelief and shock.

Her first instinct was to refuse. To shake her head and say no way in *hell* was she going to live with the boy she'd tormented in high school. This was probably his sick way of getting back at her.

But . . . no. That wasn't the kind of man Lincoln Young was. She knew that without really even knowing him. Though, Harper wasn't sure about his motivation. Why was he trying to help her?

"Why are you being so nice to me?" she whispered, almost scared to hear his answer. "I was horrible to you. You should hate me."

"Harper, that was twenty years ago. A lot has happened to both of us since then. It makes no sense to hold a grudge for that long. Yeah, you were a bitch, and when we graduated high school I was glad I'd never have to see you again. But life has a funny way of bringing things full circle.

"I don't hate you. Did I ever expect I'd be sitting here, inviting you and your son to live with me? No. But I'm also not the kind of man who's able to watch a kid I like and respect stress because he's worried about his mom. Say yes, Harper."

She wanted to. He was dangling the proverbial carrot in front of her, and it was taking all her strength not to grab for it. "How much would rent cost?" she asked, attempting to keep her voice level.

"No rent," he told her.

Harper shook her head. "No, Linc. I can't come live in your house and not pay my and Kash's fair share."

To her surprise, Linc chuckled. "You did hear me say how much work the house still needs, right? It's pretty much a shithole at the moment. You'll probably walk in, then turn around and walk right back out. The bones are good, but she's in rough shape. There's no way I'd charge anyone to live there right now."

"I can't," Harper said, sticking to her guns.

He stared at her for a beat. Harper thought she saw respect in his gaze, but she was probably mistaken. She was pathetic at best. At a very low spot in her life.

"How about this? I know you're working a lot right now, and you don't have a lot of free time. But what if when you *are* around, you help me with the house? You and Kash. I could teach him things like simple carpentry and plumbing, how to install appliances, the right way to paint, how to put insulation in . . . things like that. He could be my helper when he's not at school."

Harper wanted to cry. She knew without a doubt Kash would *love* that. He didn't have a lot of friends at school, and he already idolized Linc. Having his idol teach him "boy" things like fixing up a house would be a dream come true.

She swallowed hard. She didn't like charity. Didn't like knowing she wasn't able to give her son the things he needed and deserved on her own, the very reason she was living with her dad. But Linc was offering something that might mean she could save enough to get her and Kash their own place by summer.

Independence.

He was offering her a way to get her pride back.

But a part of her still wondered about the catch. Because she certainly couldn't see a lot in this arrangement for him. It wasn't as if she or Kash would be *that* much help around his house. She didn't know the first thing about home improvement.

"Say yes, Harper," Linc repeated firmly. "I know you don't like me, have *never* liked me. I don't know why, it's not as if I've ever done anything to you. Not back then and not since I've returned to Maine. But—"

"I like you!" Harper blurted, interrupting him. "But more than that, I respect you. Linc . . . there aren't many men, many *people*, who would do what you and your brothers did. Move back to Maine when you had your own lives and jobs elsewhere, to help out your mom. If Kash turns out half as good as you are, I'd be proud."

"You should already be proud of him," Linc said with a scowl.

"That's not what I meant. I *am* proud of him," Harper insisted. "He's my entire world. I just . . . was trying to . . . never mind." She looked down at her fingers in her lap.

She was always saying the wrong thing around this man. She felt tongue tied and inferior to him. He'd done things after high school. Had made a difference in the world. She'd wanted to, but all she'd managed was to screw up her life before eventually running back to her daddy with her tail between her legs. She and Linc couldn't be more different.

"Trying to what?" Linc asked.

She sighed. "Let you know that I admire you. That I'm grateful you've taken such an interest in Kash. That you and your family were there for him when I couldn't be. That you haven't let my dad's prickliness taint your feelings for my son."

"Victor's an asshole, but deep down—*deep* down—he's a good man. He wouldn't have reached out to Chad when he saw my mom being kidnapped if he wasn't. He wouldn't have spent all day on the water looking for Marit if he wasn't. I'm not saying I want to hang out with him or anything, but I kind of understand him."

Harper lifted her head and looked at Linc. "Understand him?"

"Yeah."

He didn't elaborate, and Harper was kind of scared to ask for details. *She* certainly didn't understand her father. He'd always been extremely hard on her. Expecting perfection when she was anything but perfect. She felt that pressure from him now more than ever. Felt his disappointment that she wasn't successful. That she'd had to come back home to live with him. That she wasn't married. That she'd had a *child* outside of marriage.

"Say yes," he said again. "If things don't work out, on either of our parts, you can always go back to your dad's. Or better yet, the smaller house on Lobster Cove will probably be fixed up by the spring. You and Kash can go there if you can't stand my piece-of-shit house—or me—any longer. Say yes for your son. He worries about you. Feels as if he needs to look out for you. He's your protector, and he should be sleeping in the middle of the night, not awake and texting me because he's concerned about where you are and what might be happening to you."

It was kind of a cheap shot, but Linc was right. Harper was well aware that her son was older than his years. That he had a tender soul.

That he wanted to take care of her. They'd been taking care of each other for years now.

"All right. Thank you, Linc. I accept. But if at any time you get tired of us, and you want us out, you have to tell me. I won't be mad. I can always go back to my dad's place. I still don't really understand why you're being so generous and gracious, but I'd be stupid to say no."

To his credit, Linc didn't look smug or crow about her giving in. He simply nodded. "You need help moving your stuff over tomorrow?"

"Tomorrow?" Harper asked in surprise.

"Why not?"

"Well, I have to work."

Linc stared at her for a beat. Then asked, "What time?"

"Ten."

"Can you go back to your dad's house and get some sleep?"

Harper frowned. "Yeah, why wouldn't I be able to?"

"Kash said Victor kicked you out."

She snorted. "He did—after I was already halfway out the door. I've learned that when things get heated, the best bet is to put space between us. He'll be fine."

"All right. I'll come over with Chad tomorrow, and you can show us what you want moved. We'll do the heavy lifting, and when you get off shift, you can come straight to my place and put things where you want them."

"You don't have to do that," Harper said, stunned that he'd even offered.

"I know I don't."

"Well . . . okay. Thank you."

"You're welcome. I usually wouldn't suggest waking a kid, but maybe you should let Kash know you're back when you get home. So he doesn't worry anymore. You can tell him about the new living arrangements and figure out the bus thing tomorrow. I don't know how that works."

It wasn't quite that easy, but in the scope of everything else, they'd figure it out.

Then something occurred to Harper—and she felt the need to be clear. "Just because I'm moving into your house, that doesn't mean I'll be obligated to you . . . sexually."

The look on Linc's face made Harper regret her words instantly. She saw shock, then anger flash over his features before he quickly masked his emotions.

"I'll follow you back to your dad's house," he bit out, reaching for the door handle.

Before he could throw himself out of the vehicle, Harper grabbed his arm. He froze with one foot on the ground, halfway out of her car.

"I'm sorry," she blurted. "I didn't mean to offend you. It's just . . . I didn't want there to be any misunderstandings."

"Did I give you any indication that there were strings with my offer?" Linc asked quietly.

"No. But that doesn't mean they don't exist. I've learned the hard way that most men have hidden agendas."

"I don't," he said firmly. Then he stood from the minivan, nodded at her, and shut the passenger door. He walked back to his SUV and climbed behind the wheel.

Harper closed her eyes for a moment. She'd screwed up. Big time. And yet, Linc hadn't rescinded his offer to have her and Kash stay with him. She still wasn't sure why he'd offered in the first place . . . but a huge weight felt like it lifted from her shoulders.

Not having to pay rent, being able to save such a big chunk of each paycheck, would go a long way toward padding her bank account. She could be independent again, which seemed surreal after so many years of struggling.

She hated that she'd offended Linc, but she had to be sure of his intentions. As she'd told him, she'd definitely seen the worst in humanity over the years. Experienced it firsthand.

Looking in her rearview mirror, she saw him waiting patiently for her to pull out of the parking lot. He didn't really need to follow her home. The weather was clear, there was no snow on the ground yet. She could certainly drive to her dad's house without worrying about getting there safely.

But she couldn't help feeling a twinge in her heart that he wanted to make sure she got there all right. Lincoln Young really was a good man. Better than so many people she'd met over the years.

She had a lot to atone for. She'd been terrible to him when they were kids, and there was nothing she regretted more.

Sighing, she started her engine, absently noting that she needed to get gas in the next couple of days, before pulling out of the parking space where she'd fully intended to spend the night.

As she headed toward her dad's, Linc's headlights stayed right behind her. And when she pulled into Victor's driveway, he flashed his lights after pulling in behind her, then immediately backed out again, turning around to head to his own house.

Harper's mind spun with all that had happened in the last thirty minutes or so. How her life had once again turned on a dime. She had no idea if she was making the right decision to move in with Linc or not. She knew her *dad* would definitely have something to say about it. He'd probably disapprove, but then again, he'd pretty much disapproved of everything she'd ever done, so why this would be any different, she didn't know.

But for the first time in ages, she was looking forward to what was to come. The change would be good for both her and Kash. Her boy was struggling, and maybe, just maybe, living with a man who was full of praise and compliments, instead of judgmental looks and frowns, would help Kash flourish.

Chapter Two

Linc hadn't really planned on asking Harper to move into his house. But seeing the exhaustion and defeat in her eyes had led to the impulsive offer.

Then, he expected to regret the words the second they'd left his mouth. Instead, he'd found himself digging in and doing everything in his power to get her to accept his help.

Yes, they had a not-so-great history, but as he'd told her, that was twenty years ago. A lifetime. They'd both changed significantly.

Thanks to his military career, Linc was well aware locals saw him as a larger-than-life hero . . . but the truth was, he felt as if he was barely hanging on most days. And tonight, he saw that same desperation in Harper.

He realized they had more in common than anyone would think. Which was somewhat amusing as, at first glance, they were nothing alike. She was a single mother with too few pennies to her name, living with her dad because her options were limited. He was a decorated Air Force pilot, medically retired, with more than enough money to do whatever he wished with his life.

But for both him and Harper, family came first. Full stop. They were also both hard workers. And they each had secrets. It wasn't hard to see there was way more to Harper than met the eye. Just as there was with him as well.

Linc had no idea if having Harper in his home was a good idea, but seeing her in her car, at the end of her rope, and reading the emotion in her son's words when he'd texted him, worried about his mom . . . Linc had no regrets in asking her to move in with him.

And he hadn't lied. His house needed a lot of work. Now that it was getting cold, he was finding all the places the insulation sucked and realizing how drafty the place was. It was going to take a hell of a lot of work to bring the house up to snuff. Harper and Kash might hate living there. Might not like the cold, the creaky floors, the slight smell of mildew that permeated the place.

But . . . what was done was done. He wouldn't take the offer back.

Linc had never lived with a woman before, and he certainly hadn't cohabitated with a kid. In fact, he'd never even *wanted* children . . . something his mom would probably have a coronary over if she ever found out.

His mother had dreamed of grandchildren since the day Linc had turned eighteen. She was over the moon that two of his younger brothers were finally giving her those grandbabies. Britt, who was engaged to Chad, was due in the spring, and Marit, who was with the baby of the family, Zach, was also pregnant, due in the summer.

But Linc had never really felt the urge to procreate. Especially since his accident, when he'd had to ditch his plane and parachute into enemy territory. The thought of leaving a kid behind, of making a child lose their father, was horrific to him. He'd actually thought about that a lot while on the run, and the decision to never have kids had basically solidified itself within him.

The week he'd spent evading the enemy was still as clear as day. He remembered every terrifying moment. Every step he took had been agony, and yet he'd had no choice but to put one foot in front of the other . . . that is, unless he'd wanted to become a "guest" of the enemy forces hot on his tail.

He'd received plenty of commendations for that week, but he didn't feel as if he deserved a single one. He'd done nothing special. Simply been lucky enough to keep one step ahead of those after him.

His shoulder still hurt after all these years, and there was the small matter of him not being able to sleep through the night.

No, he was messed up deep inside, and the last thing he wanted was to bring a child into that world. Linc was terrified his nightmares would manifest themselves into something physical. Or that he'd eventually turn his frustration, anger, and pain outward. And he'd never, ever put any child in a position where he or she might come face-to-face with the demons that lived inside his head.

To that end, inviting Harper and Kash into his home was risky, but he had no doubt as soon as Harper saved enough money, she'd move into her own place. He was counting on it. As he'd told her, he'd just finished his big suite on the main floor of the house, which meant his guests could have the entire second floor to themselves. That was really the only reason he'd felt safe making the offer. Having that separation between them was for their own good.

Would hopefully keep them from hearing any of his nightmares.

Of course, one thing he couldn't get out of his head was what Harper had said to him after she'd finally agreed to move in. How it didn't obligate her to anything sexual with Linc.

Immediate rage had swum through his veins. Hell, her statement *still* pissed him off. And her quick apology for saying it—but not taking it back—hadn't helped. He'd been highly offended. He tried to keep in mind that they really didn't know each other very well. Only had the barest bit of contact when Linc brought Kash home now and then.

She didn't know him, and he didn't know her.

But he was smart enough to realize that the fact she even felt the need to clarify he wasn't entitled to her body, no matter what he offered, spoke *volumes* about her history.

Linc hadn't entertained a single thought of sex with Harper Bates when he'd made the offer for her to move in with her son. It was the furthest thing from his mind, despite the fact that he was a red-blooded guy, and Harper was an attractive woman.

A *very* attractive woman. Tall and curvy, with beautiful red hair pulled back into a simple ponytail more often than not. She'd lived in New York City for years, had wanted to be a model once upon a time.

So he figured she'd had more than her share of come-ons and men making offers that definitely included *strings*. Big fat ones.

He sighed, begrudgingly respecting that she'd come right out and warned him that sex was off the table. Even if it pissed him off that she'd felt the need to clarify it in the first place.

He wasn't an idiot. He knew sexual harassment and gender prejudice took place. Including in the Air Force that he loved. He'd known some kick-ass female pilots, but most never rose to the ranks they deserved simply because of the "good ol' boy network." It was getting better, but prejudice was still very prevalent.

Turning his mind away from the violent thoughts creeping in about the nameless, faceless men who might've dared be inappropriate with Harper, Linc once more stood in his living room, staring out the large window with a cup of hot chocolate in hand. This was exactly what he'd been doing the night before when he'd gotten Kash's texts, the boy so clearly worried for his mom.

It was now morning. Kash would've been told that he'd be moving in with Linc, was probably eating breakfast, asking his mom a million questions.

He had no idea how mean old man Rogers might've responded to the news that his daughter and grandson were moving out. Maybe he'd be relieved? More likely pissed that they were leaving his house for one that belonged to one of the Young brothers.

Though, he kind of had advance warning. When Harper and Kash had been arranging to move onto Lobster Cove—onto land that Rogers coveted—rumor was, he hadn't been happy. That move had fallen through, but the old man had to know his daughter was still looking for somewhere else to go.

Taking a sip of his hot chocolate, Linc felt it warm him from the inside out. He was addicted to the stuff. Not coffee. Not tea. Hot chocolate. It was childish and silly, but from the time he was a young boy, he'd loved it. His mom made it with milk and double the chocolate. Sometimes she'd even put marshmallows on top. It had always reminded him of home, of winters in Maine, and even after moving out and joining the Air Force, he'd continued to drink the stuff.

The phone in his pocket vibrated with an incoming text, and Linc pulled it out, smiling as he saw it was from Kash.

Kash: is it really true r we really moving in2 your house

Linc: Sure are.

Kash: wooooooooooooooooooooooo

Linc couldn't help but laugh at the kid's reaction.

Kash: thank u 4 finding mom last night

Linc: You're welcome.

Kash: mom just told me to tell u that its no prob taking a different bus from school i should be there by 330 or 4 what project are we doing first

Linc laughed out loud again. The sound rusty and echoing throughout the room.

Linc: I was going to start with painting. Need to do that before I do the floors.

Kash: awesome

Linc: You might not think it's awesome when you see how much needs to be painted.

Kash: ive never painted b4 its gonna b fun

The enthusiasm the boy showed was endearing. Linc knew the excitement would wane after a while. After reality set in about how much work there was to be done in the house.

Linc: How about we work on setting up your room first when you get here. Then we can see what else needs to be done.

Kash: would it b ok if we set up moms room 1st she works until 6 today and will b tired when she gets home

Linc's heart lurched at how considerate Kash was toward his mother.

Linc: Of course.

Kash: cool i gotta go moms rushing me and i don't want to miss my bus c u later

Linc: Later.

Linc put his phone back in his pocket . . . and realized a couple of minutes later, he was still smiling. He didn't know what effect Harper and Kash would have on his life *after* they moved in, but he had no doubt it would change things.

Taking a deep breath, he made his way into the kitchen, putting his mug in the sink before heading for the stairs. He needed to shower, maybe get a head start on moving his stuff downstairs before heading over to Victor's house. He'd already texted Chad and asked if he'd help with Harper and Kash's stuff. Of course, his brother had agreed, asking if Britt could come too . . . although she wouldn't be lifting anything heavy on account of her being pregnant.

Linc liked Britt. She was good for Chad. Brought out the best in him.

Not a day went by when Linc didn't see one of his relatives. He hadn't been totally sure about moving home to Maine, but now that he was here, he was content. More so than when he'd lived out west. Family could be a pain in the butt sometimes, but he'd missed his. Way more than he'd ever realized.

Thirty minutes later, Linc was on the way to his mom's neighbor's house. After he was done moving Harper and Kash's things, he'd go over and spend some time with his mom. If he didn't, he knew he'd never hear the end of it. She'd want to hear all about how her pretty neighbor and her son had come to be living with him.

For his part, Linc wanted to nip any expectations she had in the bud. His mom was a romantic who probably thought this meant he and Harper were a "thing." Which they weren't. He was letting her move in because of Kash. Period.

Linc refused to let the nagging voice in the back of his head take root. The one telling him that he was a liar. He was helping out a neighbor, that was it. And he needed to make sure his mom didn't start making any more damn wedding plans. She had enough on her plate with the other two weddings she was organizing . . . not to mention baby showers.

Neither of his brothers actually had concrete plans for their weddings yet, but that didn't matter to their mother. She was so excited that two of her babies had found amazing women to spend the rest of their lives with, she was full speed ahead.

When Linc turned onto Victor Rogers's property, he immediately saw that it was in dire need of some TLC. The gravel driveway needed to be graded, there were trees that should be pruned or even taken down, so they didn't damage any structures during a windstorm, which Rockville had a lot of. Even the main house looked . . . tired.

Like Lobster Cove, Victor also had two rental houses on his property, but they looked just as neglected as the main house.

Linc had wondered once why Harper and Kash hadn't moved into one of those, but apparently Victor wasn't willing to give up the rental income they provided. It was just another thing about the old man that rubbed Linc the wrong way.

But Linc wasn't privy to Victor's money situation. Maybe he really needed the income. It was a moot point now, since Harper and Kash would be moving out today.

Pulling as close as he could to the front door of the house, Linc cut off the engine and took a deep breath. Though it was too late to take his offer back, he was suddenly having second thoughts.

And third and fourth ones.

He liked his solitude. Didn't really want anyone in his personal space. Especially in the middle of the night, when his demons usually reared their ugly heads. And what did he know about kids, anyway? Sure, he liked Kash. The boy was smart and eccentric. And so eager for positive reinforcement. Linc could practically see the kid preening anytime someone said something kind to him.

Fact was, Linc saw a lot of himself in Kash. The boy he used to be. Unsure of himself. Gangly. Slow to hit puberty. He'd been bullied by more than Harper and her group of mean girls, although they were the main instigators. It wasn't until he'd joined the Air Force that he'd grown into his body, started weight lifting, gaining confidence in himself.

He couldn't help but wonder if Kash was being bullied, and figured he probably was. Kids hadn't changed much over the years, any weaknesses or differences in their peers an opportunity to pounce. And Kash had more than his fair share of reasons to be seen as an outsider. He was new to town, was smarter than the average seventh grader, and apparently had more interest in science-y things than girls, being popular, or anything else kids his age thought was important.

Not sure what he could do to help the kid, Linc's thoughts were interrupted by Harper appearing at the front door. She stood there watching him, uncertainty and worry easy to see in her gaze.

Linc's body was moving before his brain caught up. He didn't like to see doubt in Harper's eyes, not when it came to him. No matter how many second thoughts he was having, he wasn't going to rescind the offer. That would be an asshole thing to do, and Linc prided himself on keeping his word.

"Hi," she said a little nervously as Linc approached.

"Morning," he responded with a nod. "Things okay? With your dad?"

She shrugged. "He thinks I'm making a mistake, but that's nothing new. He thinks every decision I've ever made was a mistake."

"He's probably upset that he's losing you and Kash," Linc said.

Harper blinked in surprise. "You think?"

"He's going to be alone again when you leave. It could be a rough adjustment after having you and Kash around."

"Wow, that's so not what I thought you'd say," Harper said.

"What'd you think I was going to say?" Linc asked, genuinely curious.

"I don't know. Maybe something about how my dad's an asshole, and you aren't surprised he's being a jerk about us moving out."

"Your dad *is* an asshole," Linc said without hesitation. "But that doesn't mean he doesn't have feelings. And before you keel over in shock, you should know that when I first got here, I probably would've said exactly what you thought. But with the shit that's gone down with my family, and how he's helped us . . . I'm able to see him in a different light. Your mom died a while ago, yeah?"

Harper nodded. "Before I moved to New York."

"He's lonely. Rattling around in this big house of his. He loved Carrie, and losing her had to have been hard. He's a little crusty . . . okay, a lot crusty . . . but there's good in there somewhere."

"Who are you and what have you done with Linc?" Harper joked.

Linc felt uncomfortable all of a sudden. "Again, I'm not saying I want to come over and hang out with him, but your old man's been through some shit. And now you're moving out a second time. He's probably lashing out because he doesn't want to be alone again."

"We aren't going thousands of miles away," Harper said, sounding a little defensive. "I'm going to keep my eye on him. He might drive me crazy, and I might not ever be able to do anything right in his eyes, but I still love him. He's still my dad. And Kash's granddad."

"I know. You ready to show me what to bring over to my house, so you can get to work?" It was an abrupt change of topic, but Linc was done talking about Victor. He might understand the man, but that didn't mean he wanted to be around him any longer than necessary.

"Sure. Come on in. By the way, Dad's not here. He said he didn't want to witness another one of my shitty decisions, and he wasn't going to help me make said shitty decision by assisting me in moving my stuff."

Linc winced. He felt like taking back all the semi-nice things he'd just said about Victor.

Harper chuckled. "I can see you regret everything you just said." She shrugged. "I'm used to him. His words mostly go in one ear and out the other these days."

Linc wasn't sure that was true. Victor was her father. The one person in her life who should be doing everything in his power to support her. To encourage her. To lift her up. If he had a daughter, or a son for that matter, that's what he would do. What his own dad had done for him and his brothers.

Harper led the way into the house, and Linc took the time to look around. He'd never been inside and was curious about the place. To his surprise, the house was very well kept. It wasn't dirty. Wasn't cluttered. The difference between the inside and the outside grounds was like night and day.

Harper led him to a room at the back of the house. It was small and had a tiny window that overlooked the trees between Victor's property and Lobster Cove. There was a twin-size bed and a small dresser. Harper had apparently already packed her things before he'd gotten there. Two large boxes sat on the floor, with three smaller ones stacked on top. "Here are our things."

Wait—*our* things?

"Kash's too?" Linc asked, knowing he sounded shocked.

Harper looked a little embarrassed. "Yeah. We didn't have a lot when we got here, and Kash doesn't need much beyond his telescope and books. I have to warn you, those smaller boxes are heavy because they're mostly books."

Linc stared at Harper, then looked back at the boxes. He was feeling a lot of things right then. He was well aware that material shit mattered less than things like shelter, food, and safety. But he wasn't thrilled that everything Harper and Kash had to their names fit into five fucking boxes.

Hell, he'd had more than that when he'd lived on an aircraft carrier, and he'd bet his brother Zach did too.

"Is it *too* much?" Harper asked quietly, misinterpreting his continued silence. "We can leave the books here. I'm sure my dad won't mind."

"No!" Linc exclaimed. Then moderated his tone. "No, it's not too much at all. I thought there'd be more, that's all."

"We really don't need much," Harper repeated with a small shrug.

The hell they didn't.

Linc had no idea of Harper's situation. He'd assumed she was the same spoiled girl she'd been back in high school. With tons of clothes, makeup, and other doodads that women and girls seemed to think were so important. Now he flushed slightly, feeling foolish.

Living in her car, being homeless, would've made it imperative that she narrow down her belongings to only the bare necessities.

"Right. It doesn't look like I'll need Chad's help after all. I'll get these moved out to my place, and they'll be there when you get off work this afternoon."

"Thank you so much, Linc. I mean it."

"You're welcome. And stop thanking me. It's done. We're moving on. All right?"

To his surprise, Harper smiled.

"What?" he asked. "What's funny?"

"You remind me of my dad, that's all."

Linc's eyes widened, which made her actually giggle. The sound was light, a little rusty, as if it had been a long time since she'd found anything to laugh about, which irritated Linc all over again.

"You don't have to look so appalled," she told him, still grinning. "Wasn't it you a moment ago telling me that you thought my dad wasn't as big a jerk as he shows to the world?"

"I have the right to change my mind," he muttered.

Which sent Harper into giggles again.

The sound was carefree and happy, and nothing like he'd heard from this woman in the time he'd known her since he'd been back in town. He liked it. Liked even more that he'd been the one to make her feel that way, even if just for a moment.

"I can help you get these to your SUV," Harper told him.

"I got it," Linc reassured her, looking down at his watch. "You probably need to get going if you don't want to be late."

Harper looked at her own watch and gasped. "Shoot! Time got away from me."

"You sure there's nothing else you need me to take over for you?" Linc asked.

"You do have beds . . . right?" Harper asked with a smile, indicating she was making a joke.

But to Linc's horror, he realized no, he did *not*, in fact, have beds.

He was an idiot. The invitation for her and Kash to move in had been so impulsive, he hadn't even thought about where they were going to sleep.

"Of course I do," he said as impassively as he could. He would never admit that he'd completely forgotten about freaking beds.

"Good. Although honestly, I could sleep anywhere. After you sleep in your car, which is the most uncomfortable place in the world to sleep, you pretty much appreciate any kind of couch or pillow to rest your head on."

She was wrong. A car wasn't the most uncomfortable place in the world to sleep. That honor would go to the cold, hard ground of North Korea while on the run from soldiers hunting you, while trying to decide if it would be better to head toward China or Russia.

Linc forcibly shook the memories out of his head. "Well, you don't have to worry about that now."

"Th—Right," she said, catching herself from almost thanking him again. "Well, I guess I'll see you after work then. If something happens with Kash, if he doesn't get on the right bus or something, I'll let you know. And for the record, if you get tired of him, just tell him to go read a book and he'll get out of your hair."

"I'm not going to get tired of him. I *like* Kash, Harper. He's funny, and smart, and he keeps me on my toes."

"Oh, well, yeah. I like him too. But he's a lot. Sometimes he can be exhausting with his questions."

"It'll be fine."

"All right. If you need anything, just text me. I can bring a rotisserie chicken home from work if you need me to."

The thought of her spending her money on him when she had so little for herself and her son right now made Linc feel a little sick inside. "I've got it. Don't worry."

"Okay. But I don't expect you to pay for our food, Linc. Kash eats like a horse. I've never seen a kid eat so much."

"He's a growing boy. The two of us will figure out something for dinner, and we'll have it waiting for you when you get home."

Harper stared at him for a long moment.

"What? Something wrong?"

"No. It's just . . . sometimes Kash makes dinner for me, usually just sandwiches or something, but I can't remember any other time after I went to New York that I came home to a hot meal waiting for me."

And that was just too heartbreaking to contemplate.

"Well, don't get too excited. I'm not a chef like Zach. But I'm not as bad as Knox either."

Harper smiled at that. "I've heard he can burn water."

"He can," Linc confirmed.

"I'm not picky," Harper said. "I'll eat just about anything."

And that was one more thing Linc had in common with this woman. He supposed when you were dead broke and living out of your car, you couldn't afford to be picky.

Memories of the last nightmare he had filled his head. He'd woken up almost able to taste dirt and leaves in his mouth. He was tired of the nightmares but, sadly, had gotten used to them. Tired of remembering the terror he'd felt while he'd been on the run. While he was hunted down like a rabid dog.

He didn't know why he had such vivid memories of every single nightmare. Memories that crept up on him when he least expected it. It had been years since his crash, and he was more content and settled now than he'd been in a long time.

Maybe that was why? His brain was settling down, giving him more time to think?

Whatever the reason, he hated it. Harper and Kash would be good distractions. He hoped. The last thing he wanted was to continually relive those seven horrifying days of his life.

"Good," he answered belatedly. "I'll see what Kash and I can come up with."

"I know you don't want to hear it, but thank you again, Linc. Seriously."

He nodded, then tapped his wrist, letting her know that time was ticking.

"Right. I'm out of here. See you tonight."

Then Linc was alone in the small room Harper had moved into when she'd come back home. After he heard her minivan start up and head down the driveway, Linc didn't hesitate.

He snooped.

Did a walk-through of Victor's house.

Checked out the fridge and pantries, peeked into the other rooms in the house.

His intention wasn't to steal anything, far from it. He was curious about his neighbor. About the man who was as prickly as a cactus. There were pictures of his late wife everywhere, as well as pictures of Harper. Some looked as if they were professional shots, probably taken not long after she'd gotten to New York. She was beautiful. Had a sparkle in her eye. As if she was ready to take on the world. And Linc supposed she had been. She'd been full of hope and certainty that she was going to be a huge success.

There were also a few pictures of Kash when he was a baby. The one that stuck out to Linc was obviously taken right after he was born. Harper was in a hospital bed, holding her newborn son. She looked exhausted, terrified, and a little shell shocked. Her entire life had changed, and it was more than clear to Linc that she wasn't sure what the future held.

Much as he'd probably looked when the Air Force took his picture upon arrival at the hospital in Japan, after being picked up by the Night Stalkers who'd swooped in after he'd crossed into Russian territory.

Linc picked up the picture and studied it. Harper looked . . . gaunt. Too skinny for just having given birth. He wondered what Kash's story was for the first time. Who his father was. Why he wasn't in the picture.

But it wasn't his business.

He put the picture back on the small table.

The kid was twelve, there was obviously no father in his life. The past was the past, Harper had obviously moved on.

But as soon as he had the thought, Linc winced. He was a hypocrite. The past was never just the past. It was always there, lurking, waiting to mess with your head.

Turning abruptly, Linc headed for the last door he hadn't looked in yet. Opening it, he decided this had probably been Kash's room. There were glow-in-the-dark stars on the ceiling and a poster of Saturn still on the wall. The twin bed looked sad and lonely in the empty room. The mattress sagging in the middle. There wasn't even a dresser, just a closet with a few empty hangers.

Victor Rogers kept a clean house. Uncluttered but sparse. Once again, he had no idea of the man's finances, but to Linc, they didn't seem as good as he wanted the town to believe. Seemed Victor really *did* need the income he got from his rental properties.

And if that was the case, how in the heck did he think he was going to buy Lobster Cove? He'd been pestering Linc's parents to sell for years . . . but with what money?

Linc also recalled that the man had spent all day on the water looking for Marit when she'd gone missing. The fuel had to have been expensive, and as far as he knew, Zach hadn't offered to reimburse him. Hell, Linc himself hadn't thought about it either.

Was that why Victor hadn't stored his boat for the winter yet? It was still docked in Rockville Harbor. Storage costs money. Money the man didn't have?

Making a mental note to talk to Chad about storing their neighbor's boat on Lobster Cove, Linc headed for the boxes in Harper's small bedroom. The sooner he got everything into his SUV, the sooner he could head into town to find two beds, a couple of dressers, and stop by the grocery store to stock up.

He was determined to have whatever Kash and Harper needed to feel safe and secure. Food, a roof over their heads, and a comfortable place to sleep. Basic needs he could easily offer.

She wasn't even living with him yet, and there was already something about Harper that was getting under his skin. He didn't know why, wasn't sure he even *liked* the woman. He'd gone out of his way to keep his distance from her since he'd been back in Maine, but that space was about to disappear entirely.

He still wasn't sure he'd made the right decision, inviting her and her son to live with him, but he'd help her get back on her feet, and when it was time for them to get their own place, he'd gladly help them move their things out. By then, he'd probably be itching for them to go. To have his own space back.

Probably.

Maybe.

Shit. What had he done?

Chapter Three

Shoot. What had she done?

As Harper checked her phone and saw she had another five excited texts from Kash, telling her all about what he and Linc were doing, she wondered if she'd made the right decision. Again.

It felt as if she'd made the wrong choices over and over throughout her lifetime. And this was possibly one more.

Moving in with Lincoln Young had seemed like a good idea last night. When she'd been cold and exhausted. Not to mention irritated with her dad for once again telling her that she was never going to get anywhere working at Walmart. But it was a job. And Harper was proud of herself for not being a mooch. For doing what she could to change her and Kash's situation.

But now, seeing Kash's excitement in his texts, how thrilled he was about something as simple as paint colors for the room he'd be living in temporarily, Harper was worried. Kash could easily get too attached to their benefactor. Might not understand that they were living with Linc only in the short term. That he wasn't going to be more than a friend.

One more disappointment in her son's short life.

Harper was very aware that Kash wanted a dad. He'd started asking about his own father around age five. He wanted to know why other boys had daddies and he didn't. Then, when he was a little older, he wanted to know where he was.

Why he didn't want a son.

And she'd had no idea what to tell him. How to tell him that his father was a piece-of-shit human being. No one she'd ever want to introduce him to.

Couldn't introduce him to.

Now, Harper didn't want Kash to hope for things that were never going to happen. He already had a huge hero worship thing going on with Linc. He was the first man to ever support Kash unconditionally. To let him babble on about stars and planets and nebulas, and not cut him off and tell him he should be interested in more boyish stuff, like football or girls.

Hell, Harper had a little bit of a hero worship thing going on herself when it came to Lincoln. Partly because he was so kind to her son, but mostly because . . . he was *Linc*.

She'd heard all the talk around town. About how he'd crashed while on a mission in the Air Force and survived a week evading enemies before he was rescued . . . all while severely injured. But that wasn't why Harper had a mild crush on the man. In fact, that side of him was intimidating.

It was because when she looked into his eyes, she saw a familiar isolation that she felt down to her soul.

She was surrounded by people all the time, and yet she felt alone. As if no one truly saw her. Some might admire her red hair and green eyes, or even her body—thank goodness for a fast metabolism—but very few seemed interested in getting to know her as a person since she'd moved back home.

At least, not until recently. Britt Starkweather and Marit Phillips, women engaged to two of the Young brothers, had recently begun texting Harper. And she appreciated their efforts . . . but she hadn't tried to deepen a relationship with either of them as of yet. It wasn't because she didn't want to, or because the women didn't seem interested in getting to know her better.

After years of caution, Harper was just used to keeping people at arm's length.

She felt as if Linc was a kindred soul. She swore she saw the same loneliness in his eyes that reflected back in her mirror every morning. But nothing could come of it. How could it? She would forever be the girl who'd made his life miserable in high school. If she could go back and change things, she would, but she couldn't. What was done was done. All she could do was atone for her mistakes and move on.

And move on, she would. As soon as she had enough money saved up, she'd find a place of her own for her and Kash. Get out of Linc's hair. He was probably already regretting asking her to move in with him.

Today at work had been tough. The closer the holidays got, the meaner customers seemed to become. If they weren't able to use their twenty-cents-off coupon, they went off the rails. She got it, saving money was important, she knew that better than most, but screaming at the person ringing you up, who has the unfortunate task of telling you the coupon is expired, doesn't actually help anything.

Honestly, she needed about a week off to sleep. To recharge her batteries. But that wasn't going to happen for many reasons, two of which were that she needed the money and the holidays were practically upon them. The busiest time of year for retailers. Which meant even longer hours for her and even more stress.

But at least now she was certain that Kash would be all right. She remembered holidays in the past where she'd had no idea where their next meal was going to come from, or whether or not they were going to be evicted.

Feeling way older than her almost forty years, Harper headed for home.

No, for Linc's house. She hadn't had a home in way too long. Couldn't wait to finally be able to settle into a place with her son. She had no expectations on what that home would look like. A trailer? An apartment? A tiny little house? It didn't matter. All that mattered was that it would belong to her and Kash. A place where they could finally relax. Could decorate however they wanted.

The drive to Linc's house was about the same distance as it was from work to her dad's. After she parked in the driveway, she took a moment to close her eyes and be thankful for Linc's incredibly kind and generous offer. She'd gotten to the end of her rope with her father. She loved him, of course she did, and would always be appreciative that he'd let her move in with him to get back on her feet. But the time had come for her to leave. He must've felt the same way, that had to be part of the reason he'd gotten even more critical recently.

Opening her eyes, Harper saw all the lights on inside Linc's house. It felt . . . welcoming. The low temperatures were hovering around freezing, and as November turned into December they'd only get colder. The bright porch light was a beacon. It felt like a promise. A new beginning.

Just as she was about to get out of her minivan, Linc opened the front door and half jogged toward her. For a split second, Harper had the crazy thought that he was going to say he'd changed his mind and she needed to go back to her dad's house.

"Is everything okay?" she blurted, as she remained frozen with one foot on the ground and still half in the driver's seat. "Kash?"

"He's good. I just came out to tell you to park in the garage," Linc told her, pointing toward the detached building next to the house.

Turning, Harper realized one of the doors was already open. She looked back at Linc. "Are you sure?"

"Of course. Only have one car, Harper. There's no reason for you to park outside, where your car will just get covered in snow and ice. It'll save you some time in the morning, not having to scrape your windows. Kash and I have dinner waiting, so don't take all day." He nodded at her before turning and heading back to the house.

Harper stared after him for a beat, her gaze glued to his ass.

It wasn't the first time she'd noticed that Lincoln Young was damn fine looking. They were about the same height at around five-ten, but that's where their similarities ended. He had dark hair where hers was a deep auburn. His eyes were brown and hers were green. He was muscular, and while she had a few curves, she was underweight. He filled out the jeans he was wearing very nicely . . . both the front *and* back.

She felt ashamed for even noticing.

She shouldn't be noticing the size of Linc's dick. It made no difference to her situation. Besides, it had been so long since she'd been with a man, she should've forgotten what that part of the male anatomy could do for a woman. Not that she'd *ever* really known. All her sexual encounters had been . . . less than ideal.

Once again, her mind shied away from that topic. She wasn't going there. Didn't want a man, was doing just fine without one, thank you very much.

But was she?

The doubts began to creep in. From the moment she'd left Maine, she'd struggled. Maybe she should've just stayed here and married a hometown boy. Her life would be very different if she'd done that, for sure.

"Harper," Linc called from the porch, sounding amused. "Stop daydreaming and go park! The food's getting cold!"

"Sorry!" she told him, as she climbed back into the driver's seat.

Out of all the things Linc had offered her, a parking spot in a covered garage was possibly one of the most exciting. It had been forever since she'd had the luxury of protecting her car from the elements overnight.

She needed a new vehicle, but for now it was holding on, thank goodness. She had a ton of dings in the frame, from other cars bumping into it, and from the weather and general wear and tear. But the engine was in good shape.

She pulled into the garage and climbed out of the minivan. She collected the three bags of things she'd picked up after her shift was over and headed for the house.

Surprisingly, her exhaustion seemed to lift the closer she got to the front door. Seeing Kash always had that effect on her, but she was also very aware that she felt a kind of . . . anticipation at seeing Linc as well.

Harper *was* too exhausted to analyze the complicated feelings she had toward the oldest Young brother. Of which there were many.

She'd always been a little intimidated by him when they were kids, because he was so smart, and he was even more intimidating now, as an adult. There was plenty of shame and guilt on her part, for how poorly she'd treated him. Pride for the man who'd served his country and become a hero. More than a little envy over his relationship with his mom and brothers. And a bit of wistfulness because he always seemed to have his shit together.

On top of all that, he'd obviously done well for himself over the years, enough that he was able to buy this house on the coast. Sure, it needed work, but it couldn't have been cheap. No houses with waterfront views were.

But under all those feelings was that little hum of attraction. Linc was a seriously good-looking man. He'd certainly filled out since his high school years, when she and her friends had teased him about being a scrawny beanpole. It wouldn't be a hardship to see a man like him every morning and night.

"Mom!" Kash called out the second she opened the front door. "Hurry up! Linc and me made dinner!"

"Linc and I," Harper corrected, as she walked into the house.

Linc hadn't lied. The place needed *a lot* of work. Under the smell of garlic, there was a hint of must in the air, as if it had been closed up for years and years. The floors needed replacing, there was new drywall that hadn't been painted yet, and the kitchen looked like it had been installed in the 1950s or so.

But the bones of the place were amazing. Harper took it all in, tilting her head back to look at the tall ceilings, what she thought was original woodwork around the doorframes, and the centerpiece of the room—the wide curved staircase.

"Wow," she whispered, impressed.

"That's one of the reasons I bought this place," Linc told her as he reached for the bags in her hand. "I told you that you didn't need to get any food," he said next, sounding grumpy.

Harper ignored him, but she did let him take the bags from her. "What were the other reasons?" she asked.

"Huh?" Linc asked, frowning.

"You said the staircase was one of the reasons you bought this place. What were the others?"

"Oh. There aren't any neighbors within a mile, the cove is far enough from Rockville that it doesn't get a lot of traffic, and . . ." He gestured toward the windows in the main living area with a small smile. "It's dark now, but when the sun comes up, you'll see why I didn't hesitate to plunk down an obscene amount of money for such a run-down place."

Harper could imagine. She'd dreamed of owning a place like this once. Now? She'd be content with a tiny little house in the middle of town. As long as it was her own, she'd love it.

"Mooooom, you can look at the house later. Come see what Linc and I made for dinner! He let me do most of it too! Look! Homemade pizza!"

Harper blinked. She'd kind of expected something like frozen chicken pot pies and green bean casserole. But pizza? It was such a bachelor thing to make.

As if he could hear her thoughts, Linc leaned over and whispered, "For the record, I'm no chef, but I *can* cook more than pizza."

Worried he thought she was disappointed or upset with the dinner menu, Harper said quickly, "I love pizza. For a while, that's all Kash and I ate. But I'm sure this is way better."

Linc frowned.

Shoot, she was messing this up already. Harper felt tongue tied around this man. Unsure of what she should and shouldn't say.

Kash rescued her from saying something else that might irritate Linc by grabbing her hand and dragging her to the small table next to the kitchen. It was old as well, a little wobbly, the top scarred and watermarked.

"I set the table," Kash informed her. He was practically glowing, and it was such a change from the reticent boy he'd been recently that Harper didn't care if the pizza was terrible, she'd eat every bite with a smile on her face if only to make her son happy.

"Cloth napkins and everything!" Kash said. Then he whirled around and hurried into the kitchen. "Linc says he doesn't have fancy plates, but I think the ones he has are *super* fancy," he continued, as he used his fingers to put a piece of pizza on a plate.

"Tongs, Bud," Linc drawled. "Touching food isn't polite."

"But I touched it while I was making it," Kash said with a confused frown.

Harper hid her smile. She'd been in Linc's shoes many, many times over the years. Informing her son of something that was socially acceptable, only to have him turn around and make a perfectly valid point that contradicted what she'd just told him.

"Yup. And you washed your hands before you started cooking," Linc said calmly. "Since we put the pizza in the oven, you've unpacked your books, set up your telescope, and helped me clear out your mom's side of the garage. You think there weren't any germs or dirt in any of those activities?"

Kash wrinkled his nose. "Yeah, probably."

"No *probably* about it, Bud. Why don't you go ahead and wash your hands now. I'll dish up the pizza and serve it."

"Don't start without me!" Kash yelled, as if it wasn't going to take him less than twenty seconds to wash and dry his hands right there at the kitchen sink.

"Wouldn't dream of it," Linc reassured him.

Watching her son with Linc made Harper's eyes tear up. She turned away to stare blankly at the back of the sofa nearby. She'd seen Linc be kind to Kash more than once. Hell, the entire Young family had taken him under their wing. But for some reason, seeing this interaction, something so . . . ordinary . . . had her close to crying.

She wished she could've given Kash experiences like this for the last twelve years of his life. Instead, he'd had no male role models and only an exhausted mother who felt as if she was barely keeping her head above water.

She heard Linc nearing and did her best to blink away the tears.

"You okay?" he asked softly, for her ears only.

Harper nodded. She didn't know if she was, but she'd be damned if she ruined this first meal under Linc's roof.

Looking at the plate Linc put in front of her, Harper was surprised at what she saw. Yes, it was pizza, but it was some of the best-looking pizza she'd seen in a very long time.

"It's nothing special," he told her, after glancing over to see Kash still at the sink. "Store-bought French bread, large amounts of garlic mixed with the bottled sauce, tons of cheese, turkey pepperoni, parmesan cheese sprinkled on top with a dash of hot pepper flakes your son swore you loved."

"I do love hot pepper flakes. Linc, this looks . . . delicious."

"Again, not fancy, but it was easy. I wanted to be sure Kash wouldn't fail with his first cooking experience."

He turned back to the kitchen, and while he was warning her son to dry his hands on the dish towel hanging on the fridge and not his pants, Harper was still processing his words.

The care he was taking with Kash was like nothing she'd experienced before. Of course, she did everything in her power to build up her son's confidence, but dinner for them was usually fast food, or something simple like sandwiches or a rotisserie chicken she brought home from work.

Her dad had never taken the time to teach Kash how to cook. And for Linc to go out of his way to make something Kash couldn't fail at . . .

The pesky tears she'd managed to banish a second earlier were back.

"Did you try it? How is it?" Kash asked, bouncing over to the table and climbing up onto his chair, one leg tucked under his butt while he hovered over the plate.

"Sit, Kash. On your butt," Harper ordered. "At least pretend like you're civilized."

Kash laughed. The sound never failed to make Harper smile. She'd fucked up a lot of things in her life, but her son was always a bright spot in an otherwise very tough few years.

"We toasted the bread, and Linc even let me use the oven mitts to put it in and take it out of the oven. I mixed some spices into the sauce and made sure the pepperonis were perfectly spaced out. Is it good? It's good, right?"

Harper had just taken a huge bite, and she smiled at her son as she chewed. After she swallowed, she said, "The best pizza I've ever had." And she wasn't lying. Sitting here at Linc's table, seeing how happy her son was, warm and satisfied, it *was* the best pizza she'd ever had.

"Linc says it's because of the bread crust. It's garlic bread. So it's extra flavorful."

Harper had a feeling she'd be hearing "Linc says" a lot in the next few weeks. She didn't mind though, especially if it meant seeing her son so content.

Dinner went by quickly, partly because Harper was so hungry, but mostly because the pizza was so good. Kash insisted on doing the dishes, since "Linc says it's the responsible thing to do."

Harper offered to help, and with the three of them washing, drying, and putting dishes away, the chore was done in record time.

"Can we show her now, Linc? Please?"

"Show me what?"

"Come on!" Kash said with a huge grin on his face. He grabbed her hand again, this time tugging her toward the stairs.

They went to the second floor, but Linc stayed downstairs. Harper wondered if he was ready for some alone time . . . Kash *could* be a lot.

"We were going to paint today but ran out of time. Linc says we'll have plenty of time to do it this winter. He also found out he has to replace some walls up here, so he didn't want to paint and then have to do it again after putting in new walls. But he said once it's all done, I can pick out the color I want for my room. Isn't that *cool*?"

It was cool, but also worrisome. They weren't going to be here permanently. Her son was going to be disappointed if they moved out before he got to pick the color for his room. Harper had a feeling even if she promised he could paint his room in the color he chose wherever they landed next, it wouldn't be the same.

She made a mental note to talk to him. Explain that living with Linc was temporary and they wouldn't be there long.

But all thoughts of the difficult conversation she needed to have with her son flew from her mind when he threw open one of the closed doors in the hallway.

"Ta-da! It's your new room! Isn't it *awesome*? I worked really hard to unpack your stuff."

The room was . . .

It was like a dream.

The walls needed work, as did the floors. The paint on the ceiling was chipping off, and there was a noticeable draft coming from the window . . . but it was still the most beautiful room she'd ever seen.

There was a queen-size bed taking up most of the space. It wasn't anything fancy, but there was the fluffiest, most comfortable-looking comforter on the bed that made her immediately want to cuddle up and sleep for days. It was a dark green with white swirls all over it. There were two pillows, and even a ruffly thing around the bottom of the box spring.

But there was more than just a bed. There was a dresser with five drawers, a table next to the bed that had a couple of her books on the top, as well as pictures of her and Kash, and she could see her clothes already hanging in the closet.

The last touch was the rug on the floor under her feet. It was thick, and her toes curled in her shoes, thinking about walking on it in her bare feet. It was a warm cream shade, with circles of bright colors all over it—fuchsia, green, and pink, with browns to even out the brightness.

Harper wanted to lie down on it and cry. When was the last time she'd had a rug in her room? A clean one? A brand-new one? She knew it was new because she spied the tag in the corner that Kash and Linc had forgotten to remove.

It was too much. All she'd expected or needed was a little corner somewhere to stash her things and lay her head. This was . . . it was amazing.

"Wait until you see *my* room!" Kash exclaimed, grabbing her hand once more and attempting to pull her toward the door.

Harper was almost afraid to. She was already overwhelmed with how above and beyond Linc had gone for *her*, she couldn't imagine what he'd done for her son.

And she was right to be afraid.

The second she walked into Kash's room next to hers in the hallway, she was overwhelmed all over again. There was another queen-size bed, with a navy blue comforter this time. Another rug on the floor and a dresser for his clothes. But he also had a bookcase that was already full.

If she wasn't mistaken, there were books on those shelves that Harper didn't recognize.

"Look, Mom! It's *full*!"

Kash was standing next to his closet, a huge grin on his face as he gestured to the clothes hanging there. More than he'd had that morning.

"And socks! New underwear too!" he said gleefully, as he pulled open one of the dresser drawers.

It was too much. Linc had done way, way too much.

"That's awesome, baby. How about you give me some time to talk to Linc . . . alone."

Kash's smile slowly died. "Are you mad?"

She forgot how easily her kid could read her. How sensitive he was. "No, sweetheart. I just want to make sure Linc knows that he's not expected to buy us things. That we're only going to be here a short time."

"Oh."

It was one word, but there was so much emotion behind it that Harper flinched. Still . . . she had to be strong. Make sure her son knew they wouldn't be staying. That this living situation was fleeting.

"Why don't you read one of those new books I spy on your shelf while I talk to Linc. I'll be up soon to tuck you in."

"I'm not a baby. I don't need tucking in," Kash told her a little peevishly. "You aren't going to fight, are you?"

"No. We're just going to talk."

"Promise?"

"Promise."

Harper didn't want to fight with Linc. She simply wanted to understand. Why had he gone to so much trouble to set up their rooms the way he had? She had the sudden feeling *everything* in their rooms that hadn't been packed in their five boxes was brand new.

She felt uncomfortable with the amount of money he must've spent. She had no way to pay him back and didn't like feeling indebted to him . . . more than she was already.

She headed for Kash's door but turned at the last minute. "How was school today?" Kash had admitted recently that things weren't great at school. The middle school was attached to the high school, and there was a group of upperclassmen who loved to pick on the younger kids. Kash was apparently in their sights.

It wasn't a huge revelation. He was thinner and shorter than most of his classmates. Add in his red hair and the fact that he loved science, and Harper wasn't surprised he was a target. Winning the crate race apparently hadn't helped either. It had just put a spotlight, and target, firmly on his back.

"Fine," Kash mumbled, as he went over to his bookshelf and pretended to look at the books.

This was karma doing her thing once more. Harper knew it. Because she'd been a mean girl when she was younger, her son was paying the price. "And robotics club? Is that going well?"

"Yeah."

"You like it?"

"Uh-huh."

It was like pulling teeth. Harper was torn between staying and trying to get her son to talk to her and confronting Linc. Figuring Kash wasn't going to open up tonight, she opted for the latter.

"All right. I'll be back up to check on you in a bit. You showering tonight or in the morning?"

Her son looked at her then. "What time do you work tomorrow? Will you need the bathroom in the morning?"

He was *such* a good kid. Always looking out for her. "I don't go in until noon."

Kash wrinkled his nose. "Which means you work until like eight, right?"

"Unfortunately, yes."

"All right. I'll shower in the morning then."

"Okay." Impulsively Harper walked over to Kash and leaned down, kissing the top of his head. "Thank you for the wonderful dinner. I love your room, and mine. We're very lucky Linc extended the offer for us to stay here. We just have to be careful not to wear out our welcome. He's not used to living with anyone. He probably likes his space."

Kash shrugged. "He said he liked having me here. That the house got lonely. That he could use my help."

Harper had no doubt Linc had said those words to her son. But had he meant them? Or was he just being nice? She really needed to have a discussion with the man. To set boundaries. And to request he also set some when it came to Kash. Her son was desperate for positive male attention, and he could easily become a pest.

"Love you, Kash," Harper said, as she backed toward the door once more.

"Love you too."

At least her son hadn't grown up enough to think saying "I love you" was for babies. The time was coming though, all too soon, when he'd not want to openly show his affection. When he'd want to spend all his free time with his friends. Harper dreaded that day, but was all too aware it was part of growing up. Part of Kash finding out who he was and spreading his wings.

And there was every possibility that staying with Linc, flourishing under his influence, would make that time come faster than she wanted.

Harper closed his door almost all the way, leaving it open a crack, then took a deep breath as she headed down the hall. As she glanced into the bathroom on her way, she saw it too looked full of brand-new things. Thick, fluffy towels on the rack, all her toiletries on the counter, bright shower curtain that still smelled like plastic. There were even some deodorant and body spray on Kash's side of the counter that Harper certainly hadn't bought for him.

Her resolve firmed as she continued toward the stairs. Linc shouldn't have bought all the things he had for them. They weren't charity cases, and she didn't like feeling as if she owed him.

But a small part of her, deep down, felt a *little* warm and fuzzy that he'd gone so far out of his way to make them both happy. That he was trying to take care of them.

Was that what he was doing? Or was he manipulating them? Was this all some weird way of getting back at her for all those years ago, when she'd done her best to make his life miserable? Providing things for her son that she couldn't?

No. Linc wasn't that kind of man. She knew that without a doubt. It was more likely he was simply trying to make a single mother and her son feel welcome in their new space. Comfortable.

It wasn't that she didn't *want* to feel that way, but a part of her didn't feel as if she deserved it. Kash? Yes, he absolutely did. But her? She'd made too many mistakes in her life that she needed to atone for.

Straightening her shoulders, she started down the stairs, determined to find Linc.

Chapter Four

It was only a matter of time.

Harper wasn't going to be thrilled with all the things he'd bought for her and Kash today. But once he'd started shopping, he couldn't seem to stop. They needed beds, but also a place to put their clothes. And Kash needed a bookshelf. That had him thinking about what other books Kash might like, which led to him thinking about how few clothes both Kash and Harper had.

He'd ended up spending way more than he'd anticipated, but Linc didn't feel one ounce of buyer's remorse. Both Harper and her son needed more than the pathetically meager amount of belongings they possessed. And he could afford to buy them.

But he knew without a doubt that Harper wasn't going to be as appreciative as Kash had been when he'd seen his new room. The new sheets, blankets, rugs . . . it was kind of like putting makeup on a pig, as the rooms still needed a lot of work. But he'd wanted to make both their private spaces feel like a sanctuary . . . for as long as they'd be here.

He had no idea how long that would be, but surprisingly, he wasn't too worried about it. Kash was a good kid. He'd spent enough time with him before today to know that, but spending one-on-one time with him, while they walked through the house and Linc told him what his plans were, and as they "cooked" side by side, it was even more obvious what a good person Kash was. Harper was doing an amazing job raising him. He was sensitive, kind, and protective.

Though . . . Linc had seen a hint of a very familiar emotion in his expression when he'd asked about school. He'd allowed Kash to change the subject, but it wasn't hard to see that the boy didn't really like school, which was a shame, since he was so smart he should be excited to go every day. To learn something new.

Linc got the immediate feeling Kash didn't like school because of how he was treated. Which Linc *hated* for him. Kash was amazing, and just because he was a late bloomer who enjoyed astronomy and science more than sports, that shouldn't put him in the crosshairs of school bullies. But it probably had. And that sucked.

Linc knew all too well how it felt.

It was ironic that it was Kash's mother who'd made Linc feel that way.

He shook off the melancholy. Those days were well and truly behind him. He needed to concentrate on the here and now. And that meant hearing whatever Harper wanted to say. And it was obvious she had lots of thoughts running through her head as she walked down the stairs toward him.

To his surprise, Linc wanted to grin. She was actually cute. She still had on the khaki pants she wore to work and the navy blue polo shirt that did nothing for her shape or coloring. She looked tired but determined. He liked seeing her in mama-bear mode. And he had no doubt that's what she was. She might not stick up for herself, but for Kash, she'd face her enemies head-on . . . not that he was an enemy. Far from it.

It had been less than a day since he'd offered to let her and Kash move in, and he was already getting to know a completely different Harper than she showed the rest of the world. A more vulnerable one. Unsure of herself. Hanging on by a thread. It was a far cry from the self-assured, almost conceited girl she'd once been.

"It's too much, Linc," she said without preamble as she approached. She kept her voice low, likely so Kash wouldn't overhear her.

"What is?" he asked, acting confused. He knew exactly what she was talking about.

"You know what. The beds, the clothes, the books, the freaking shower curtain!"

"You'd rather water get all over the bathroom? Sleep on the floor? Keep Kash's books in stacks around his room?"

"Well, no . . . but you said you had beds," she accused.

"I lied," he said easily.

Harper's mouth fell open. "I can't believe you just admitted that."

"Why not? It's true. Look, you needed a place to go. Kash needed a place where he didn't have to worry about his mom storming off in the middle of the night to sleep in her car. I have the room, it's not a big deal."

"It *is* a big deal," Harper said, quietly and a little calmer. "To me, it's a huge deal."

Linc supposed she was right, and he said so. "I don't mean to belittle your feelings. Look, I like Kash. He reminds me a lot of myself. I was a scrawny, quiet little kid in school too. I was obsessed with planes, and he's obsessed with space. He's going to do great things, Harper, I just know it. But he needs a safe place to land. One without judgment. And I can offer that to him. *And* you."

Harper just stared at him.

Linc took advantage of her speechlessness and went on.

"Your rooms are drafty, and will only get more so as we head into the heart of winter. Warm bedding was necessary because it'll get chilly in your rooms, until I can get the windows replaced and resealed. I know you noticed how much work there still needs to be done, but that doesn't mean you can't be comfortable in the meantime. And it's not as if the beds and bedding will go to waste after you're gone. They can be reused. I needed to get some furniture, and your arrival just sped up that process a bit. That's all."

"And the stuff for Kash in the bathroom? And the books?"

Linc shrugged. "Those were spontaneous purchases. I thought he'd like them."

He could see emotions flitting across Harper's face. "He does."

Linc nodded.

"I just . . . I don't want him getting too attached. We're leaving as soon as I save up enough money," Harper said.

For some reason, that sent a pang of pain through Linc. But he pushed it down. Wasn't he just thinking about how difficult it would be to live with someone else? How hard it would be to keep his insomnia and nightmares from them? He'd known when he'd made the offer that this was temporary.

"I understand that. And I hope you'll take all the things I got for Kash with you when you go. But that doesn't mean he won't always have a place here."

"You aren't his dad."

The four words were said sharply and with an intent to hurt. Which they did.

"I understand that too. But from where I'm standing, he *has* no father. And Victor certainly hasn't acted like a loving grandfather. Kash is starved for some positive male attention. I don't want to be his dad, but I wouldn't mind being his friend," Linc bit out.

Harper sighed and looked at the floor. She ran a hand through her hair, pulling out the ponytail holder, letting her auburn hair spill around her shoulders. She lifted her head and looked him in the eye. "I'm sorry. That was uncalled for. Rude. And you're right. About all of it. I'm grateful that you're letting us stay here. That you're being as cool as you have been with Kash. He looks up to you, and there's no one I can think of who'd be a better role model. I swear, I can't remember a time he voluntarily offered to do dishes. He's been here less than a day, and you've already been a good influence. Thank you."

Linc nodded.

"But . . ."

He knew there was a *but* coming.

"I don't want him to be disappointed when we leave. Don't want him to resent me in any way. We've always been a duo. We've only ever had each other. I don't want to lose that closeness."

"You and Kash will always have a bond that can't be broken," Linc said gently. "Nothing I do or say will ever change that. I don't know anything about what the two of you have been through together, but Kash always has your best interests at heart. He insisted you get the bigger room, and he made sure yours was perfect before he touched any of his stuff.

"All he talked about was how hard you work and how excited you'd be to have dinner waiting when you got home. He asked me if I'd teach him how to make other stuff, so he could make sure you had food waiting when you got home after you moved out. He knows staying here isn't a permanent thing, Harper. He's a great kid. Loyal, protective, and you've done a hell of a job raising him in what I'm guessing were difficult conditions.

"But he *is* growing up. Will want time to himself more and more. I can offer that to him here. He'll always have an open invitation to hang out. Spend the night if he wants. There are no strings attached to that offer either."

"Thank you."

"You're welcome. And before you find out yourself, I should tell you that I stocked the pantry and fridge today as well."

"Um . . . all right?"

"No, I mean, I *stocked* it," Linc informed her. "Here, let me show you." He walked over to the pantry and opened the door.

The shelves were packed from floor to ceiling with pasta, canned food, crackers, potato chips, protein bars and drinks, and everything in between.

"There wasn't room for it all, so I cleared out the front hall closet and turned that into a second pantry," Linc said a little sheepishly. "And I bought an upright freezer as well. It's in the mudroom off the back door, because there wasn't any other good place to put it. It's stocked as well."

Harper stared at him incredulously.

"Kash is a growing boy," Linc defended himself, feeling a *little* embarrassed at how overboard he'd gone.

"This makes the three bags of snacks I brought home seem pretty lame," Harper said under her breath.

"They're not lame. While Kash was showing you the upstairs, I put away the things you got. I had no idea he liked wasabi peas."

"He loves them."

"Things aren't always going to go as smoothly as they did tonight. I'm sure I'll irritate Kash at some point, because I can definitely be annoying. I've gotten used to living alone. And Kash is almost a teenager. They get moody. And you're probably just as used to being on your own, with no one else to help you with Kash. We'll figure it out. Give each other space when we need it. This is going to work, Harper. We just have to put in the effort."

"Yeah. But I want to be clear that you don't have to keep buying us things. We're good, Linc. We might not have a lot, but we have each other."

"And no one can ever take that away from you. What time do you work tomorrow? Kash wasn't sure when I asked."

"Not until noon. But that means I won't be home for dinner. I get off at eight."

"Okay. Depending on what time Kash gets up in the morning, maybe we can make you something to bring with you."

"He's an early riser. Which I am not," Harper said with a small grin.

"Then you can sleep in, and I'll make sure he eats a good breakfast and gets out to the bus on time."

"You don't have to do that. I'll get up."

"I know I don't have to, but I'll be up anyway. Sleep in for a change."

"So you're a morning person too?" she asked.

"You have no idea," Linc responded before thinking. He didn't think she meant two or three in the morning, which was when he usually woke up.

"We'll see," she said with a small shrug. "Is there anything I can do while I'm down here? Any chores? I want to do my fair share of stuff around here."

Linc wanted to tell Harper that she did enough. Working her ass off, taking care of Kash, shouldering all the responsibility for him on her fragile-looking shoulders. But he wasn't about to say that. Besides, he'd already told her that she could help around the house instead of paying rent.

"Sure. Anything you see that needs doing. Vacuuming or sweeping is almost useless with these floors, but there's always the trash to take out and recycling. Maybe you can swing by the transfer station on your way to work some days with the big boxes I've broken down or with other trash. Lord knows with the amount of reno this house needs, I've got a lot of trash for the dump."

"Of course. And I can cook. On the days I'm not working."

"I'd like that," Linc told her, meaning it. He'd never expect her to cook for him, but he wouldn't turn it down either, if she felt like tinkering in his incredibly outdated kitchen.

"I'll also do mine and Kash's laundry."

"He already asked if I had a washer and dryer and told me he'd take care of that for himself."

"He did?"

"Yup. Mumbled something about not wanting you to mess up his new clothes?"

Harper chuckled, and the sound made Linc relax.

"Do you really think this will work?" she asked. "We don't even know each other. Not really."

"Yes," Linc said firmly. "We've both got Kash's best interests at heart. If that doesn't make us a team in this, I don't know what will."

"Yeah." Harper looked him in the eyes once more. "We should talk about what happened back in high school."

"No, we shouldn't."

"Linc, I was awful," she protested.

"It was decades ago. I hold nothing against you, Harper. I admit that having you living next door to my mom wasn't something I was thrilled about at first. But you're a different person now, as am I."

"I *am* a different person. And I'll do everything in my power to prove it to you."

"You don't have to prove anything. I know how different you are, because if you weren't, Kash wouldn't be the amazing, kind, caring kid that he is."

Every muscle in her body seemed to sag at his compliment. "Thanks," she whispered.

"Not blowing smoke up your ass, Harper. Just stating facts."

"I still appreciate hearing it. Being a single mom is hard. Some days it feels as if I've screwed everything up, and others I couldn't be happier with how things have gone."

"Understandable," Linc agreed. "But speaking of school . . . do we need to talk about Kash and present-day mean girls and bullies?"

Harper sighed.

"I'm not saying this next thing to be cruel . . . but the first time you and your friends called me Rinky-Dink Linc was when I was in the seventh grade."

Harper winced and turned away from him. But since it was dark outside and there were lights on in the house, Linc could see her unhappy reflection in the floor-to-ceiling windows.

"He's skinny, Harper. Sticks out like a sore thumb with his red hair. And that's not even including the fact that he's into science, is a member of the robotics club. He's also new to the area. To the school. If he's not being bullied, I'd be shocked."

"I think he is," she admitted in a low tone. She had her arms wrapped around herself defensively. "But he won't talk to me about it."

"I'll see what I can do. Get him to open up."

She turned her head and met his gaze. "I'm so sorry," she whispered.

"Stop, Harper. Don't go there. We're starting new. From today. I admit it took me a few years to get over my anger at you and your friends, but anger serves no purpose now. I lived my life and you lived yours. Our paths have crossed again, and we're starting over."

"You're being very gracious about this," she said.

He shrugged. "I learned the hard way that life isn't fair. That when push comes to shove, holding grudges is useless. You have to put one foot in front of the other and keep going, no matter what. It's either that or lay down and die."

How the conversation had turned so serious, Linc wasn't sure. But he regretted steering it in the direction he had. The last thing he wanted was Harper asking about the accident that took his career and caused his less-than-restful nights.

"There's not much we can do about the bullies, but we can make sure Kash knows we're here if he wants to talk, and that he can rise above whatever shit they're saying to him," Linc said firmly.

Harper still looked uncomfortable, and Linc knew she was thinking about some of the things she and her girl posse had done and said to him. But he truly *was* over it.

Before tonight, he would've said there was no way he'd ever want to get friendly with Harper Bates. But now? With Kash's help, he saw a completely different Harper. Insecure, tired but determined. He wanted to help her, almost as much as he wanted to help her son navigate the muddy waters of middle and high school.

For someone who'd never wanted kids, Linc found himself looking forward to spending more time with the preteen. To encouraging his love of science and seeing where his interests might take him. What kind of man he'd become.

Linc had a feeling he'd do amazing things with his life.

"I didn't want to come home. Back here to Rockville," Harper admitted. "Thought it was a failure. That everyone would see *me* as a failure. I mean, I didn't exactly do anything I set out to do when I moved to New York.

"But you know what? I'm glad to be here. Even though my dad's extremely hard to please and there was no way I could continue to live with him, I love him, and I'm glad to get to know him better as an adult. I think Kash can flourish here, more so than in New York, as long as he can find a good friend group and stay away from the bullies.

And even though my job isn't anything I wanted to be doing, I'm proud of myself."

"You should be," Linc told her. "I'm going to turn in. Make yourself at home. Watch TV, get a snack, do whatever you want in the house. You aren't going to bother me."

It was early, way too early for him to go to bed, but Linc was feeling the need to put some space between him and Harper. He didn't like her body language, closed off and stressed. It was taking all his control not to take her in his arms and give her a huge hug. If anyone needed one, it was Harper Bates.

But he wasn't going there. They were friends of a sort. That was it. She wasn't his to soothe. Nor was he a shrink, even though Lord knew he'd *seen* his fair share over the last several years.

Linc had provided her and her son a safe place to land, to regroup, to get their bearings. She'd be leaving soon enough. He simply needed to be a good host until that time came.

"Okay. I'm not much of a TV watcher, I prefer to read," she told him.

"Well, I've got a ton of books you can choose from. Not sure if they're your genre or not, but you're welcome to take your pick," Linc told her, gesturing to the bookshelves on the far wall. "There are more in boxes in one of the rooms on the second floor. I'm happy to let you or Kash rummage through them."

"Awesome."

"Good night, Harper."

"Night, Linc."

Linc walked toward his bedroom, knowing he was going to be up most of the night because he wouldn't be able to shut his brain off after everything that had happened today. Because of his change in circumstances.

At the last second, before he entered his room and shut the door, Linc found himself turning back toward the living room, and Harper.

"My mom's planning a big Thanksgiving. With all of her sons home, and with two grandbabies on the way, she's almost giddy with happiness and wants to have a traditional Thanksgiving dinner with all the trimmings. She's going to make way too much food, and I have it on good authority that she's asked Zach to help as well. Will you and Kash come? And invite your dad too?"

The offer to invite Victor was impulsive, and one he'd probably regret. But hearing Harper talk about the love she had for the man, he couldn't exactly leave him out of the invitation. And if he wanted Harper and Kash there, Victor would have to be included as well.

Linc was very aware that none of his brothers would be thrilled to share a table with their old neighbor, but wasn't that what the holidays were about? Forgiveness and togetherness? Like it or not, Victor Rogers was *still* their mom's neighbor. And Chad and Britt's, actually. He was a curmudgeon, and he had done some *not*-so-neighborly things in the past when it came to Lobster Cove, but he'd also been vital in finding Marit, and informing everyone about Camden kidnapping Mom and Britt.

"I don't know . . ." Harper said.

"Think about it. You know my mom. Know she'd be over the moon to have you and Kash there. And your dad too. Her heart is huge, and the more the merrier as far as she's concerned."

"Thanks, Linc. I know you didn't bargain on any of this."

"You're right, I didn't. But I'm not sorry about it either. My life had gotten . . . well, let's just say you and Kash are a good distraction."

"Distraction?"

Linc wasn't ready to discuss this, even though he'd brought it up. "Good night, Harper. Let me know about Thanksgiving so I can tell Mom."

He gently shut his door, knowing he'd made the right decision by inviting Harper and her family to Thanksgiving. It might be awkward having Victor join them—if he even accepted—but *someone* had to extend an olive branch. The man would never win any neighbor-of-the-year awards, but it was past time to put differences aside and attempt to mend fences.

Linc heard Harper puttering around in the kitchen for a few minutes, then her footsteps on the stairs. It wasn't until he heard her door close that he relaxed. He hadn't realized he was so tense until that moment.

His life had already changed immensely, and it hadn't even been a full day. If anyone had told him twenty years ago that he'd be living with the girl who'd tormented him every day, he would've called them insane. And yet, here they were. And the weird thing was . . . he actually liked having Harper there.

Life had kicked her in the teeth, but she was still plugging along. He admired that in her. Hell, he simply admired Harper. She was no longer the spoiled brat she'd been all those years ago. He hated that she'd had to go through such tough times in order to learn what was important in life, but her experiences had turned her into a woman that Linc respected.

Was . . . attracted to?

No, no, no. He couldn't be attracted to Harper Bates. Wouldn't that be hilarious, if he and the girl who'd bullied him relentlessly ended up together? It was like a bad Hallmark movie.

Though, Linc couldn't deny the attraction was there. She was beautiful, even in her exhaustion and worry about Kash. She worked hard. Wasn't afraid to apologize for her past behavior or make amends. Was a damn good mother.

In fact, Linc pretty much hadn't found anything that majorly turned him off.

He needed to be careful. *Very* careful. Because she was going to leave, of that he had no doubt. Her goal from the moment she'd come back to Maine was to find a place of her own for her and Kash. He had to keep that in mind. The last thing he wanted was to become another decision she regretted.

Taking a deep breath, Linc grabbed a book off the stack on the table next to his bed and climbed onto the mattress. He arranged his pillows behind his back and got comfortable. He hoped to read until he got tired, and with any luck, he'd sleep for a few solid hours before his nightmares woke him once again.

Chapter Five

The transition from living with her dad to living in Linc's house was going surprisingly well. Harper expected to feel awkward around Linc, but he truly seemed to have put their past history behind him. Though *she* found it harder to forget how she'd treated him once upon a time, since he was being so cool about it, Harper was beginning to come to terms with her past as well.

And Kash was already flourishing living under Linc's roof, being around him all the time. As each day passed, Harper saw her son doing more and more things to mimic their host. He was more polite, calmer, and seemed to sincerely enjoy things like cooking, doing his own laundry, and taking out the trash.

He'd always gone out of his way to take care of her, but being around Linc had made those instincts even more prevalent in her son. When Harper came home from work, she didn't have to do much of anything. Kash insisted on setting the table, doing the dishes, and even finishing his homework without any nagging on her part.

And seeing him and Linc discuss what he was learning in science class, and hearing the stories Linc told him about the weather phenomena he'd witnessed firsthand from the cockpit of a plane, was as eye opening to her as it was to her son.

Almost a week had passed since they'd moved in, and to Harper, it felt as if they'd been here much longer. Linc was an easy man to live with. If anything, she wished she had more time to simply sit and talk to him. To get to know him better.

But she had a feeling if she did have that time, it would make things . . . complicated. Harper liked Linc. A lot. He was a good man, a good son, a good brother, and an excellent role model for Kash. It was as if he'd been a father for years. He seemed to know exactly what to say to Kash to make him happy, to motivate him or cheer him up.

Harper hated how much she had to work as the holidays approached, because that meant she was away from Kash even more than usual. School wasn't going well for him. Not academics, those were great as always. But socially, he was struggling to find his place. To find a group of friends who would have his back.

And much to her dismay, bullies *had* homed in on her son as an easy mark.

Kash didn't say much, but what he did admit to was heartbreaking. And Harper knew all too well that what he *wasn't* saying was probably twice as bad as what he was.

There was one boy in particular, an upperclassman, who seemed to delight in tormenting Kash and other younger kids at lunch . . . one of the only times the high school and middle school kids mingled. He'd gotten his friends involved as well, including his girlfriend.

It was disheartening, and even though Kash didn't talk much about what went on while he was at school, it was obvious he was miserable.

Thank goodness this was a holiday week, and they both had a little bit of a break.

It was Wednesday, and Kash had today and the rest of the week off from school, and Harper had Thursday and Friday off from work. How she'd managed to get Black Friday off, she had no idea, but she wasn't going to complain.

Of course, she had to work until ten o'clock this evening, but it was a small price to pay for having the next two days off in a row.

Every morning when Harper got up, Linc was already awake, and had usually prepared breakfast for her and Kash. And when she got home from work, no matter the time, he was always still up. She honestly didn't know when the man slept.

This morning, Kash was sleeping in since he didn't have to go to school, and she wasn't leaving until after noon. So she had a little bit of time to actually sit and enjoy her morning, for once. And to talk to Linc, which she was more excited about than she probably should be.

"Morning," she said with a smile, as she walked into the kitchen.

"Morning, Harper. Did you sleep well?" Linc asked.

"Like a rock. You?"

"Like I always do," he responded. "I made an egg casserole last night. Eggs, sausage, cheese, peppers—both hot and sweet—and hash browns on the bottom. That okay?"

Harper frowned. "I got home at nine. You made that after I went to bed?"

Linc shrugged. "Yeah."

"Well, thank you. It sounds delicious."

"I'm going to make cinnamon rolls with Kash when he gets up . . . if that's okay."

"Why wouldn't it be okay?" she asked, genuinely curious.

"Because it's junk food that'll rot his teeth."

Harper chuckled. "He's a teenager. And I think his teeth are safe. Besides, he needs the calories."

"True. My plan was to have him eat the casserole before we started on the rolls. I saw a video online that takes the regular cinnamon rolls in a can and adds a shit ton more butter and sugar to make them even gooier and tastier."

"Yum!" Harper said with a smile. The thought of Linc seeing a recipe online and saving it to make something with Kash made her heart flip-flop in her chest. "When in the world do you have time to scroll through the internet, looking for recipes?"

If she wasn't mistaken, she thought Linc looked a little embarrassed at her question.

"Not that there's anything wrong with that," she added quickly.

"Sometimes I have trouble sleeping, and I end up going online to try to pass the time and to make myself tired enough to fall back asleep," Linc admitted.

"I don't know what that's like," Harper joked. "I don't have that problem. I can usually always sleep. Well, recently. Not so much when we were in our car, but here? Now that I know my boy is warm, safe, and happy? I'm out like a light."

Linc didn't even twitch. "I'm glad I could help give that to you."

"Me too." Swallowing hard, butterflies in her belly, Harper forced herself to change the subject. The more she got to know Linc, the more she *wanted* to get to know him. She'd had no idea that he had trouble sleeping. She wanted to help him, but of course there wasn't much she could do about it. "So . . . is there anything I can pick up from the store for tomorrow?"

"Nope. I guess Mom's been in a cooking frenzy. She's totally in her element and very excited for tomorrow," Linc said.

"Yeah, Britt added me to a group text with her and Marit, and she's been keeping us updated on the crazy that is your mother," Harper said with a smile. "She says she's been like an Army general, ordering everyone around, worrying about making everything perfect."

Linc chuckled. "Sounds like Mom. She was always like that. A ball of energy, when all us kids ever wanted was to sleep in on our days off. She'd make us get up early to have 'family time.' Your dad is still coming, right?"

"As far as I know. He tried to claim he didn't want to come, that he wouldn't be welcome, but your mom drove over to his place, told him to his face that he'd better be there or else, then drove back to Lobster Cove."

"I wish I could've seen that," Linc said, grinning.

"I have the video," Harper said.

"*What?* You do?"

"Yup. He got a camera for the front door when Kash and I moved back home. He said he wanted us to feel safe. I downloaded the video from my phone and saved it. It's priceless. Here, I'll show you." Harper slipped her phone out of her back pocket and walked over to where Linc stood in the kitchen. She pulled up the video and leaned toward him so they could watch it at the same time.

It wasn't until Evelyn's voice was echoing through the room that Harper realized just *how* close she and Linc were standing. He'd put his arm around her waist, seemingly without thought, and she was leaning into him. Since they were the same height, their cheeks were practically touching as they watched his mom point her finger in Victor's face and order him to show up to Thanksgiving, "or else."

She also told him they were neighbors, and it was way past time they started acting like it. Adding that she felt Kash was as much *her* grandson as he was Victor's, and she didn't want the boy feeling torn about which grandparent to spend the holiday with.

She said some other stuff, which was as funny as it was endearing, but Harper stopped paying attention. She couldn't think about anything other than how . . . *right* it felt to basically be in Linc's arms. He was warm, muscular, and smelled so darn good. Harper wanted to turn her head and bury her nose in his neck.

She refrained . . . barely. This was the first time she'd been this close to the man, and it was taking every ounce of strength she had not to sag into him.

She felt more at home in his arms than she had in any other man's embrace. Ever. And that thought scared the shit out of her. This was Lincoln Young. The man she'd tormented. The guy who'd selflessly invited her and Kash to stay with him so she wouldn't feel the need to sleep in her minivan to get away from her overbearing father.

The man she was discovering she liked. A lot. Like . . . *a lot* a lot.

"My mom," Linc said with a small chuckle that seemed to reverberate through Harper.

Harper stepped away from him more abruptly than she'd intended. Ignoring the confused look on Linc's face, she managed to return his smile. She hoped it looked more natural than it felt. "Yeah, so as far as I know, Dad's still coming over tomorrow. If he doesn't show, I'll go over there and get him. Or maybe I'll send Kash."

"If he doesn't show, *I'll* go over there and drag his ass to Lobster Cove. My mom's worked her butt off for this Thanksgiving, and she's looking forward to him being there as much as she is the rest of us."

Harper was still feeling a bit off kilter from her sort-of embrace with Linc, and she desperately wanted to change the subject to something safer . . . for her own peace of mind. "Have you talked to Kash about school in the last couple days? Every time I ask about it, all I get is 'It's fine.'"

"Not yet, but I thought I'd take him to the airfield like he's been begging me to, on Saturday. Ever since I told him that's what I liked to do when I was his age, he's been asking if I'll take him. I figured since you'd be working, and I need a break from paint fumes, it would be a good day for it. I thought I'd try talking to him then."

Harper wanted to cry, and she wasn't sure why. Maybe she was still reeling from her close encounter—and the realization that she had a crush on the man—but it took an immense amount of control to keep the tears from falling. "I trust you, Linc. I know you'll tread carefully."

"Of course I will."

"He looks up to you so much. Admires you."

Linc shrugged as he turned back to the casserole he'd apparently made the night before. He was putting it in the oven to warm it up before they dug into it. "I'm nobody special."

Harper couldn't and *wouldn't* put up with this man saying things like that. She took a step toward him without thought and put her hand on his back.

He turned his head toward her.

"You can't really think that," she said with a small frown.

Linc finished fiddling with the oven timer and turned to face her. Harper's hand, still connected with him, was now resting on his chest. They were standing toe-to-toe and staring into each other's eyes. It was nice, not having to crane her neck to look up or down at him. They were the perfect height together. Their bodies would line up flawlessly.

She wasn't sure if he'd gotten closer, or if she'd made the move, but suddenly there was only a hairsbreadth between them. One of his hands rose to rest on her hip, and the other brushed a lock of hair away from her cheek.

"I'm *not* special," he insisted. "I'm antisocial, except when it comes to my family. I'd rather spend my time here, being a hermit in my house, than going out and trying to improve my community. I've got demons, Harper. Demons you have no idea about. Couldn't even imagine."

"We all have them," she insisted.

But Linc shook his head. "Not like mine."

She frowned, and somehow her hand slid upward until it had curled around the back of his neck, her other hand now on his chest. Now they were touching from their chests to their hips. Both his arms were around her, hands clasped together at the small of her back. She licked her lips, and she couldn't help but notice how his gaze immediately dropped to watch.

"Related to what happened? Your crash?" she whispered.

"Yes."

It was one word, yet Harper couldn't help but feel pleased that he was opening up to her. "Do you want to talk about it?"

"No."

"Okay. Can I do anything to help?" she asked.

"You're doing it."

"I'm not doing anything."

"You're here. With Kash. Keeping my mind occupied on other things."

"Except I'm not here much," she said with a small laugh. "I'm always at freaking work."

"But you are. You're up here," Linc said, lifting a hand to tap at his temple, before lowering it once again to hold her against him.

"Oh." Harper didn't know what to say to that.

Wait—yes she did.

"You *are* special, Lincoln Young. You always have been. I think that's why I was so willing to go along with my girlfriends all those years ago. Because even when you were a gangly teenager, more angles than muscles, I knew deep down that you were going to be someone. Do great things.

"I had goals, but they felt superficial compared to yours. I knew you wanted to be a pilot, that you wanted to go into the military. What did *I* want? I wanted to be famous. To be a model. So I did my best to bring you down. But you didn't let me or my friends crush your spirit. You left Rockville and soared, *literally.* While I crashed and burned. And now, as an adult, you might pretend to be a hermit, but you actually have a way of drawing people in. Of making them feel comfortable and safe."

"You feel that way?"

Harper licked her lips again. Scared to admit what she was feeling. But she wanted to be honest with this man. "Yes."

"Good."

"Good?" she asked.

"Yeah, good," Linc repeated. "Because I like being the person who makes you feel that way."

Harper's fingers tingled. Hell, her whole body was tingling. She felt as if they were on the verge of . . . something. Something important.

But she was scared to make any kind of move. What if she was wrong? What if Linc was just being Linc . . . protective and concerned, in a friendly way and nothing more? She'd be mortified if she did what she couldn't stop thinking about doing—namely, leaning forward and putting her lips on his—only to have him reject her.

"Harper?" he whispered, leaning forward a fraction of an inch and pressing the pads of his fingers into her lower back.

"Yes," she told him, giving him the consent she hoped he was clearly asking for.

The gleam in his eyes as he closed the distance between them sparked an immediate fire deep within Harper. A fire of desire she hadn't felt for years, if ever.

Her fingers tightened on his nape as his lips brushed against hers.

It was a fleeting caress. Too quick. Too light. Not even a kiss, really. And still she let out a small moan. Felt his hips twitch against hers at the sound.

She was a giant ball of nerves right then. Feeling more than she had in forever.

"Mom?"

The sound of Kash's confused and sleepy voice jerked her back to the present.

God. What was she doing?

The last thing she wanted was to ruin the good thing she had going on here. If she started something with Linc, and he decided he was done, she and Kash would have nowhere to go. Well, they could go back to her dad's house, but that would be less than ideal . . . and include a resounding "I told you so" from Victor.

Harper took a step back—or tried to, but Linc's hands on the small of her back wouldn't budge.

"Your mom got something in her eye, Bud. I was just trying to see if I could find anything in there," Linc said smoothly. He'd put a bit of distance between them, but they were still standing way too close. Harper was grateful for his quick thinking, disappointed though she was that they'd been interrupted.

"Oh. I'm hungry. Whatever's cooking smells really good. It woke me up. What is it?"

Linc's hands finally dropped from behind her, but not before brushing against her oh so slowly as they did. Harper took a step backward and saw Linc's gaze was still locked on hers. The desire and regret in his eyes made her feel not so alone in her feelings.

Though, *her* feelings didn't matter. Kash's interruption was for the best. She couldn't kiss Linc again. She couldn't mess up this living situation. Not for her sake, and definitely not for Kash's.

But a tiny part of her couldn't help wondering if kissing Linc actually *would* mess things up.

Maybe it would make things better?

She wasn't sure. But now wasn't the time or place to explore whatever was going on between them. Not when she had a long workday ahead of her. Not when tomorrow was Thanksgiving and they'd be surrounded by family.

Not when Kash was wandering into the kitchen, ready to help Linc with breakfast.

"I think I'll go and shower while you men get breakfast ready," Harper announced, proud that she sounded so normal.

At least she thought she did. When she looked at Linc, she saw lust in his gaze for a split second before he banked it. Was thinking about her in the shower the image that put that look on his face? Of course, thinking about bathing made her think about Linc, naked in *his* shower. Which made her tingle between her legs.

Damn, she had it bad. She had to get a grip.

"You want me to see if I can spot anything in your eye before you go?" Kash asked, sounding concerned.

It didn't go over her head that Kash was mimicking Linc once again. He was such a sweet boy. Always wanting to take care of her. She tore her gaze from Linc's and looked at her son. "I think I'm okay now. But thanks. I heard you and Linc are going to make cinnamon rolls today. And on Saturday, he's going to take you to the airfield."

Kash beamed. "Yeah, I'm so excited! And don't forget about Thanksgiving! It's been forever since we've had a real Thanksgiving, hasn't it, Mom?"

"Yeah, baby, it has." Harper didn't want to think about the last few Thanksgivings they'd had in New York. Getting their holiday meals from a shelter, or in the form of a bag from the food pantry. And last year, how they'd actually been living in the minivan over the holidays.

She never wanted to go back to that kind of situation. Didn't wish it on anyone.

"Come on, Bud. I'll show you the video about how to make the cinnamon rolls. The casserole will be reheated by the time your mom is done showering and changing," Linc said.

"Cool."

The last thing Harper saw when she turned around at the base of the stairs was Linc leaning over the counter, holding his phone, his head right next to her son's as they intently watched how to make the world's best cinnamon rolls.

She paused for a moment, wanting things she had no right to want.

For this to be her life.

But life was much more complicated than her simple wishes and dreams. She'd learned that the hard way, from the moment she'd left home all those years ago. Just because she wanted something didn't mean it would actually happen.

She liked Linc. A lot. Wouldn't mind seeing where things between them could go. But why in the world would a man like Linc want someone with her baggage?

Sighing, Harper turned her back on the cozy kitchen scene that she desperately wanted to join, instead trudging up the stairs toward the bathroom. She had a long day at work to get through. Then hopefully a relaxing, if not possibly chaotic, Thanksgiving. She could only pray her dad behaved himself and that everything went all right. Then a day off before the grind of the holidays *truly* started at work.

She had no time and no right to be attempting anything with Linc. No matter how much she wanted to. Kash came first. Would always come first. She'd made that vow the day he was born and wasn't going to deviate from it now. If she and Linc started dating and it ended badly, Kash would be the one who got hurt the most. And she'd already done enough to hurt her son in his short life. She'd be damned if she did anything else.

But even as she showered, she couldn't forget the way Linc's lips felt brushing against hers. How she'd felt in the circle of his arms. The softness of his hair against her fingertips as she'd pulled him close.

Her nipples hardened and, without thought, Harper's hand snaked between her legs. It didn't take her long to make herself come, not with thoughts of Linc urging her on.

So much for her resolve to keep things friendly between her and Linc. He might just be the man who broke her resolve. Time would tell if that was a good thing or not.

Chapter Six

Linc was tired, which was nothing new for him. But it seemed as if lately, he was even more exhausted than normal. Between working on the house to make it more comfortable for Harper and Kash, entertaining Kash when he got home from school, making sure both his houseguests ate nutritious meals and didn't just grab junk because it was cheap and easy, and working through his evolving feelings for Harper . . . Linc had gotten even less sleep than normal.

When he'd invited Harper and her son to live with him, he truly hadn't had any expectations in mind. He figured he would help her out for a few months until she could afford rent on a place of her own. Now he had a feeling, even after they'd only been with him for days, that when they left it would make the house seem even emptier and lonelier than it did before.

When Linc had bought the five-bedroom house, he knew it was too big for one man, but he figured he could use the extra space to have sleepovers with his nieces and nephews . . . when his brothers gave him some and when they got old enough. While Linc didn't want kids of his own, he genuinely loved children. Would enjoy spoiling the crap out of his brothers' kids. Teaching them about all the things he liked . . . flying, the outdoors, birds.

Spending time with Kash after school was awesome. He was energetic and funny. And so damn smart it was almost scary. He was also like a sponge, soaking up everything Linc taught him. Hanging on his every word. The afternoon they'd gone out into the crisp November air to look for different kinds of birds—and only seemed able to spot seagulls—was a fail, but Kash had turned the day around by explaining why the moon was sometimes visible in the daytime sky.

When Harper came home and found them sitting on the floor in front of the living room fireplace, wrapped in blankets and drinking hot chocolate, the smile on her face seemed to light up the very air around her.

And that was the problem.

Linc liked her. A lot. The adult Harper he was coming to know was empathetic, worked her ass off for pennies, and didn't accept help easily . . . for just about anything. As if doing so would somehow make her seem weak.

But Linc didn't see her that way at all. She couldn't be weak and live through what she'd endured—and he had a feeling he didn't know the half of it. Like him, she kept a lot of her past close to the vest. Didn't share about her time in New York at all. He knew the basics, but nearly twenty years was a long time to live somewhere and not talk about it.

Kash, on the other hand, was very open about New York. About how he'd hated their tiny little apartments and rooms they'd rented. How scary it was to sleep in their car. How he'd stay awake all night to guard his mom while she slept. How he'd befriended a few homeless men and women and still worried about them to this day.

In short, there were depths to Harper that Linc hadn't expected. And the more time she and her son spent under his roof, the more he was already wishing they'd never leave.

Doing his best to push away thoughts of rattling around his big house by himself when the pair found their own place, Linc's focus returned to the here and now with the sound of Britt's laughter.

She, Marit, Harper, and his mom were sitting out on the deck at Lobster Cove. It was chilly, too cold to be sitting outside, really, but they'd piled blankets on their laps and Chad had lit the portable heater he'd bought earlier in the fall, when it became obvious Mom and Britt's favorite place to sit together was out on the deck.

They were watching Kash and Knox down on the beach, hunting for treasures. Linc wasn't sure what they'd find, since Lobster Cove wasn't known for sea glass or cool driftwood, and it was rare that there were any neat shells that washed ashore. But that wasn't deterring the pair. They were still scouring the beach for anything of interest.

The women were chatting and drinking wine—well, his mom and Harper were—and seemed to be getting along as if all of them had known each other for years rather than a few months.

Britt had one hand on her belly, which had finally started to round with her and Chad's child. And Marit seemed to glow. She was a tiny dynamo who'd proved herself resilient and tough as nails recently, when a lobsterman decided he was going to kidnap her and leave her to die on an uninhabited island. She'd turned the tables on him, and by the time Linc, Victor, and Zach had arrived, she'd subdued the asshole who'd dared try to kill her.

Now the Young family had *two* court dates they were waiting for, which sucked. Linc hated that for his brothers and mom. Things had settled down a little bit in the meantime, and he felt blessed to be spending the holidays with everyone.

"She fits in," Chad said, coming up next to Linc. He took a long drink of the beer he was holding.

Linc didn't have to ask who he was talking about. "Yeah," he agreed.

"Things between you seem good."

His brother was fishing, but Linc didn't mind. "They are."

"Not feeling talkative, huh?" Chad joked. Then he got serious. "I wasn't sure about her, you know. I remember how miserable you were in high school. Harper and her friends really did a number on you."

Linc pressed his lips together and nodded. As the brother closest to him in age, Chad remembered more about Harper from back then. Linc hadn't talked much about how her and her friends had treated him when he was at home, but it was hard to hide how difficult they'd made his high school years.

"But she seems different," Chad went on. "Vulnerable. On edge. As if she expects everyone to turn on her at any time."

Linc nodded. His brother had summed up what he'd sensed perfectly. She seemed to be waiting for the other shoe to drop. For the good things in her life to turn to shit.

"She's had a rough go of it since returning. I had the room, so it wasn't a big deal to offer a place for her and Kash to stay until she gets her feet under her again."

"And Rogers? He's okay with her staying with you?"

"Don't know. Don't care what he thinks, to be honest," Linc said.

"And he's still coming over today, right?"

"As far as I know, yeah. Kash and Harper love him, he's just . . . difficult to live with."

Chad barked out a laugh. "Ya think?"

Linc hid a small smile behind the bottle of beer he brought to his lips.

"Never thought I'd see the day Victor Rogers was sharing a Thanksgiving table with us," Chad mused. "What's the saying, 'Keep your friends close, but your enemies closer'?"

"Rogers isn't our enemy," Linc felt obligated to say. He didn't particularly like the man, but listening to Kash chat about him in a positive light had him thinking about their neighbor in a different way.

And it was a testament to the kid's huge heart that he could say *anything* good about his grandfather, considering how the old man treated him sometimes. But Kash had mentioned in passing how hard it was for his granddad to live by himself. And how much he missed his wife. Had also commented about how smart he was and how fast he could read. Things Linc wasn't sure made him grandfather of the year, but he wasn't going to contradict Kash.

The man *was* lonely though, as Kash pointed out. That was easy to see. He'd liked that his daughter and grandson moved back to Maine, but at the same time, he'd obviously gotten used to having his own space. And they'd definitely been a disruption. Victor also didn't know what to do with Kash, who was a quirky kid, not into the same things Victor was, and that seemed to frustrate them both.

Having Harper and Kash move out would hopefully be a boon for all their relationships. It gave them space from each other, but still allowed them to enjoy having family nearby, which would maybe bring them closer as a result.

"I know he's not," Chad said with a shrug, responding to Linc's comment about their neighbor not being their enemy. "If not for him, we might not be here today. Happy, carefree, enjoying the holiday."

His brother was exactly right. The truth was, the Young family was indebted to Victor Rogers. They might not like it, but it didn't change facts. Their mom seemed thrilled that he was coming over, saying earlier that if he didn't show up by the time the food was ready, she'd march her happy butt over there to drag him to the house by his ear if she had to.

None of her sons would allow *that* to happen, but they'd make sure the man appeared somehow or another.

In the meantime, Zach was hard at work behind them, and even though everyone had offered to help, he'd done nothing but scowl and tell them all to get the hell out of his kitchen. The amazing smells had Linc's belly growling, and he couldn't wait to see what Zach was cooking up . . . besides the traditional turkey, of course.

Their mom had made a ton of appetizers, which everyone had been nibbling on all afternoon, and homemade rolls that she was forced to put away, since over half of them had been consumed within thirty minutes of her putting them out. Her rolls *were* Thanksgiving, at least for Linc. He couldn't remember a holiday without them. They were so damn good. *No one* made bread like their mom.

There were also veggies and homemade sour cream dip, pretzels, smashed brussels sprouts, chicken sausages in a blanket, jalapeño poppers, arancini—which were basically crispy rice balls with a ton of cheese—and of course, deviled eggs.

Everyone was in good spirits. Except for maybe Zach, who was busy muttering to himself in the kitchen and threatening to gut anyone who dared invade his space. But he'd be fine once the food was on the table and he could concentrate on Marit once more.

Hearing more laughter from the deck, Linc looked through the window and saw Harper laughing at something that was said. She looked more relaxed than he'd seen her in quite a while. And he couldn't take his gaze off her lips. Lips he'd touched with his own.

Their light kiss hadn't been nearly enough. It was a taste of what could be. And Linc was almost shocked to realize how much he wanted to not only taste Harper Bates, but devour her. He didn't understand why. She wasn't his type. But then again, the women in his past who he'd thought *were* his type had all ended up being disasters.

Never in a million years would Linc have thought he'd actually be attracted to his childhood tormentor. That he'd look forward to the moment when Kash was dropped off by the bus. That he wouldn't enjoy being by himself anymore.

That last thought was still one of the most difficult to wrap his mind around. Linc had always been content to keep his own company. He spent a lot of time in his own head when he was in the cockpit of a jet. Never had a lot of close friends in the Air Force. He did his job, did it well, then usually went back to his room on whatever ship he was on to read when he was done.

But now? Barely a few days in and he felt restless when Harper was at work and Kash was at school. Found it harder and harder to concentrate on projects around the house.

Hearing Kash open the door and yell out "I'm home!" immediately made his restlessness settle.

It was fun to think of new ways to stimulate Kash's young mind. To introduce him to new things, but also to simply sit and read a book while Kash was on the opposite side of the couch.

While the boy reminded Linc of himself in many ways, Kash also reminded him of Zach, the baby of the family. He was a mama's boy, and Kash was just as devoted to Harper as Zach was to their own mother.

It was a beautiful thing, and also kind of sad. Sad because the protectiveness Kash had inside him for his mom, and others, was most likely a direct result of the hardships they'd lived through in New York. He was an old soul, having seen too much bad in the world at a young age.

But those experiences also made him very sensitive to others. Aware of his surroundings. More perceptive.

A knock on the door tore Linc's thoughts from Harper and Kash. Putting his beer down on a coaster on a small table in the living room, he and Chad both headed for the door at the same time.

Chad reached it first, opening it to a scowling Victor Rogers.

"Wasn't sure if you'd have anything decent to drink, so I brought over a couple six-packs of Rock Harbor Brewing Company's craft beers. I personally like the Storm Surge IPA the best, but will also drink the Spruce Head Stout."

It was a nice gesture delivered in an assholey way. Typical Victor. But Linc was starting to understand the man. He wasn't good at saying thank you, or even being very friendly, but deep down—very, *very* deep down—it was obvious he wanted to be included.

"Thanks. Love our locally brewed beer," Chad said, clearly amused, gesturing for him to enter.

Victor glared at Linc on his way by but didn't say a word.

He was aware he wasn't on the top of Rogers's list of favorite people at the moment. He'd taken his daughter and grandson away from him . . . sort of. Even though their relationship was hopefully getting better as a result, he still saw Linc's offer to let them live with him as interference.

"The women are on the deck, if you want to say hello," Chad said.

"Why are they out there? It's too cold for any rational person to sit outside in November in Maine" was Victor's response.

Linc internally sighed. It was going to be a long afternoon if their neighbor didn't lighten up.

"Where's Kash?" Victor asked, sounding eager to see the boy.

"He and Knox are out on the beach, looking for treasures."

"Think I'll go join them." Victor took a beer out of one of the six-packs, setting the others on the kitchen counter before heading for the door that led out to the deck.

"He's a prickly little asshole, isn't he?" Zach asked no one in particular.

"Absolutely. And I hate to admit this, even a little bit, but he kind of grows on you. Once you get past the bullshit—past the fact that he tried to get Dad's businesses shut down so many times, past all the times he called the cops and said we were trespassing on his property when we were growing up, and past the scowls and pointed barbs he mutters under his breath," Chad said with a smirk.

Linc had to agree. Having Victor here for Thanksgiving would definitely make things interesting, that was for sure. But the fact that the first thing he wanted to do was see his grandson went a long way toward making Linc forgive some of the man's rough edges. That, and the idea that he seemed concerned about the women sitting outside in the cold. He wasn't unfeeling, he was simply . . . crusty.

He watched Victor stop to say hello to the ladies before walking down the deck stairs toward Kash and Knox.

Reaching out, he snagged one of the craft beers Victor had brought—smiling at the fact they were ice cold—and headed for the deck himself.

All four women looked over at the door when he came out. The air was chilly, but the propane heater was doing its job at making the space around it almost comfortable.

"He came!" Harper said with a smile on her face.

"Yup."

"Took him long enough," Evelyn grumped, but she also had a small smile on her face, regardless. "Next year's Thanksgiving is going to be so different from this year's," she continued, changing the subject as smoothly as a backcountry gravel road. "We'll have two babies to entertain. I can't wait for five years from now, when we go from ten people around the table to who knows how many!

"Oh! I have an idea," she added excitedly. "We need to find a big tablecloth. I mean *big*, and some fabric paint. We'll have the kids put their handprints on the cloth each Thanksgiving. Write their name and year under each print. Eventually it'll be full of handprints, and it'll be such a wonderful reminder of all our amazing holidays together."

"That's a great idea," Marit agreed.

"I can order the paints and tablecloth," Britt offered.

"I'm just sad we can't start this year. I mean, it's only fair that Kash has the first year to himself," Evelyn mused.

Harper looked surprised. She glanced at Linc, as if asking him to help her navigate these tricky waters. But he wasn't going to touch this one with a ten-foot pole.

First and foremost, because the thought of Kash spending more holidays with the family was too appealing.

"But we're just your neighbors. I mean, we *were*, but kind of still are . . . and not family," Harper stuttered.

"Nonsense. Kash is one of us. He's used the lobster swing. He has Fort Bad Assery out in the woods, and he's been over here helping with the rental houses that are no longer rentals, several times. I've fed him cookies, and we all cheered him on when he won the crate race. He's most certainly earned the right to be the first handprint on my grandkid tablecloth. I'm sure I've got something I can use this year. Maybe a napkin. We can sew it onto the tablecloth when we get it. We'll outline his hand with a Sharpie. It might look a little wonky and weird, but I don't care. I want his handprint!"

His mom was sounding a little fanatical, and Linc wondered how much wine she'd actually had already. He gestured for Chad to join him outside before turning back to the women. "We'll figure something out, Mom. How about some more appetizers? Zach says it'll be another hour, hour and a half before everything's ready."

"I think I need more wine," Evelyn countered.

"I'd love some deviled eggs. They're so delicious. Evelyn, will you share the recipe with me?" Harper asked.

"Of course, child. It's all about the spices, you know."

Chad had stuck his head out and heard Linc's suggestion about the appetizers. He went back in and returned with a tray full of a mixture of finger foods. He put it on the table in front of the ladies, and Linc was relieved when his mom reached for a brussels sprout as she continued to school Harper on the best way to make deviled eggs.

"Thank you," he mouthed to Harper, as he nodded to the food, then to his mom.

She winked in return, then turned her attention back to his mother.

Chad leaned over Britt, covering her hand over her belly with his own as he whispered something into her ear. Linc was thrilled to see his brother so happy. It was obvious he doted on his fiancée. He would make an amazing father, and Linc was anxious to see them both blossom as parents.

Chad stood up and said out of the blue, "Britt and I are going to get married before Christmas. We thought we'd have a small ceremony here at Lobster Cove. On the deck. Weather permitting, of course."

That announcement was enough to get their mom to let out a little screech as she stood up, knocking her chair over in the process. And that was all it took for Knox and Kash to look up at the deck, then come running. Zach also appeared at the doorway, looking worried.

"Your brother's getting married! Here!" Evelyn exclaimed, then promptly burst into tears. She threw herself at Chad and hugged him as hard as she could. "I'm so happy!"

Everyone was standing and congratulating Chad and Britt, and Linc took the time to sidle up next to Harper. She was smiling, but she also looked a little uncomfortable.

"You'll get used to it," Linc reassured her.

"To what?"

"This. The crazy that is my family. Poor Marit's first date with Zach was here at the house, and she had to endure Britt and Chad getting engaged and the excitement that went along with that. My mom was beside herself, even more giddy than she is right now."

Harper giggled a little. Her cheeks were flushed, probably from the wine and the warmth of the heater.

"We thought something was wrong," Kash said, as he hugged his mom around the waist.

Linc realized that Kash was growing like a weed. He was taller than he'd been even a few months ago, when he ran the crates at Lobster Fest in town. He wasn't much heavier, but it would only be a matter of time at the speed he was growing.

"Can I go back to the beach and look for cool stuff with Granddad?"

Victor hadn't come up to the deck, but he'd wandered closer so he could eavesdrop on what was happening.

"Of course, baby."

"I'm not a baby," Kash muttered, before hugging his mom once more and running back down the stairs. He and Victor wandered off, with Kash talking a mile a minute and his granddad nodding now and then.

"They're getting along so much better now that they aren't living under the same roof. Thank you for that, Linc. Seriously."

He'd told her over and over that she didn't need to thank him, and she'd done her best to stop, but there were times, like now, when it seemed she couldn't help herself.

"You're welcome," he said simply. He couldn't resist putting his arm around her waist and giving her a small sideways hug. He wanted to do more; but since their circumstances were so new, he refrained.

Dropping his arm from around her, he took a sip of his beer as the women settled back down into the chairs and began to talk about the upcoming wedding.

Linc didn't really care about the details of his brother's nuptials, just that he was happy. Being in the kitchen with Zach wasn't an option, and Knox had gone back to the beach to join Victor and Kash. Chad had sat down and pulled Britt onto his lap, and seemed content to listen to the women make plans for his own wedding.

Linc found himself restless again. Honestly, he felt a little left out. But he didn't really mind. Lately, he'd felt a touch disconnected from his family. Maybe it was exhaustion catching up with him from so many nearly sleepless nights. Maybe it was the house he'd bought, taking up all his time.

Maybe it was because his brothers were moving forward, getting married, starting families, and as the oldest, he felt as if he should've already done what they were doing by now.

Whatever the reason, he decided to take a quiet walk around Lobster Cove. Make sure all was well. He entered the house, told Zach he'd be back shortly, and left out the front door.

First, he wandered over to the auto body shop. He was as proud of the place now as he'd been when his dad had first opened it. He remembered the hours upon hours he and his father had spent with their heads under the hoods of cars. Their fingers covered in grease as they attempted to get a lawn mower working again. The joy they felt when they got a snowmobile started after replacing the engine.

The fact that it was still operating today made it feel as if their dad was still with them. Of course, he wasn't, which sucked. Austin Young would've been thrilled that two of his sons were engaged and soon-to-be dads. He'd already be planning on introducing his new grandchildren to his beloved engines. Hell, their first gift from him would probably be a tiny little T-shirt with Lobster Cove Auto Body emblazoned on the front.

Next, Linc headed over to the rental houses. He peeked into the window of the smaller one and winced at what he saw. It had been gutted, and it was obvious it would be months before it was ready to rent again. Possibly even later than spring, which meant Harper and Kash wouldn't be moving in there anytime soon.

From the houses, he made his way toward the massive boat storage area. There were boats everywhere he looked, all covered with the white shrink-wrap they used to protect them from the elements and critters in the winter. When he and his brothers were little, they loved to play hide-and-go-seek around the boats. They never went into the boats themselves, but crawling around and under them seemed like the most fun ever back then.

Laughter rang out from the house . . . and Linc sighed, wondering what he was doing. Why was he out here by himself and not with his family?

Feeling drawn to the house, back to Harper, wanting to see her enjoy herself and relax for once, Linc decided to do one more thing before he rejoined everyone.

He headed for the woods, taking a direct path through the trees instead of going the long way around by the water, which had been his plan. It didn't take him long to get to the fort that he and his brothers had all played in at one time or another. Chad had found Kash there in the early summer, and had made up a name on the fly for the decrepit structure. Fort Bad Assery.

Thinking about that still had the ability to make Linc smile. There was nothing badass about the sticks and wooden planks they used to play in. Kash had improved the structure, but it was still looking a little shaky, especially now that the boy wasn't there to continue the upkeep. The things he'd stored inside had been removed for the winter, and all that was left was the dirt floor and a mouse nest in the corner.

Linc wasn't sure why he was there. Why he'd felt the urge to check on the pathetic little fort. Maybe because he wanted to be able to reassure Kash that it was still standing? To reminisce?

Whatever the reason, now that he was there, Linc suddenly felt himself falling into the dark place in his head that he did his best to keep locked away.

Looking at the rotting wood, hearing the wind in the trees, seeing the rodents . . . it all reminded him of the week he'd spent on the run for his very life. How he'd hidden under sticks and branches like the ones in front of him as he'd attempted to get a few minutes of sleep before he started walking once more.

His shoulder throbbed with remembered pain as he stood there, staring blankly at the fort. The cold seeped into his very bones, chilling him the same way it had back then. He hadn't been able to start a fire because that would have given away his position as clearly as a giant arrow pointing down from the sky, saying HERE I AM, COME GET ME!

"Linc?"

He didn't hear the soft, feminine voice saying his name. He was too far gone into his memories of that awful time in his life. He stood there shivering, one hand clutching his shoulder, as it had so often back then. The bottle of beer he'd been drinking had dropped to the ground, forgotten, as he struggled to cope with the memories.

Slowly, ever so slowly, Linc heard someone speaking to him in a low, steady tone.

"You're okay, Linc. I'm here. You just stand there as long as you need to get your bearings. I won't leave you. You're safe. You're here at Lobster Cove. It's Thanksgiving. Dinner's ready, but I'm sure no one will mind waiting a little longer. Your mom sent me out here to find you. You're all right, Linc. I promise."

Blinking, he turned his head and saw Harper standing next to him. She wasn't touching him, but he swore he could still feel the heat of her body.

"Linc? Are you back?"

He supposed he was. Although the memories still danced at the edges of his mind, teasing, tormenting him.

Linc moved without thought, reaching for Harper. She came willingly, burrowing into him as he wrapped his arms around her. She buried her head in the crook of his neck and held on as he continued to shake.

He was grateful she didn't speak, didn't ask him what was wrong or what he was doing. She was aware of his past, just as he was aware of hers. Neither knew the details, but she obviously knew whatever he'd been through, it was bad.

She'd been smart enough not to touch him, thank goodness. He shuddered to think what he might've done if she'd dared to touch him while he was lost in his memories. He probably would've thought she was the enemy. That they'd found him.

If he'd hurt her . . .

Closing his eyes, Linc mentally swore. Used all the bad words he'd learned over the years but knew better than to voice out loud anywhere within a mile of his mother. Evelyn Young would somehow know he'd uttered the words, using that mom intuition she had, and would make him regret saying such vile things.

"I knew about Fort Bad Assery, you know," Harper said after a long minute in his arms. She didn't raise her head, simply spoke into his neck. The warmth of her breath wafted over his chilled skin, warming him from the inside out. "Britt let it slip one day, and I came over here to check it out myself when Kash was at school. Unlike my dad, I had no problem with him being out here, on Lobster Cove property. He needed the alone time as much as I did, but I didn't have a cool fort to escape to."

She continued to babble on about her son and the fort and how much he loved looking up at the stars, and how she could picture him out here in the summer, reading and simply enjoying nature and doing what he loved.

Linc appreciated this woman more than he could express. He'd just had a monster of a flashback, and she was giving him the time he needed to regain control. He supposed he should explain what happened. Give her some sort of reason why he was standing in the trees, shaking like a leaf and staring off into space. But somehow he knew that she'd never demand any explanation. She'd simply be his anchor until he could stand on his own.

"Thank you," he whispered when she took a breath. It was his turn to voice his gratitude.

"You're welcome. Are you hungry? Do you want to go eat? Or leave? I can come up with a reason why I have to go, and why you need to take me home. Kash can stay here. Spend the night at my dad's house."

Respect for this woman grew within Linc. She was offering to use herself as an excuse, so he wouldn't have to come up with a reason why *he* wanted to leave.

Linc shook his head. "No. I'm okay."

"Are you sure?" she asked, lifting her head and looking into his eyes. "Because I have no problem using menstrual problems as an excuse. Your brothers will all hear *menstrual* and immediately nope out. Won't ask any questions. Britt, Marit, and your mom might know better, but they're all too polite to say anything."

For normal men, she wasn't wrong. But his brothers were a different breed. If she went inside and claimed she was having any kind of womanly issue, they'd immediately want *more* details, want to know if she needed a doctor. They'd probably even offer to get her pads or tampons and whatever else she might want. It was what *he'd* do. But Linc appreciated her desire to shield him from his own family.

"I want to go back. Zach's been slaving all day, and I've been smelling the delicious things he's been making. I'm okay now. I just needed a moment."

"You don't sleep enough," she said, her gaze still boring into his.

"I know." It was as close as he'd ever come to admitting his insomnia.

"What can I do to help?"

Her unselfishness was the balm he needed to banish the lingering aftereffects of his flashback. It had been a bad idea to come out here on his own, but in his defense, it hadn't been an issue before. He supposed it was his lack of sleep that had let his mental shields slip down enough for the nightmares to sneak back in.

"You're doing it," he told her.

Harper rolled her eyes. "I'm not doing anything," she protested.

She was, more than she knew.

Linc took a deep breath, then took her hand in his. He saw the beer bottle on the ground and bent to pick it up. "Nothing I hate more than wasting good beer," he said, trying to inject some humor into this situation.

"I knew you and my dad had *something* in common," Harper quipped. "He's always loved his craft beer. And claims Maine beer is better than anywhere else in the world."

"Has he been anywhere else in the world and had their beer?" Linc asked.

"Of course not," Harper joked.

Linc made a mental note to maybe order some German beer, from Germany, and sit down with Victor to sample it. Neither of them would probably have much to say, but that was all right.

They walked back toward the house hand in hand, and with each step, Linc felt more like himself. But something had to give. He'd never wanted to take pills to help him sleep, but he was getting to the point where that might be necessary. It would be better than zoning out at the wrong time and place.

Dropping Harper's hand at the front door, he gave her a small smile, and she returned it before pushing past him and opening the door.

"Found him!" she called out. "Let's eat!"

Linc got a few hard and probing looks from his brothers, but thankfully they didn't push for answers as to where he'd been and what he was doing.

Zach had outdone himself as far as Linc was concerned. He'd not only made traditional dishes, like turkey, green bean casserole, and sweet potatoes, but he'd also incorporated the best of Maine into their Thanksgiving as well. The broiled lobster tails with scallop stuffing were to die for. And the lobster cornbread stuffing was a hundred times better than anything Linc had ever tasted.

Victor had shocked the hell out of all of them by saying with a frown, "I'm allergic to lobster," when Zach described the dishes before putting them on the table. Everyone froze in surprise and a bit of horror . . . until Victor smiled slightly. It was rusty, and almost a little creepy looking, because he did it so infrequently.

"Just kidding," he added.

The fact that Victor Rogers had made a joke was a Thanksgiving miracle. Everyone had laughed until their bellies hurt, then Zach continued to load up the table with the rest of the food he'd prepared.

There was also the usual mashed potatoes with gravy, and the rest of the rolls their mom made were gone within seconds. By the time dessert rolled around, everyone was completely stuffed. But not too full to indulge in pumpkin pie and the not-as-traditional chocolate pie.

The table was full of laughter, and even though Victor didn't exactly join in the conversation, he was listening intently. Linc even caught him smiling a time or two.

When they were kids, the time after eating was spent outside playing with his brothers as their parents cleaned up and sat down to take a break. This year, everyone piled into the living area together after working as a team to put everything away.

But not before Evelyn had convinced Kash to put his hand on a white napkin while she traced the outline with a Sharpie, just as she declared she would. The kid looked pleased as punch to be the first in what would hopefully be a long tradition of handprints on cloth.

Afterward, his mom settled into her usual chair with a blanket over her lap.

Britt was sitting on Chad's lap, Marit was snuggled up next to Zach, snoring. Victor had left after dinner, but not before graciously thanking Evelyn for inviting him, and Zach for making all the food. He'd even hugged Kash, though he'd merely nodded at his daughter before leaving.

There was a football game on the TV that Knox was absorbed in, while Kash was curled up at the end of the sofa with a book, oblivious to everyone around him.

Linc was sitting next to Harper on the couch, simply enjoying being with his family. The conversation flowed easily, and he felt almost as if he were floating. His belly was full, Harper's body heat was warming his side, even though they were both careful not to let on that their relationship was ever so slowly shifting from simple roommates to . . . more?

Linc wasn't sure where they stood, not really. But he wasn't in a mood to rush anything either. Didn't want to hurry things along, only to find out they might be compatible physically, but relationship-wise . . . not so much.

That was a potential issue more on Linc's part than hers. Anyone who ended up with Harper would be lucky. Would get a hardworking partner who didn't hesitate to jump in with both feet and do what needed to be done. He'd seen it more than once in her interactions with Kash, and with the repairs around his own house. She didn't complain about working all day, then coming home to help him scrape hideous wallpaper off the bathroom walls . . . and ceiling.

Who put wallpaper on the freaking ceiling anyway?

"Today was good," Chad said after a moment.

"No. It was perfection," Evelyn corrected, with a happy smile on her face. "When are we doing it again?"

Zach chuckled. "Christmas."

"Goody. That's not too far away!" Evelyn said, sounding like a kid.

She seemed more carefree, happier than she'd been since her sons had moved home. The pain of losing her husband was still there, Linc knew, but time had a way of dulling the loss of a loved one. As did gaining two daughters-in-law and the anticipation of grandbabies on the way.

"Thank you all for inviting Kash and me to join you," Harper said.

"Of course."

"So glad you could be here."

"Wouldn't have been the same without you."

Everyone spoke at once, making Linc grin.

"With that, I think we need to get going," Harper continued.

"I didn't think you had to work tomorrow," Britt said with a small frown. "You're lucky to get Black Friday off."

"I know, but I've got a ton of things I need to catch up on, since I've been working so much. And Saturday starts the beginning of the holiday season . . . and grumpy shoppers."

Everyone groaned at that.

Harper stood, and Linc followed suit.

"We're headed out, Kash," she told her son.

He was so lost in whatever he was reading, he didn't even hear her.

"Kash," Linc said in a louder tone.

At that, the boy immediately looked up.

"We're leaving now."

"Oh, okay." He closed the book and stood. Soon, everyone was on their feet, exchanging goodbye hugs, and Britt and Marit were making plans with Harper to get together soon.

"I'm happy to help in any way I can with your wedding," she told Britt.

"Thanks. We want to keep the ceremony simple. But I'll let you know if we need anything."

"Good luck with that," Knox mumbled under his breath.

Chad smacked the back of his brother's head. "Shut it," he said with a grin.

Before he knew it, they were in his SUV and on their way back to his house. Looking in the back seat, Linc saw Kash was snoozing minutes into the drive. Apparently, car rides didn't just put babies to sleep. The kid was out like a light, his book still clasped in his grip.

Keeping his voice low, Linc asked Harper, "Do you really have a bunch of things you need to do?"

"No. But you're tired. You need to get some sleep."

Linc was literally speechless. He couldn't remember the last time someone had put him first. Her care of him made him feel . . . mushy. It was a strange feeling, being taken care of. He'd always been the one taking care of others. Looking after his brothers, his mom, the men and women under his command.

Words wouldn't come, so he kept silent as he drove them back to his house. He parked, and the three of them walked to the front door together. Kash was like a zombie and didn't complain when his mom ordered him upstairs and to bed.

"You think you can sleep? Is it too early?" she asked him.

There was no way in hell he was going to sleep, but Linc nodded anyway.

As if she saw right through him, Harper said, "Why don't we watch TV for a while? Neither of us have anything pressing to do tomorrow. I thought we could maybe go out for a matinee, there's that new Christmas movie Kash was interested in seeing, and then try out that board game I brought home from work the other day."

Honestly, it sounded like a perfect day to Linc. He nodded. "You want another glass of wine?"

She grimaced. "I think I had enough wine tonight. Maybe some tea?"

"Sounds good. Go get settled. I'll meet you at the couch."

"It's a date," she quipped with a smile.

The words echoed in his head as Linc prepared their drinks in the kitchen, tea for her, hot chocolate for him. A date. Things between them weren't the usual way couples got to know each other. They were doing things backward. Moving in together, then learning more about each other. But he didn't hate it.

As far as he was concerned, this *was* a date. Pretty much their first one. Unconventional though it might be.

By the time he got back to the living area, Harper was standing next to one of the oversize chairs with a blanket . . . and a small questioning smile on her face. "Is it okay if we share? It's a little chilly in here tonight."

It might've been an excuse, but Linc didn't mind. He nodded and put their drinks on the table next to the chair, then sat. Harper settled herself on his lap and covered them with the blanket. Linc handed her the mug of tea, then grabbed the remote with the hand that wasn't wrapped around the woman in his lap.

Soon, they were relaxed against the cushions and engrossed in a comedy series that had gotten great reviews on one of the streaming apps.

The last thing Linc was aware of was the feel of Harper's hair against his chin as she snuggled closer. He fell into a deep, dreamless sleep for the first time in years.

Chapter Seven

Linc couldn't stop thinking about Thursday night as he and Kash lay on the warm hood of his SUV, watching planes take off and land at the small airstrip near Rockville the Saturday after Thanksgiving.

He'd learned the trick about using the engine's residual heat to stay warm from his dad. When he'd take him to do exactly what they were doing now, watching the planes. The hood would eventually cool down, but when it did, he'd simply get up, start the engine, and leave it running for ten minutes or so.

Thanksgiving night, he'd fallen asleep with Harper draped over him. He'd woken up at three thirty-two in the morning, with Harper still sound asleep in his lap. Some people wouldn't think that was anything special, but for Linc, it was *everything*. He didn't remember any of his dreams. Hell, he didn't think he'd *had* any dreams.

Getting five solid hours of sleep was unheard of for him. He wasn't sure if Harper was a miracle worker, or if he'd just been so exhausted that his body had literally shut down.

He didn't think it was the latter, because there'd been times in the past when he'd been just as exhausted and still woken up with nightmares after only an hour of rest.

So that left Harper as the reason he was able to sleep. *Really* sleep.

He'd sat in that chair, holding her for another two hours, until she began to stir. Two hours that he'd usually spend pacing, or rehashing the events that had led to him being chaptered out of the Air Force.

She'd been adorable upon waking. Groggy and confused about where she was, then mortified that she'd slept on top of him all night. But Linc refused to let her dwell on it.

All day Friday, he'd felt energized. As if he could take on the world. They'd done just as Harper had suggested. Went out to see a movie, then came home and played games, cooked, read books, and just enjoyed spending time together.

Linc had hoped to repeat the night before, but Harper went upstairs to bed the same time as Kash. She was working today, and had wanted a decent night's sleep before dealing with the craziness of the holiday shopping season.

If Linc had any doubt that Harper was the reason he'd actually slept—and slept well, at that—it was confirmed when he'd woken up sweaty, with his heart racing, only ninety minutes after going to bed. He'd done everything he could think of to get back to sleep, but it was no use. He'd ended up pacing the house, trying to outrun his demons . . . with no luck.

As a result, he was grumpy and kind of a jerk when Harper made her way downstairs this morning. He felt bad now, but at the time, in some warped way of thinking, he'd blamed her for his shit night. It wasn't her fault, not in the least, but he'd been short with her anyway, not saying much before she'd headed out the door.

After Kash had come downstairs and asked if they were still going to the airfield, Linc almost said no, that something had come up. But he didn't want to lie to the boy, and because Kash was so excited about the outing, it was impossible to say no to him.

So here they were. Lying on the hood of his SUV, watching planes take off and land in the chilly November air, while memories assaulted Linc. Memories of the boy he used to be. Of lying just like this with his dad, talking about his future, what he wanted to do, where he wanted to go, of how he wanted to save the world.

There was no doubt that he'd done some heroic things, had saved lives, had taken lives as well. Linc was proud of his service to his country.

And it was funny how he'd ended up full circle. Back here in Maine, doing exactly what he'd done so many years ago, with another boy who was eager to grow up. To make a difference in the world.

He had no doubt that Kash would make those differences too. Not in the way Linc had, by joining the military, but with his brain. His smarts. He was going to find new planets, maybe even discover sentient life somewhere far beyond their skies.

They'd talked about nothing in particular for a while, the weather, the food they'd had at Thanksgiving, Zach's lobster shack, The Lobster Buoy, and about the crate race that Kash had won.

There was a break in planes coming and going, and Linc figured this was as good a time as any to bring up the topic he very much wanted to talk about.

"How's school going?"

"Fine," Kash said quickly. Almost too quickly. "Science is fun. I don't mind math, but English . . . yuck. And art feels like a waste of time. I suck at it, and it's not making me a more well-rounded individual or any of that crap that people say it should."

Linc couldn't help but laugh at that. "Well, all you have to do is pass. You don't have to get an A."

"Yes, I do," Kash countered. "If I want to get into MIT, Harvard, or my first choice, the University of Arizona, I need a four point oh. I can't let freaking art class mess that up."

"The University of Arizona?" Linc couldn't help but ask. It was a long way from Maine, and he had a feeling Harper wouldn't like her baby being so far from home.

"Yeah. It's the best astronomy program in the US. It receives the most government funding and gets money from NASA. It even has an optical engineering program . . . which is where people learn the science behind optics and design and build objects that use light. Like lenses, microscopes, and of course . . . telescopes."

"Right," Linc said, impressed that even at twelve years old, Kash was already thinking about where he wanted to go to college. At that age, all Linc could think about was planes. Although, given that he'd gone into the Air Force, maybe he'd *also* known what he wanted to do way back then.

"I'm sorry you aren't enjoying art, but what about the social aspect of school? I don't hear you talking about your friends that much."

Kash was quiet for a moment, then he shrugged. "I hang out with the kids in the robotics club."

It was like pulling teeth. Linc decided to stop beating around the bush.

"When I was your age, I was bullied in school. I was a late bloomer, scrawny, and a bit of a nerd. There was a group of mean girls who delighted in calling me names and making my life miserable. I did everything I could to try to avoid them, but that wasn't really possible."

He wasn't going to tell Kash that his mom was one of those girls. It was water under the bridge, and the last thing he wanted was to do anything that might undermine the close relationship between mother and son. But he wanted to make sure Kash knew that he could empathize with him.

"*You* were bullied?" Kash asked, sounding absolutely shocked.

"Yup."

"I don't believe you," he mumbled after a brief silence. "And it's not very nice to lie, you know."

"I'm not lying," Linc insisted. "Hang on." He sat up a little and pulled out his phone. "Mom sent pictures to all of us boys a while back. She was going through her albums after our dad died, and I guess feeling nostalgic. She sent them off to be digitized, then sent the link to the albums when they were done."

Linc had saved the link, of course. The pictures made him laugh at the time. They'd brought back such good memories of growing up with his brothers on Lobster Cove.

He found the email and clicked on the link, scrolling through the folders until he found the one with the year he was in the eighth grade. He opened it, then passed his phone to Kash. "That was the year I turned thirteen. I was in the eighth grade. I'm the tallest of the boys in the various pictures."

Kash took the phone and began to scroll through the images. He was quiet as he took in the Young family from all those years ago.

He stopped on one picture that still had the power to make Linc wince. He was an awkward-looking kid. Tall, skinny, his hair too long and, as usual, not brushed. He was standing by a table full of model airplanes that he'd spent hours upon hours building.

Linc remembered being so proud of those models. He'd done everything in his power to make them as accurate as possible. He was grinning like a dork and wearing shorts that were too small for him and a T-shirt with the words "Air Force Academy" on the front.

"I brought one of my models to school once," he said quietly, as Kash stared at the picture. "I wanted to show it to my best friend, a kid who was just as into planes as I was. I was carrying it down the hall when I first got to school, and who did I run into? The mean girls. They surrounded me, taunted me, made fun of my model, told me I was the biggest geek they'd ever met. Said I was going to be a virgin the rest of my life because no girl would ever want to date such a huge nerd. Rinky-Dink Linc. That's what they called me. They were relentless.

"By the time the bell rang and they finally wandered off, giggling like a bunch of hyenas, I was devastated. I'd worked so hard on that model, and they'd made it seem like such a stupid thing. I threw it away in the first trash can I came across. I still regret letting them get to me like that."

Kash looked up from the phone and glanced at Linc. "They call me Trash-Kash," he admitted in a soft voice.

"Are they older than you or in your grade?"

"Older. The guy who picks on me the most is in the eleventh grade. His name is Donny. And his girlfriend, Ginger. I mostly just see them at lunch, but they always look for me. Make fun of me being in robotics club. My red hair. How skinny I am. It doesn't matter if I ignore them or try to think of things to say back, it just eggs them on more. I hate it. I hate *them*. School sucks because of them."

Linc's heart broke for the boy. He knew exactly how he felt. "I wish I had some magic advice for you. Something you could say to those kids that would make them leave you alone. But I don't. All I can do is tell you . . . it gets better. Maybe not tomorrow. Maybe not next year. But eventually they'll graduate and be gone. And you'll fill out and gain weight and height. Your hair will always be red, but that's not a bad thing. It's unique, just like you. Like your mom.

"There's nothing wrong with doing what you love. For me, it was planes. I used to sit out here for hours and watch the planes and dream about flying myself one day. For you, it's the stars. You can sit outside and watch the sky for just as many hours. Don't let *anyone* tell you what you love is wrong. Or stupid. Or make you feel as if you're less because of it.

"Karma is a real thing, Kash. That might sound like a cop-out response, but it's not. Donny and Ginger? They'll reap what they sow. That means they'll get what's coming to them. Again, maybe not tomorrow, but one day."

"Did your bullies?" Kash asked.

Linc was walking a fine line here. But he honestly believed that, yes, karma had come for Harper. He hated that for the woman he knew today, and she'd more than paid for the sins of her childhood. "Yes." He left it at that.

To his relief, Kash nodded as he handed Linc's phone back to him.

"You're smart," Linc went on. "Really smart. I have no doubt you're going to do great things. No matter what field you study, you'll make a difference in the world. Believe that. When those bullies get to you, remind yourself that you're tougher than most kids. You and your mom have been through some stuff that they have no idea about. You think Donny would know what to do if he was plunked down in the middle of the night in New York City? No way. Or Ginger would be able to handle it if she had no idea where her next meal was coming from? I'd say definitely not. Just be you, Kash. Because you're a hell of a person. Inside and out. And I'm proud to know you."

He could practically feel the kid soaking in the compliments. Linc was well aware words alone wouldn't make the bullying better. It would take thick skin and the ability to ignore the mean things others said about him. But hopefully with enough positive reinforcement—not only on his part, but also on his brothers', his mom's, and even his grandfather's—Kash would come out the other side of adolescence without being broken by the kids who sought to raise themselves up by tearing others down.

"Just be honest, Kash," Linc went on, wanting to say this one last thing. "You shouldn't lie to your mom, or really to anyone. And be honest with yourself. If you're having a bad day, don't be afraid to say so. If your mom asks how school went, you're allowed to say 'Not great' and tell her why. The one person in this world who wants the absolute best for you is your mom. She'd move mountains for you. Would do absolutely anything."

"I know."

"Do you? Do you really?" Linc pressed.

Kash looked over at him. And Linc could see the seriousness in his eyes. "We were staying in a shelter in the city. It was one of the better ones. It wasn't scary like some of them, and the food was actually good. The mattresses on the beds were comfortable. They kept the heat on all night, so it was warm. It was also close to my school. But there was this one guy. He gave me the creeps. He'd stare at me, and sometimes he'd come into the bathroom when I was showering.

"I didn't say anything to Mom because she was working really hard to find a good job so we could get another apartment. And because that shelter was primo, and I knew it. But one day, when I got back from school, Mom had already packed all our stuff into the minivan and said we were leaving.

"The creepy guy tried to get her to change her mind. Came over as we were walking out and told her she was making a mistake, and she'd regret leaving. Mom looked him straight in the eye and said she wouldn't spend another second under that roof as long as *he* was there. That she saw the way he looked at me, and over her dead body would she stand by and let anyone hurt me.

"That's when we started living in the car. She left that shelter, a place where we were comfortable, and warm, and our bellies were full, and put up with living in a minivan. And she did it for *me*. I knew what that guy wanted. But I didn't say anything to Mom because we were more comfortable than we'd been in a long time. So yeah, I know she'd do whatever it takes to keep me safe. I feel the same about her."

As Linc listened to Kash speak, a newfound respect for the boy rose within him. He might only be twelve, but he'd lived more than most grown men Linc knew. He understood the importance of loyalty and protecting those he loved. He'd never felt prouder of Kash than he did in that moment. Harper was a lucky woman. She might've been through hell since leaving Maine, but the one thing she'd absolutely done right was sitting right next to him.

"I've heard you in the middle of the night," Kash said abruptly.

It was quite a change of subject, but Linc mentally shrugged and went with it. "Why are you awake to hear me up and moving around?" Linc asked.

"I have to pee sometimes. Why are *you* up?"

"No reason."

"I thought you said I should be honest. Not to lie," Kash countered, throwing Linc's words back at him.

Linc sighed. "I don't sleep well."

"Because of what happened to you?"

"Because of what happened to me," he agreed.

Silence lay between them for a long moment. There was no way Linc was going to tell Kash about the things he'd done, seen, experienced. Especially not in the week after he'd crashed his jet and been on the run.

After a long moment, Kash reached out and took Linc's hand in his. "I'm sorry that happened to you, Linc. But for the record, I think you're the strongest man I've ever met. I don't care if you don't sleep well and you have nightmares. I admire you so much. Thank you for telling me about being bullied. It helps some. Knowing the person you are today, it gives me hope that I can be just like you when I'm old."

Linc wanted to laugh. Some days he felt ancient, but honestly he didn't feel *that* old. He had a lot of years left in him . . . he hoped. And surprisingly, Kash's words settled deep in his soul.

He would miss him desperately when he and his mom moved out. He'd gotten used to him being around, even though it had been little more than a week. His questions. His nonstop chatter. The quiet way he took care of others around him, even though he was the kid and Linc was the adult.

"Thanks, Kash."

"You're welcome. What kind of plane is that?"

He'd changed the subject again, but Linc was relieved. He was much more comfortable talking about planes than his insomnia or the reason behind it. And while he was glad he got to talk to Kash about bullying, he didn't want to say too much and let it slip that his own mom had been one of the people who'd tormented him in his middle and high school years.

Before he knew it, hours had passed, and both he and Kash were chilled to the bone, despite the trick with the running motor. They'd stopped by the store on the way home and gotten ingredients to make tacos. It was an easy meal, and one that could mostly be made ahead of time by prepping the veggies and making the meat. They could throw the latter in the microwave when Harper got home from work.

She arrived home late . . . and crabby. Apparently the day after Black Friday was just as busy as *actual* Black Friday. People had not been on their best behavior, and it was clear Harper was struggling to keep a smile on her face for her son. Kash took it upon himself to get dinner ready, and when they all sat down to eat, Linc saw the first honest smile on Harper's face that night.

"Did you two have a good day?" she asked.

"We did," Kash said. "We were at the airfield for hours. Did you know Linc knows the name of every single plane ever made?"

"I'm not sure I'd say that, Bud," he said with a chuckle.

"Well, he knew the names of every single one we saw today. And he knows how much fuel they carry, how many hours it takes to qualify to fly them, and he was really funny when he critiqued the takeoffs and landings."

"I bet he was. Tomorrow's Sunday, and I'm working the morning shift, but I should be home by four. You want to go see Granddad for dinner tomorrow?"

"Sure."

"All right, but you have to get your homework done before I get home, so we don't have to rush through our visit," Harper warned.

Kash scoffed. "It'll take me like two seconds. It's easy."

"All right, just get it done, Superboy."

"I will."

"You want to come with us?" Harper asked, looking at Linc.

He smiled. "I think I'll pass. Victor's growing on me, but let's not push our luck."

"Growing like a fungus," Kash mumbled.

For a second, Linc and Harper both froze. Then she giggled, making the smile Linc had been trying to hold back come forth.

"He's something," Linc agreed. "But he loves you both very much."

"We love him too. Even when he's being weird and overbearing. Right, Mom?"

"Um . . . right, honey."

"Don't worry, I've got the dishes. You guys just chill," Kash said, as he stood and reached for his mom's plate.

"Thanks, Kash. You're a good kid."

"I know."

"Modest too," Linc joked, once Kash was out of earshot. "Why don't you head upstairs? Maybe take a bath or something. Try to relax."

"You wouldn't mind?" Harper asked.

If he had his preference, she'd stay down here with him and sit in his chair and fall asleep on his lap again, but that was Linc being selfish. Harper needed her alone time, especially after being around people all day. "Of course not."

"I think I'll take you up on that. You really are welcome to come with us tomorrow night."

"I need to work on some stuff around here, but thank you for the invite."

"Any time."

They stared at each other for a beat, and Linc could feel the awkwardness between them. He hated it, but he wasn't sure how to fix things. Grabbing her and kissing her the way he longed to probably wouldn't work, but that didn't stop the craving to do just that. It was a weird thing . . . to want this woman so much after she'd been the bane of his existence at one point in his life.

But that was forever ago. This was now. And now, he wanted Harper Bates.

"Why is your last name Bates and your dad's Rogers?" he blurted.

Harper chuckled. "How long have you been stewing on that?" she asked.

Linc shrugged and could feel his cheeks heat. "I don't know. I've just been wondering."

"I changed my last name when I moved to New York. I thought Bates sounded better than Rogers, for some reason. At least, my eighteen-year-old brain found that perfectly logical." She shrugged. "Got used to it and never changed it back. When Kash was born, I figured I'd go with it. My dad wasn't thrilled, but by that point, he was disappointed with every decision I'd made since graduating high school, so it didn't really faze me."

"I don't think it was disappointment, more like worry, probably."

"Maybe. I'd like to think I shed the Harper Rogers I was in high school for a newer, better version with Harper Bates."

"You did," Linc said with certainty. He made a mental note to tell her about the talk he'd had with Kash about bullies at some point, when the boy wasn't around to overhear. Kash probably wouldn't mind him telling Harper, but he'd still tell her in private . . . just in case.

"All right. I'm going to head up. Will you make sure he doesn't stay up too late?"

"Of course."

"Thanks. I feel like I've been the worst mom lately. Leaving so much to you."

"I don't mind in the least. I enjoy his company."

"And he loves hanging out with you too. Good night, Linc."

"Night, Harper."

Linc watched as she headed for the stairs, his gaze glued to her ass as she went. She really was a beautiful woman, even tired, grumpy, and frazzled after a long day on her feet. All Linc wanted to do was pamper her, but he didn't have the right to do more than give her some much-needed time to herself, while he looked after her son.

Which he supposed *was* pampering her, in a way. She hadn't been able to rely on others for a while, and knowing Kash was safe and happy had to go a long way toward taking a burden off her shoulders. He felt good about that.

"So, kiddo, anything you want to watch tonight?"

"*How the Universe Works.*"

He wasn't apologetic in the least about watching the series for the eight hundredth time in a row. It was pretty much all Kash wanted to watch, but Linc didn't mind. It was good background noise, and he could read the next book from the huge stack next to his bed. He used to read thrillers, but they were a little too close to what he'd lived and breathed, and brought back too many memories, so he'd switched to fantasy. It was a nice change, escaping into the worlds of dragons, ogres, and other fantastical creatures.

He even found that he enjoyed the occasional "romantasy," which was a fancy way of saying there was sex between the other scenes.

After going into his room to grab a book, and as he settled into his chair—a chair that felt too big without Harper in it—he heard the water rushing through the pipes in the walls as Harper started her bath upstairs.

Visions of her naked in a tub full of bubbles swam in his mind, and Linc did his best to turn them off. Harper was his houseguest, that was all. He'd never do anything to make her think her living here was contingent on anything he might want.

And Linc wanted a lot. Wanted to see if her lips tasted as good as he remembered. Wanted to know if their chemistry carried over into the bedroom. To see if maybe, just maybe, they could put their pasts behind them and forge a new future together.

It was cheesy and sentimental, but the more time Linc spent with Harper and Kash, the more time he *wanted* to spend with them. He was proud of Harper for how hard she worked, but also resentful of how much her job took her away from him.

Shaking his head at how pathetic he was being, Linc did his best to concentrate on the words on the pages of his book. As the narrator of the TV show spoke about dark matter, he got lost in a story of aliens intent on taking over Earth, and the one woman who might be able to save them all.

Chapter Eight

Three weeks. That's how long it had been since Linc had kissed her . . . sort of. But he hadn't attempted to do so again, and Harper didn't understand why. Well, she kind of did, actually. Her hours were very irregular, and she was on edge from working in retail around the holidays. She wasn't in any kind of mood to be intimate with anyone, barely had enough energy to make sure Kash was doing his homework and eating properly.

Thank goodness for Linc. He'd taken responsibility of watching over Kash as if he'd been doing it since the kid was born. He may not have wanted children, but he was doing a damn fine job as surrogate father to her son.

He'd even taken Kash to downtown Rockville to see the lobster trap tree the town put up every year. It was exactly what it sounded like: lobster traps stacked up in the shape of a giant Christmas tree, with lights wrapped around the entire thing. It was quirky and cute and something Harper remembered from her own childhood. The town had also put up a lobster buoy tree, stringing up the iconic buoys in the shape of a tree as well.

Harper loved Christmas in Maine, and loved that her son was getting to experience all the things she had when she was a kid. She just wished she could enjoy all of it with him.

The only positive thing about working so much in December was the way her bank account was growing. Harper had even been able to splurge and buy Kash a subscription to something called a Hack Pack, which he'd raved about at dinner one night.

He'd learned about it from other kids in his robotics club. It was a science-based box that came every other month, and it integrated engineering principles into programmable robots the recipient had to make, using components like an infrared receiver, an H-bridge, and a stepper motor.

Harper had no idea what those things were, but Kash did, and he'd been super excited as he'd described them during that dinner. And anything that got her son *that* excited about learning was something Harper desperately wanted to give him.

So she'd bit the bullet and paid the exorbitant—at least for her—amount of money for the subscription. Now she couldn't wait to see the excitement on his face when he opened the first box, which had come earlier in the week and was hidden away in her bedroom.

She'd been able to get a few smaller things for his stocking, to open on Christmas Day, as well. It was going to be a very good holiday for mother and son. One like they hadn't had in years. And Harper was proud that she'd been able to make things work.

Of course, she couldn't have managed it without Linc. He'd taken her and Kash in when she'd been desperate for somewhere to go. And in the process, her relationship with her dad had improved by leaps and bounds. Apparently they were just a little too alike for living together to be viable.

Today was Chad and Britt's wedding. They were having it out at Lobster Cove, and Harper had been touched and shocked when Britt had asked if she'd be part of the ceremony. They weren't having bridesmaids and groomsmen, per se, but of course, Chad's three brothers would be at his side, and Britt had asked Marit and Harper if they'd stand up with her.

Britt didn't want anyone to have matching dresses and said she didn't care what colors they wore. All she wanted was to spend the day with the people she loved the most while she married her soulmate.

Harper had agonized over what to wear. It wasn't as if she had a ton of options. Once upon a time, it was her goal in life to wear designer clothes and high heels on the world's most famous runways. Now? She mostly wore khaki pants or jeans with a polo shirt . . . and of course, the blue vest she hated. Her shoes were cheap joggers she'd picked up secondhand, and it had been so long since she'd worn a pair of high heels, she wasn't sure she'd even be able to walk in them anymore.

Her life had changed so much, it was almost hard to believe. It had taken her a while to readjust to small-town living, but honestly, being here in Maine, living a slower lifestyle . . . she liked it. Didn't mind not having to worry about what to wear and who she might see if she went out. And she definitely didn't miss the constant noise, the pollution, the lack of trees, the crowds, and the increased crime rates.

But she *did* want to look nice for Britt and Chad's wedding. They'd been so kind to her, especially considering they were well aware of the history between her and Linc. They'd been forgiving and gracious, and Harper appreciated that more than they'd ever know. Not to mention the way they'd taken Kash under their wing. How they'd welcomed him into the Young family even before Harper knew about his fort on their property.

She'd found what she thought was a pretty dress last week at work, while walking around on her break looking for stocking stuffers for Kash. Years ago, Harper would've rather slit her wrists than stoop to wearing anything from the big-box store. The clothes were cheap and ill-fitting, and she and her friends were too snotty to shop at her current workplace.

But now, having experienced what it was like to literally feel as if she were starving, she wasn't nearly as picky. And when she'd tried on the dress, she was shocked to find it actually looked good on her. It was a dark green—always a good color with her hair—and the hem stopped just above her knees. It was formfitting around her chest and waist, and the skirt flared out a little, flattering her figure. The neckline showed just enough cleavage to be sexy, but not slutty.

Most importantly, when she'd slipped it on, Harper felt pretty for the first time in longer than she could remember.

Shoes were a little trickier. Chad and Britt were getting married a week before Christmas. While shopping, Harper had to consider the day of the wedding could be snowy, or it could be raining buckets. It might also be a freak warm day, with the sun high in the sky. Figuring if it was either of the first two, she could wear boots and change shoes once she arrived at Evelyn's house, Harper had bought a pair of silver platform heels. They were more sturdy than traditional heels and weren't uncomfortable when she'd tried them on.

Now, having just finished putting on makeup—something she hadn't bothered with in ages—she stood back as far as she could in the bathroom at Linc's house, trying to take in her entire outfit. She felt good, but a little uneasy.

What if everyone could tell her dress was from Walmart? What if the shoes she'd bought fell apart after she took more than a few steps? There was always that possibility. Had she overdone her makeup? Would everyone think she was trying too hard?

Doing her best to shake off her uncertainty, Harper turned her back on her reflection and looked at her watch. They needed to leave soon, so they could get to Lobster Cove in time to help out wherever they could. She was fairly certain Evelyn had things well under control, but she was eager to do whatever needed doing once she got there.

To her surprise, Linc had taken Kash shopping, insisting he'd take care of his clothes for the wedding. Her son had seemed excited after the outing to the shops in downtown Rockville, but he wouldn't show her what Linc had bought for him. She'd tried to pay Linc back, but he'd actually looked offended when she offered him money, so she'd let it drop.

Eager to see what her son had chosen to wear, Harper took a deep breath, then exited the bathroom. Kash's bedroom door was open, and he wasn't inside, so she assumed he was downstairs with Linc, waiting on her. She grabbed her purse from her room, then headed for the stairs.

Her gaze went to her son as she descended the steps—and she almost couldn't believe what she was seeing. She was so used to seeing Kash in jeans and T-shirts, or sweatpants and hoodies, it was hard to reconcile the person she saw standing in the living room, talking to Linc.

"Kash! You look awesome!" Harper exclaimed with a huge smile.

He had on a pair of what she thought were new jeans, but they were black. His long-sleeve button-down shirt was dark green, almost perfectly matching her dress. And to complete the look, he was wearing a bow tie. An honest-to-God *bow tie.* Seeing her little boy look so grown up was a shock, but it also made her extremely proud.

"Look, Mom! My tie has the Milky Way on it! Linc ordered it online for me. It's specially made just for me. The material really should be black like space, but it wouldn't match as well, so we decided to make it dark green like my shirt. And it's a *real* bow tie. Not a clip-on! Linc taught me how to tie it. It took me like a million times to get it right and it's still crooked, but it's so cool! Like Bill Nye! You know, the Science Guy? I loved that show so much when I was little."

Harper did her best to control her tears. To her, Kash was *still* little, but it was obvious he was growing up. A little too fast for her liking. Before she knew it, he'd be moving out to go to college. "It's wonderful, Kash. You look great. And we match!"

"Yeah, I hope you aren't mad, but I snuck into your room and took a picture of your dress before I went shopping with Linc. Just enough so he could see the color though, I know you wanted it to be a surprise. We matched the color of my shirt as best we could to your dress. I think we did good."

"You did amazing, baby."

"Not a baby," he muttered with a roll of his eyes.

Laughing, Harper turned her attention to Linc for the first time. And what she saw had her heart suddenly beating faster and her legs feeling like Jell-O.

The expression on his face could only be described as feral. He looked as if he was two seconds away from pouncing on her.

Harper felt herself blush, but she couldn't tear her gaze away from his. She had a feeling if it was just the two of them, they might not even make it to the wedding. That's how intensely he was staring at her.

Or maybe it was her imagination? Maybe she was projecting what she wanted to see on his face right now.

"Mom looks good, doesn't she?" Kash asked innocently, breaking whatever trance the adults were in.

"She looks amazing, Bud," Linc said, in a voice that seemed deeper than usual. More husky.

"You clean up pretty darn well too, Linc," Harper told him. And he did. He had on a pair of dark slacks and his own button-down. But his was a deep-maroon color. Between the three of them, they embodied the colors of Christmas. And he was also wearing a bow tie.

When Harper stepped closer, drawn to him like a cat to a bowl of cream, she saw it had tiny red lobsters all over it. She smiled.

"Lobsters."

Linc chuckled. "I had to do it. Their wedding is at Lobster Cove, after all."

"Yeah."

"Oh, you know what else we bought?" Kash said, sounding almost giddy with excitement.

"What's that?" Harper asked, forcing herself to look away from Linc. She wanted nothing more than to press herself against him and ask him to take her upstairs, but that would be inappropriate as hell, not to mention they didn't have time—*and* Linc hadn't given any indication that he wanted to repeat the gentle kiss he'd given her three weeks ago.

Not until today, that was. Not until he saw her in something other than the day-to-day jeans and sweats she usually wore. She liked knowing she could affect him. That she could surprise him by not always looking like the harried single mother he'd probably gotten used to, the one who worked too hard and stressed too much.

"Little lobsters!" Kash crowed, as he held up a bag full of teensy plastic lobsters.

Harper frowned. "What are those for?"

"We're going to go into Britt and Chad's house and hide them *everywhere* while they're on their honeymoon in Portland. There's two hundred and fifty of them in here. We even numbered them all, so they can keep track of how many they find. It's going to be *so* much fun!"

Harper looked back at Linc in surprise. "That's . . . um . . . kind of mean?"

"Naw, it's all in good fun. I've seen it done with ducks or frogs mostly, but you know . . . when in Maine . . ."

"What about the baby? Won't he or she choke on them?"

"We'll mostly put them up high. You know, on top of picture frames, inside cabinets, in their silverware drawer. They'll have found most of them by the time the baby comes anyway. But I'm hoping there will be some hanging around for years. Chad'll find one and roll his eyes and think of his oldest brother."

"I can't wait!" Kash gushed. "I've been watching videos online of other people who've done something like this, to get some good ideas about where to hide them. And I've got some *great* ones!"

"Well, count me out. I don't want Britt to think I had anything to do with it."

"No worries, she'll know it was all me and Kash. Right, Bud?" Linc held up his hand to high-five the boy, and they both grinned like lunatics.

It was in that moment that Harper felt herself falling completely for the man. He'd not only gone out of his way to take her son shopping, but he'd also ordered him a custom bow tie, and now he was including him in his shenanigans with his brothers. Kash had never looked so happy and carefree. Had never had a chance until now.

It was a bittersweet moment. Both because of her son—knowing she, alone, hadn't been able to give him the life he had now—and because she had no idea what to do about her intense attraction to Lincoln. She wasn't the kind of woman who could have a no-strings-attached affair.

Never had been. If she gave in to her attraction to Linc, it would hurt like hell when things ended.

And she had no doubt that things *would* end. She was only a temporary houseguest. Eventually, he'd want his house back. Would want to return to his quiet, private life, the one where he didn't have to constantly watch over and entertain someone else's kid.

As much as she respected and admired the man—and wanted him physically—she couldn't have him. Not if she thought it might end in her heartbreak . . . and *especially* not in Kash's.

With that thought running through her mind, she took a deep breath and turned away from the temptation that was Lincoln Young. "Ready to go, Kash?"

"Yup!"

"You need to be on your best behavior today," she warned.

"Mooooom, of course I will be."

"All right, I'm just saying, this is an important day for Britt and Chad, and we want to do whatever we can for it to go perfectly."

"There's no such thing as perfect," Kash said.

Harper let out a little huff of laughter. Figured her son would choose that moment to parrot back to her words she'd said to him more than once.

"Right. As perfect as it can be then."

"Do you think we'll be able to sneak away to do the lobster attack before the ceremony?" Kash asked Linc as he headed for the door.

"Doubt it. Don't worry, we'll figure out a time. Even if we have to pretend to leave, then sneak back around to the house in the dark."

"Ooooh! A covert operation! Yes! Let's do that."

Harper couldn't help but chuckle. Leave it to the former badass Air Force fighter pilot to want to sneak around in the cold dark night and break into the home of his brother—the former Army sniper—to plant hundreds of plastic lobsters anywhere and everywhere.

All right, *breaking in* was a stretch, as Harper knew for a fact Chad had given each of his brothers a key to the house for emergencies.

The drive to Lobster Cove was uneventful, but the closer they got, the more anxious Harper became. What was she even doing here? She wasn't a part of the Young family. No matter how much she might want to be. Yes, her father was invited, but he would most likely come over right at the time the ceremony was set to start and leave right after, if he showed at all.

By the time Linc parked, she was a nervous wreck.

"I'm leaving the lobsters in here so no one figures out what's up," Kash said, before opening the back door and hopping out. Thankfully the weather was cooperating, and no one had to wear boots. It wasn't exactly sunny, but it wasn't raining or snowing either.

She reached for her own door handle, but Linc stopped her by putting a hand on her arm.

"Wait a sec, Harper."

Even the simple touch of his hand on her arm made tingles shoot through her body, settling between her legs. This was a problem. A big one. She wasn't sure she'd be able to handle being around this man much longer without seeing where their amazing chemistry went.

She looked at him expectantly.

"You look beautiful."

She blinked. That wasn't what she thought he was going to say at all. But the surprise morphed into pleasure immediately. He thought she was beautiful. Harper had heard people talking about her looks in a positive way all her life. Especially while attempting to get into the modeling scene in New York. But hearing Linc say it? Nothing made her feel better.

"Thanks. You look great too."

They stared at each other for a long moment.

"You've been working really hard lately, I hope you can relax a little today. Enjoy the day."

Had he moved closer? Or had she? Harper wasn't sure, but they were definitely a little closer together than they had been when they'd first pulled up.

"I'll try. You too. You've been a huge help with Kash, and I know you're still working extremely hard on the house. And not getting enough sleep in the process."

His gaze was alternating between meeting her own and flicking down to her lips. His hand moved on her arm, caressing upward, his thumb gently moving back and forth on her bare skin. The dress had short sleeves, probably inappropriate for December, but since it fit so well and Harper loved it, she hadn't cared.

She was doubly grateful now that her arms weren't covered, so she could feel the calluses on Linc's hands. Hands that had controlled multi-million-dollar jets, had toiled attempting to remodel his house, and had high-fived her son over something as silly as a bag full of plastic lobsters.

He was a multifaceted man, and Harper had never met anyone like him. He also wholeheartedly and unashamedly loved his family, and he wasn't afraid to voice that love.

"This isn't the time or place, but fuck it," he muttered—then he closed the scant distance between them.

His hand tightened on her arm, as if he was afraid she was going to bolt. But Harper wasn't going anywhere. No way. She wanted this. Wanted to see if the taste she'd had of his lips three weeks ago was as good as she remembered, or if she'd blown the encounter out of proportion in her mind.

The second his lips closed over hers, Harper realized she hadn't blown *anything* out of proportion. And he didn't hesitate this time, simply took what he wanted.

Harper gave it to him, because she wanted the same thing.

A small moan left her throat as he devoured her. Taking control of the kiss. His tongue surged into her mouth, tangling with hers as he tasted her properly for the first time. After a moment, the desperation between them lessened a bit, and the kiss gentled. Became more erotic for it. Linc's hand slipped under the sleeve of her dress, and Harper could feel her nipples harden at his touch.

The console was between them, and the angle was awkward, but she'd never been more turned on than she was right this second.

After a last caress of her tongue, and a nip of her lip, Linc lifted his head. He didn't speak, simply stared at her as he licked his lips, as if attempting to memorize her taste.

"We should probably go in before people wonder what we're doing out here," she whispered after a moment, unsure as to what else to say. She figured grabbing him and pulling him into the back seat was out, so the alternative was acting almost as if that amazing kiss hadn't happened.

"We're moving forward from here," Linc promised in a low, growly voice, as if he could hear her last thought. "We can go as slow as you want, but I'd like to explore this chemistry we have."

Giddiness filled Harper. She wanted to let out a girly screech and jump up and down with joy. He wanted to see where things between them could go! Forgetting her negative thoughts from earlier, she smiled at him a little shyly and nodded.

"Yes? You want to date?"

"Yes, Linc. I'd like that a lot."

"Good. Me too. Come on. Let's go see what chaos awaits us inside."

He caressed her arm one last time before turning to get out of the car. In a daze, Harper did the same, and while he didn't take her hand when they met up at the front of his car, he did walk a little closer to her than usual.

Moving back to Maine hadn't been anything like she'd thought it would be when she'd made the decision. Living with her dad hadn't worked out, but somehow she'd been accepted as part of the Young family, something she never would've guessed could happen in a million years. Kash was thriving, even with the bullying situation, and Harper knew it was all because of Linc. And if someone had told her twenty years ago that she'd be dating the boy she'd tormented relentlessly, she would've laughed in their face.

And yet, here she was.

Life was funny. It moved in twists and turns, and you just had to keep moving forward, hoping for the best when it gave you its worst. Harper could only hope and pray that she'd already experienced the worst life had in store for her, because she didn't think she'd survive being given a glimpse of heaven and having it snatched away again.

She didn't deserve Linc, but she damn well sure was going to try. Was going to do her best to be a better person than she had been in the past.

As they neared the front door, they could hear laughter inside.

"Ready?" Linc asked with a small grin.

"Ready," Harper agreed.

He lifted a hand and smoothed a lock of hair behind her ear in a tender, intimate gesture, before reaching for the door handle.

~

"Do you, Britt Starkweather, take this man to be your lawfully wedded husband? To have and hold. In sickness and health. For richer or poorer. And when he's being so annoying, all you want to do is throw him out the window?"

Everyone chuckled at Knox's question. Harper had been surprised to learn he was officiating his brother's wedding ceremony, but he was perfect for the role. Both poignant and funny at the same time.

Everyone was standing on the back deck. The sun wasn't shining, and it was kind of a bleary December day on the coast, but no one noticed the weather. Everyone's attention was on Britt and Chad. She had a baby bump that could clearly be seen under her white wedding dress. It was a simple long-sleeve sheath that flowed gracefully over her hips, reaching the deck.

Harper knew she was wearing white sneakers under her dress. Sneakers that had been covered with hundreds of sequins, so they sparkled like diamonds. She was carrying a handkerchief that Evelyn had carried at her own wedding, decades ago, and there was a picture of Austin Young on the table nearby.

There weren't many decorations, no gaudy balloons or streamers. There was one bouquet of flowers that, surprisingly, Victor had brought over when he'd arrived ten minutes ago. They were a touch wilted and weren't in a fancy vase. In fact, they were still wrapped in the paper from the grocery store where he'd bought them.

But the fact that he'd gone out of his way to bring something wasn't lost on anyone in attendance. He was trying to be more neighborly, and that was what mattered.

Kash was bouncing from foot to foot as he watched intently, completely focused on the couple in front of them. Evelyn was standing between Zach and Marit, an arm around each of theirs, smiling from ear to ear.

And Harper was standing so close to Linc, she could feel his body heat. Which was good because she needed it. The short-sleeve dress wasn't warm in the least, and standing outside was quickly making her chilled.

"Yes."

Britt's answer was short and sweet, and all her attention was on her soon-to-be husband. They were holding hands as they stared into each other's eyes.

"Do you, Chad Young, take this beautiful, amazing, too-good-for-you woman to be your lawfully wedded wife? To have and hold. For richer and poorer, in sickness and health. And promise to get up in the middle of the night when your kid is puking his guts out so she doesn't have to?"

Everyone laughed again.

"Absolutely," Chad said with a firm nod.

"I understand you have your own vows you want to share? As if mine weren't good enough?" Knox quipped.

Harper loved this. Loved how everyone was having a good time. How the ceremony wasn't formal and fussy. She even saw a half smile on her dad's face, which was something she'd always remember.

Britt released one of Chad's hands to reach into the neckline of her dress and pull out a piece of paper.

"What else do you have in there?" Chad asked, as he leaned forward and peered down her dress. Britt smacked his head with the folded paper and put a hand over her chest.

Laughter rang out again, as she unfolded the paper and cleared her throat.

"I promise to always respect and admire you, Chad, and to appreciate you for who you are, as well as the person you want to become in the future. I promise that your dreams will be my dreams, and that I will do everything in my power to make them a reality for us both. I promise to encourage you and hopefully inspire you, to laugh with you, and to comfort you when needed. I promise to nurture the love between us in good times and bad, when life is simple and when it's not, when loving you is easy, and when it takes a whole lot of effort."

Everyone chuckled at that, and Britt turned her head to smile at her new family before continuing.

"I promise to be faithful to you, and place you and our family above all else. And finally, I promise to love you with everything I am and everything within me, today and every day. To walk beside you, in front of you when necessary, and even behind you, letting you take the limelight and accolades you deserve. I promise to be with you, heart and soul, wherever life takes us . . . together."

Harper sniffed. She didn't think she'd ever heard such heartfelt vows in her life.

Chad leaned down and kissed Britt gently.

"Hey! It's not time for that yet, bro. Chill out!"

Shaking his head at his brother's antics, Chad pulled his own piece of paper from his back pocket. He took a deep breath, cleared his throat, and licked his lips before speaking.

"Britt, I vow to love you to the end of my days. To grow *with* you, and not apart. To make my accomplishments ours, and your challenges mine. To love you deeply and honestly as your teammate and partner. I choose you. To stand by your side and sleep in your arms. To learn and grow with you, even as time and life change us both. To laugh with you in the best of times and carry you through the worst. To never take your actions, words, and kindness for granted. I vow to consider your well-being as important as my own. From this day forward, you're my family, whether you like it or not."

Once again, everyone chuckled.

"I vow to fight for life, for joy, for us. For our future, for your dreams, our love, and to uplift you and make you a better person for choosing to be with me. To always do what's best for you and our children, and to be the kind of father I had . . . patient, kind, and embarrassing." Chad grinned and winked at his mom before finishing.

"I will be the best husband and person I know how to be. And when I screw it up, I know you'll be there to guide me. I love you, Britt. You make me a better man, brother, son, and partner. I can't wait to see where life takes us. Together."

There was a long pause. And then Knox said, "Oh, you're done being mushy? Good."

Chad rolled his eyes at his brother, but he was smiling, so it was obvious he wasn't too annoyed by his jokes.

"My turn to be a little mushy," Knox said. "Please look down at the hands of the person you're holding right now. These are the hands of your best friend, young and strong and full of love for you, today on your wedding day. These are the hands that will work alongside yours as you build your future together. They are the hands that will hold you when fear or grief fills your mind and heart. They'll wipe tears from your eyes, both of joy and sorrow.

"They're the hands that will hold your children, will hold your family together, and will give you strength when you need it most. And when these hands are wrinkled and aged, they will still be reaching for yours, giving you the same unspoken strength and tenderness you feel right this moment."

Harper didn't feel bad about the tears coursing down her cheeks, since *all* the other women in the small group were crying. Even the men looked moved by Knox's words.

"Time for the rings. I blew my wad with the amazing speech about your hands, so do your thing and put them on each other."

Chuckles rippled through the group as Chad and Britt exchanged rings.

"Now that we've heard your vows to each other, and my incredibly heartfelt speech, it's my deepest honor to pronounce you husband and wife. Chad . . . *now* you can kiss your bride. And make it a good one. None of this wimpy lip touching that some people feel is appropriate. Kash, Mom, you guys might want to look away."

Kash muttered, "Gross," before doing as Knox suggested and turning to look out at the cove, but everyone else watched as Chad bent Britt over his arm and kissed the daylights out of her.

"Is it time to eat now?" Kash asked, when Chad finally brought Britt upright once more. "I'm starving."

Her kid was always hungry, but Harper didn't hold it against him. He was still growing, and soon, hopefully, he'd start to fill out and would need all the calories he could get even more.

"I don't know about that, but I'm freezing. Time to go inside!" Evelyn announced.

Everyone shuffled into the house, and Harper sighed in relief as the warmth surrounded her once she stepped into the living room.

The rest of the day was spent laughing and simply enjoying each other's company. They'd all gotten together recently at Thanksgiving, and today was just as satisfying as the holiday had been. The food was amazing, Zach had once again stepped up and done most of the cooking, and seeing the joy on Britt and Chad's faces throughout the night was rewarding on a visceral level.

Evelyn had insisted on making the "cake," and it was probably the best thing Harper had ever tasted. It was untraditional, just like the rest of the wedding—a chocolate peanut butter pie, which she'd learned was Britt's favorite.

Britt and Chad had even had a first dance as a married couple right there in the living room, after the men pushed furniture out of the way. Harper's eyes teared up once more when Chad danced with his mom. All in all, it had been as close to a perfect day as Harper had ever experienced.

As she'd warned Kash time and time again, there was no such thing as an *absolutely* perfect day . . . as predicted, her dad had left not long after the ceremony, and Marit dropped a bottle of wine, sending dark red alcohol flying all over the kitchen floor. The shoes Harper bought had indeed been comfortable at first, but soon began rubbing her heels unbearably, and she'd had to borrow a pair of socks from Evelyn to save her poor feet.

But even with the small issues, the day was still unforgettable.

Everyone joined in picture-taking duties, and at the end of the night, they shared the photos by using their phones' built-in features to drop them to each other in batches. As a result, Harper's cell was full of the smiling faces of the Young family, and she loved each and every pic.

Her favorite was one Evelyn had taken. Harper and Linc had moved to the "dance floor" to share a slow dance, along with all the other couples. She was gazing at him with what she could only describe as longing on her face, and Linc was staring back with the same expression. One of his hands sat at the small of her back, the other holding their clasped hands up by his shoulder.

The picture captured all the emotions she was feeling at that moment perfectly. Desire, satisfaction, happiness, contentedness.

Her other favorite picture was of her and Kash. They were holding hands and swinging around in a circle as they danced. They were both laughing their heads off, and the joy on her son's face was priceless to Harper. His hair was mussed, he had a stain on his shirt from where he'd dropped something while he ate, and his bow tie was untied, hanging around his neck.

He was a boy on the cusp of manhood who still had no problem being silly with his mom. She loved that picture so much.

And at the end of the night, after everyone had said bye to Britt and Chad—who were going to spend their wedding night at a B&B in Rockville before heading to Portland—and after Harper, Linc, and

Kash had said their own goodbyes, Linc pretended to drive off, but he turned out his lights and pulled into the boat storage yard instead.

Somehow, Harper was convinced to go with the boys to execute Operation Lobster, as they called it. Hiding those tiny lobsters all over the small house Britt and Chad were living in was actually hysterical fun. Finding places to stash the little critters was quite a challenge. Especially two hundred and fifty of the suckers.

By the time they were done, Harper had a feeling the couple would be finding lobsters years from now. It was a harmless and fun prank, she'd decided, and weirdly, she felt honored to have been included.

It was late when they got back to Linc's house, and Kash was dead on his feet, trying valiantly to keep his eyes open but walking like a zombie into the house and straight up the stairs.

He turned after a few steps and said, "Tonight was awesome. Thanks for the clothes, Linc. And the bow tie. And for including me in Operation Lobster. And Mom, thanks for everything you do for me. You're the best mom in the world." Then, without giving either of them a chance to respond, he disappeared up the rest of the stairs.

Then it was just Harper and Linc. She felt shy all of a sudden. She was tired, and she knew he had to be too. There'd been a lot of emotion throughout the day, and she felt weighed down by it all.

"Go to bed, Harper. You look exhausted. You're working in the afternoon, right?"

"Yeah. Two to ten."

"Sleep in as long as you can. I've got Kash."

Gratitude and longing hit Harper hard and fast. He was *such* a good man. She walked over and put her hands on his chest as she leaned into him. She felt his arms go around her, and she rested her forehead against his shoulder. They stood like that for a long moment before she straightened.

"Thanks for sharing your family with us. You have no idea how much it means to me."

"You're welcome," Linc said simply. Then he licked his lips and said quietly, "I've wanted to kiss you again all night. Seeing you smile, your happy tears, you laughing with your son, I don't think I've seen anything as beautiful as you in a very long time."

Pleasure bloomed within Harper. No compliment she'd ever received meant as much as the ones coming from this man's lips.

"Then kiss me," she encouraged.

Her hand went to his nape as he leaned forward. This kiss wasn't as . . . desperate . . . as the one they'd shared in the car. It was easy and affectionate. He kept it short—shorter than Harper would've liked.

"Good night, Harper. See you in the morning."

She didn't want to drop her hand from his neck, but his words were obviously meant as an ending to the wonderful day they'd shared.

Smiling as she backed away, Harper gave him a dorky little wave, then mentally winced at how stupid she was being. Turning, she headed for the stairs where Kash had disappeared moments earlier. Just like him, she turned after going up only a couple of steps.

"Do you think you'll be able to sleep tonight? After all the excitement?" She worried about Linc. Kash had told her a little bit about how he had trouble sleeping, but since she usually slept like a rock, she hadn't caught him awake in the middle of the night.

"Sure," Linc said with a smile.

He was lying, but Harper didn't know what she could do about it. Linc was a grown man, and if he wasn't getting enough sleep, he'd know what to do to fix it. Wouldn't he?

But Linc didn't give her a chance to question him, he simply nodded and headed for his bedroom.

Wishing she had the guts to ask him to stay with her, even if just to sleep in his oversize chair again, Britt walked up the stairs toward her room. She took off the dress and kicked off the shoes, making a mental note never to buy shoes from her workplace again, no matter how cute they looked. She put on an oversize T-shirt and padded out to the bathroom.

By the time she got back to bed, she was dead on her feet. She'd planned on staying awake long enough to go over the wonderful memories of the day, especially Linc's kisses. But as soon as her head hit her pillow, she was out like a light.

Chapter Nine

All was not well in the house.

Linc knew he was a big part of the reason why.

Christmas and New Year's Eve had come and gone.

Kash loved his Christmas presents, and afterward they'd all gone over to Lobster Cove to spend a few hours with Evelyn and the rest of the family. Operation Lobster was a huge hit, and Britt and Chad continued to laugh at how many lobsters they were finding all over their house, in places they never would've thought to look.

Chad complained that the one Linc had put inside a bottle of Italian dressing in their fridge had scared the crap out of him.

For Christmas, Linc had bought Harper the softest, fluffiest bathrobe he'd been able to find. The house was drafty, and she always seemed to be chilled, and since he didn't feel as if he had the right yet to warm her with his own body heat, the bathrobe had been the next best thing.

For Kash, he'd splurged and bought a top-of-the-line telescope. Harper had protested when they'd had a moment alone, after opening presents, but he'd simply shrugged and told her to think of it as furthering the boy's education.

Harper had gotten him an autographed hardback special edition book by one of his favorite authors, and Kash had presented him with a certificate claiming that a star had been named after him.

For New Year's Eve he, Kash, and Harper had celebrated by staying up until midnight and lighting a few sparklers . . . the handheld pyrotechnics. He refused to actually set off fireworks for many reasons. Even though his house was pretty isolated, sound carried across the water, and there were many dogs that were especially sensitive to the loud boomers.

Not to mention men and women like him, who might be triggered by the sounds of the explosions.

Now, it was nearing the end of February. School had been back in session for weeks . . . and Kash was struggling. It was easy to see. Linc was relieved when the boy actually had an honest conversation with Harper about Donny and Ginger and their friend group picking on him. Being bullies. But she didn't really have words of wisdom that would help him any more than Linc's had.

However, knowing her son was going through the same thing she'd put Linc through had obviously begun to eat at her. When she looked at Kash, Linc could see guilt in her gaze more often than not. Being on the other side now, seeing how badly someone suffered from bullying, had to strike deep for her.

Then there was Linc.

He was being an asshole.

He knew it, but he wasn't sure how to fix things. His sleep cycles were even worse than they'd been before the holidays. Night after night of barely any sleep, and trying to hide the fact that he was always dead on his feet—not only from his family, but from the boy and woman living with him—was taking a toll.

He'd started drinking over-the-counter cough medicine at night in an attempt to knock himself out. And while it worked, the effects didn't last any longer than if he hadn't taken anything at all. He still woke abruptly after an hour or two, max. The stuff also seemed to make his dreams even more vivid.

He was at the end of his rope, and he wasn't sure what to do.

Talking to a shrink hadn't worked, and he really didn't want to have to start taking sleeping pills. Doing so felt like a failure.

How could he have been strong enough to walk for miles and miles through hostile territory, with an arm that was completely useless, and *not* be able to fucking sleep for more than two hours a night? It was pathetic, and Linc hated feeling that way.

As a result of his constantly being on edge, his relationship with Harper hadn't progressed as well or as fast as he would have liked. They'd shared a few kisses, had begun to hold hands when they were outside the house, but that was it.

Linc's mouth watered every time he thought about how beautiful Harper had looked at Chad's wedding. He thought she was pretty all the time, but when she'd made an effort to dress up, she'd been stunning. And it was more than the physical trappings. Her joy over being with his family, watching her son flourish, celebrating his brother's wedding—it made her even more exquisite in his eyes.

He wanted her.

Wanted to bury himself in her and never come up for air.

Wanted to lose himself in her arms and her touch.

But with every day that went by, and he was too chicken to make a move, he felt more and more awkward about taking their physical relationship to a higher level.

He was pitiful. Seriously. He couldn't get control over his own mind and body when it came to sleeping, and he felt as if Harper was slipping away before they'd ever really made an effort to see if a relationship between them could work. Something had to give, and Linc was afraid it was going to be *him* that broke. Who ruined everything.

For a man who was used to being in complete control while flying a multimillion-dollar fighter jet, he was floundering with the lack of control he felt in his life at the moment.

With Kash back at school and Harper's hours at work back to normal, Linc was trying to get back into the groove with his house renovations. Today, his plan was to get serious about the floors in his living room before tackling the upstairs bedrooms. He had the materials in one of the empty guest rooms, and he and Kash had finished painting toward the end of Kash's winter break.

He'd intended to start ripping up the old floors way before now, but he'd started trying to take naps while Harper and Kash were gone, and when they returned, his time was spent with them, making dinner, watching science shows on TV, or playing some kind of board game.

His life had completely changed since they'd moved in, and Linc wasn't upset about it. Not in the least. In some ways, he felt more alive than he had in years, even with the lack of sleep. They'd totally upended his routine, but in a good way.

He'd just started carrying the wood flooring downstairs to the living room when he heard a car pull up outside. Wondering if one of his brothers had come to see him, Linc quickly set the boxes down and went to look out the window to see who'd arrived.

He was confused to see Harper's minivan pull into the garage next to the house. Panic hit hard and fast. Why was she home from work so early? Was she all right? Was it Kash?

He had the door open and was halfway to the garage when she met him.

"What's wrong? Are you okay?" he asked a little frantically.

She stared at him for a beat, then grabbed his arm and tried to pull him toward the house.

But Linc dug in his heels. "Talk to me, Harper. Why are you home?"

"Linc, you've only got a short-sleeve T-shirt on. It's freaking cold out here. Let's go inside and I'll tell you."

"Just tell me that you're all right first!"

"I'm fine," she said dutifully.

Linc ran his gaze up and down her body, trying to figure out if she was lying.

"Promise. I'm good. Kash too. And as far as I know, so is everyone in your family. There's no emergency. Now, come on, let's get inside and I'll tell you why I'm here."

Relief made Linc feel almost dizzy. He'd had enough emergencies in his family, but somehow thinking about Harper or Kash being hurt was enough to send him into a full-blown panic. So much for the levelheaded fighter pilot he used to be. His houseguests had changed him irrevocably.

He let Harper pull him toward the house, enjoying her concern and her bossiness. She'd also changed since she'd first moved in. In the beginning, she'd been afraid to contradict him on anything. She was fairly quiet, unwilling to make any kind of waves or change anything in his house.

Since then, she'd become a little more assertive. Making suggestions as to how to decorate and where to place furniture to make rooms seem as if they had a bit more square footage. And she'd been right every time. As a result, Linc's house seemed more . . . homey. Comfortable. There were throw pillows on the chairs and cozy blankets draped over the backs. He had place mats on his table and decorative towels in his kitchen, instead of the utilitarian ones he'd always used. They were small changes that made a big impact.

But his favorite new item in his house was a picture Harper had gotten blown up for him for Christmas. She'd had it framed as well. An image of Linc and his three brothers out at Lobster Cove, taken at Thanksgiving. They were on the back deck, with the water behind them and their arms around each other. It was hanging on the wall near the television, and it was the first thing he saw every time he entered the living room.

Family was why he was here in Maine. And it was a great reminder of what was important in life. Not the accolades you got at work, not what others thought of you, but being there for those you loved.

As soon as the door shut behind them, she turned to him with her hands on her hips.

"Enough is enough," she said sternly, meeting his gaze. "I don't know what's up with you, but something's wrong. You're tense all the time, you're constantly squinting as if you have a migraine, and you've done so much baking recently there's no way you're getting enough rest, because I know you're doing it at night when Kash and I are sleeping.

"I took the next two days off. I thought maybe we could go to Boothbay Harbor. I know it's the offseason, but there are still some restaurants open, and I've already made a reservation at a B&B near downtown. You need a *break*, Linc. And I think we need some time together too. Without all the distractions we've got here, like work, the house repairs, your family."

Linc was stunned. When was the last time someone had gone out of their way to take care of him? He couldn't remember. When he was a kid, probably. As the oldest brother, he'd always been charged with watching over his siblings. And he'd moved back to Maine for the express purpose of looking after his mom.

Was this how things were between Britt and Chad? And Marit and Zach? He figured it probably was. They looked out for each other, lifted the other up when needed.

Now that he thought about it, his parents had done the same thing. There were plenty of times when he could remember his dad telling everyone to keep their voices down because their mom was napping. Or when his mom would make a special dinner in the middle of the week for no real reason, except she said she wanted to pamper their dad.

Linc had never been in a relationship where his girlfriend went out of her way to spoil him. He was always the one doing the spoiling. He wasn't resentful of that, not then and not now, had always simply assumed that was his role in a relationship.

But even though he and Harper were still feeling each other out, hadn't moved things between them to a physical level, she'd done more for him with this simple gesture than any past girlfriend ever had.

"Linc? Is that okay? I've already arranged for Kash to stay with my dad. They both seemed kind of excited about it, which is a relief. This space between us all has been the best thing for our relationship with him. If you want to stay here, that's okay too. I can help with the floors, which I know you've been wanting to get started on."

Linc stepped toward Harper, crowding her, pushing her back until she was pressed against the wall. He put his hands on her face, his thumbs brushing against her cheeks as he lowered his head until they were only a hairsbreadth apart.

"Yes, it's okay. It's more than okay. It sounds fucking fantastic. Thank you."

She breathed out a sigh of relief. "You're welcome."

"Are we leaving today or tomorrow?"

"Today. As soon as you're packed, actually. After school, my dad will bring Kash over here to pack a bag. I packed this morning before I left for work, my stuff is upstairs. All you have to do is put your stuff together and we can head out."

Linc didn't really know what to say. He was more excited for two days alone with this woman than he could adequately express. He could still remember the feel of her in his arms as they slept in his chair. How amazing she'd felt, and how well he'd slept. He still wasn't sure if it was a fluke or not, but he was looking forward to seeing if she somehow had the magical ability to put him to sleep . . . and keep him there.

But he wanted to be clear about where things stood between them. Didn't want there to be any misunderstandings. "One room or two?" he asked.

Her brows furrowed for a moment, before it dawned on her what he was asking. She blushed but didn't drop her eyes. "One. Is that okay?"

"Okay? Harper, I haven't been able to think about anything other than being with you for weeks. Every time I hear the water in the pipes when you're showering, all I can think of is you, naked upstairs, how the water and soap might look as they slip over your body. I probably shouldn't admit this, but I've jacked off to thoughts of you almost every day."

Her blush deepened. "You have?"

"Yes."

"Oh."

"Does that turn you off?" he asked gently, wondering if he should've kept his mouth shut.

"Does it turn *you* off that it *doesn't* turn me off?" she asked with a small smile. Her hands were at his sides, and he could feel her fingers tighten on him as she spoke.

"No way."

"Good. Because when I'm in the shower? When you hear the water in those pipes? I'm usually getting myself off to thoughts of *you*."

And just like that, Linc was hard. He wanted to grab this woman and drag her into his bedroom and take her right then and there. The thought of waiting even one more minute to have her was almost physically painful.

"I'm going to make love to you tonight. And tomorrow. And tomorrow night. And probably before we leave Boothbay. I'm not sure I'll be able to get enough of you. You've gotten under my skin, Harper, and I'm not even mad about it. I like you there. And I like you *here*. In my house. Your stuff strewn around the rooms. I'm looking forward to spending time away with you, more than I can say. And not just in bed. Talking to you, laughing, shopping, eating, all of it. I can't think of anything better than a couple days off with just the two of us."

"Ditto."

He chuckled. He had packed a lot into his words. But he wanted to be sure they were truly on the same page. "Are you on birth control?"

She swallowed hard and shook her head. "There hasn't been a need."

"All right, we'll have to stop at a store on the way there. I don't have any condoms . . . because there hasn't been a need for me either. Are you truly okay with this? It'll change things. I hope for the better, but it'll definitely change our relationship."

"I'm ready for it. I want it, Linc. I want you."

Moving slowly, giving her a chance to pull away, Linc lowered his head. She leaned forward, meeting him halfway. Their kiss was surprisingly gentle. Maybe because Linc knew that tonight, he'd finally be able to do all the things he'd fantasized about.

Anticipation churned inside him, and he knew it would make tonight all the better. Kind of like Christmas morning when he was a kid. He looked forward to it all month, and when it finally arrived, he felt almost giddy. As if something deep inside him had finally been fulfilled.

He'd felt the same way while he was training to fly fighter jets, and the first time he sat behind the controls was like Christmas morning all over again. Linc had no doubt being with Harper in the most intimate way would be exactly like the satisfaction of anticipation fulfilled.

"I need to go pack," he said, after he pulled back.

"Yeah."

Neither moved.

Linc grinned. "You have to let go of me before I can do that."

"*You* need to let go of *me* so I can go get the suitcase I packed this morning," she countered.

"You first." It was childish and silly, but their banter made Linc feel lighter than he'd felt in weeks.

She had a huge grin on her face, but she sighed as if extremely put out and dropped her hands from his sides.

"I win," Linc crowed, then kissed her hard and fast once more before stepping back.

"I think we've both won," Harper said in a low voice.

She couldn't be more right.

They went their separate ways, moving at a quick pace. As reluctant as they'd been to stop touching each other, they were apparently just as eager to be on their way.

It didn't take Linc long to pack. He threw in a pair of jeans, some shirts, a sweatshirt, underwear, and socks. Grabbed what he needed from his bathroom, pausing for a beat as he stared at the bottle of cough medicine, then aggressively zipped up his toiletry bag.

No. He wasn't going to bring that bottle. If he didn't sleep, at least he'd get to appreciate holding Harper as *she* slept.

It was time. Time he figured out a way to get the sleep he needed to be able to function. If the next two nights didn't change anything, if it turned out sleeping with Harper in his arms was a one-time fluke thing, he'd call his doctor and make plans to discuss his options. He'd probably do that no matter what happened. He couldn't go on like this. It wasn't healthy. Physically or mentally.

And he never wanted Harper to take on the burden of his insomnia. If having her near helped him sleep, great. But he didn't want her to ever feel obligated, or like his health was on her shoulders. The crash and subsequent flight through the jungle to keep from being captured was in the past. Over. Done. He wasn't going to let it keep affecting him any longer. He'd worked too hard to get where he was today to let those assholes who'd hunted him win.

Harper was waiting by the front door when he came out of his room. He walked around the house, making sure everything was secure. He turned the heat down a notch or two, then, satisfied that everything was good, he shrugged into his jacket.

Finally, he smiled at Harper. "Let's do this."

"Let's do this," she echoed with a huge smile.

They walked out together, and after Linc locked the door, he picked up her suitcase and led the way to the garage. He had a feeling the next two days would completely change his life. He could only hope it was changed for the better, and he didn't screw anything up between them. He wanted their relationship to work. More than he could express out loud.

The thought of losing Harper, and Kash in the process, was too painful to think about. He'd do whatever it took to show this woman that he was the kind of man who'd always be there for her. Someone she could count on. Who she could respect and admire. Because she was all that for him, and so much more.

Chapter Ten

Harper was extremely relieved she hadn't overstepped when she'd made the reservations for the two of them. Something was wrong with Linc. He was on edge, and he had dark circles under his eyes. Kash had confirmed that he didn't sleep well, and it was becoming more and more obvious to Harper that it was a serious problem, not just a night here and there.

She wouldn't be surprised to learn he had PTSD from his crash. She didn't know much about what happened, just enough to know it had been extremely harrowing, and that he'd almost been captured. Post-traumatic stress would certainly explain his sleep troubles.

Whatever the reason, instead of resting, he'd been going completely overboard in the kitchen. He might not be as good a cook as Zach, but the man could bake. Every morning when she woke up, the house smelled like cookies, or some kind of bread, or a casserole he claimed to have made for his brother Knox . . . who was *completely* hopeless in the kitchen.

And then there was the look in his eyes. A haunted look. Hopeless. Defeated. As if his demons were winning. And it tore at her heart, made Harper desperate to do something to help him.

She'd felt that way herself. Like she couldn't last one more day. As if everyone looked *through* her instead of *at* her. Didn't notice how hard she was fighting to keep Kash safe and happy.

Life was hard. Damn near impossible at times. And for that reason, it was the fleeting moments of kindness she remembered most. So she wanted to give one of those moments to Linc. She thought a few days away would do them both a world of good. And in the process, would hopefully nudge their relationship to the next level.

Because she wanted that. Badly. Holding hands and kissing was great, awesome, but she wanted more. She wanted all of Linc. The good, bad, and ugly. She wanted to feel as close to him as a person could get. Naked. Raw. Completely open.

In order to do that, she felt as if she needed to open parts of herself that she'd kept locked away for years. That she hadn't ever shown anyone. Share things she hadn't *wanted* to tell anyone . . . until now.

The desire for Linc to know her was overwhelming. He might reject her. Might decide she had too much baggage . . . but she didn't think so. If he hadn't kicked her out of his house by now, she didn't think he ever would. If for no other reason than he loved Kash, of that she was sure.

She didn't think learning the truth about how her son came into the world would change that.

But would it change his feelings toward *her*?

Harper wanted to sleep with Linc. Wanted to feel him moving deep inside her. Wanted to experience lust and sexual satisfaction again. It had been forever since she'd had any kind of desire to be with a man. But she wanted Linc. It was why she'd booked a room with only one bed. To make sure he understood that she was choosing him. Choosing to sleep with him. Giving consent. Because that was very important to her . . . and he'd know why before too long.

Thankfully, he seemed quite pleased with her taking control of their physical relationship. With making the first move. Harper felt more like the woman she used to be. Someone who knew what she wanted and did whatever it took to get it. She'd lost her way for a while, but she was getting back to that woman . . . thanks in part to Linc.

Before night fell, he'd know everything. All her deep dark secrets. He'd either turn out to be the man she needed, or he'd turn his back on her. They could still be just friends, if that was what he chose.

But if he slept with her, gave himself to her fully, and *then* decided he just wanted to be friends? Wanted to go back to just being housemates? It would destroy her.

Harper was taking a huge risk with this trip. It wasn't just to ease some kind of sexual desire on both their parts. It would be either a new beginning, or the end of what could be. She hoped and prayed it would be the former, but she'd accept whatever his decision was. She'd take the first step, after that it was up to Linc.

The trip to Boothbay Harbor was fun. They decided to stop in Damariscotta, a cute little town along the way, not far from Rockville. It didn't take long to walk through the downtown area and browse the shops that were open.

They ate lunch at a place called King Eider's Pub, named after the duck that was iconic in the area. Harper had the seafood pot pie, which was amazing, and Linc had the untraditional fish n' chips. She wasn't sure why it was called untraditional, but he assured her it was delicious. They also shared a serving of the firecracker green beans, which had her lips and tongue tingling even after they left.

They considered going to the Maritime Museum in Bath, but decided to leave it for another day. The trip down to the coast was peaceful in terms of traffic, and Linc told her it would be a much different trip in the summer when all the tourists were around.

She gave him directions to the small B&B and was thrilled with how cute the place was when he pulled into the driveway.

The owner met them at the door and showed them to their room, which was really the entire upper floor of the house. It was huge, and decorated in typical coastal décor . . . lobsters, of course, and anchors, and blue and white everywhere they looked. The window faced the harbor and was across from the little touristy town. All they had to do to get over there was cross the Boothbay Harbor

Footbridge, and they'd be right in the middle of the shops and restaurants.

The bathroom was large, and Harper couldn't help but notice the shower was more than big enough for the two of them to share. She had lusty thoughts about what they could do in that shower, and couldn't wait to try it out . . . after she had her talk with Linc.

They decided to head over to the town and wander around, since the sun was still shining and they had some time to kill before dinner. As soon as they exited the house, Linc took her hand in his, and they walked side by side across the bridge. There weren't many people out and about, but those they passed nodded politely or told them good afternoon.

It felt decadent to not be working. It had been years since she'd taken the time to do something just for herself, and Harper was enjoying the day immensely.

There were a lot of after-Christmas sales still going on, and she found herself splurging on both an oversize sweatshirt that said "Boothbay Harbor" and a sweater with a large lobster on the front. It was impractical, as it was hand-wash only, but it was adorable and Harper couldn't resist. It didn't hurt that Linc urged her on, saying it was perfect for her and looked amazing with her auburn hair.

Even better, Linc didn't insist on paying for her purchases. He'd come to understand that she needed to be able to pay for the things she wanted on her own. That she didn't need or want him to step in and hand over his credit card. It might be silly, but being capable of paying for her own things made Harper feel as if she was finally climbing out of the hole she'd been in for so long.

However, that didn't keep Linc from going overboard when it came to Kash. He found so many knickknacks that he thought her son would like, and was so excited about every item, she didn't have the heart to tell him no when he wanted to buy them.

By the time they'd walked off their lunch, Harper was more than ready to get off her feet. And amazingly, she was hungry again.

They were hoping to eat at McSeagull's, a restaurant right on the waterfront, but it was closed for the season. So instead they headed down the street to Ports of Italy, a tiny little Italian restaurant that smelled delicious from the outside.

Linc had the ravioli di astice, which was ravioli filled with lobster and ricotta in a light sauce, so good he was literally moaning with every bite. He also decided he was going to urge Zach to put the dish on his menu, or at least his version of it, so he could have it whenever he wanted.

Harper finally decided on the tagliatelle alla bolognese. Tender homemade pasta with meat-and-tomato ragù. They both had wine with their meal, and they shared a chocolate torte for dessert. By the time they left, Harper was stuffed to the gills and glad they had to walk back to the B&B.

The closer they got to the house, though, the more nervous she became. About the talk she wanted to have with Linc. She had no idea how he would take what she needed to tell him. If she was smart, she'd put it off. Enjoy the night with him. Experience how combustible their chemistry would be when they were finally able to explore it fully. Without the pressure of work, time, or the fear that Kash might walk in on them.

"Breathe, Harper," Linc said gently, as if he could feel her tension. "Nothing's going to happen that you don't want to happen."

"I want everything," Harper blurted. "I mean, I want to be with you. That's why I got one room and one bed. But I want to talk first."

He looked over at her. "Talk?"

"Yeah. There are things I want you to know. About me. Kash. About my time in New York."

"All right. But for the record, there's nothing you can tell me that will change my mind about tonight, or about wanting to be with you."

God, he was a good man. But it was easy to say those words, especially when he had no idea what she wanted to talk to him about.

Harper was silent as they walked into the B&B and up to their room. She was trying to figure out how to start as he put the bags with their purchases in a corner of the room. Then he reached for her hand and tugged her over to the small love seat at the foot of the bed and pulled her down next to him.

"I'm here, Harper. I'm listening. I'll always be open to anything you want to tell me, whenever you want to talk."

"I'm afraid it'll change things."

"Nothing you tell me will change anything. You'll still have a place in my home with your son. I'll still want you as much as I do right this moment. Will we always be together? I don't know. I'm not a fortune teller. But I can tell you that you being honest about whatever is on your mind will never be a reason for me to turn my back on you. On us. On what we could have."

His words made her feel a little better. Maybe she was being silly. Letting her own insecurities and shame about what happened color her perception of reality. The only way she'd really know was if she opened her mouth and spoke.

Nodding, she took a deep breath. Then told him what she'd never told another soul in the world.

"When I left Rockville to move to New York, I was so full of myself. Thought I was so beautiful that modeling agencies would take one look at me and fall all over themselves to sign me. I honestly didn't consider that there were thousands of tall redheads out there who looked just like me. I was a small-town girl completely out of her depths in the big city.

"My dad tried to warn me, tried to get me to go to college instead, but I was having none of his advice. I thought I was smarter than him. More worldly. I was going to be rich, and he'd apologize for every doubt he'd ever had about what I wanted to do. But I quickly found out how out of my league I was."

"Relax, Harper," Linc said quietly. He squeezed her hands gently. "I don't think anything you're saying is too out of the ordinary.

Most eighteen-year-olds have no idea about the real world. I know I didn't."

"I worked my ass off for seven years. With each new year, I just knew *that one* was going to be mine. The year I was discovered. When I finally made my mark. I worked shitty jobs, mostly waitressing, to be able to afford the tiny apartment I was sharing with three other wannabe models. We ate a lot of ramen and food we got on the sale racks at the store. You know, cans of stuff that expired and meat that was a day or two past its sell-by date. I saved money to constantly update my headshots, and walked my ass off going from agency to agency, trying to find an agent who would finally see my potential.

"When I was twenty-five, I thought I'd finally done it. There was this guy who seemed blown away by my pictures, by me. He was employed by one of the more prestigious modeling companies in New York. An agent he worked with had gotten a hold of my portfolio from another company I'd sent it to, and he'd brought me to the guy's attention. He told me I was exactly what he'd been looking for. That I'd be the next big thing, and he was one hundred percent sure he could get me big parts in TV shows and maybe even a movie.

"I was so *beyond* excited, I had blinders on. My roommates tried to tell me this guy sounded too good to be true, but I wouldn't listen. I thought they were just jealous. I was stupid . . . so stupid."

Harper took a deep breath. She hated to admit how dumb she'd been, especially to this man, but she'd come this far. She had to keep going.

"But there was a caveat. Before he agreed to sign me, he needed to get the approval of three of his fellow agents. Said that's how they worked. That there needed to be a consensus that any model they hired was *right* for the agency. He explained there was this big shindig his company was throwing, the perfect place to introduce me to coworkers and get the approval we needed. He also said there'd be film producers and representatives from Hollywood there, a potential springboard to get a jump start on my new career, once I was approved by his colleagues.

"I splurged and bought a skintight black dress and four-inch heels. The material clung to my curves, and I felt so damn good about myself. I remember thinking how lucky I was when I entered the nightclub where the party was taking place. How that night was going to be the beginning of a whole new life. One where I was the talk of the town, with everyone wanting me to star in their projects. How I'd get calls from all the big designers, wanting me to wear their clothes . . .

"It was the start of a new life, all right. Just not the one I'd envisioned.

"The party was weird from the start. There were only a handful of women there. It was mostly men. *Older* men. Everyone was drinking, and I didn't really like the look of lust on the men's faces. But honestly, I'd gotten pretty used to that. You can't be a woman in the fashion industry and not learn to recognize when someone thinks you're hot.

"And I felt safe enough, because my new agent hung on to me all night, walking me around and introducing me to people. I was flattered, and I did what I could to impress everyone so they'd agree I'd be perfect for their agency. I was happy to smile at those strangers, drink the drinks that were pushed into my hand, and bask in the glow that came with being the center of attention."

She felt Linc stiffen next to her but forced herself to continue. To finish what she'd started.

"I don't remember the rest of the night. My next memory is waking up the next morning in an alley. A fucking *alley*. My dress was on inside out, I had no underwear and no shoes. And I *hurt*. All over. Inside and out.

"I knew what happened—of course I did. How could I not? But I was in denial. I somehow made it home, and the looks of pity from my roommates were almost more than I could bear. I took a long hot shower, and I cried the entire time. When I finally dragged myself out, I immediately called my alleged *agent*. He'd blocked my number. And when I did an internet search to find out more about him, I realized he'd given me a fake name. He apparently didn't exist in the industry. I didn't even know if he had an actual office, because we'd always met in a park, or a diner, or a coffee shop.

"I'd fallen for his lies, hook, line, and sinker. I have no idea how he actually found my headshots. But he used me, and probably sold me and all those other women to the highest bidders that night. Hauling me around to meet everyone like he was parading a prize steer in front of potential buyers.

"I found out I was pregnant two months later. I'd immediately gotten an STD test done, but I hadn't even thought about asking for emergency contraception. I was too freaked out about having a potential disease, too traumatized about what had happened to me, and too upset about being *so stupid* to believe that asshole's lies about being an agent and wanting to sign me.

"I have no idea who Kash's father is. Don't want to know. Don't ever want *Kash* to know. I thought about an abortion at the time, even made an appointment to do it, but in the end . . . I couldn't. I wanted the baby. That baby inside me was innocent, regardless of how he was created. I wouldn't let him suffer for my stupidity of not doing more research on the sleazeball who'd pretended to be an agent.

"Despite the circumstances of his conception, I wanted my baby. It was probably selfish of me, but for the first time in a long time, I was looking forward to my future. To being a mom.

"I had Kash alone in the hospital, no friends, no family, no one there to hold my hand, to tell me it would be all right. I was terrified about what was to come, but the second they put Kash in my arms, everything else seemed to fade away. He was definitely my kid. He had a head full of red hair from the moment he came out. And my green eyes. And my dad's chin. I looked into his eyes and swore

I'd always put him first. That I'd do whatever it took to be the best mom possible.

"Nothing else I've ever done compares to him. He's my entire life. While I hate the circumstances that brought him into the world, I don't regret making the decision to keep him. I've struggled almost every day to make sure he has food and shelter, but it's never been difficult to give him love.

"When I finally realized I was hurting him by continuing to try to make a life in New York, I called Dad. Begged him to let us come home. I put aside my pride, something I should've done years ago, and crawled back to Rockville feeling like a failure.

"But because of you and your family, I finally feel as if I'm getting some of my dignity back. I can't change the past, the decisions I made, the things I've said and done, but I'm trying to do my best to be a different person today. A better one."

She paused, taking several deep breaths. "I just wanted you to know the whole sordid tale. Of where I've been, what I've done, and how Kash was conceived. Again, I don't know who his father is, I didn't even try to find out. No good could ever come of it. And I never pressed charges because I didn't even know the name of the man who sold me out, literally. I'm sure the men at that party all had fake names too. For years, I lived in fear I'd come face-to-face with one of them in the city, but I never did. At least, I don't think I did.

"And . . . that's my story. I wanted to be completely honest with you before . . . before we go any further down the road we're traveling."

Harper hadn't looked up the entire time she was speaking. Simply stared at her hands. Hands that were being held in Linc's large, strong, capable grip.

When he let go of her and stood, Harper looked up for the first time.

And almost stopped breathing at what she saw.

Linc. Looked. Pissed.

Absolutely furious.

He took a deep breath, then shut his eyes, cutting off the emotion Harper had seen there.

She stared at him, her hopes for what might've been crashing and burning in that moment. She'd always known there was a possibility Linc might be mad at her for what she'd done. For how stupid she'd been. Though she'd hoped that wouldn't be the case.

But there was no mistaking the anger she'd seen on his face. It was as clear as day.

Despair shot through her body. Looking around the room, she felt ashamed as the silence dragged out. Humiliated. She'd completely opened herself up . . . and he'd not said a word. Was still standing there with his eyes shut, as if he wanted to be anywhere but in her presence.

She couldn't stay in that room for another second. Not where she'd hoped to finally be able to experience all that was Lincoln Young for the first time.

She needed to go. To get out of there.

She wouldn't be able to bear his disdain when he finally got himself together enough to speak. To hear him point out her mistakes. She'd made many, she knew she had, but she didn't need to hear them from the man she was beginning to care for so deeply.

Hell, who was she kidding? She was falling in love with Linc. With the man he was with Kash. With his family. With the hardworking man, the imperfect man, the guy who could be sweet enough to buy her a bathrobe for Christmas because he'd noticed how cold she got while puttering around his house. The man who'd opened his home to a single mom in need of a safe haven.

She stood and silently grabbed her suitcase to pack her things, tears falling down her cheeks as she thought about what might have been.

Her thoughts were going a mile a minute. Things would change from here on out, that was for sure. She wasn't quite able to afford her own place yet, but she couldn't stay with Linc. Not after this. Oh, he'd probably try to convince her to stay for Kash's sake, insist he wasn't mad at her. But she'd seen his face before he'd been able to hide his feelings.

Sniffing quietly, she ran a hand over her eyes, trying to hide the fact that she was crying. She had no idea how she'd get back to Rockville, since Linc drove them here, but she'd spend some of her precious savings on a taxi if she had to. Anything to put some space between them. To try to shore up her shattered shields once more.

She'd be okay. She always was. She had no choice, Kash was depending on her.

It felt as if minutes had passed as all these thoughts raced through her head, but in reality, it hadn't been more than thirty seconds. She was just putting her suitcase on the bed so she could shove her stuff into it and get the hell out of there when Linc asked in a confused tone, "What are you doing?"

Turning, Harper saw he looked just as intense as he had right before he'd closed his eyes. She didn't see the anger on his face anymore, but he was obviously still upset about what she'd told him.

"Packing," Harper said, sniffing again, doing her best to stop more tears from falling from her eyes.

"Why?"

"Why?" she repeated.

"Yes, Harper—why?"

She couldn't read the emotion in his voice. It wasn't anger, per se, but it was . . . something. "Um, because you're mad?" It came out more as a question than a statement.

"I *am* mad," Linc agreed. "I'm furious. At the men who took advantage of you. Who drugged and raped you. Who haven't been held accountable for their despicable fucking actions."

Harper straightened, abandoning her attempts to unzip her suitcase. "You are?"

"Of course I am! I wouldn't be a decent goddamn human being if I wasn't! Did you think I was mad at *you*?"

She stood there in shock, staring at Linc.

"You did. Why in the world would I be angry at you, Harper? You did nothing wrong. *Nothing.* Hear me? You went to that party thinking you were going to make connections in your industry. Thinking you were going to find someone who wanted to sign you. Mingle with people who were on the up-and-up. Instead, you were fed to the wolves. I *hate* assholes like that fake fucking agent. Vampires who feed on others. Do nothing but take. And I'm glad you don't know which of those monsters is Kash's father, because their names shouldn't ever cross your lips. Or his."

"Linc," Harper whispered, overwhelmed with relief. That he hadn't tuned her out because he was upset with her.

The next thing she knew, she was in Linc's embrace. He was holding on to her so tightly it was hard to breathe. But she didn't care. She held him just as tightly.

He pulled back and used his fingers to wipe away her tears. "You honestly thought I was mad at you?" he asked.

She gave him a small nod.

"Never, Harper. I'm sorry I zoned out like that. I was just so . . . overwhelmed with emotion. I needed a second to understand everything I'd just heard. I should've told you that I needed a minute to process what you'd told me. You were the wronged person here, not me."

"It's okay," she told him quietly. Her heart had lightened considerably since she'd found out he wasn't angry *at* her, but on her behalf instead.

"It's not. I . . . it's hard for me to process things normally now. After my crash . . ." He sighed, then pressed his lips together. "You shared your darkest secret. It's time I did the same."

"You don't have to—"

"I want to. I want to be the kind of man you can trust. You chose to confide in me, hopefully because you see a future between us. I want the same. And you need to know what kind of man you're attaching yourself to."

"I *do* know, Linc."

"You don't. But you will. Come on, let's sit back down. It's my turn to open up. To be completely honest. I want no secrets between us, Harper. There can't be if we want this to work."

Harper nodded. She couldn't deny she was curious as to what he had to say. She assumed it was about his crash and what he went through, but she didn't want him to feel forced to do or say anything.

When they sat, and she looked into his eyes, she saw a rawness there that surprised her. A desire to get things off his chest, just as she'd done.

"I'm here," she told him, echoing what he'd told her not too long ago. "I'm not going anywhere."

"We'll see," he said morosely.

Chapter Eleven

Linc couldn't believe he was about to tell Harper the full story of what happened after he'd crashed his jet. He swore to himself a long time ago that he'd never tell anyone the absolute worst parts of his experience. There would be no tell-all book, no one would ever know the specifics of what he'd done and felt during that week on the run.

And yet, here he was, about to spill all his secrets to the one person who could destroy him with her disdain. How could he do anything else after her bravery in telling him about Kash's conception? He was still beyond furious about what had happened to her. The fact that she'd literally been thrown away in an alley like trash after who knows how many men had violated her had him wanting to track down every single one and kill them with his bare hands.

But that was impossible. She'd come to terms with her past; he had no choice but to let it go.

He could make sure her bravery didn't go unrewarded, however. Even if hearing his story might not be the reward he thought it was. He might lose her as a result. But better to know now than after he was too invested in this relationship.

He knew it was already too late though. He loved this woman. It was almost laughable that the bullied boy had fallen in love with his tormentor. But as he'd told her time and time again, they weren't the same people they were back then. They were . . . seasoned. Maybe they clicked now *because* of their experiences. Because they'd been through hardships. Could appreciate what was right in front of their faces in a way they couldn't when they were younger.

Focusing, Linc realized several minutes had gone by while he was lost in his head. But Harper didn't look impatient in the least. She held his hands and waited to hear what he wanted to say.

"You know about my crash."

He waited until she nodded.

"I was on a recon mission over North Korea. I was flying high, above radar range with two other birds . . . jets . . . when something happened. Later, I found out it was a freak thing, something that had only happened one other time before, and engineers believed they'd fixed what had caused the first crash. It's technical, but suffice it to say, it wasn't anything I'd done, or anything that could've been prevented. It just happened at the worst possible time.

"I immediately started losing altitude. I knew I'd be picked up on radar any second, and that wasn't good. Not at all. I had time to hear my wingmen tell me they'd send help before my seat auto-ejected. I'd been well educated in the mechanics of ejecting. Had even trained for it. But the reality is something else entirely.

"I broke my collarbone and felt my arm break when I hit the aircraft canopy. I watched the jet crash, the fireball erupting below me as I descended. It seemed to take forever for my parachute to open. And when it did, the pain as my body jerked was immense. I knew I was still in North Korean territory, and I needed to get the hell out as soon as possible. Unfortunately, my only options were China or Russia. Neither were very friendly, especially toward a US Air Force jet pilot who was flying in airspace their governments wouldn't be happy about.

"My landing was hard, but I was alive. I took precious minutes to use some of the parachute material to make a sling for my useless arm and gather up some of the ropes to maybe use in traps later on, dumped my helmet, and headed north."

Linc recited what had happened almost emotionlessly. He'd talked about the crash itself many times before. To doctors as they tried to put him back together and to the Air Force personnel who were tasked with investigating.

It was what came next that he'd kept to himself. At least, the details.

Harper was stroking his hand, her gaze locked on him, all her attention completely focused. If it had been anyone else, Linc might've felt uncomfortable with that kind of scrutiny, but all he saw was empathy and sadness for him in her gaze. No pity. Thank goodness.

"I estimated I was about a hundred miles from China, and just slightly less from Russia. And that made my decision for me. The second I started walking, I knew I was in trouble. Every step was excruciating. I'd been in training accidents before, but my spine hurt like hell from the ejection. The sight in my left eye was blurry, and I was extremely dizzy, probably with a concussion. Those slightly fewer miles to Russia could've literally meant the difference between life or death. And not just because being caught inside North Korea was the worst-case scenario.

"So I walked toward Russia. It was cold and the terrain was hilly, with deep, narrow valleys. Thankfully there were a lot of trees, which served as great camouflage. I walked all day, every day, putting one foot in front of the other, even when I was almost delirious with pain. If I'd been captured, the pain I was in would've seemed like a walk in the park compared to what the soldiers would do to me to get intel about why I was in their airspace.

"I was fairly sure the US government would be coming for me . . . if I could get out of North Korea. I had a tracker. It was an experimental program; the Air Force had worked with a former Navy SEAL to obtain them. But I was on my own at that moment, and I knew it.

"It was a weird experience. To feel so completely alone. To know people were probably watching a small red dot on a computer screen, so they could see where I was, but could literally do nothing for me. I was being hunted, I could feel it, and my only saving grace would be reaching the border before they found me."

"I can't imagine," Harper whispered.

"No, you can't. And I'm glad," Linc said fiercely. "I wouldn't wish what I went through on my worst enemy . . . well, that's not true. I one hundred percent wish it on those assholes who violated you. On Kash's biological father."

He was startled when Harper let out a small huff of laughter.

Looking up at her, he was surprised to see her smiling. It wasn't huge, but it was there. She amazed him. Her strength. She'd also been through something *he* couldn't even imagine, and yet she could still find humor in her experience.

As he watched, she sobered. "Finish it, Linc. Tell me all of it."

She was right. He was dancing around the worst of what happened to him. He needed to get this done so he could never speak of it again.

"I drank water where I could find it, and that was my mistake. I had nothing to filter it with, but I had to drink. I couldn't keep walking at the pace I was without liquid. The stomach cramps started first, then the vomiting, then the diarrhea. Sometimes all three at the same time. I soiled myself . . . shit was literally dripping down my leg inside my coveralls, but there wasn't a damn thing I could do about it. I had to keep going.

"I had nothing to eat, couldn't stop to try to trap something, I was too worried about who was behind me and how close they were. I ate grass, leaves, and even dirt once, just to have something in my belly. I was on autopilot, putting one foot in front of the other, not really even seeing where I was going at that point.

"And I was always on alert. Twenty, thirty, forty times a day I would think I'd heard something, someone, and would dive to the ground. I'd crawl with one arm, burying myself under anything I could use to hide . . . shrubs, leaves, whatever. I'd wait a couple of minutes, and if I didn't hear anything, I'd force myself to get up and walk again.

"I honestly don't know how I did it. I was filthy. My stomach hurt so bad from whatever was in the water and from the random crap I'd swallowed, trying to fill the emptiness that felt like it was devouring me from the inside out, that I couldn't walk upright anymore. My ass and thighs were raw from the diarrhea, and my feet were torn to shreds inside my boots. But I didn't dare take them off to check on them—my boots, not my feet."

Linc didn't know why he was trying to make a joke, other than because he felt completely exposed. Turned inside out. Talking about what he'd been through made it feel real all over again. Even now his belly clenched, remembering about how he'd felt back then.

"I only slept for ten, fifteen minutes at a time, terrified that I'd wake up to soldiers standing over me, pointing their rifles in my face. I had no idea when I actually crossed the border. It's not as if there's a line on the ground indicating where North Korea stops and Russia starts. I did know that I couldn't cross straight into Russia though, there's a river that separates the two countries, so I had to go into China, and then over to Russia.

"Luckily for me, it was dark when I must've crossed over, and in the north of the country the borders aren't as heavily secured as they are in the south, or in other more populous places. I thought I should've gone far enough to be out of North Korea, but I wasn't completely sure. So I just kept walking. Staying in the trees, away from people. I figured eventually I'd either be caught, I'd fall over dead from whatever bacteria was wreaking havoc on my body, or my own countrymen would come get me.

"Thankfully, the latter happened. One moment I was stumbling along, delirious, munching on a fucking pine cone, and the next thing I knew, I heard a helicopter over my head. I thought that was it. I was dead. But in fact, it was the United States Army. Night Stalkers, more specifically. They'd attempted to get permission from the Russian government to come in to get me and were denied. But thankfully, my countrymen didn't take no for an answer.

"Those hotshot Army pilots came swooping in anyway. One chopper landed . . . well, kind of hovered over this huge boulder . . . and six Delta Force operatives leaped out of the helicopter, surrounded me, and basically carried me back to the chopper. The whole rescue took less than thirty seconds. One second I was a walking zombie, sure each step would be my last, and the next I was lying on my back, staring up at the men who'd come to get me as we zoomed away from the China–North Korea–Russia tripoint.

"I was taken straight to a military hospital in Yokosuka, Japan. I still feel sorry for the nurses who had to clean me up. I was a mess. I was unconscious for days, apparently hours away from death. The bacteria level in my body was off the charts and was doing a number on all my organs. I'd lost about twenty-five pounds in a week, and my feet were in such bad shape, I couldn't walk for ten days while they healed.

"My shoulder had been torn from its socket, and I'd broken not only my collarbone, but three ribs as well. I did have a concussion, and some bleeding on the brain. The doctors kept telling me it was a miracle I was alive. I started hearing the word *hero* being bandied about when I woke up, and it felt . . . wrong.

"I'd done *nothing*. Soldiers in World War One and Two were heroes. Vietnam. Operation Desert Storm. The men and women who led their fellow civilians out of the World Trade Center were heroes. The firefighters and police officers who died on September eleventh were heroes.

"Me? All I'd done is hang on as my plane ejected me and then walk for miles, hoping against hope someone was tracking me and I'd be picked up. I shit on myself, ate fucking dirt like an animal, and they were calling me a hero? It was a joke.

"The worst part was, that was the last time I was ever in one of my beloved jets. The Air Force decided my injuries were bad enough that I wouldn't be able to safely fly again. They were right, as my arm and shoulder don't have the range of motion they used to, and my left eye sometimes still goes blurry at random times. But it hurt. Having what I loved most taken away from me, and having the humiliation of what happened to me repeated in my head every night when I close my eyes . . . it affected me. Badly.

"I don't sleep. Not more than an hour or two a night. I go to sleep, but wake up from nightmares of being pounced on by soldiers as I'm lying in the dirt. Or I wake up feeling as if I've shit myself again. Or with the taste of dirt in my mouth. My mind relives that week over and over, the second I'm asleep."

"Have you talked to someone about it?" Harper asked gently.

She was still stroking his hand, and it kept Linc grounded. The fact that she hadn't let go of him, even after hearing the depths of his humiliation, was a balm to his soul.

"Just the facts. Not what I was feeling or thinking. It was mandatory for me to talk to an Air Force shrink. I actually had to talk to a few. One was horrified by what I told her about the crash, then tried to pretend she hadn't made such awful faces when she heard what I went through. I never went back. Another seemed uninterested and just prescribed me narcotics, even after I told him I didn't want to take drugs. The one good therapist I saw was nice, but she honestly didn't say anything that actually helped. I finally gave up. Talking about what happened didn't help. It only made my nightmares worse."

"Have you talked to your brothers? They would probably understand better than anyone."

"No. No one knows. No one but you. I don't want them to look at me differently. I'm their big brother. They've always looked up to me. I don't want them to have the image of me eating fucking dirt with shit running down the inside of my pants in their head."

"Has *anything* worked?" she asked with a frown.

"Yes."

"What?"

"You," Linc told her, taking a deep breath and looking into her eyes as he said it.

"Me? What'd I do?" she asked, sounding completely confused.

"You let me hold you while we slept. That night, when we fell asleep in the chair? I slept. For five solid hours. I don't know why you seemed to keep my nightmares at bay, but you did."

She didn't say anything for a long moment. Then she got that determined look on her face that he loved so much, and said, "Well, tonight seems like a perfect night to try it again. To see if it'll work for a second time."

The relief Linc felt was *intense*. If he'd been standing, he was afraid his knees would've gone out from under him. Tonight had started out with her opening up to him, sharing the worst thing that had ever happened in her life, and somehow, she was the strong one right now.

"I'm sorry I worried you."

She rolled her eyes. "It doesn't matter now. How much sleep did you get last night?"

"Uh . . . about forty-five minutes."

"And the night before that?"

"The same."

"Linc, you can't function on that little amount of sleep. No wonder you've been baking so much."

"I think I've proven that I *can* function on very little sleep," he said dryly. "I have no choice."

"Well, that stops now. You're going to sleep, damn it! I mean it."

Linc couldn't help it. He laughed. Then he got serious again. "Does it make a difference? I mean, with us? Now that you've heard all the disgusting stuff I did?"

"Does it make a difference now that you know how Kash was conceived? How stupid I was?"

"No," Linc said firmly. "It doesn't make one damn bit of difference. I love that kid. He's funny, smart as hell, considerate, and protective of you. He's awesome. As are you. And you weren't stupid. Maybe a little naïve, but that's not the same thing."

"And you didn't do anything disgusting. You *survived*. There's a huge difference. And I don't think any one of the doctors, nurses, or those Delta Force and Night Stalker guys cared that you were covered in dirt and poo. I bet they were all in complete awe that you'd made it out alive, without being captured. They were probably proud of you for doing what you had to do in order to survive. Just like I am."

A huge weight felt as if it had been lifted from Linc's shoulders. Tonight had been a night for revelations, and for the first time, he *truly* felt as if he could start over with Harper. The slate had been wiped completely clean once and for all. They were two humans who'd been through the worst of the worst, and had somehow found each other.

Maybe that had been their fate all along. To know each other as kids, to experience the lowest of the low, and then come together once more, changed. Stronger together than apart.

"How about we shower away our respective experiences? I don't know about you, but I feel dirty after talking about what those men did to me," Harper suggested.

"And I feel disgusting after reliving what I went through," Linc agreed.

"Yeah. I've been dying to check out that huge shower," Harper said with a shy smile.

This woman. She was amazing. But as much as he wanted to shower with Harper, this didn't feel like the right moment.

"There's nothing I want more than to see you slicked up with soap and feel you against my naked body, but right now . . ." His voice trailed off. He wasn't sure how to explain what he was feeling.

"It's okay. You just unloaded a lot of stuff, and I'm being selfish. Thinking about my own needs and wants."

"It's not that . . . I just . . . when I see you naked for the first time, I want it to be after a good night's sleep. Not when memories of the mountains are so fresh in my head. I want nothing to taint our first time together."

Linc could see understanding and affection in her eyes, and it was a huge relief. He brought one of her hands up to his mouth and kissed her knuckles. Then he did the same with the other hand.

"Thank you for being honest with me," Harper told him. "I would've been horrified if you did something you didn't want to."

"Make no mistake, Harper. I want you. We'll shower together and more. Much more. But not tonight."

He loved the blush that tinged her cheeks pink. "I'm going to hold you to that."

"Go ahead and take your time in the bathroom. I'll shower when you're done."

She nodded. And after a small nod and shy smile, she turned and entered the bathroom, closing the door behind her.

Half an hour later, they were both clean and lying in bed together. Harper had her head on Linc's shoulder and one arm flung across his chest. Her knee was hitched up and resting against his thigh. She was a comfortable weight against him, and once again, Linc felt grounded by the feel of her.

"Is this okay? I'm not hurting your shoulder?"

"It's the other one that was hurt," Linc told her.

"Oh. Good. Linc?"

"Yeah, sweetheart?"

"I'm sorry you had to go through what you did. But I disagree about the hero part. I mean, I understand why you think the way you do, but being a hero isn't just about grand gestures or surviving huge newsworthy disasters. I think heroes are made every day, by people doing extraordinary things when they really want nothing more than to give up. You surviving the way you did, putting one foot in front of the other, even though it hurt like hell and you didn't think you could continue, and staying out of North Korean hands . . . that *is* heroic."

Her words settled over him like a warm blanket. Kind of the way she physically felt lying against him. He thought about what she said for a moment. He didn't think he'd ever see himself as any kind of hero, but he could understand where she was coming from.

"If that's the case, then you're just as much a hero as I am. You picked yourself up from that alley and kept on going. You made the incredibly unselfish and difficult decision to keep your baby. A child conceived because of rape. And you haven't held that against Kash, not for a single day. You've raised him to be an amazing kid, and he'll be an even more amazing adult. That's heroic in my eyes."

He heard Harper sniff against him. "Thanks, Linc. That means a lot, coming from you. Someone I admire and look up to."

"And your words mean the world to me too for the same reason," he said softly.

"If you wake up later . . . if you have a nightmare, wake me up," she ordered.

"Okay." But he was lying. There was no way in hell he was waking Harper if he couldn't sleep.

"I mean it," she said sternly, lifting her head to glare at him.

Linc chuckled. She was adorable when she tried to mama-bear him. "All right, all right. Don't go all feral on me."

"Don't think I didn't notice you didn't agree to wake me," she grumbled, as she put her head back on his shoulder.

Smart. This woman was too smart for his own good.

"I'm a little raw right now, Harper. I have no doubt that my dreams aren't going to be good, considering I just relived the worst week of my life. But I promise that when I do wake up, I'll try not to think too much, and I'll be much better off lying here holding you than pacing the house like I usually do."

Harper hugged him and sighed. "I wish there was more I could do for you."

"You're doing it. Listening, being here, not turning away in disgust when you heard about the poop thing."

She chuckled a little next to him. "Linc, I've had a baby. Not only is childbirth messy, I think there was also poop involved. Not to mention, babies are pretty disgusting themselves. I've been pooped on, peed on, thrown up on, and washed more urine-soaked sheets in the middle of the night than I can count. Of *course* I wasn't turned off or disgusted by what you went through. The human body is amazing and repulsive all at the same time. You have to forgive yourself for what you had no control over. *That's* what you should concentrate on—not bodily fluids."

Linc was silent as he digested Harper's words.

She was right.

Damn it, she was *right*. He'd spent years beating himself up for the way his body had failed him in that jungle. But if it had happened to one of his wingmen, if it had been one of their jets that had crashed, and they'd been through what he had, would he think less of them?

No. Definitely not.

So why was he being harder on himself than he'd be on literally anyone else?

"You're right," he whispered.

But there was no response from Harper. She was dead weight against him, breathing heavily, sound asleep.

Linc smiled. The trust she'd shown him tonight by opening up about what happened to her, the empathy while listening to his story, not pulling away, not even for one second, and for being in his arms now, especially after what had happened to her at the hands of her fake agent . . . it was humbling.

Walking for a week through enemy territory didn't seem nearly as difficult as what she'd been through. Harper had been struggling for over twelve years. Linc almost felt ashamed for being as affected as he was by what had happened to him. He'd had it easy compared to what Harper had endured.

He could almost hear her scolding him in his mind. Telling him that comparing horror stories wasn't cool. That it wasn't a competition.

And she'd be right again.

He closed his eyes and tried to simply be in the moment. To enjoy having Harper against him. To feel her warmth all along his side. To appreciate the soft bed and warm blankets. To listen to the wind blowing outside, and be glad that he was inside. With one hell of an amazing woman in his arms.

Chapter Twelve

Harper woke up with a start. She'd dreamed of being held down and staring up at six faceless men looming over her. Her heart was beating hard, and she had a sheen of sweat on her brow. It was still dark in the room, and for a second, she was disoriented. Where was she? What time was it?

A split second later she remembered. All of it. And understood why she'd woken up sweating.

Then she heard something she'd never heard before . . .

Linc.

More specifically, Linc *snoring*.

She was still lying next to him, except this time she was on her back and he was the one snuggled up to her. His arm was heavy over her breasts, and one of his legs was thrown over her own. His head was buried in the crook of her neck, and his hot breath against her was part of the reason she was so warm. That, and his body heat was intense. And they still had the comforter on top of them as well.

But Harper didn't care. Not one little bit. She could lie there until she was a pile of sweat with eyes and still be completely happy. Linc was sleeping. Snoring quietly. Completely out and relaxed in her arms.

She had no doubt it was because he'd purged all the hateful things he'd been thinking about himself earlier. And he was exhausted from days and weeks of not sleeping enough. But she couldn't help but be proud of the fact that maybe, just maybe, she had something to do with it as well. He'd said that he'd slept that one night when they'd fallen asleep in his chair, and she'd like to think that being next to her brought him a form of comfort.

Most women would be offended that their boyfriends considered them some kind of sleep aid, but not Harper. Not after hearing what he'd been through. How bad his insomnia really was.

She lay there with a huge grin on her face, and risked bringing the hand that wasn't pinned to her side to the arm thrown over her chest. She gently stroked him, loving that he could relax his mind enough to sleep.

How long she lay there, grinning, forgetting all about her own nightmare, she had no idea. But eventually she dozed off again.

When she woke a second time, the room had lightened. And the first thing she saw was Linc up on one elbow, hovering, staring down at her. She was still on her back next to him, and his leg was no longer pinning her down, although his arm was resting along her sternum.

When he saw she was awake, he smiled.

"Morning."

"Hi," Harper said, suddenly feeling shy. They'd opened up last night. Been vulnerable with each other in ways they hadn't been with anyone else before. She felt as if this morning was a new start for both of them, but she wasn't sure how *he* felt.

"I slept," he whispered, his tone full of awe. "I mean, like *real* sleep. For hours. I *knew* it was because of you."

Harper chuckled. "I think it's more that you reached the end of your rope. Your body finally shut down."

"Nope. It was you."

She rolled her eyes, blushing. "Whatever. I'm just glad you finally got some sleep. You look much better this morning. I mean, you always look good, but you look rested now. You don't have those dark bags under your eyes."

It was his turn to laugh. "Yeah, I was kind of turning into a zombie there."

"I think your brain was glad that you got some of that self-recrimination off your shoulders."

"Maybe. But I still think it was you. You're an amazing pillow."

Harper laughed again. When had she started out a day with so much laughter? Never. That's when. "Maybe I can market myself that way. Make a body pillow that looks like me and make millions of dollars."

"Nope, I'm keeping you all to myself. I'm selfish that way."

Harper warmed from the inside out. She wouldn't mind being kept by Lincoln Young. It definitely wouldn't be a hardship. "What do you want to do today?"

"You."

She blinked. Had she heard him right?

His arm moved then, his hand slowly inching down until he was palming her breast. She still had on the T-shirt she'd brought to sleep in, but it had hiked up considerably, leaving her covered by nothing but her underwear from about her belly button on down. And suddenly it still felt as if she was wearing way too many clothes. She wanted this man's hands on her.

But she also didn't want him to make love to her out of some warped sense of gratitude. She wanted him to want her because she was Harper Bates. Because he couldn't wait another moment to get inside her.

Because that's how she felt about him.

She reached up and grabbed his wrist. He immediately stilled.

"Don't. Not if all you're feeling for me is gratitude. You didn't sleep because of *me*, Linc. Not really. It was just being able to unload all the things you've been holding inside for too long. I gave you permission to forgive yourself, and you did. That's why you were finally able to sleep."

"You're right. You said some things that made me think after you fell asleep in my arms. I've been punishing myself for something I literally had no control over. And I hate not having control of anything."

"Not a surprise," Harper muttered.

Linc grinned, but he went on. "Me wanting you has nothing to do with last night. Nothing to do with whether or not I sleep. And fuck all to do with gratitude. It has to do with the fact that I've lusted after you for weeks. Because I admire the hell out of you. Because you're an amazing mom, hard worker, and you've won over my family without even trying. And because you have a spine of steel. Life has done its best to knock you down over and over, and yet you refuse to yield. To bend. You have no idea how fucking rare that is.

"I want you because you smell good. Because your body is incredible. Because I can't wait to see your red hair strewn across my pillow as I take you. Because thinking about you masturbating in the shower gets me harder than I've ever been. I want you because you're *you*, Harper."

"Oh. Okay then, carry on," she said, letting go of his wrist with a small smile.

He chuckled. "If at any time you want to stop, all you have to do is say the word. Consent is important to me, Harp. Especially after knowing what you've been through. Nothing could hurt me more than you going through with something you aren't sure you want, simply because you don't want to hurt my feelings or because you think we've gone too far to stop."

His words meant the world to her. But he was delusional if he thought she didn't want him. "I want you just as much, Linc. I think I've *always* wanted you . . . yes, even back when I was a royal bitch. There was something about you that drew me in, but I was too young to understand it then, and even if I had, too cowardly to stand up to my friends and do anything about it. I knew you were going to do great things, and I think I was jealous.

"Now, watching you with Kash, the most important person in my life, makes me want you even more." Then she grinned cheekily. "And of course, you're *hot*, Linc. You're what girls call a silver fox."

"I'm not *that* old!" he protested with a chuckle.

"I don't know, I see some gray hairs coming in," she teased.

Linc growled and covered her completely.

She giggled, loving the feel of him over her.

Then he froze. "Is this okay?" he asked.

Knowing what he was referring to, Harper was quick to reassure him. "I don't remember any of it. Just waking up in the alley."

"Still . . ."

"It's okay. More than okay. I love the feeling of you on top of me. In the middle of the night, when I woke up from my own nightmare, you were all snuggled up next to me . . . it felt amazing."

"Wait, you had a nightmare? Are you all right?"

"Focus, Linc. You. Me. Bed. Sex."

"I'm serious . . . was it about . . ."

Knowing he wasn't going to let it go, and secretly loving that about him, she nodded. "Yeah, but the second I realized where I was and who was snoring in my ear, I forgot all about it. Fell back asleep within minutes."

He eyed her for a long moment, as if trying to decide if she was telling the truth. Finally, he nodded. "Okay."

"We were discussing what we wanted to do today," Harper reminded him, wanting to get back to him touching her.

"That's right, we were," he said, moving a hand to her waist and slipping it under her T-shirt. Harper held her breath as he eased that hand up her body, barely making contact with her skin. "First, we can see what our hosts have made us for breakfast."

His fingers brushed against the underside of her breast.

"Then we can take a walk. It's cold, but the exercise will be good for us."

He was driving her crazy with his light touches. Tickling but not touching her nipple, which had gotten hard the second he got close with his fingers.

"Maybe some more shopping. There's that store you wanted to go to with the yard-spinny things."

"Linc," Harper whined, as he continued to tease her with his words and hand.

"It's too bad the botanical gardens are closed for the season. We should've gone in December, when they had all the lights up."

"I swear if you don't touch me right now, I'll—"

"I *am* touching you," he interrupted, mock innocently.

She had no idea he was such a tease. Harper arched into his touch.

"Lunch, maybe come back here and relax. Watch something on TV. Read a book. Then I want to take you out to dinner again. Find a nice restaurant where we can have some wine, enjoy each other's company, take a couple hours to eat."

Finally, *finally*, he circled her nipple, and Harper sighed with pleasure.

"Or maybe we'll stay in all day. Right here in bed. A place I used to hate. Resent because I was never able to sleep. But with you in here with me, I think I'll work off enough energy to be sleepy again tonight."

"More, Linc. I need more."

His teasing smile died. "You'll get all of me, Harper. I hope you're ready."

"I'm ready," she said firmly. "I need you. Stop messing around and *touch* me already."

In response, he curled his hand around her breast and pinched her nipple—hard.

Harper arched into him and gasped. It hurt, but it felt so good.

It was hard to believe they were finally here. In bed. About to make love. She'd dreamed of this moment for so long, and it had finally arrived.

She wasn't willing to be passive though. She wanted to touch too. Wanted to run her hands up and down his chest, take his dick in her hand, see if she could make him lose his legendary control.

As he played with her nipples—he had both hands under her shirt now—she ran her own palms under his T-shirt and up his chest. He didn't have a six-pack, but he didn't have much extra padding either. She liked that. Liked that he wasn't completely built. He felt more human as a result. Not quite so out of her league. Harper was well aware that her boobs were a bit saggy and her belly not very toned and . . .

Self-deprecating thoughts about her body flew from her head as Linc got impatient and growled, "Arch."

She did, and the next thing she knew, the shirt she'd worn to bed was gone. She had no idea where Linc threw it, and she didn't care, because suddenly his mouth was around one of her nipples.

She let out a little mew, and her hand immediately went to the back of his head, both to anchor herself and to make sure he never, ever moved.

The only word for what he was doing was . . . *feasting*. He bit, sucked, and tormented her as he switched from one nipple to the other. It was too much and not enough. And through it all, he made hungry growly noises in the back of his throat. It was sexy as hell, and almost hard to believe it was happening to her.

But the tingling between her legs made it very clear that it *was* happening to her. And Harper wanted more.

Grabbing the hem of his shirt, she tried to pull it up and over his head, but Linc wouldn't lift himself from her chest.

"Linc," she complained.

She saw his wicked grin as he sat up before the material of his shirt blocked his face for a split second. Then he swooped down and went back to playing with her tits.

"I've dreamed about this," he said between sucks. "I wondered if you had freckles . . . and now I know."

"I've always hated them," Harper said breathlessly. "I was also glad they were only on my body and not my face."

"They're adorable. And sexy as fuck. I want to kiss every single one." He lowered his head and proceeded to do just that. But it was when he latched on to the side of her breast and sucked, hard, that Harper arched once more.

"Wh-What are you doing?" she asked, when he didn't let up. "Wait—are you giving me a hickey? Stop it, Linc!" She began to laugh and squirm in his grip.

When he finally lifted his head, he was grinning from ear to ear, his gaze glued to her chest.

She tried to look down, to see how much of a mark he'd made, but he put his hand over it, still grinning.

"I can't believe you did that!"

"Couldn't help it. I love seeing my mark on you."

Harper flushed. She liked *knowing* his mark was on her.

He was still grinning when he began to shift down her body.

Harper's breath sped up. Was he doing what she thought he was? When he took hold of her underwear and raised a brow at her, as if asking permission, she couldn't do anything but nod.

As he peeled her underwear over her hips and down her legs, Harper felt herself blush once more. His head was between her legs, and she'd never had a man as enthralled with her body as Linc seemed to be. In fact, she'd never had a man go down on her. She wasn't sure if she'd like it or not. It seemed way too intimate.

Of course, she'd given blow jobs in the past, all men seemed to crave those, but none of her scant few lovers had wanted to reciprocate. She'd suck them until they were hard, then they'd fuck.

But Linc didn't seem to be in any kind of hurry.

She squirmed a little. "Linc?" she asked, sounding unsure—and hating it.

"Hmmm?" he asked, his tone distracted.

"You don't have to . . ." she started, as she tried to pull him back up her body.

He didn't budge, but he looked up at her. "Don't have to? Of course I don't. But if I don't taste you in the next ten seconds, I think I'll die. I've wanted to be right where I am now for longer than I care to admit. One of my favorite things in the world is going down on a woman. Do you not enjoy it?"

"Um, I don't know."

He frowned. "You don't know?"

"No one has ever . . ." Her voice trailed off again. She was almost forty—it was embarrassing to admit that she'd never experienced what he was about to do.

Linc looked shocked for a moment, then he grinned. "Seriously? I get to be your first? I've never been anyone's first before."

Harper opened her mouth to say something—she wasn't sure what—but the words died in her throat when his head lowered and his mouth got to work.

He licked, he sucked, he nibbled. He did a lot of what he'd done to her nipples, but it felt so much better between her legs. And when he took her clit between his lips and alternated sucking hard and flicking the small bundle of nerves with his tongue, Harper thought she was going to fly out of her skin.

Good Lord, his touch felt so much better than her fingers! And way better than the hard plastic of the vibrators she used.

She couldn't stay still. She bucked up against him, and he had to grab hold of her hips so he could keep his mouth on her. Harper would've been embarrassed at how much she squirmed and trembled, but she was beyond that now. Was too lost in the pleasure Linc was giving her.

He moved so he had one hand pressing on her belly, his elbow and arm holding her leg open and down, and with his other hand, he pressed a finger inside her as he sucked on her clit.

Harper squeaked, and her other leg flew up, her foot finding purchase on the mattress as she attempted to inch away, get respite from the too-intense feelings he was evoking inside her. But in the next second she was pressing against his mouth, wanting him to flick her clit faster.

He added another finger and began to gently fuck her as he feasted. Harper could see and feel how wet she was. Linc's entire five-o'clock shadow was drenched in her juices. She was on the verge of an orgasm—a big one.

And Linc wasn't backing off. He was bringing her higher and higher. It was frightening. Too overwhelming.

"Linc," she protested, "too much!"

But she didn't think he heard her. He wasn't the kind of man to ignore a woman when she wasn't sure about something. Especially her, not after knowing her history. Her voice got stuck in her throat when he lifted his head and used his thumb to roughly caress her clit, harder and faster than his tongue had been able to manage.

"Come for me, Harp. Give it to me. All of it. I want it. I want to see you fly."

She couldn't do anything but obey. Not with his fingers caressing her from the inside, his thumb moving faster than she could track on her clit, and his gaze glued to her soaking-wet folds where his fingers were fucking her, as he probably imagined his cock would be soon.

Every muscle in her body went taut, her ass came up off the bed, and she froze for a split second on the precipice.

Then she flew over the edge. It was scary as hell—and freeing. She'd never felt such all-consuming pleasure. Black spots obscured her vision and she closed her eyes, frantically grabbing onto Linc's shoulders so she wouldn't fly away.

When she began to come back down to earth, she felt as if she'd run a marathon. Her heart was beating out of her chest, she was sweaty, but she felt a rush of endorphins like she'd never experienced before. But instead of feeling exhausted, as if she could sleep for hours, like she'd heard other women describe, she was ready for more. Needed it. Needed Linc.

Her eyes opened, and she saw him still between her legs.

As if he'd been waiting for her to look at him, he lowered his head, still holding her gaze, and ran his tongue between her pussy lips, licking up the juices there.

"Fucking delicious."

The sight was so erotic, seeing her come on his tongue, that Harper couldn't wait one more second to have this man.

She sat up suddenly, startling him and giving her the advantage. She pushed on his shoulder until he flopped back on the bed. Her hands went to his boxers, and she roughly pulled them down. His cock burst forth from the material, precome already weeping from the tip.

She didn't wait, couldn't wait, to get his underwear all the way off. She needed him. Wanted to taste him as he'd tasted her. Wanted to thank him for the amazing experience he'd just given her.

Wrapping her hand around the base of his cock, she lowered her head and took him straight down her throat in one fast movement.

He groaned, and seemed to grow even thicker and longer in her throat. Smiling, she mentally vowed to give him a blow job he'd never forget. She might not be *his* first, but she'd damn well make sure she was the best.

Chapter Thirteen

With the taste of Harper still on his lips and tongue, Linc almost came as soon as her fingers closed around his cock. And when she went down on him, taking him all the way into her throat without hesitation, he thought he'd died and gone to heaven.

One of his hands went to her head. He pulled her hair out of the way so he could have the best view of his dick disappearing between her lips. He'd never seen anything sexier. Her enthusiasm was erotic as hell and made him feel more wanted than any other woman had ever managed.

In the past, he'd felt as if most of his partners had gone down on him because they'd thought it was expected. Harper was making love to his cock with her mouth. When he wasn't in her throat, she was licking, sucking, and nibbling, just as he'd done to her. Precome was leaking from the tip of his cock like a sieve, and she either used it as lubrication or licked it up with a Cheshire cat smile.

"Fucking hell, Harper," Linc muttered.

She smiled around his dick as she bobbed up and down. He was going to come, and the last thing he wanted was to blow his wad in her mouth. Not when her juicy pussy was waiting for him. He'd been nervous about making love to her after hearing her story, but the woman currently devouring him as if he were a popsicle obviously wasn't thinking about the past. Which was a huge relief.

Turning his mind away from what she'd told him, because it would kill his erection faster than jumping into Lobster Cove on a winter day, Linc licked his lips, still tasting her there.

He took another moment to enjoy the sight of Harper slurping and deep-throating him. He wasn't a small man, and seeing how easily she took him was such a turn-on.

"That is so damn sexy," he told her, as she continued to suck him. "Seeing your lips around me, it's a dream come true, sweetheart. I can't wait to do this while you're on your knees in front of me. I want you to suck on me until right before I blow, and then I want to come on your tits. See it dripping from your nipples."

She moaned at his words, and the sound reverberated around his cock, making him even harder.

"You like the sound of that?"

She nodded but didn't let go of his dick. In fact, she sucked harder, making *Linc* moan this time.

She took her mouth off his cock, using her hand to jack him off while turning to kiss his inner thigh. Then she latched on to him—and proceeded to give him one hell of a hickey.

Linc couldn't help but laugh. He knew exactly what she was doing, and he didn't give even the smallest shit. She could mark him any way she wanted. He'd wear the bruise with pride, knowing she gave it to him. And remembering what she was doing while she did.

Except, his boxers were in the way. She was having trouble keeping the material out of her face as she marked him. Linc reached down, dislodging Harper from his leg with a pop, and he shoved the offending material farther down his thighs. He kicked it off and reached for Harper.

She was still pumping his cock with her hand, but he pulled her on top of him. He wanted to fuck the shit out of her, though he remained cognizant of her past. And while she said she didn't remember anything, the last thing he wanted to do was trigger some long-buried memory by taking her in the missionary position.

She smiled down at him, going up on her knees and reaching for his cock once more. She started to notch him between her legs, but something occurred to Linc at the last minute. He literally wanted to cry, but he wouldn't take her without protecting her first.

His hand flew out and he covered her pussy as he said, "Fuck . . . condom, Harper. They're in my bag."

She didn't protest, didn't hesitate. Simply swung her leg over his and hopped off the bed. He watched with appreciation as she leaned over to grab the bag from the pharmacy they'd stopped at along the way. Bent in front of him, he could see her thighs glistened with her juices, and her pussy lips were puffy and equally wet.

It took all Linc's control not to leap out of the bed and take her right then and there. With Harper leaning over, him fucking her from behind like an animal. He felt like one. His mind was hazy, and he'd never been so desperate to get inside a woman.

And not just any woman. This one. Harper.

She turned with a smile of triumph as she held up the box of condoms, opening it as she walked back to the bed. Linc couldn't keep his gaze from her tits. From the hickey he'd given her earlier. It was going to bruise like hell. He regretted sucking so hard. He'd have to keep in mind in the future how easily her skin damaged. His intention was never to hurt or embarrass her. Just to have her think about him every time she saw it.

She'd succeeded in opening the box by the time she reached him, and while the thought of her putting the condom on him was crazy hot, Linc didn't have the patience at the moment. He held out his hand, and he had the package open and the rubber rolled down his dick before she'd even climbed back onto the bed and hitched a leg up to straddle him.

As soon as she was in place, Linc reached for her hips and held Harper steady as she once more took hold of him.

It took a shitload of control not to thrust up the second the head of his cock breached her pussy lips. But somehow, he managed to lie still and let Harper take the lead. Thankfully, she didn't prolong the moment. She sank down on him in one long thrust, taking him to the hilt.

Their pubic hair meshed together, his dark and hers red. Another erotic sight he'd remember and jack off to in the future when he couldn't be with her.

She shifted on his lap, and he slid in another fraction of an inch.

"You feel so good," she whispered, smiling down at him. Her hands were braced on his chest, her legs spread wide across his lap. When she tightened her internal muscles, Linc was a goner.

"Hold on, Harper. This is gonna be hard and fast. That okay?"

"Perfect."

The word was barely out of her mouth before Linc was moving. Thrusting into her from below. He lifted her off him slightly and held her aloft as he fucked her. They both moaned. The sounds their bodies made were loud in the quiet of the morning, but they were too swept away to care.

Pleasure made Linc's entire body tingle as all the blood rushed to his cock. His balls tightened, and he knew it was only a matter of moments before he came. It was too soon. Too fast. But after the blow job, still tasting her on his tongue, and the tightness of her pussy around his dick, Linc was a goner.

"Fuck," he growled, his body shaking as he orgasmed. It seemed to go on and on. The world turned inside out. Nothing had ever felt like this. *Nothing.*

Through it all, Linc kept his gaze locked on her face. Memorizing this moment. The small smile, the flush on her cheeks. The way she bit her lip when his orgasm finally waned. She was proud that she'd been able to make him come. It took away the sting of how quick he'd been.

As soon as he could think again, his hand moved from her hip back to her clit. She was still spread eagle around him, and he had easy access to that magic button of hers. He held her hip with one hand while the other forcefully strummed her clit.

"Linc!" she exclaimed, as she squirmed on top of him. Her inner muscles spasmed around him, caressing him from the inside out. Amazingly, Linc felt his cock hardening once again. He needed to get the condom off and put a new one on, but not until she came for him.

"S-S-Sensitive," she stammered, but she didn't push him away.

"Come around my dick, Harp," Linc ordered. "I want to feel it. I'm getting hard again. Seeing you ride me, my mark on you, seeing your tits bounce and sway . . . I'll never get enough. You make me feel as if I'm eighteen again. I want to fuck you slow next time. Put you on your back and take my time, throw you over the edge again and again until you beg for mercy."

"Yes! Do it!" she cried.

"Not until you come," Linc said, gritting his teeth. The truth was, he wasn't sure that he had enough control to do as he'd promised. He was legendary for his control, but at the moment, he felt as if he had none. This woman turned everything he knew about himself on its head. And he couldn't even begin to care.

He loved it. Loved *her*. She'd changed him. How he felt about the world, about himself, about kids, about what was important in life. And he wanted to bury himself inside her and never leave.

He'd finally found a place where he felt like the old Linc . . . here. Between her legs. Inside her body. Her heart. And he was never letting her go.

She let out a sound between a moan and a squeak, and just like that she was coming once more. And the grip she had on his cock was life changing. It almost hurt, but in the best way possible. Her rippling muscles caressed him into full hardness.

Growling, Linc pulled out while she was still coming and ripped off the used condom. Looking around, he spotted his boxers and quickly wrapped the used rubber in them before dropping them to the floor and grabbing the box of condoms. He had another rolled onto his cock in seconds.

He pushed Harper to her back and nudged her legs apart before notching himself back between her soaking-wet folds and pushing inside.

He slid all the way in easily, and it felt like coming home.

They both sighed, and Linc took a deep breath. He needed to slow down. To get control.

Harper smiled sweetly and lifted a hand to palm the side of his face. She wiped a thumb over his cheekbone. "You're a mess," she said softly.

Linc knew what she was talking about. He could feel her juices drying on his face. Between her two orgasms and his one, the smell of sex was heavy in the air, their musky scent filling his nostrils. And he couldn't get enough.

"I'm *your* mess," he said softly.

"Yes," she said with a nod. "You are."

Her hair was spread out on the mattress, and it was everything Linc had dreamed of and more. The only thing that could make it better was if it was *his* mattress. *His* pillow. When he'd become such an alpha caveman, he had no idea. He'd never been this way before. But Harper was changing all the rules.

"You ready for more?"

"With you? Always," she said.

"This time will be slower. I won't be so fast to lose it."

"I like knowing I can make you lose that legendary control you're so known for," she said with a proud smile.

"You do," he said, not ashamed in the least to admit it. "But I'm going to do my damnedest to last longer than ten seconds this time. You too sensitive? You think you can come again?"

"No, and yes. Maybe not right away, but you feel so good, Linc. You've done things to me that I've never experienced before. It's always been difficult to make myself come, but I swear all you have to do is look at me with those fuck-me eyes and I'm a goner."

Linc chuckled, then jerked in surprise with how good that felt as he was buried deep inside her pussy. "I think *I'm* the goner," he told her.

The next thirty minutes were some of the most erotic of Linc's life. He managed not to come right away, and to get Harper to orgasm twice more before he finally let himself go. The sheets were a mess, they were both sweaty, and he had no idea where their clothes ended up. But he'd never been more satisfied.

To his amazement, he fell into a light doze with Harper in his arms after he came deep inside her body for the second time—only slightly resentful of the condom as he removed it right before they fell asleep.

He woke up before Harper, as he'd done earlier, and had the chance to study her as she slept. She really was the most beautiful woman he'd ever seen, even more so after several orgasms and absolutely relaxed. He had no idea what was wrong with the modeling agencies in New York. Why they hadn't snatched her up the second she'd sauntered onto the scene all those years ago.

"How long was I asleep?" she asked groggily when she finally stirred.

"Not too long. Just over an hour."

"Hmmmmm." She stretched against him, and while his cock twitched, it seemed as if it'd had enough . . . for the moment. Linc had no doubt tonight would be another story, and he'd be going at her as if it was their first time all over again. He'd probably always be quick to come with her, but he honestly didn't mind. He knew it was because she was so sexy and he loved her so much. But he'd always make sure she was satisfied, even if he was a two-second wonder.

"Thanks for remembering the condom," she said after a moment. "I was a second away from taking you without it."

"How do you feel about more kids?" He hadn't meant to ask, but it was another important discussion, especially since he had no plans to lose this woman.

"Honestly?"

"Of course."

"I don't want them," Harper admitted. "Don't get me wrong, I love Kash with everything I am. He's the best thing that ever happened to me, even if the circumstances of his creation were horrible. But being a mother is the most difficult thing I've ever done. I don't think I have it in me to do it again. Even if I had a partner this time. I just . . . maybe I'm selfish, but I feel as if I'm just starting to find myself again. Having kids is a full-time job, and I want to experience life not being stressed all the time."

"Shhhh, you don't have to justify your feelings. Not with me. I hadn't thought much about children, never really wanted any, but since spending time with Kash, I could see myself raising a kid . . . with you. But I don't need a child with *my* DNA to feel complete. I love Kash. He's awesome, and I love teaching him stuff, and having him teach me things as well. But babies?" He shook his head. "I don't really want one."

Harper stared at him for a long moment. "So we're on the same page?"

"Looks like it."

"I've wanted to get my tubes tied for a while now but couldn't afford it. Just as I couldn't afford birth control."

"I know you don't like to use my money, but I hope you'll reconsider in this case, because it affects both of us. We can talk about it more later, but in the meantime, I'll be responsible for birth control for us. I'll protect you. I can even go a step further and admit that I've already talked to my doctor about a vasectomy."

"You have? Isn't that a permanent thing? What if you change your mind?"

"They can be reversed, but in my case it would be permanent. I'm not going to change my mind."

"Will your mom be upset?"

Linc's eyebrow rose. "My sperm belongs to me, not my mother."

Harper grimaced. "Yeah, that made more sense in my head than it did when I said it out loud. Sorry."

Linc took a deep breath and decided to say what he was thinking. He could either crash and burn or put their relationship on a sturdier heading with what he said next. "I was actually afraid that you'd say you might want one, or two, or three more kids . . . because I think that's the only thing that could keep me from admitting that I'm falling for you, Harper. I look forward to you coming home from work, and I like taking care of you, watching you blossom, now that you don't have the weight of the world on your shoulders. And I like how you take care of me in return."

Harper licked her lips as she stared up at him.

"Like this trip. You took it on yourself to plan it, to get the room reservations, to plan things for us to do. It means a lot. But wanting more children . . . it would've been a deal-breaker for me."

"Linc—" she started, but he shook his head, stopping her from saying anything else.

"No, I'm not done. I was scared to tell you about my insomnia. Thought you might see it as a weakness. My own family doesn't know the extent of my nightmares and inability to sleep through the night. But you didn't even blink. Even scolded me for thinking you'd care.

"I love you, Harper Bates. It scares me to death because you've become so important to me in such a short period of time, but I'm no coward. And I want you to know . . . even if you don't or *can't* return my feelings, I'm a better man for loving you. For knowing you. If you want to move yourself and Kash out because you thought this was a casual thing, or because you thought we were friends with benefits or something, I'll understand. I'll hate it, but I won't stand in your way."

"Linc—"

"But I hope you'll let me continue to see Kash," Linc added almost desperately, talking over her. Not willing to risk hearing her admit she didn't want him the way he wanted her. That she just wanted to be friends. "He's incredible. And I think he needs more masculine influence in his life. *Good* influence. I promise I won't ever be condescending to him. I'll support him in whatever he wants to do, and if he continues to have issues with bullies, I'll do what I can to help. I'll even go to school and confront the assholes if I have to."

"Stop interrupting me!" Harper demanded, sounding exasperated when Linc finally paused.

He held his breath, hoping against hope she wouldn't admit his feelings were too intense. Would say he had a chance to win her heart. Even if it was a small one, he'd take it. She was worth however long it took to woo her.

"I love you too."

Linc opened his mouth to tell her that he'd wait forever for her to reach where he was—but closed it when her words sank in.

"You do?" he asked, sounding as unsure as a brand-new recruit at boot camp.

"How could I not? You're everything I've ever dreamed of in a partner. But if you had wanted children, it would've been a deal-breaker for me too."

Linc could hardly believe what he was hearing. "You aren't just saying that? You and Kash have a place to stay as long as you want it regardless."

Harper frowned. "Are you kidding me? You think I'd say I love you just because I want a place to *live*?"

"Um . . . no?" Linc felt off kilter. He'd fucked things up, and it hadn't even been a minute since they'd shared their first *I love you*s.

"Men," she said with a roll of her eyes. Then she pushed at his shoulder until he turned onto his back. Linc's heart beat faster as she climbed on top of him once more. Her skin was so warm, and he freaking loved the feel of her naked body against his own. His cock twitched with interest.

"I love you, Lincoln Young. You're an amazing man, and Kash and I are lucky to have you in our lives."

"I'll talk to the doc about that vasectomy," Linc blurted. "I want you bare. I want to fill you with my come over and over. Want to see it dripping out of you without worry of any consequences. It'll be less invasive if I take care of it than if you have surgery. And I know an implant or something would be quick and easy for you, but why have you get anything injected when I can take care of it for us permanently?"

"That's what you're thinking about right now? After we said we loved each other?" Harper asked with a small chuckle.

"Well . . . yeah. I love you, you love me. Neither of us want babies. I'm staring at the mark I put on your tit, seeing your nipples brush against my chest, feeling my cock stir between your legs, smelling sex in the air . . . how could I think of anything else *but* sex? Wanting to be able to take you whenever and wherever I want, without having to worry about condoms and messy cleanup, or worrying about them failing, and being able to fall asleep still connected to you in the most intimate way possible?"

"Right. But . . . and I hate to bring this up . . . messy cleanup will still be a factor," she said wryly.

"Oh, yeah . . . well, I'm happy to take responsibility for that too. And for doing the laundry."

"Deal. You can do laundry for the rest of our lives."

Linc couldn't help but grin hugely at her words. "The rest of our lives. I like the sound of that."

She blushed but met his eyes bravely. "Me too. What are we going to tell Kash?"

"The truth. That we're dating."

"No, I meant about why I'm suddenly sleeping in your bed."

"You're willing to do that? I was going to suggest we take things slow. Introduce him to the idea of us dating first, before we moved on to sleeping together."

"Linc, I think he knows we're dating. He's seen us holding hands and kissing. He's also a smart kid, and he's going to be *beyond* thrilled with the change in our relationship. He's even hinted to me that you'd make a great husband."

"He has?"

"Yes. And if you think I'm going to let you go back to not sleeping, you're crazy. I'm still not convinced I'm the *reason* you're sleeping, but

I'm also not willing to put it to the test by sleeping upstairs while you wander around like a zombie, baking like a man obsessed."

Linc was overwhelmed. He'd gone from being at the end of his rope, completely exhausted and stressed, to having everything he'd ever wanted overnight. It was hard to wrap his head around.

"I love you, Harper," he whispered.

"I love you too," she whispered back with a smile. Then she lowered her head and kissed him. It was the first time they'd kissed since being in this bed. But Harper kept it short and sweet, didn't let Linc deepen it like he longed to.

"I'm hungry," she said. "And I want to check out those yard spinners like you said we would. And I need to brush my teeth. No more kissing until then."

Linc couldn't help but chuckle. "Woman, you took my cock down your throat and you don't want to kiss me with morning breath?"

She blushed and nodded firmly. "Yes."

"All right. I suppose if we don't get out of this bed, we'll end up staying here all day. And since I really do want to kiss you properly, we have to get up to brush our teeth. So, fine. Food, shopping, sightseeing, and then bed again."

"Maybe we should stop at another pharmacy, just in case?" Harper suggested, with a sexy little smirk.

"Hell yes, we should," Linc agreed. He suddenly sat up, wrapping his arms around Harper as he did. She let out a small sound of surprise but returned his hug.

Linc sat there with his face buried in Harper's neck for a long moment, loving the feel of her naked body against his. Appreciating that they'd been able to overcome their emotional sharing of their pasts and been brave enough to tell each other how they felt.

This trip felt like a new beginning. Linc was putting his past behind him and looking toward the future. He didn't know what it held for either of them, but he hoped it was devoid of any drama.

He'd talk to his doctor again about getting a vasectomy as soon as possible. He'd been thinking about it for a while now, even before Harper came back into his life. Kids simply weren't in his future, and he'd wanted to do something to make sure it wouldn't happen accidentally.

An accident he wanted to avoid even more, now that he was with Harper and they were on the same page as far as babies went.

Their future was looking bright, and he couldn't wait to get on with it.

Chapter Fourteen

Two weeks had passed since the trip to Boothbay, and Harper had never been happier. She'd immediately told Kash about the change in her and Linc's relationship, and as she'd thought, he'd been over-the-moon happy. He loved Linc just as much as she did, and he was thrilled with the thought of his mom finally having someone to lean on . . . other than him, of course.

She and Linc were still figuring out how to be in a relationship. He constantly wanted to pay for everything, but she'd put her foot down. There was still a part of her that needed to prove to the world that she could make it on her own. She didn't want or need Linc swooping in to take over. She'd worked damn hard to build up her bank account, to prove to her father, to Kash, to herself, to *everyone* that she was a good mother who could provide for her child.

So things were still a little shaky as far as that went, what with Linc's strong provider instinct. But she still brought food home from work and still continued to work on his house as much as possible, in lieu of rent. Gas was a hefty expense, since she drove herself to and from work and Linc didn't exactly live close, but she continued to pay for that on her own as well.

But pretty much everything else was going exceedingly well, as far as being officially boyfriend/girlfriend. And the best thing was, Linc was still sleeping more than he'd been since he was medically discharged from service. Not eight hours, but at least a solid five each night, sometimes even a little more. Which was a huge step up from the two or less he was getting before Harper slept in his bed.

They didn't make love every evening. Sometimes they were too tired, or she worked late, or they were worried about Kash hearing them. But when they did, it was always just as combustible as it had been the first time.

Today, Harper had taken a day off, and she'd made plans to spend the afternoon with Kash one-on-one for the first time in a good long while. They'd had breakfast with Linc, and then he went to Lobster Cove to put up new shelves in Evelyn's pantry. Why she'd decided to completely redo the small room, Harper had no idea, but because Chad and Britt were busy, she'd asked if Linc could come over to help. And since he was an amazing son, of course he said yes.

When Kash begged to assist him, Harper couldn't deny his request. She spent the time they were gone taking a long, leisurely bath. She couldn't remember the last time she'd been able to do something so decadent.

The boys got back to the house around two, and Harper made a snack for Kash, and lunch consisting of dill pickle chicken salad, biscuits, and potato soup for Linc. She felt as if he was constantly giving to her, so it was a good feeling to do something for *him* for once.

After promising to drive safely, and to call if she needed anything—anything at all—Harper and Kash left around three o'clock. They were going to have a late lunch / early dinner, then go to the Blueberry Pond Observatory. To say Kash was excited was an understatement. He would never be the kind of kid who'd like going for a hike or to a stuffy museum. But he could literally spend hours staring up at the night sky.

Thankfully in the winter it got dark early, so they could still get home at a decent hour. The observatory was about an hour and a half away, so it wasn't exactly close, but this was one of Kash's Christmas presents, and Harper was excited to see him in his element.

Not only that, but she wanted to talk to him. Felt as if she hadn't had a chance to really sit down and have a good chat about how he was feeling, both about school and about things at home. They'd had a lot of adjustments in a short period of time, and she wanted to know where his head was at. The car ride was a perfect time and place to do that.

They stopped in Damariscotta at the Oysterhead Pizza Company. The pizza there was some of the best Harper had ever eaten, and Kash certainly seemed to agree. He ate almost an entire pepperoni pizza by himself. She wasn't sure he'd even breathed after picking up the first slice.

Her little boy was certainly changing right in front of her eyes. He used to pick at his food, and there had been that point in time when he didn't want to eat unless he knew she was too. He'd caught on that she was giving him their only food, and he wasn't happy.

When they were on the road once more, Harper brought up the main thing she wanted to talk about. "Are you sure you're okay with Linc and me dating?" she asked.

"Yeah."

"Just yeah?" she pushed.

Her son gave her a look. "*Duh*, Mom. I like him. He's awesome. He looks after you, and he's nice to both of us. Why? Are *you* okay with him? You aren't just going out with him because of the house, are you?"

"What? No!" Harper said firmly. "I would never, ever be with someone because of money. Or a house."

"Good. Because you deserve love. And it's obvious Linc loves you," Kash said simply.

His sweet words felt good, and she had to bite her lip not to tear up. "Obvious, huh?" she said, knowing she was fishing, but wanting to know what her son saw when he looked at her and Linc.

"Uh-huh. His eyes follow you everywhere you go. If you get up to get a drink, he watches you. And the look on his face of . . . I don't know . . . satisfaction? Contentment? Happiness? I'm not sure *what* it is, but when you come back, it's easy to see. And he's sleeping better, which is cool. It used to be when I'd get up in the middle of the night, he was always awake. Sometimes pacing, but most of the time in the kitchen making something. It didn't matter if it was midnight, one, two, three . . . whenever I'd wake up to go to the bathroom, he'd be downstairs doing something."

"I'm also very happy he feels more comfortable and can mostly sleep through the night now."

"You know what, Mom?"

"What?"

"I think us moving in was good for him. It let him think about something other than what happened to him."

"You know about that?" Harper asked, worried about what he might've heard.

"Just that he crashed and had to walk for days and days to safety."

Relief filled Harper. Linc would hate for her son to know the details about what he'd gone through. She certainly wasn't going to say anything to him, and it's not as if Linc would've told him. She guessed that his brothers probably had a good idea of what he'd been through, because they'd been in the military and had training on evading the enemy when necessary. But Kash, as smart as he was, was still a kid and didn't need to know all the horrible details of Linc's ordeal.

"Well, I agree with you. I definitely think he's better off with us being around."

"And we're definitely happier because of him," Kash said firmly. "You aren't so stressed, and we have food whenever we want it, and a safe place to sleep. You were able to clean out the car too. It's nice."

It *was* nice. But guilt still ate at Harper that she'd made her son go through what he had. She should've moved home years ago.

"You talked to Granddad lately?" Harper asked, wanting to change the subject.

Kash shrugged. "Yeah. He called the other day to see how school was going. Wanted to know how I did on my Spanish test."

"That's good. How *did* you do? You never said."

"B-plus. It would've been an A, but I got bored and turned in the test without doing the last two matching questions."

"Kash Bates! Why would you do that?"

He didn't answer for a beat, then he sighed. "Honestly?"

"Of course. You should always be honest," Harper told him.

"I didn't want to blow the curve. Everyone's always getting mad at me for getting perfect scores. And I didn't want to deal with the grumbling and comments under people's breath after we got the tests back. So I just . . . blew those last two questions off. And it *worked*," he said, almost belligerently. "Everyone was happy, since no one got a hundred on the test and the teacher added four points to everyone's score."

Harper sighed. She was proud that her son was smart, way smarter than she ever was, but hated that he was still dealing with being bullied—and apparently dumbing himself down because of it. "How are things with Ginger and Donny?" she asked, referring to the older kids who were the worst of the ones who picked on him.

"They broke up."

"They did?"

"Uh-huh."

"So, are they leaving you alone?"

Kash was quiet a long time. Harper waited for him to answer. Didn't badger him. Didn't press for details. She wanted them, wanted to march to the school and tell the upperclassmen to leave her son alone, but that wouldn't do anything but make them treat Kash worse. She felt helpless, and with every story about what her son endured at school, Harper hated the girl she'd been when she was in high school even more.

"Ginger is," he said finally. "I think she was just following Donny's lead because they were dating. But he's still being a dick."

She would've scolded him for his language, but she didn't have the heart. Kash was growing up, and besides, *dick* wasn't the worst word ever. She was positive he heard way worse at school and was toning down the words he used for her benefit.

"I'm sorry. Still mostly at lunch?" Harper asked.

Kash nodded.

"Did you try what we talked about before? Going to the lunchroom early or late?"

"Yeah. Didn't work. He still singles me out. Calling me Trash-Kash and making fun of what I'm wearing, what I'm eating, my backpack, my friends . . . anything he can. Why are people so mean, Mom?"

Karma. This was karma doing her thing. She'd been a horrible person to Linc and others when she was an adolescent, and her son was paying the price. Harper wasn't sure what to do or say, how to make this better for him.

"I don't know, baby. Maybe because their home life isn't good. Maybe he doesn't get enough attention, or he's learned that negative attention is better than no attention at all. Or maybe he's doing it to fit in with his friends." She sighed heavily, her stomach in knots. "I have a confession."

When her son looked at her with curiosity, Harper almost changed her mind about sharing her secret with her son. Almost. "I was a bully. When I was a kid."

"What?"

"I was awful," she whispered, feeling the shame all over again. "Especially to Linc. I called him names and made his life miserable. I felt horrible about it. Then and now."

"Why?"

She sighed. "I think mostly, like I said just now, because I wanted to fit in. Because my friends were all doing it . . . and it was kind of like a mob mentality thing. Once I started, I wasn't sure how to stop. I didn't feel as if I could speak up and tell them it wasn't right, because then I'd lose all my friends, and they'd probably turn on *me*. It was stupid and selfish, and I'm not proud of myself."

Kash was silent for a while, then he said, "But Linc forgave you, because you guys are dating."

"Yes, thankfully."

To her relief, Kash reached out and squeezed her arm. "I'm sorry you felt that way when you were young. I'm sorry you didn't have *real* friends."

Figured her kid would have empathy for her, even when she admitted to being a mean girl. "I love you, Kash. And I'm sorry that you're having to deal with someone like me when I was your age."

"You and Linc turned out all right. Gives me hope that I will too," he said a little cheekily.

Harper chuckled. Then sobered. "Is there anything I can do to help you? Maybe we can find a private school for you to go to? Or homeschool?"

Kash scoffed. "As if you can afford private school. And I don't want to have to wear a uniform. I like my classes and most of my teachers. And I love the robotics club. I wasn't sure I would. I mean, astronomy is my jam, but it's still pretty cool. Putting together robots is fun. And, I love you, Mom, but . . . homeschool? Really?"

Harper giggled. "Right. I'm not smart enough to teach you anything."

"I didn't mean that," he said quickly. "But we already spend most of our time outside of school and your work together. Do we really need to spend every moment of every *day* together?"

Harper smiled over at her son. "I don't mind being with you, Kash. But you're probably right."

"Besides, all I'd do is stare at a computer all day if I was homeschooled. My brain would rot and I'd lose all my social skills . . . not that I have all that many, but the last thing you'd want is to find me glued to my chair with cobwebs all over me one day, when you peeked into my room to make sure I was still alive."

Harper threw her head back and laughed. Kash was funny. He hadn't always been that way; one more thing she could credit to Linc and his family. They were constantly teasing each other and laughing, making jokes. Kash had obviously been paying attention and soaking it all in. She liked that he could make fun of himself in a lighthearted manner.

"Right, so, private school and home school are out. What do we do about this Donny situation?"

"*We* don't do anything," Kash said, wise beyond his years. "He's in the eleventh grade. He'll be graduating—hopefully—in a year and a half. By the time I'm in the ninth grade, he'll be gone. I can deal with his stupid taunts at lunch for that long."

"Does he have friends who think what he's doing is funny?" Harper asked. She thought back to her group in high school. What one of them did, the rest went along with. They were truly a mean-girl pack. She doubted Donny was acting alone. He probably had a bunch of boys being assholes right along with him.

"Yeah. But ever since he and Ginger broke up, he hasn't been quite as bad. He's mad at her for ending things. He's kind of turned on her, one day being mean and the next being sickeningly sweet, trying to get her back. If she's smart, she'll stay away from him. His friends kind of do whatever he tells them to, so right now they're talking him up to *her* friends. I think he's kinda trying to get her back through them."

"You see a lot, don't you?" Harper asked, kind of astonished at how in tune Kash was to the situation with his bullies.

"Have to. Don't want to end up getting a swirly during lunch."

"People don't still do that, do they? I mean, it's gross."

"It *is* gross. And my friends and I have all heard the rumors . . . I don't want to find out what it's like getting my head put in a toilet while it's flushed, thank you very much. So I have to stay on my toes. Stay alert. Be two steps ahead of Donny and his buddies."

Once again, Harper was sad that her son was dealing with bullies. Just because he wasn't into sports, and enjoyed learning and school, and had bright-red hair, didn't mean he was less than anyone else. Donny and his friends had no right to treat him like shit because he wasn't like them . . . but then again, hadn't she done the same thing?

"All right, but if there's anything I can do, let me know. Pack a lunch for you so you don't have to eat in the cafeteria, go all mama bear on Donny's parents, speak to the teachers or principal. Promise to let me know."

Kash gave her a horrified look, and Harper couldn't help but chuckle.

"*No*, Mom. I've got this. I can outsmart Donny. Stay out of it."

"Fine, but if you don't think I can help, you know Linc and his brothers would be happy to step in as well."

"I know. And trust me, if it comes to it, I'll use them as weapons in my arsenal if I need to."

Was this her son? Weapons in his arsenal? Where was he getting this?

"I finished the first robot I got from the subscription you got me for Christmas, did you see?"

Relieved that he was changing the subject, Harper nodded. "It's cool for sure."

Kash went on to chatter for ten minutes straight about what it took to build the robot and what it could do. Pleased as she could be that she'd gotten him a gift that he genuinely loved, Harper nodded in all the right places and was content to simply listen to her son talk.

When he finally wound down, she asked about the robotics club again. "You think you can use some of what you learned building that robot in your club?"

Kash shrugged. "Maybe. We have that competition coming up, and we've already made our robot for it. But I have some ideas for what we can do next."

"That's right, when is the competition again? You okay going? It's two nights away from home."

"It's in two weeks. And why wouldn't I be okay? Mr. Simpson is driving one of the school vans, and we're psyched to see how our robot will do in the competition. We should at least win a ribbon for construction. But how it'll hold up in the arena is a huge question mark. That's the hard thing . . .

you have to build something cool that will look interesting and do what it's supposed to do, but won't get smashed in the first round of fighting."

All Harper knew about the robotics club was that the kids built robots they used to fight *other* homemade robots during a fight-club kind of thing. She'd seen bits and pieces of a show on TV that did the same thing, but she didn't exactly enjoy watching.

"Well, it's just over in Portland, so if something happens or if you want to come home, all you have to do is call. Or text. You know Linc and I will come get you in a heartbeat."

"Mooooom," Kash complained. "I'm not a baby. I think I can survive two nights without you. Besides, you and Linc will have the house to yourself. You can do anything you want while I'm gone." He smirked and raised his brows up and down suggestively.

"Kash!" Harper exclaimed, genuinely embarrassed at what her son was suggesting.

He laughed uncontrollably. When he had himself under control, he was still smiling as he said, "Seriously, Mom. It's gonna be fun. I'm looking forward to hanging out with my friends and kicking some robot butt. I'm glad you have Linc now to look out for you. If we weren't living with him, I probably wouldn't have gone on the trip because I wouldn't have wanted to leave you alone."

Her kid was the sweetest. "I love you too, kiddo," she told him.

He blushed, then looked down at his phone when it dinged. "How much longer?" he asked. "Linc just texted and wanted to know."

She loved that Linc constantly texted Kash, and that he seemed to enjoy the attention.

"About twenty minutes, according to my phone's directions," she told him.

He tapped out a reply to Linc, then smiled at whatever he said in return.

"Mom?"

"Yeah?"

"Thank you."

"For what?"

"Everything. For Christmas. For tonight. I can't wait to look at the stars through their huge telescope, and to use their digital camera afterward to get super-up-close pictures. But also for taking care of me. For working so hard and moving us to Maine. For being open enough to date Linc. Just . . . everything."

This kid. He killed her.

"You're welcome, baby. I'll do whatever it takes to keep you happy and safe."

"I feel the same about you. If you ever disappeared, like Marit, or Britt and Ms. Evelyn did, I wouldn't stop looking until I found you."

Harper wasn't sure where this was coming from, but she nodded solemnly. "Thank you. And you know I'd do the same for you, right?"

"Uh-huh."

"How about we change the subject to something a little more lighthearted than either of us disappearing?" Harper asked.

"Sure. Did you know that black holes can cause spaghettification?"

"No, I did *not* know that. What's spaghettification?" Harper asked.

"It's what happens if you fall into a stellar-size black hole, your feet would be sucked in more than your head would be, stretching you out like spaghetti."

Harper winced. "Sounds painful."

Kash giggled, sounding more like the boy he still was, rather than the boy on the cusp of manhood who'd proudly thanked her for doing what any other mother should do.

He then proceeded to tell her more facts about black holes. Then he moved on to nebulas. And dark matter. It never ceased to amaze Harper how smart her son was. How excited he could get about astronomy. She loved that for him. That he'd found his passion at such a young age. She still wasn't sure what *her* passion was. Besides Kash.

For the last twelve years, every decision she'd made had been based on what was good for her son. What would disrupt his life the least. What he needed to thrive. And for the first time, Harper felt proud of what she'd done. How she'd raised Kash by herself to be the kindhearted, too-smart-for-his-own-good kid he was today.

By the time they pulled into the parking area for the Blueberry Pond Observatory, Kash was practically vibrating. Harper felt kind of sorry for whoever would be their tour leader. He, or she, would have their hands full. Kash would test their knowledge of the skies for sure.

~

Three hours later, Harper was back in the car with one happy little boy. He was staring down at a picture in awe. As if he still couldn't believe he was holding it. That he'd seen it with his own eyes.

"This is the best night of my life," Kash said quietly, once they were on their way again. It was fully dark outside now, and Harper had already called Linc to let him know they were on their way. He'd told her to drive safely and that he'd be waiting to hear all about their day when they got home. He added that the house seemed way too empty without them in it tonight, and next time he wanted to go with them.

It wasn't a stretch for him to think they'd be coming back. If Kash had his way, they'd return to the observatory tomorrow. And the next night. And the next. She had a feeling this was what he'd be requesting for birthdays and Christmases for years to come.

"Mom. This is amazing. You saw it, right? The M20 Trifid Nebula. It's in the constellation Sagittarius."

"That's the archer, right?" Harper asked, vaguely remembering their guide mentioning that when Kash had gotten overly excited at seeing it through the camera.

"Uh-huh. It's over six thousand, seven hundred *light*-years away . . . and we can see it today! I mean, I can see it with the telescope Linc got me, but not like I could with the one tonight. Isn't this cool?"

"It *is* cool," Harper agreed. To her, the picture just looked like a gray smudge on a paper with lots of white dots, but to her son it was pure gold. She loved that she'd been able to share tonight with him. Seeing his focus on the guide as she spoke, and how intensely he concentrated when he looked through the telescope and cameras, made it all the more obvious this was what Kash was meant to do. She had no doubt he'd be a famous scientist someday.

Well, famous in his own field. *Famous* was relative, and even though she couldn't name one astronomer, she was well aware there were plenty of men and women out there who'd discovered amazing and one-of-a-kind things in the sky.

Her son would be one of those people. Of that she was certain.

It took an hour, but he finally fell asleep around Damariscotta. The car had always put him to sleep, and even at twelve it was no exception. He held the picture close to his chest as he snoozed, and Harper sighed as silence filled the car.

As scary as the nights had been when the two of them slept in this very minivan in New York, there was also something especially intimate about them. They'd bonded in a way not many mothers and sons ever could. Being with him now, watching over him while he slept, brought back plenty of memories. Both good and bad.

When she pulled into the driveway at Linc's house, the door to the garage was already open, and Linc was standing at the doorway of his home. Harper gently shook Kash awake, and he stumbled out of the car and headed toward the house. Harper grabbed the bag with the posters she'd bought him of other pictures taken at the observatory.

When she caught up to Kash at the door, he was talking a mile a minute, telling Linc all about his experience and showing him the picture of the nebula. Harper had already forgotten the name of it.

Linc listened patiently with a smile on his face. He didn't look away from Kash as he spoke, but held out his arm toward Harper. She went to his side and leaned into him as he draped his arm around her shoulders.

"How about we go inside and talk about it, Bud. It's cold out here."

Kash nodded and walked as he continued to tell Linc everything he could about the night. Twenty minutes later, when he took a breath,

Linc interrupted him and told him it was late, and he needed to get to bed since he had school in the morning.

He probably could've talked all night, but he didn't even complain. Simply nodded and said, "I'll tell you all about the M57 Ring Nebula we saw tomorrow. It was so *cool*!" He grabbed the bag of posters Harper had leaned against the stairs. But after going up two steps, he turned and said, "Oh, and the pizza was the bomb! We'll have to stop there again next time we go through town so you can try it too!" Then he ran the rest of the way up the stairs.

"Posters tomorrow," Harper called up after him. "Not tonight."

"Okay, Mom!"

Harper looked at Linc with a sheepish grin.

"Sounds like he had the time of his life."

"I love watching him get so excited about the things he enjoys. Why anyone would want him to be anything other than who he is, I can't imagine."

"You talking about your dad? Or the bullies at school?" Linc asked with canny insight.

"Both. Although my dad has gotten a lot better about nagging him to get involved in sports."

"You had a good talk with him about school?"

Linc knew she'd planned to see if she could get Kash to open up a little more about what was going on at school with the bullies.

"I don't know that I'd say it was good, but I do feel a little better about it. Kash said Donny and Ginger broke up, and that for now, at least some of Donny's attention is on winning her back. Which is something, I suppose. He's also looking forward to him graduating and being gone by the time Kash joins the high school."

"Sounds as if he's taking things in stride."

"I guess." Harper turned to Linc and dropped her face into the place where his shoulder met his neck. "Karma sucks. I never spent time thinking about how you and the others we made fun of must have felt. All I knew was that it made *me* feel better to be part of some stupid clique. I didn't want to rock the boat with my friends and speak out against what we were doing. I was a horrible person, and my son is paying for it today."

"Shhhh," Linc soothed, running a hand over the back of her head.

She appreciated that he didn't minimize what she'd done. That he didn't insist she hadn't been that bad. Because she'd been a terror.

"And you should know, I talked to Kash about how I was . . . what I did to you."

"Wow. And? How'd he take it? Are you two . . . okay?"

Figured Linc would be more worried about the relationship between her and Kash, and not about whether her son would look at him differently for being bullied by his mom. "He was surprisingly cool about it. Totally let me off the hook, which is crazy, considering his school life is being made so miserable by bullies."

Linc took her face in his hands and gently tilted her head up so he could look into her eyes.

"He's a good kid. And smart. Too smart to let Donny and Ginger and whoever else get to him. He has the ability to let that shit run off his shoulders and not affect him. And you're his mom. He loves you, as do I, so it's easy for him to forgive you just like I have. You want to know why?"

"Why?" Harper whispered, gripping his sides.

"Because he knows what's important in life. Food, shelter, love. He knows without a doubt that you love him and will do anything for him. That I will. That he has my brothers. He has a whole tribe behind him now, and the self-confidence in him has risen tenfold since Lobster Fest and winning the crate race. He's coming into his own, and I can see it in him. He doesn't give a shit what others think. He's gonna do what he loves and to hell with everyone else."

"You had your brothers behind *you*, and I still made your life miserable," Harper couldn't help but point out.

"Kash isn't me. I didn't have half the brain your son does."

"He purposely didn't answer questions on his Spanish test to throw the curve, so the rest of the class wouldn't be mad at him," Harper blurted.

"See? He knows how to work the system. He's going to be fine, Harper. I know it."

"I hope so."

"You look tired. How was the traffic?"

"Fine. No accidents and the roads were dry. There was some snow in a few parking lots, but nothing major."

"Good. We're supposed to get cold this next week again."

Maine was nearing the end of winter, and while they didn't get any massive snowstorms this season, one could still blow in at any time.

He could remember growing up thirty years ago, when they'd get snow in November and it would stay on the ground until April . . . even on the coast. The water in Lobster Cove would freeze, and if they were very lucky, he and his brothers would get to go out and play on the ice. Now it was rare for the cove to freeze over at all, and they certainly didn't have snow on the ground for nearly as long.

"I don't mind," Harper said with a shrug. "Better than snow. Trying to get to work before the plows do their thing sucks. And snow makes work so much crazier. People have to go out and stock up on toilet paper, bread, and milk. I'd much rather it be ten degrees outside. It makes people stay home where it's warm."

"Spoken like a true Mainer," Linc joked.

"Well, I *am* a true Mainer," Harper said, pretending to be offended.

"So you are. It just took you a hot second to remember that and get your butt back here."

She laughed. "True. Linc?"

"Yeah, sweetheart?"

"I love you. It was really nice to come home to you waiting for us tonight instead of an empty house, or my dad, who was usually scowling and demanding to know why it took so long for me to get home."

"I worried about you the entire time you were gone. I can't wait to go with you guys next time."

"Kash would love that."

"He was texting me most of the time you were gone."

"I know. He say anything interesting?"

"Well, I know the name of every nebula he saw, and the name of the fancy telescope, and how much it costs, and I think he has a crush on the guide you guys had."

Harper giggled. "He did hang on her every word, but I thought it was because she was so smart."

"Why do you think he has a crush on her?" Linc asked.

"Today was a good day. A great day. The only thing that would've made it better was if you were there to share it with us."

"You needed the time with your son. You haven't had one-on-one time with him in months."

"I know, but that doesn't mean I didn't miss you."

"And that feels amazing. Thank you. I missed you too. It wasn't the same puttering around here without you."

Harper smiled. "You ready for bed? Think you can sleep?"

"Wellllll," Linc drawled. "Maybe not immediately. Can you think of anything that might tire me out?"

Harper grinned, her nipples already tightening at the naughty thoughts running through her head. "I might have an idea or two."

"I thought so. By the way, I talked to my doctor today. I have an appointment next week for a checkup and to discuss my vasectomy."

"So soon?" Harper asked with a small frown.

Linc had dropped his hands from her face and clasped them at the small of her back. "I see no reason to wait. I'm ready to ditch the condoms, and it's not as if I'm going to change my mind about children in the future."

"I just don't want you to regret it."

"I won't. Unless you've changed *your* mind."

"No," she said immediately.

"And you should know, you're it for me. I want to make you mine officially. And be yours officially. Not today, not tomorrow. But when you and Kash are ready. If that's this year, great. If it's in five years, no problem. But I need you to know where I stand. I'm not making any rash decisions here, Harper. I'm old enough to know what I want, and I know when I've found it. And you're it. You and Kash.

"I just need to make sure to protect you, that there are no accidental pregnancies. Condoms can fail, and I don't want either of us to go through extreme stress or heartache. I'm a man of action. If I can mitigate a problem before it happens, that's what I'm going to do. Thus calling my doctor and setting up an appointment."

Harper thought her heart was going to burst. Some women wanted roses. Wanted extravagant presents or gestures from their boyfriends. Not her. The fact that Linc was putting her and Kash first was the biggest gesture she could ever imagine.

"I love you," she said almost fiercely as she hugged him.

Linc picked her up and walked toward his bedroom, holding her in his arms. "And I love you too. You need a snack or anything before we hit the hay?"

She chuckled, her legs bouncing against his as he walked. "What am I, three? A snack before bedtime? *You're* my snack, Linc."

She felt his dick lengthen against her as he walked, and grinned.

"I'm feeling hungry myself," he said, as he kicked his door shut.

Harper had no idea how she'd gotten so lucky, but she'd do whatever she could to hold on to this man with everything she had. He was her world, and she'd fight like hell to keep him.

Chapter Fifteen

"Are you really waiting to find out if it's a boy or a girl?" Marit asked Britt as they sat outside on the deck at Lobster Cove. Evelyn was in town with a friend, having lunch. Kash was at school, and Harper had the day off, after working four ten-hour shifts in a row. She was more than ready to put her feet up and relax for a hot second.

Linc had asked if she wanted to go with him to Lobster Cove, as he had something he needed to do. She'd agreed immediately. It was the last week of March, and they had a fluke "warm"-weather day in the upper forties. This weekend it would get cold again, back down below freezing, as was the norm for this time of year. Kash had his robotics competition in Portland, and Harper was looking forward to snuggling in the house with Linc. She worked Saturday morning but had Sunday off.

So while Linc did whatever it was he came over here to do, she, Britt, and Marit, who'd also come over to visit—claiming Zach was working like a maniac in their kitchen and she needed a break from his grumpiness as he perfected a new recipe—sat on the deck in the sun and enjoyed each other's company.

Britt was due to give birth in another month, and claimed she was more than ready. Marit wasn't as far along, about four months behind Britt, but she looked just as pregnant, probably because of her small size.

"Yeah, we decided it would be fun to be surprised on his or her birthday."

"How's Evelyn feel about that?" Harper asked.

Britt chuckled. "She's not thrilled. But honestly, that's kind of why we're waiting. Not to torture Chad's mom, but because we know if she finds out, she'll go overboard buying all blue or pink stuff for the baby. As it is, our baby room is already full of green and yellow."

Both Marit and Harper laughed.

"Yeah, she's a little excited," Marit said with a knowing nod. "She keeps asking Zach and me if we know the gender of our little one yet." She had one hand on her belly and a soft smile on her face. "I keep putting her off, but the truth is . . ." She leaned forward and looked right, then left, before whispering, "We already know."

"You do?" Harper asked with wide eyes.

"Yup. My ob-gyn gave it away accidentally during a routine sonogram. She felt awful afterward, but Zach and I wanted to know anyway, so it wasn't a big deal."

"And?" Britt asked with a huge grin.

"You want to know?" Marit asked.

"Duh!" Harper exclaimed. "Yes!"

"Promise not to spill the beans to Evelyn?"

Harper and Britt both crossed their hearts and hoped to die.

"It's a boy," Marit said, with a happy grin on her face.

"A boy!" Britt exclaimed. "I bet Zach is thrilled!"

"He is, but I don't think it mattered if we were having a boy or a girl. He just wants kids."

"I get that. Chad's the same way. He's already talking about our next one . . . how long we want to wait and all that," Britt agreed.

"What about you? Is Linc baby-crazy too? You should know the Young brothers apparently have very potent sperm," Marit warned Harper with a grin.

Harper knew the topic was going to come up at some point. But honestly, she'd expected it to come from Evelyn first. The woman was positively giddy that she was getting two grandbabies so close together. She couldn't wait to spoil them rotten. And when she'd found out that Linc and Harper were officially dating, she'd been beside herself. Harper could practically see the baby question in her eyes every time she saw her and Linc together. She hated to disappoint anyone, but there would be no babies in her future.

"Uh . . . about that," she hedged, not wanting to bring down the conversation.

"What? Did I say something wrong? Shoot, I'm so sorry." Marit bit her lip in consternation.

"No. You didn't say anything wrong at all. It's just . . . Linc and I . . . we don't want kids. Any more, that is. Kash wasn't planned, and raising him was the hardest thing I've ever done. He's finally at an age where I can breathe again. And being here in Maine has helped tremendously too. It's not as dangerous as New York City was. We just . . . we don't want kids," Harper repeated lamely.

Britt leaned over and grabbed Harper's hand. "I think that's awesome."

"You do?"

"Yes. That you and Linc know what you want and what you don't. That you've been able to talk about things like children now, before things get too deep and you find out you're on different pages."

"I agree," Marit said with a nod. "And I can see Linc not wanting kids. Not because he isn't great with Kash, and he'd be an amazing dad to a baby. But he probably had to look after Zach a lot when he was young, because they're ten years apart."

"He's okay with you having Kash though, right?" Britt asked with concern.

"Yes! Oh yes." Harper was quick to defend Linc. "He's amazing. He loves him so much, and he's great with him."

"Of course he is. He's Linc," Marit said simply.

"And you know what? It doesn't matter if you want babies or not, because you've already given Evelyn her first grandchild. You and Linc being together means Kash is officially a Lobsterite! I know Chad already told him that he was, but now that you're dating Linc, it's *official* official," Britt said.

Harper chuckled. "I know what you mean."

"I think you need to make it clear to Evelyn that you and Linc love each other. That you're together in a long-term kind of way. You are, aren't you?" Britt asked.

"Yes," Harper confirmed.

"Right. Then I think Linc should make sure his mom knows that Kash is now her grandson too. For real. I mean, I know she already sees him as part of the family, the whole handprint thing at Thanksgiving is proof of that. But I also think she's so caught up in her baby frenzy, she's missing the obvious fact that Kash is, in actuality, her first true grandchild. Not the baby I'm carrying," Britt said.

"It's not a big deal," Harper said with a shrug.

"Are you kidding? Yes, it is!" Britt countered. "It'll take some of the pressure off of me!"

They all laughed hard at that.

"Will she be disappointed, do you think?" Harper asked.

"No," both Marit and Britt said at the same time.

"He has an appointment to get a vasectomy," Harper blurted. She usually wasn't one to talk about such personal things with others, but she'd been worrying about this ever since Linc told her it was a done deal. That the operation was planned for a few weeks from now.

"That's probably smart if neither of you want kids," Britt said.

"And you won't have to take the pill or deal with messy condoms. Bonus!" Marit agreed.

"You don't think it's . . . extreme? What if he changes his mind? Or we break up?"

"First of all, this is Lincoln Young we're talking about. He's one of the most decisive men I've ever met," Britt started. "If he says he doesn't want children, he's not going to change his mind."

"And you aren't breaking up," Marit said.

Harper couldn't help it, she chuckled. "You don't know that."

"Well, I'm married to his brother, and I know the way the Young men work. Like Britt said, once a Young makes up his mind, it's *seriously* made up. And Linc has definitely decided you're it for him. So I don't think you have to worry about breaking up."

Both their comments eased Harper's worries a little more.

Then she realized what Marit just said. "Wait—you're *married* to Zach?"

To her amazement, Marit's cheeks turned bright red.

"Oh my God! Really?" Britt asked, gaping at Marit.

She shrugged. "We really didn't want a whole shindig like you and Chad. It was kind of a spur-of-the-moment thing. We applied for the license with the intent to decide later when to have a ceremony, and when we went to the courthouse to pick it up . . . decided to just do it. We made the appointment that day, and now we're married."

"Holy crap, that's awesome! Congratulations!" Harper told her.

"Thanks. We're both super happy and relieved we don't have to worry about all the stuff that comes with a ceremony, particularly the cost. Zach can use that money toward expanding The Lobster Buoy, and we'll also need it for the baby, especially since I'll have to take some time off in the height of lobster season. Eliot has been awesome about it, but I hate thinking about the money we'll be losing."

"I'm happy to babysit when I'm not working," Harper volunteered.

"Me too. Might as well have your son and our baby get close from the start. And you know Evelyn will be itching to spoil him."

"Yeah. I keep forgetting that I actually have a whole support system now," Marit said with a shrug. "I want to stay home with him for a while, but I'm sure I'll be back on the *Wave Rider* before Zach thinks I should be."

"Do you have a name picked out?" Britt asked.

Harper was relieved the spotlight was off her. Honestly, she'd expected her announcement that she and Linc wouldn't be having babies to be a much bigger deal. But she should've known better. Marit and Britt were extremely easygoing and kind.

"Mark Austin," Marit said.

"Oh my God, Evelyn is going to lose it when she hears that," Britt said.

Harper agreed. Zach and Marit giving their baby his late father's name as his middle name was a huge honor.

"You don't mind, do you?" Marit asked Britt. "I mean, were you going to use Austin's name?"

Britt shook her head. "I don't mind at all. We haven't fully decided on names, but Austin isn't in the running. But you know what is?"

"What?" Harper and Marit asked at the same time.

"Evelyn . . . as a middle name, if it's a girl."

"Is it bad of me to hope it's a girl?" Harper blurted. "I would love for Evelyn to have a namesake. And for there to be more girls around here. Boys certainly have the upper hand. With the four Young brothers, Kash, and your little one, Marit. We need a girl."

"I agree," Britt said with a smile. Her hand rubbed her belly. "Personally, I'm hoping it's a girl too. And I have a feeling it is . . ."

Marit and Harper both squealed with excitement.

"I didn't say it *was* a girl," Britt cautioned. "Just that I kind of feel it is."

The three women all smiled at each other.

"I can't believe how nice it is today. I don't mind winter, but it's great to get a hint of spring every now and then too," Marit said, turning her face up to the sun.

"Agreed. Hey, Harper. What was it Linc said he had to do today?" Britt asked. "Chad didn't know he was coming over."

"He didn't say. I was too excited to see you guys and hang out to get details. I just figured it was something for Evelyn," Harper said. But now that Britt had brought it up, she also wondered why Linc had wanted to come over to Lobster Cove.

Mentally shrugging, she supposed he'd tell her later. For now, all she wanted to do was relax and enjoy some girl time. She was surprised at how well she clicked with Britt and Marit. On the surface, none of them had much in common. Well, besides the fact that Britt had lived in her car for a short time. And yet, they all got along as if they'd known each other for years rather than just a few months.

"So . . . when are you telling Evelyn that you and Zach got married?" Britt asked after a moment.

Marit shook her head. "Oh no, *I'm* not telling her. That's Zach's job. Or maybe . . . one of you could spill the beans . . ." she said, her voice trailing off.

Harper immediately shook her head and held up her hands. "Not it!" she exclaimed.

"If I were you, I'd do it just like you did with us. Casually slip it into conversation. Maybe when you're all at the hospital, waiting for me to give birth. Around his brothers. They'll be too busy worrying about the baby to care. And Evelyn will give you shit later, but in the moment, she'll be all about the baby."

"And you. They'll all be worried about you," Harper added.

Britt shrugged. "Yeah, but we all know the baby will be the focus. As it should be."

Harper was sure that Chad would disagree. As would all the Young brothers. They were all peas in a pod. Putting their women's health and safety first. She'd seen it with their mom, and how they all treated Britt, Marit, and even her. Even Knox, the confirmed bachelor, was always asking about the women and how they were doing. If Britt thought for one second the only person anyone would care about when she gave birth was the baby, she was very wrong.

"That's not a bad idea. I'll mention it to Zach. Again, it's his secret to tell. I'm not getting between a mama and her son's wedding ceremony."

"I'm home!"

All three women turned to look back inside the house. They could hear Evelyn through the closed sliding glass door. She had a grin on her face as she held up two bags with an easily recognizable logo . . . Ruckus Donuts.

"She's determined to make me even bigger than I already am," Britt mock complained, already struggling to stand with her pregnant belly.

"I freaking love those donuts. I don't know what's in them, but they're addictive as hell."

"Sugar," Harper said with a laugh. "That's what's in them."

"I love sugar," Britt sighed.

"You sound like Buddy the Elf, from that movie," Marit joked.

The three of them moved toward the door, happy to head inside and see how Evelyn's trip to town had gone.

After visiting with his mom for a bit, Harper wondered where Linc was, how much longer he'd be. Not that she didn't enjoy spending time at Lobster Cove, but she was ready to go. She and Linc were going to make a cold pasta salad together for dinner. There were tons of veggies and cheese to chop up, and she wanted it to be ready before they had to go pick up Kash from school.

He'd been staying late every day this week with the robotics club, getting ready for the competition this weekend. He was nervous and excited at the same time. Every night, he babbled nonstop about the strengths and weaknesses of their robot and how he thought they'd do in the competition. The boys, and one girl, had been studying the other schools' past robots and tweaking their design and specifications, trying to figure out what would be most effective.

Hopefully Linc would finish up whatever he was doing so they could head home soon.

Home. She loved the sound of that. But then again, she'd learned the hard way that home wasn't always four walls and a roof. It was wherever your loved ones were.

When she'd lived in her minivan with Kash, that had been home. Now, home was wherever Linc was, and that thought gave her goose bumps as she thought about spending the rest of her life with the man. He was quickly becoming her everything, and she was very lucky he forgave her for being such a horrible person all those years ago.

~

Linc wasn't nervous about what he was going to do. He was more determined.

He needed to talk to Victor Rogers. Explain to him that he was going to marry his daughter—and there was nothing the man could say or do about it.

He expected him to be unhappy. Not that Victor was ever happy about anything . . . but *really* unhappy about this. About his only daughter marrying one of the Young brothers.

He'd seemed to mellow out over the last few months, but Linc wasn't going to chance him being a dick to either his daughter or his grandson about this. He could hate Linc all he wanted, but if he dared say one bad thing about him and Harper being together to either Kash or his daughter, he'd regret it.

So Linc figured he'd cut the man off at the pass. Make his point loud and clear. That he needed to be all right with them being together, or risk losing two of the best things that had ever happened to him.

He hadn't told Harper what he was planning to do, because he didn't want her to needlessly worry. It would be all right, because he'd make it so. He still didn't particularly like Victor, but the man *was* Harper's father. And she loved him, even when he was being an ass.

He had a secret weapon in his hands as well. Something he'd picked up specifically for this moment. To hopefully win over the grumpy asshole neighbor. Or at least make him less likely to explode and kick Linc out of his house.

The one thing he couldn't plan was whether or not Victor would actually be home. He didn't know the man's schedule. It seemed he spent almost every day hunkered down inside his house, but it was possible he could be out shopping or something.

After leaving Harper with Britt and Marit, Linc took the shortcut through the path in the trees that separated Lobster Cove from Victor's property. He was relieved to see Victor's old Subaru Outback parked under the lean-to next to the main house.

He knocked loudly on the front door, stepping back to wait for Victor to appear.

When he did, he was frowning and looking irritated at being disturbed. Not a great start to the visit.

"What do you want?" Victor asked with a scowl.

"Got a moment to talk?" he asked.

Victor crossed his arms over his chest and braced his feet shoulder-width apart. Apparently he wasn't going to be invited in.

"I brought you some Schloss Steinheim . . . it's a German pilsner from Trinken Brewing over in Bath. I know how much you like German beer." Linc held up the six-pack he'd taken the time to go get one day while Harper had been at work and Kash at school. It was a peace offering of sorts. He figured since this man was eventually going to be his father-in-law, he should do what he could to calm the waters between them.

But it didn't look as if Victor was going to bend an inch. Linc knew the man wasn't thrilled about his relationship with Harper, but that wasn't going to make him back off. It had taken too damn long to find the one person he wanted to spend the rest of his life with, he wasn't going to lose her because her dad was a dick.

Linc mentally sighed. This wasn't how he wanted this to go, even if it was what he'd expected. He leaned over and placed the beer on the deck. Victor could drink it after he was gone.

"Right. I came over to talk to you about my relationship with Harper."

"I don't want to hear it," Victor said without hesitation. "I stayed quiet when she said she and Kash were moving in with you, but I'm done with that. You're not good enough for her. You've always been disrespectful. When you were young, you had no problem trespassing on my land, even though I told you a thousand times to stay away. Don't think I didn't know it was you who TP'd my house. And that time the code enforcement officer came out because he heard my rental properties weren't up to code . . . I know that was you as well."

Linc couldn't help it. He laughed. "I can't believe you're still hung up on something that literally happened thirty years ago, when I was *ten*. News flash, Rogers—kids like to run and play. And if I crossed over onto your property while playing in the woods between our houses, I didn't even realize it. It was only *you* who was so tight assed that you didn't want anyone stepping even one toe over the property line.

"And yeah, I *did* TP your house." Linc shrugged. "Again, that's what kids do. If you remember properly, I also came over and helped clean it up.

"Lastly, I have no idea what you're talking about in regard to code enforcement. I was probably gone by then, already in the Air Force.

"I know you don't like us Youngs, and I don't really know why. All we've ever done is try to be nice to you, and you've thrown it back in our faces time and time again. We invited you over for Thanksgiving as an olive branch, and that seemed to go well. What's changed?"

"What's changed is you taking advantage of my daughter! And stealing my grandson to boot!"

Linc's eyes widened. "I haven't stolen Kash from you, and I'm certainly not taking advantage of Harper." He ran a hand through his hair. This was going nowhere. He needed to say what he came to say and get the hell out of here before he said something he'd regret. "Look, I'm here as a courtesy to let you know my intentions when it comes to Harper. I love her, and I'm going to marry her. I don't know when, but it's gonna happen."

"Fucking hell," Victor said, pressing his lips together in anger after he spat the words out.

"Harper loves you, as does Kash, and it would mean the world to them if you were supportive of our relationship. But the truth is, it's going to happen whether you approve or not. I prefer to have you as an ally instead of an enemy, but nothing is going to stop me from making Harper my wife."

"You'll take ownership of my property over my dead body," Victor growled. "And not even then!"

Linc blinked. "What?"

"You think I don't know the Youngs want my property? Want to expand Lobster Cove? I'm not an idiot! I've known for years. And what better way to get your greedy hands on it than to marry my daughter? Well, I'm here to tell you that I'll do whatever it takes to make sure it *never* falls into your family's hands."

Linc was truly shocked. It was Victor who'd always wanted *their* land, not the other way around. Why he was making such a crazy claim now, he had no idea, but Linc wasn't going to let the man turn his greed around on the Youngs.

"I don't want your property," Linc said honestly. "The thought never crossed my mind. Or my mom's, for that matter. She has her hands full with Lobster Cove. She doesn't want to expand. Never has."

"Bullshit. This is prime waterfront property, of course you all want it. Your brother and his wife could move in over here and get out of your mother's hair."

"First of all, they aren't *in her hair*, as you say. Secondly, I'm telling you, we don't want your land, Rogers."

"Well, you aren't getting it no matter how low you stoop, including convincing Harper to marry you."

The man was delusional. "I love your daughter," Linc said, irritated beyond belief. He hadn't exactly thought this meeting would go well, but he'd never thought it would go *this* bad. "And Kash too. I have no ulterior motives. I simply want to be with them. Love them. I would think that's what *you'd* want too."

"I want her to be with anyone other than a Young."

And that was the crux of the issue. Victor hated the Young family so much, he'd deny his only daughter happiness, simply to hang on to the bitterness he for some reason held in his heart toward his neighbors.

"I came over today to let you know my intentions. Let you know that you've got an amazing daughter and grandson. And to make sure you know that I will take care of them and love them. To reassure you that Harper will never have to live in her car again. Will never go hungry. Will never have to worry about if she has enough money for rent. They've had a difficult life, and it'll be my honor to make sure they're happy, healthy, and loved for the rest of their days. I'm not here to ask your permission, and I don't give a damn if you approve of me and my family or not.

"But think about this, Rogers . . . if you continue to be an ass, you're going to lose them. You'll die in this house a lonely old man. I'm offering another olive branch. But if you're an asshole to them, if you continually bad-mouth me and my family, they're going to pull away. Stop calling. Stop coming to visit. Not because I told them to—but because they won't like being around you. Enjoy the beer."

Linc turned around and walked away without looking back.

"We aren't done here!" Victor called out.

But Linc ignored him. He'd said what he had to say. If the old man didn't like it, the ball was in his court. He could either accept the inevitable or not. For his sake, and Harper and Kash's, Linc hoped like hell he'd accept the fact that his daughter was in love with a Young.

He walked back through the trees, stopping at Fort Bad Assery. It was looking a little forlorn, now that it was winter. And because Kash hadn't been there in months. He had no need to get away from Victor's place anymore. No need to escape a household full of tension. No need to be alone, because he didn't have to face the disappointment of a grandfather who felt he should be into more "manly" hobbies.

Kash was flourishing, and Linc was proud of that. He had no doubt the boy would grow into his frame way sooner than he had. Linc was bullied throughout high school because he'd been such a late bloomer, but Kash was already growing. Filling out. Like he said, Donny and Ginger would graduate and move on, and hopefully his high school years would be easier as a result.

Linc stared at the ground, his hands in his pockets. He wished things with Rogers had gone differently. For Harper. Though, he didn't have to tell her that her dad wasn't thrilled with them being together. She already knew.

Talking to Victor one-on-one hadn't even put a dent in the man's resentment and disapproval of their relationship, as he'd hoped. It wouldn't stop them from being together, but it would stress out Harper and Kash. Which Linc hated.

Sighing, he headed for the house. He hadn't told Harper why he wanted to come to Lobster Cove today, and he wasn't looking forward to letting her know about the outcome of his talk with her dad. But he wouldn't keep it from her. He wanted her to promise to tell him if Victor got too vocal about his displeasure when she and Kash visited. Or if he started trying to turn Kash against him.

Time would tell how this played out, but Linc was determined that nothing and no one was going to come between him and Harper. He'd make sure she and her son knew they were loved and appreciated every day of their lives. Because the truth was, he was one lucky son of a bitch. Harper loved him for some reason he couldn't fathom. He was moody, had some mental baggage from what happened to him, and would probably have medical issues with his injured shoulder in the future. His house needed a shit ton of work, and his family was big, loud, and had no problem sticking their noses in each other's business.

But she'd never find another man who would love her like he did. He needed Harper way more than she needed him. And he vowed to never let her regret loving him. From this moment on, she was his number one focus.

With renewed determination to make sure the woman he loved never went one day without hearing the words from his lips, Linc made his way back to the house.

~

"Are you okay?" Harper asked, when she and Linc were driving to his place. He'd been . . . off . . . since he'd returned to the house. He'd shared a donut with them, then asked if she was ready to head out. After hugs all around, they left, and now she was wondering what had put him in such a pensive mood. He wasn't upset, not really. But whatever he'd done while he was at Lobster Cove seemed to have unsettled him.

"Yeah. I went to talk to your dad," Linc said without preamble.

"Oh. Okay."

"I told him that we were getting married."

Harper wasn't sure how to feel about that. She got tingles every time she thought about marrying Linc, but she wasn't quite ready to take that step. She supposed she was still worried he'd change his mind. That he'd wonder what the hell he was doing, tying himself to a woman who worked at Walmart, had no college degree, and had an almost-teenage son with his own share of drama.

"No comment?" Linc asked, glancing over at her.

Harper could see the worry in his eyes.

"I'm guessing it didn't go well."

"It didn't go as well as I'd hoped," Linc admitted.

"And that's who the beer was for?" Harper asked. She'd noticed the six-pack he'd put in the car, but figured he was bringing it to Chad or something.

"Yup."

"That was a nice gesture."

Linc shrugged.

Her boyfriend was considerate. Even knowing her dad wouldn't especially appreciate the gesture, he'd gone out of his way to buy it and bring it anyway.

"What'd he say?"

"He's convinced the Young family wants his land."

Harper rolled her eyes. "I don't know why he thinks that. He's always been obsessed with Lobster Cove. Even when I was young."

"Why?"

"I think some of it is jealousy. He saw how well you guys were doing with the rentals and the other businesses, and I think it upset him that the things he'd attempted weren't nearly as successful. It just kind of became a habit from then on to dislike everything about Lobster Cove. He's not a bad guy," she felt obligated to say.

"I know he's not," Linc said without hesitation, which Harper appreciated. "If he was, he wouldn't have helped find Marit and wouldn't have gotten involved when he saw Britt and my mom being kidnapped. I just . . ."

It was interesting, seeing Linc at a loss for words. He was usually so self-confident. Harper didn't hate this side of him. It made him seem more vulnerable.

"I just don't want him turning you or Kash against me," Linc finished in a rush.

Harper was speechless for a moment—then she laughed. She couldn't help it. Before Linc could get offended, she rushed to explain what was so funny. "Linc, there's no way in hell my father could ever do or say *anything* that would turn either of us against you."

"He's your father," Linc said softly. "I don't want to come between the two of you."

"We've always had a complicated relationship," Harper explained. "He's overly judgmental, wants things done his way. He's competitive and grouchy and isn't afraid to say what's on his mind, no matter who he hurts in the process. But he's still my dad. The only one I have. He might not understand me or agree with the decisions I've made, but when push comes to shove, I have no doubt he'd bend over backward to help me. Regardless . . . he's not going to turn us against you, because both Kash and I love you. We see the man you are, and nothing my dad can say or do will change that."

"I don't want you to lose him because of me."

"If he decides to continue to hold this grudge, he'll lose us because he's being a stubborn, stupid asshole. Not because of you," Harper said firmly. "It's going to take time, Linc. He's got to come to terms with our relationship, because I'm not giving you up. If he makes me choose? It won't be a hard choice. I'd choose you every time. And I know Kash feels the same."

She watched as Linc swallowed several times, trying to control his emotions.

"Just don't give up on him," she said quietly. "I know he's not the most pleasant person to hang out with, but I think if we give him time, maybe *lots and lots* of time, eventually he'll come around. He'll see the kind of man you are, just as I have."

"For the record, I don't want his land. I've got my hands full with my own house and land. I love where we live, and as much as I adore my mom, I don't want to move in next door."

Harper smiled at that. "I know," she reassured him. "But thank you for telling me."

"Needed to give you a heads-up. The texts from him to Kash might stop for a while. And he's probably going to give you the silent treatment too."

"I can handle him, and I'll talk to Kash. He's old enough to understand how his grandfather is. He lived with him for a while too."

"I don't want to come between him and his grandfather either," Linc said with a small frown.

"You won't. You know how protective Kash is. Of me, and of you too. And he inherited the stubborn gene from *both* my dad and me. Once he hears that my dad wasn't very nice to you, he'll refuse to talk to *him* until he apologizes. That's just how he is."

"He's amazing," Linc said softly.

"Yeah."

"Harper?"

"Hmmm?"

"This weekend, when Kash is at his robotics thing . . ."

"What about it?" Harper asked, when Linc didn't finish his sentence.

"I'm gonna show you exactly how much I love you. In our room, your old room, the living room, on the kitchen table, the kitchen counter . . . I want you to remember me saying 'I love you,' and showing you how much, everywhere you look in our house."

Harper's nipples immediately tightened, and she squirmed in her seat. "I can't wait," she said, with a small smile.

She loved her son with everything she was, but she couldn't deny she was looking forward to a couple of days in the house alone with Linc. They wouldn't have to hold back because Kash might see or hear them. Even though the kid didn't mind them being together, was thrilled actually, that didn't necessarily mean he enjoyed seeing them being all lovey-dovey and kissing and stuff. So him being gone would give both her and Linc a chance to express themselves fully.

Linc held out his hand, and Harper took it without hesitation. They held hands the rest of the way back to the house.

Chapter Sixteen

"Text your mom when you get to Portland," Linc told Kash before he left for school the next morning.

"I will."

"And if you aren't too engrossed, let us know how things are going too," Harper said.

"Mooooom. I'm gonna be busy. We have to strategize and make adjustments after each fight," Kash complained.

Linc smiled at that. Kash might be protective of his mom, but he was also nearly a teenager. Other things in his life were becoming more important, which he approved of. A twelve-year-old shouldn't be worried about their mom every second of the day. If she was working too hard or getting enough to eat. He was finally relaxing enough to be a kid. Which Linc thought was healthy.

"I know. Just try to answer when I text, okay?"

"*Okay*, Mom. Can we go? I'm meeting Abigail and Brad to make a few tweaks to our robot before classes start."

"Right, we're going. Give me a second to say bye to Linc."

Kash rolled his eyes. "Don't take ten years," he warned. "You can smooch him when you get home after work."

"Smart aleck. Go on with you. Go start the car and warm it up," Harper said with a laugh.

Kash waved to Linc. "Bye, Linc. See you Sunday!"

"Good luck, Bud! Knock 'em dead!"

"That's the goal," Kash said with a grin, before snatching the car keys off the counter and heading out the door.

"I wish I didn't have to work today or tomorrow morning," Harper said, as soon as Kash was out of earshot.

Linc reached out and grabbed Harper around the waist and pulled her into him. He didn't respond verbally, instead kissing the hell out of her. Every time he put his hands on her felt like the first time. He still got tingles, and his cock got hard. Linc wondered if that would ever change . . . maybe in twenty years or so.

When he lifted his head, they were both breathing hard. "I love you. I'll have dinner waiting for you. And maybe a bath. I can't wait to have you all to myself starting tomorrow afternoon."

"You aren't making it any easier for me to go to work," Harper complained.

Linc grinned. "Sorry."

"No, you aren't," she countered, but she was laughing while she said it, so Linc knew she wasn't really upset.

"You sleep all right last night? I didn't get a chance to ask you this morning."

"I did," Linc said. And he wasn't blowing smoke up her ass either. He didn't exactly sleep like a rock, like she did, but he'd still gotten a respectable four and a half hours. And the best thing was that he didn't have any nightmares. He counted that as a win in his book for sure.

He knew she wasn't a cure for his insomnia and PTSD, but she helped him relax, which in turn helped him sleep. And slowly but surely, the bad memories from his accident were being pushed further and further to the recesses of his brain as new memories, with Harper and Kash, took over.

"Good. I'll see you around three-thirty when I get home. I thought, since you're going to be busy installing the floors in here today, maybe we could go to The Lobster Buoy and pick up dinner tonight."

"You just want to try the lobster-mac-and-cheese-stuffed baked potato Zach said he was putting on the menu for this weekend," Linc accused.

"No offense, but . . . duh. Your brother is an amazing cook. The things he can do with lobster are amazing."

"No offense taken, because you're right. Zach is a fucking genius in the kitchen. Fine. We'll head out to his shack and get dinner. I'm going to miss you today. I want to spend every second I can with you and only you."

Harper smiled at him. "I'd like that."

"Good."

The horn blared from outside.

Linc chuckled. "Sounds like Kash is getting impatient."

"I think his teenager years are going to be the death of me," Harper said with a sigh.

"Enjoy them, because they'll go by really fast. The next thing we know, he'll be headed off to college, and who knows when we'll get the time to hang out with him after that."

"I know. You're right, but man, I'm dreading the time when his hormones kick in."

Linc could only grin. He remembered those days. When he'd discovered girls and how much he liked them.

"Right. I'm going. See you later. Love you," Harper said, kissing him briefly before pulling away.

Linc would never get tired of hearing those words. "Love you too. Be safe."

"I will."

He walked her to the door and watched as she headed to the garage, then backed the minivan out. He stood at the door, freezing his butt off in the chilly March air as she drove down the driveway. Only then did he close the door and take a deep breath. He had a lot to do to *finally* get the floors down here finished before she arrived home from work that afternoon.

But he did it with a smile and not feeling as if he would fall flat on his face because he hadn't gotten enough sleep. He was a new man because of Harper. He wouldn't change his life for anything . . . which wasn't something he could say a few months ago.

Kash had gotten good at avoiding Donny and his jerk friends. He'd learned that if he got to the cafeteria at the very beginning of his lunch period, he could get in before Donny got there, get his food, then leave and eat lunch in the robotics club's meeting room.

Today, he had a question for his Spanish teacher after class, which meant a late start for lunch. He knew without a doubt that he'd have a run-in with Donny as a result. But . . . that was okay. Because surprisingly, it was becoming a little easier every day to just ignore the bully's taunts.

Maybe it was because he'd found a group of people he enjoyed hanging out with, who didn't judge him for liking science and other so-called "nerdy" things. Maybe it was because he knew without a doubt that Linc liked him exactly the way he was. That he didn't wish he was more athletic or "manly." Maybe it was because his mom was so happy now, and it made everything around him seem not quite so . . . dire.

Whatever the reason, Kash walked to the cafeteria with his head held high. He decided he wasn't going to let Donny get to him anymore. He wasn't going to provoke the kid, he wasn't *that* stupid, but he was done skulking around and going out of his way to avoid him.

He walked into the cafeteria and looked around for his robotics club friends. He didn't see them, so he headed for the line to get his food.

Except he didn't make it to the line. Owen and Scott waylaid him. They came up beside him, each taking one of his arms and turning him back the way he'd just come.

"Hey! Let go of me!" Kash exclaimed, trying to pull his arms out of their grasp, but they simply tightened their grips enough that it hurt—*a lot*. And since they were taller and heavier than he was, there wasn't much Kash could do. The last thing he wanted was to make a scene. Bringing attention to yourself at school was never a good thing, so he kept quiet and went where the two boys led him . . . occasionally trying to jerk his arms free.

The next thing Kash knew, they were headed for the door that led out into the courtyard between the high school and middle school.

"Donny wants a word with you," Owen told him.

"Why? I haven't done anything to him. Let me go!" Kash said, deciding his earlier decision not to make a scene was dumb. He writhed, trying to twist out of the bullies' grips, with no luck.

"Calm down!" Scott growled, as he struggled to hold on to a squirming Kash.

He was sure he was going to be taken to one of the restrooms in the high school and given that swirly he'd joked about with his mom, but instead of heading toward the building, Owen and Scott headed away from *both* schools.

Before he knew it, they'd left the property and were walking into one of the small neighborhoods that surrounded the schools.

His heart was in his throat, and his mouth was dry as dust. He was also cold, because it wasn't as if he had his coat with him. Owen and Scott hadn't exactly stopped to let him grab it from his locker.

All he had was the backpack with his schoolbooks. He found it easier to carry them around all day, rather than go back and forth to his locker before and after every class. Since his last name started with a *B*, and the lockers were assigned in alphabetical order, his was all the way at one end of the school. So, he carried his books with him.

Donny had made fun of him for that, along with what seemed like a hundred other things, but Kash didn't care. His backpack made his life easier, and he wasn't going to suffer simply because someone didn't think it was "cool" to carry it around.

Realizing his mind was wandering, Kash blinked and found they'd cut across a few lawns and were approaching a house that looked as if it hadn't had anyone living there for quite a while. Owen and Scott pulled him around back—and Kash's hopes fell even further when he saw Ginger and Donny already there, standing under a dilapidated deck.

"I'm serious, Donny, give it back," Ginger ordered, hands on her hips. "I need my phone!"

"And I'll give it back, I just—oh, *finally*. Took you long enough to get here." Donny had turned when his friends appeared with Kash.

Ginger looked annoyed . . . and confused. "What's going on? Why is *he* here? All I want is my phone. Give it back, and I'll leave you guys to do whatever stupid thing you're planning on doing."

"Oh, but we need *you* to make what we're planning work," Donny said with a smirk. Then he moved fast, grabbing Ginger's upper arm much the same way Owen and Scott were holding Kash.

"Ow! Stop it! Let go!"

"Nope. I gave you a chance to come back to me, to get whatever bug you had up your ass out and come to your senses. But you didn't. And now I hear you're dating *Alistair*? He's in the fucking *band*! What a joke! So . . . I decided since you humiliated me, and you seem to like nerds, I'd let you spend some quality time with the biggest nerd at school—Kash Bates."

"This isn't cool, Donny," Ginger said, sounding scared now.

Kash wasn't sure what the hell was going on. Donny had brought him here to get back at his ex-girlfriend? He was being used as punishment for her? It didn't make sense. But he had a bad feeling about this. About whatever Donny had planned.

"Grab his backpack," Donny told Owen and Scott. "And make sure you get his phone. We need his password too. Oh, and the combo to his locker." He turned back to Ginger. "I've got this all planned out. It's gonna be hilarious!" Then he got in his ex's face. "You shouldn't have broken up with me. Now you have to pay the price."

"Donny, *no*."

"Ginger, *yes*," he mocked in a mean tone. Turning to look at his friends, he said, "Well? What are you waiting for? Get that phone and his combo!"

Kash didn't bother trying to fight. Why should he? It wouldn't do any good. Not when it was three against one. At this point, it was obvious Ginger wasn't involved in whatever Donny had planned. She was as surprised as he was. Kash figured Donny had stolen her phone just to lead her away from the school, to this deserted house.

Ginger was *always* on her phone. She'd be desperate enough to get it back that she'd have followed him anywhere. Never thinking he'd do anything to hurt her.

Scott found his phone, and Owen knocked Kash to the ground. He straddled his chest and curled his fingers into a fist, lifting his arm and preparing to punch. "What's the password?"

"Three-one-four-one-five-nine." He didn't think these guys would appreciate knowing that those were the first six numbers in pi.

"And your locker combo?"

He told them that too, without hesitation. He didn't want to get punched in the face. Didn't want to do *anything* to antagonize them. He didn't know what they had planned, but the last thing he wanted was to piss them off.

Ginger was crying now, begging Donny to let her go, to give her phone back, to basically leave her alone, but all three boys ignored her.

Scott was scrolling through Kash's phone. "His mom's number is easy, since she's in here under 'Mom,' but I don't know who all these other people are," he told Donny.

"Here, hold her," Donny told Owen, after he'd climbed off Kash. He shoved Ginger toward him.

Kash saw Owen checking Ginger out from head to toe as he grabbed her arm, holding her still. And all of a sudden, he was scared for the girl. She'd been his tormentor, had allied herself with Donny, had no problem making fun of him right alongside her boyfriend.

But the look in Owen's eyes was scary. He was staring at her like she was a piece of property.

Kash wasn't stupid, he'd seen that look many times when he was living in the city. It meant the guy wanted sex from her.

He hoped these boys wouldn't do anything to Ginger. She was mean, but she'd broken up with Donny, and she was obviously scared out of her mind right now. She didn't deserve to be hurt that way. No one did.

"Who are all these people?" Donny asked. "Linc, Knox, Britt, Marit, Zach . . . they all sound stupid."

Which made no sense to Kash. How could names on a screen sound stupid? He wasn't about to say that out loud though. "Friends of my mom's."

"Whatever. Doesn't matter," Donny muttered. "I know Brad, Chuck, Abigail, and Jamie are your nerd friends. And 'Granddad' is self-explanatory. Okay, I have what I need. Let's go, boys."

Donny glared at Kash, who was still on the ground. He wasn't going to move until he was told. He was in self-preservation mode right now. Wanting to comply with everything he was told so he wouldn't get hurt.

"You're going to do everything I say and keep your mouth shut, got it?"

Kash nodded.

Donny turned to Ginger. "You too. We're walking to Scott's car, and you're gonna get in all nice and calm. In the back. Owen and I will be by the doors. Don't try anything stupid and everything'll be fine."

"Where are we going?" Ginger asked between sniffs.

"No need for you to know that," Donny told her with a smile. "But it may or may not involve a boat."

Then he laughed. A sound that grated on Kash's nerves like nails on a chalkboard.

He was almost frozen in fear. A boat? Marit had been kidnapped and taken away by boat, and she almost hadn't been found. Was Donny really that psychotic that he was going to kill his ex-girlfriend? And why was *he* here? Donny was a bully—but was he really a *killer*?

No. Kash had to believe he wasn't. He was just trying to scare them. Make Ginger regret breaking up with him. He wouldn't actually *hurt* them.

He hoped.

Donny kicked Kash's legs. "Get up, Trash-Kash. We got a trip to take. And I'll be sure to text everyone, so no one will worry about you being gone for the weekend." He laughed again, an ugly sound Kash knew he'd never forget as long as he lived.

As Scott grabbed his arm once more after he stood, to make sure he didn't run, Kash couldn't help but think about Linc. About what he'd gone through. Of course, this situation didn't compare in the least to being ejected out of a fighter jet into enemy territory, but he vowed to be just as brave as Linc had been. To keep going. Putting one foot in front of the other.

Someone would realize something was wrong. That he wasn't at the robotics competition. And as soon as they did, they'd rally, just as they'd done to find Marit, and Britt and Ms. Evelyn. He simply had to keep calm until he was found.

~

Mom: Are you at the hotel yet? You were supposed to let me know when you got there.

Kash: Sorry, Mom. I'm here. Everything is fine.

Mom: Are you excited about tomorrow? Is your robot ready to kick some other robot butt?

Kash: Oh yeah! Can't wait!

Mom: Good. Try to get some sleep tonight. If you can, let me know how it goes tomorrow.

Kash: I will.

Mom: Love you.

Kash: I love you too.

Harper smiled down at her phone. She'd just pulled into the garage at the house Friday after what seemed like a never-ending shift and was exhausted. She'd ended up staying an extra two hours for a coworker whose babysitter fell through, and it took her extra time to find someone to watch her kids. She understood how frustrating that could be, as she'd lived it herself when Kash was little.

Now, she was more than ready to relax in the bath Linc had promised. And eat lobster mac and cheese from The Lobster Buoy for dinner. However, she'd eat a cardboard box right now if that was the only option.

Happy that Kash was in Portland, safe and sound, she got out of her minivan and shivered. There was a cold front moving in that would drop the temps at least ten degrees tonight. It would stay chilly throughout the weekend, then start warming again next week. Not for the first time, she was relieved that she wasn't living in her car. Winter nights had been the worst . . . then again, summer wasn't great either. Basically, living in the car had been the lowest point in her life. And she was still ashamed that Kash had to experience it as well.

The front door opened as she approached, and seeing Linc waiting for her wiped all the bad memories from her head. She was here now. She and Kash were happy and healthy, and she had Linc.

"Food or bath first?" he asked, after he kissed her hello.

"Food. Definitely," Harper told him. "It smells awesome, and I'm starving."

"I thought since you had to work later than planned, we'd go to The Lobster Buoy tomorrow for the potatoes. Tonight, I made a simple chicken-and-rice stew."

Harper smiled. "Thank you. I appreciate you so much," she said in a soft tone. "It's been a very long time since anyone's taken care of me the way you have. The way you *are*."

"Tomorrow I'll take even better care of you," he said with a small smirk.

Harper laughed and rolled her eyes. "Boys. All you think about is sex."

"Who said anything about sex? I'm talking about taking you to work and picking you up so we can go straight to Zach's lobster shack."

She giggled. "Uh-huh, suuuuure you are." But she wasn't upset that her boyfriend—fiancé?—was so attracted to her. She'd taken her looks for granted for a very long time, and now that she was nearing forty, and no longer felt as if life was beating her down, she appreciated Linc's attraction all the more.

"You hear from Kash?" Linc asked.

"Uh-huh. He's good. In Portland. Ready for the competition tomorrow."

"When is he supposed to get back to the school on Sunday?"

"They have a competition in the morning, then the awards ceremonies, then they'll head back. So probably around three or so."

"Awesome. We'll have almost twenty-four hours all to ourselves," Linc said, the satisfaction easy to hear in his tone.

Harper shivered. She was just as excited as he was. She hadn't forgotten what he'd said about making love to her in every room in the house. It would feel amazing not to have to worry about what they said or did for a short while.

She stepped into Linc's personal space and ran a hand up his arm to the nape of his neck. She was leaning forward to kiss him when a huge yawn came out of nowhere. She was blushing by the time she was finished, and Linc was grinning like a loon.

"Hold that thought until tomorrow afternoon, Harp. Tonight, let me pamper you. Food. Bath. Maybe a massage."

"Be still my heart," she said, only half kidding. She'd never had a massage before. Had always been leery of a stranger touching her all over when she was half dressed. But having Linc massage her from head to toe? Yes, please.

"I love you," she told him.

"I love you too. Come on. Let's get you fed so you can go read that new alien romance book you downloaded."

"You don't think I'm weird for liking that genre?" she asked.

"Nope. Don't give a shit *what* you read, as long as it's relaxing for you. And as long as you enjoy it."

"Cool. Because it's *so* good! It's book three in a series where six women have been kidnapped from Earth and rescued from the bad aliens who wanted to sell them in an auction. But now they're trapped on *another* alien planet, where they were all separated and are trying to find each other . . . with the help of the big, hunky male aliens whose long-buried instincts are triggered and they realize the female humans are actually their fated mates."

"Sounds good," Linc said.

Harper was surprised to realize he wasn't patronizing her. "They are," she said firmly. "The women are like, 'Dude, slow your roll because I'm freaking out. I have no idea where I am and there are five-legged lionlike things trying to kill me.'"

Linc chuckled. "Yeah, I can see why they'd be less than excited about the alien guys wanting to shag."

"Shag?" Harper said, giggling.

"Yup. And I'm assuming their tails can do some freaky stuff."

"Of course they can."

"Right. So . . . food, bath, book, then sleep. Work in the morning for you, and then I'll see if I can manage to get creative, and be just as good or better as aliens with tails."

Harper loved this. Loved being able to talk about things she enjoyed with another adult. And not be mocked for it. She was more than tits and ass, which was all she'd ever felt she was in New York. She was judged for her looks and only her looks. No one had cared about whether or not she had a brain in her head.

Being with Linc was refreshing, and it made her regret how much of her life she'd wasted in the city. Thank God she was done caring what others thought. She was living her life the way *she* wanted. With the man she loved, and enjoying each and every day.

There was no guarantee of happiness in life. You had to take each day as it came. Because you never knew when things could change. Harper was aware of that more than a lot of people. For now, she was deliriously happy, and she was determined to do whatever she needed in order to stay that way.

Chapter Seventeen

"We're going to die out here!"

Kash did his best not to roll his eyes at Ginger's dramatics. He, for one, was actually relieved. Ultimately, Donny and his friends had dropped them off at their current location and left. And that sucked. But all they really had to do now was wait to be found.

However, Ginger was acting as if they'd been left on an island with man-eating dinosaurs or something. Of course, their situation wasn't *great* . . . but it could've been worse. *A lot* worse.

Scott had driven them to a run-down dock way outside Rockville. Kash had no idea where it was, and Ginger wasn't any help, because all she'd done was cry and beg Donny to let her go.

During the drive, he'd watched as Donny used his phone to text Brad, telling him that he was puking his guts out and wouldn't be able to go to Portland. He'd asked him to tell their club adviser, so they wouldn't wait for him after school.

Then he'd used Ginger's phone to text her friend, Heather. Basically telling her the same thing. That she was sick and couldn't come over for the weekend anymore.

But the thing that hurt the most was when Donny smirked and told Kash that he'd text his mom later, to let her know everything was good and how well the robotics competition was going.

Kash had to give Donny points, he'd thought this out pretty well. And it would probably work. For a couple of days. Until Sunday came around, and he didn't show up back at school. Until Ginger didn't come home from her friend's house. Then people would start to wonder.

Would the police think they were runaways? That Kash couldn't handle the bullying and had just fled? Would they think the same of Ginger? That she'd run away? He highly doubted anyone would think they ran away *together* . . . that was, if they even connected the dots that they'd disappeared at the same time.

All he knew for sure was that he only needed to hang on for a little while, and then surely people would come looking for them.

The first thing Kash had noticed when Donny shoved him out of the car was a motorboat, tied up to the little dock. There were no houses around, no one who could've witnessed what was happening and wondered what was up. It was the end of March. And cold. No one in their right mind would be taking a tiny boat like the one at the dock out onto the water at this time of year.

Donny had grabbed Kash's arm and Owen took hold of Ginger, and they force-marched them down to the dock. They were shoved into the boat, and Owen started the engine while Donny sat on the seat, grinning at him and Ginger, who were left to sit on the bottom of the boat.

Scott untied them and said he'd be waiting when they got back. Then Owen had gunned the engine, and they flew over the water.

The ride was freezing, and Kash had leaned down to try to stay out of the wind. He hadn't watched where they were going, simply attempted to preserve whatever warmth he could and tried to brace for what was to come.

It took forever for them to get where they were going. How long exactly, Kash had no idea, but at least an hour or more. When the boat slowed, Kash had glanced up to see another tiny dock. Everywhere else he looked, there was only water—except for straight in front of them. He'd assumed they'd reached one of the many islands around Rockville, but had no clue which one.

He'd made a mental note to learn more about the geography of the area, so if he was ever in this kind of situation again, he wouldn't feel as helpless.

Donny had told them to get out of the boat, and Kash did as ordered, helping Ginger out.

As soon as they were on the dock, Owen backed up.

"You can't leave us here, Donny!" Ginger had cried frantically.

"Sure I can. Got the idea from the news story about that chick, the one who was brought out to one of the deserted islands around here by that crazy dude."

Kash knew *exactly* who Donny was talking about—Marit.

He froze. Was Donny going to try to kill them, like that Lucas guy had planned for Marit?

But Donny had just laughed and called out, "Good luck! Have fun with the nerd!"

And with that, Owen had turned the boat and zoomed away.

Kash was extremely relieved Donny and the others hadn't joined them on the island. Leaving them alone was definitely better than them trying to hurt them.

"Oh my God! We're going to die out here!" Ginger wailed.

Even as he rolled his eyes, Kash was turning to examine the island. It was definitely deserted. There were no boats, no cars, no sound whatsoever.

But what there *was*?

Houses. Well, cabins, to be exact. They looked to be completely closed up, but that would be easy enough to deal with. Immediate relief filled Kash.

They'd been left on some random island, but there were cabins. Which meant they wouldn't have to build a shelter, and maybe, if they were lucky, there'd even be some food inside the structures. It wouldn't be fun to be stuck here, but at least they wouldn't freeze, and hopefully they wouldn't starve.

Kash wasn't that great at outdoorsy stuff, much to his grandfather's disappointment, but he didn't mind getting dirty. Hell, he'd sat in Fort Bad Assery all summer, pulling more ticks than he could count off his body and happily lying around in the dirt. He could handle hanging out for a couple of days in a deserted cabin. Piece of cake. It would be like Fort Bad Assery on crack.

And crazy as it might sound, Kash couldn't help but think about how dark the sky would be at night out here, with absolutely no light pollution. He smiled.

"What on earth are you smiling about? He left us! No one knows where we are! We're gonna die!" Ginger yelled, then promptly burst into tears—*again*.

Even though this girl had been totally awful to him, Kash felt sorry for her. She was obviously spoiled, and if she'd ever been camping, it was probably in an air-conditioned RV, and never in the winter.

Thinking about the times he'd slept freezing his butt off in his mom's minivan, but refusing to complain because there was literally nothing his mom could do about the situation, determination swam through him. He and his mom had been through some pretty bad stuff, and this absolutely wasn't great, but it couldn't touch what he'd already endured.

Donny didn't want to kill them, he only wanted to scare them. To feel superior. To get back at Ginger for breaking up with him. This was temporary, he had no doubt.

Moving toward Ginger, Kash put his arm around her shoulders. She was a few inches taller than he was, and the angle was awkward, but he couldn't *not* try to comfort her. Protecting was in his genes. He'd been taking care of his mom for years in whatever way he could. He'd do the same for Ginger, even if she'd been nothing but mean to him. She was Donny's victim, just as he was. Like it or not, they were in this together.

"We'll be okay," he told her. "Look, there's a cabin. We'll go up there and find a way in. It'll be warmer inside, and maybe we can even find something to eat. If not, I'll go looking through the other cabins."

Ginger sniffed and nodded miserably.

Kash led her off the dock and out of the cold wind. As they reached the trees, it felt considerably warmer. The next couple of days would be uncomfortable, but they'd be all right.

Kash worried more about what his mom would think when she finally discovered he never made it to Portland. Hadn't been texting her. That she'd been tricked.

She'd panic. Be scared out of her mind. And he hated that most of all. Hated Donny even more for that. He could handle the asshole's taunting. But making his mom frantic with worry? That was unforgivable.

Thank God she had Linc. He'd take care of her. Keep her calm. Organize search parties to find him. He wouldn't give up until he figured out what happened and where he was.

"Come on, there's a trail," he told Ginger, pointing out the rough path through the trees.

She sniffed. "I'm cold. And hungry. I want to go home!"

Kash sighed. It was going to be a very long couple of days if Ginger did nothing but complain. It wasn't in his DNA, or his mom's, to complain about things that didn't go their way.

He ignored Ginger's whining and led her uphill, toward the nearest cabin. He was actually looking forward to seeing what he'd find inside. Since he couldn't change his circumstances, he decided to look at it as kind of an adventure . . . as long as he wasn't stranded here for weeks, he'd be fine.

Donny had to have a plan for retrieving them. Maybe he'd even show back up on Sunday morning, laughing, enjoying the scare he'd given them, before taking them back to the school. He couldn't be planning on leaving them out here forever.

Kash shook his head. *Obviously* it wouldn't be forever. There were cabins here. Eventually the owners would come back to open them up once the weather warmed. Even if no one found them soon, they'd eventually be discovered. Or Owen or Scott would spill the beans. One way or another, he'd get home.

He just regretted the worry and stress the people he loved would experience in the meantime.

Taking a deep breath, and pushing those thoughts away, he trudged uphill, practically pulling Ginger with him. He had a cabin to break into and explore.

~

Saturday afternoon, when Linc picked Harper up from work, she was more than ready for a day off. After she got into the car, he leaned over and kissed her. Long, hard, and deep. Just like that, the tiredness she felt melted away, and excitement and anticipation swept through her body. She couldn't wait to get home and have this man to herself.

"How was work?" he asked, when he came up for air.

Harper shrugged. "Busy."

"You still want to go to The Lobster Buoy for that lobster-mac-and-cheese-stuffed baked potato?"

She was torn. Yes, she still wanted the absolutely amazing-sounding baked potato, but she also wanted to go home and have wild monkey sex with Linc.

He smiled as if he could read her mind. "I've already called and ordered the potatoes. I think Jack is working, and you know how grumpy he is. I don't know if Zach will be there or not, but I'll just grab the food and run. We can take it home, eat, and then . . . figure out what we want to do from there."

Harper grinned. "Sounds like a plan."

Linc lifted a hand and smoothed an errant piece of hair behind her ear as he licked his lips. "I can't wait to have you all to myself. I'm turning off my phone, not answering the door for anyone. I'm going to get you naked and keep you that way until we have to go pick up Kash. That okay?"

She was grinning like an idiot, but she didn't even care. "Yeah, that's more than all right. You have enough condoms?"

He chuckled. "Eight boxes."

Harper's eyes widened. "*Eight?* Um . . ."

"Not saying we're going to use all of them in the next twenty-four hours, but you never know."

"*I* know," Harper laughed. "I wouldn't be able to walk!"

Linc laughed as well. "I'm too old to get it up that many times anyway. Besides, I'd rather spend my time pleasuring *you*. I love that women can have orgasm after orgasm."

Shivers shot through Harper.

Linc leaned over and kissed her again before reaching for the gearshift. "Gotta feed my girl, then get her home," he muttered, as he looked over his shoulder to back out of the parking space.

Harper leaned against the headrest and smiled. Her cell vibrated in her hand. Looking down, she saw she had a text from Kash.

Kash: Having fun at the competition.

Mom: Good. Are you winning?

Kash: We're doing good.

Mom: Glad to hear it. Linc and I are headed to get lobster potatoes from The Lobster Buoy. Then home to relax.

Kash: Awesome.

Mom: Thanks for checking in. Let me know what time you expect to be back at the school tomorrow, so we can be there waiting for you.

Kash: Okay.

Mom: Love you.

Kash: Love you too.

"That Kash?" Linc asked, as he headed for The Lobster Buoy.

"Yeah. He seems to be doing okay. But . . . something seems off."

"Like what?"

"I don't know. It's . . . just a feeling, I guess."

"You want to call him?"

Harper shook her head. "No, I'm sure he's busy. I can't put my finger on what's different though."

"What can I do?" Linc asked, sounding concerned.

Harper took a deep breath and did her best to relax. Kash was fine. He was texting, so she was simply being a worrywart. "You mentioned something about lots of orgasms," she teased.

"So I did," Linc replied, smiling over at her. But then he sobered. "But if you're worried about Kash, you won't be able to relax. So if at any time you need to take a break and call or text him, don't hesitate, okay? And if there's *anything*, anything at all I can do to make you feel better, just say the word."

"You're too good to me. To us," Harper told him.

"No such thing," Linc said firmly. "I worry about Kash too. He's growing up before our eyes. I swear from August to now he's filled out and has grown at least two inches. His jeans are too short now. It's crazy. By this time next year, we're going to have to worry about all the girlfriends he has instead of bullies."

"I don't know about *that*," Harper said with a little laugh. "Remember what his room looks like? With all those posters of nebulas? He's always going to be too smart for his own good. Probably too smart to put up with girly crap."

"True. And there's no rush. He's got time to win the Nobel Prize for science before he settles down with a nice girl . . . or boy. Hell, don't care which. Just want the kid to be happy."

The anxiety she'd felt about something she couldn't put her finger on faded away. Her son was okay. He'd tell her if something was wrong. She was so happy that Linc loved her son just as much as she did. "Are we there yet?"

"Where? The Lobster Buoy? Almost. Why?"

"Because I want to show you how much I appreciate you. How much your concern for Kash means to me. You ever had a blow job while driving?"

Linc almost choked. His cheeks flushed and his fingers tightened around the steering wheel. "No. And I don't want to start now. Because if I crashed, you could get hurt. Hang on for another fifteen minutes, Harp. When we get home, and are carefully parked, you can suck me off. In fact, now I can't think of anything else."

Looking at his crotch, Harper could see that he was, indeed, hard, his pants tented in his lap. She gave him a satisfied smile, loving that she could affect him as much as he did her. If he could tease about multiple orgasms, she could tease about blow jobs in the car. Licking her lips, she said, "All right, Linc."

"Fucking hell," he muttered, shifting in his seat. "Now I have to get out of the car with a damn erection. Hopefully no one notices."

Harper wasn't sure how someone *couldn't* notice the huge bulge in his pants, but she kept her mouth shut. She hadn't had this much fun with sex in . . . well . . . ever. The teasing, the anticipation, the laughter. She loved it. Loved Linc.

Thoughts of her son pushed to the back of her mind, Harper concentrated on the here and now. The rest of the afternoon and evening were going to be full of erotic fun with the man she couldn't get enough of. She couldn't wait.

~

Kash shivered. He was cold. But not as cold as he would be if he hadn't been able to break into the house he and Ginger were currently hunkered down in. He felt bad that he'd had to bust out a window, but he vowed to do whatever was necessary in order to pay for it once he got back home.

Inside, he'd found blankets in a box in a closet and some canned vegetables. He was disappointed that there hadn't been more food, but he'd certainly been hungrier than he was right this moment. All in all, this experience sucked, but it wasn't as bad as it could've been. He kept that thought in the back of his mind at all times.

Remembering what Marit had been through, he rationalized that at least he wasn't sharing the island with someone who wanted to kill him. And even though he'd technically been kidnapped, like Britt and Ms. Evelyn, it wasn't with the purpose of taking out his entire family.

No, Donny was an asshole. And he'd done something that was stupid and illegal, but he hadn't tried to kill Ginger or Kash. He wanted to make them suffer, to humiliate them. And Kash was well aware the only reason *he* was on this island was that Donny thought it would make Ginger's experience even worse.

But the joke was on him.

Without Kash, Ginger would be screwed.

Kash wasn't thinking that to be a jerk. It was just a fact. The girl had absolutely no self-preservation skills. He wasn't exactly Mr. Outdoorsman, but he sure wouldn't have sat by the dock and cried for hours after Donny left with the boat, like Ginger wanted to do. As they'd neared the cabins, she'd begged him to go back with her to the dock, *positive* Donny would return.

He refused, saying if she wanted to sit out in the cold, she'd have to go alone. Kash knew she'd been kidding herself, thinking her ex would come back . . . at least anytime soon.

He still thought Donny would return *eventually*. He had to. He couldn't actually mean to leave them out here all winter. He reminded himself over and over that Donny was an asshole, not a killer . . .

Kash hoped.

In the meantime, he was making the most of a horrible situation. After practically dragging her away from the dock, they headed to the closest cabin. But as soon as he approached, Kash knew it wasn't ideal. Yes, it was closest to the dock, but the door was standing wide open. He supposed it had blown open in one of the winter storms. There was still snow inside the one-room cabin, and there were clear signs that animals had taken the opportunity to make themselves comfortable inside. The couch was ripped to shreds, and there were animal feces all over the floor.

Kash felt bad for the owners. They wouldn't be happy when they came back after the weather warmed and saw what had happened to their cabin over the winter. He'd closed the door as best he could and continued on to the next place.

That one had looked much more promising, except he couldn't get inside. The windows were all covered in boards that were nailed on, and without tools, he couldn't figure out how to get in.

The next two cabins were the same—but the fifth cabin they approached was the one. There weren't any boards over the windows, and while the door was securely latched, he was able to bust out one of the smaller windows and crawl inside. He couldn't help but smile at the fact that one of the only reasons he was able to get in so easily was because of his skinny frame.

He'd unlocked the front door for Ginger and left her huddled on the small couch, still crying, while he explored.

He'd found the blankets and the food, then tried to reassure Ginger, but she was still lost in her own misery.

The night had been long and cold. Even with the blankets, the house was freezing. Figured that Donny would choose to strand them on this island on the coldest weekend they'd had in several weeks. At one point during the night, Kash had lain down next to Ginger on the couch, under several blankets, and held her as she cried in his arms. He had no problem sharing body heat, and it felt good that he'd been able to comfort her a little—at least, he *hoped* he had.

He felt no attraction toward the girl. He couldn't forget all the awful things she'd said and done to him. But he also wasn't a monster.

He didn't understand why Donny couldn't simply move on. If a girl said she didn't want to be with him anymore, Kash wouldn't waste his time trying to win her back. Why would he want to date someone who didn't want to date *him*? It made no sense.

Now it was morning, and Kash needed to pee. But he dreaded getting out from underneath the covers. It was going to be downright icy, but the longer he lay there, the more he had to go.

"Ginger? Are you awake?"

She mumbled something that Kash didn't catch.

"What?"

"We're going to die out here."

Kash rolled his eyes—again. The drama was starting first thing. It was more than obvious that this girl had never had to struggle a day in her life. Which, good for her, but it made being stuck in this situation with her very annoying.

"I need to pee," he said bluntly. "You want to come with me?"

"To *pee*?" she said, almost hysterically. "No!"

"I didn't mean to watch or anything. But you probably need to go too."

"I'm holding it. There's no way I'm peeing outside."

"Suit yourself," Kash said, thinking she was being ridiculous. It wasn't as if they had running water in this cabin. He'd already checked.

He scooted out from under the blankets and shivered as the cold morning air hit him. It would be even chillier outside, but he couldn't wait another second to pee.

Walking outside made Kash catch his breath. It was *definitely* colder out here, but as he looked around, he found it surprisingly peaceful. He could see the water between the trees and was drawn in that direction. He wanted to see if he could spot something . . . anything. Maybe land, or a boat, or some kind of civilization.

He stopped to piss against a tree on his way toward the water, and felt much better now that his bladder was empty. Kash wasn't sure where they were going to find fresh water to drink, but he'd worry about that later.

Just as he cleared the trees near the house they'd commandeered, the sun peeked out over the horizon.

Kash knew a lot of details about the sun. It was a yellow dwarf star, it traveled at an average speed of seven hundred and twenty thousand kilometers an hour around the Milky Way, and it was absolutely *huge*—about one point three million Earths could fit inside it.

But staring at it rising, as if coming out of the ocean, had him forgetting all the facts he'd learned and simply appreciating its existence.

It was silly, but he could've sworn he felt warmer when the first ray of sunshine hit his face. He closed his eyes and inhaled deeply. The cold air almost burned his lungs, but he felt alive. There was absolutely no sound out here. There was nothing but Kash and nature all around him. He didn't think he'd ever be the kind of person who enjoyed hunting or spending a lot of time doing outdoor stuff, but in this moment in time, he could understand why people climbed mountains, hiked across the country, or otherwise chose to spend large amounts of time camping.

He felt alive in a way he hadn't in a very long time. Even spending time in Fort Bad Assery didn't make him feel like he did right this moment. He felt tiny in the big scheme of the universe. He already knew how big the universe was, but right then, the scope of it really hit home.

Kash stood there, staring at the water and enjoying the feel of the sun on his face, for what seemed like forever, but in reality was probably less than a couple of minutes before he heard Ginger calling his name.

"Kash? Are you out there?"

He sighed. So much for his peaceful morning. But he wasn't heartless. Couldn't let Ginger think he'd somehow disappeared and left her all alone. He turned to leave, but immediately paused. He looked back at the water and closed his eyes.

"I'm okay, Mom. But if you and Linc could please come find me sooner rather than later, I'd appreciate it."

He felt stupid saying the words out loud, but he hoped that maybe, just maybe, they'd fly across the water and make it to his mom. And Linc.

Kash had never been more grateful his mom had Lincoln Young. When she discovered he was missing, that he hadn't made it to the robotics competition, she'd be a complete mess. But Linc would reassure her. Would do whatever needed to be done to find him. Of that, Kash had no doubt.

His job was to stay calm. To wait for whatever was going to happen next. Either Donny would come back to get them, or someone else would find them. Today, tomorrow, a week from now, a month. However long it took, he'd try to be patient. Because no way would his mom give up. She'd turn over every rock, browbeat whoever she needed to in order to get them to get off their butts and find him.

With the image in his head of his mom yelling at Donny, threatening him, Kash headed back into the trees toward the cabin.

All the while, Ginger continued to yell.

"Oh my God, Kash?! Are you okay? Did you get eaten by a bear?"

He sighed. Ginger was pretty stupid. Kash couldn't believe she thought there were bears on this island. But he had to be patient with *her* too. She might be older than him, but she was naïve and clueless in a lot of ways.

When he got back to the house, she was standing in the doorway with one of the blankets wrapped around her shoulders.

"I thought you were gone!" she accused, as soon as he got within earshot.

"I told you I was going to pee. Besides, where would I go?" He asked what he thought was a very reasonable question.

"I don't *know*! But I'm scared! I want to go home! I'm hungry and cold and thirsty. We're going to die out here, aren't we?"

Drama queen for sure. "I want to go home too. I'm also hungry and cold and thirsty, but we aren't going to die. We just have to wait for either Donny to come back and get us, or someone to find us."

"Donny's not coming back," Ginger wailed, her shoulders slumping. "He always told me I couldn't leave him. That I was his forever and ever. If he can't have me, no one can. That's always what he said."

Kash didn't understand that. Not at all. "Well, you *did* leave him, and when everyone finds out what he did, he'll be in big trouble. You think your parents won't look for you?"

"Of course they will," she said, sounding offended.

"Then what are you worried about?"

She scowled. "I know you're smart and all, but in case you haven't noticed, we're on a random freakin' island! One that no one lives on at the moment. How are they going to find us? It's not as if they can search every single island. It'll take days, even weeks for them to search them all."

"If it does, it'll be warmer by then, and whoever lives in the cabins on this island will return and find us and take us home," Kash said reasonably.

"I can't stay out here for *weeks*! I'll miss prom! And my birthday! And Alistair's solo in the band recital! We'll *starve*! There's no food out here. No stores. And I can't even wash my clothes! I'm already smelly and it hasn't even been a day!"

Kash was holding on to his patience by a thread. He wasn't getting a girlfriend. *Ever.* He couldn't deal with this level of stupidity and drama.

"Look, we're actually lucky. We have a house, a couch to sleep on, and blankets. No, there's not a lot of food, but there are still a few houses we haven't checked out. Maybe there are tools around somewhere, so I can get the boards off the other windows. We've been here for less than a day. If we have to, we'll figure out how to survive. It won't be fun, but we *aren't* going to die out here."

Ginger mumbled something under her breath that Kash didn't catch.

"What was that?" he asked.

They'd gone back inside the house by now and were standing in the middle of the one-room living area.

"Nothing."

"No, what'd you say?" Kash insisted.

"Fine. I said that *you* might be used to being homeless, but I'm not!"

Kash saw red—and he forced himself to breathe through his anger. He wasn't surprised Ginger knew that he'd once lived in his mom's car, but the fact that she was throwing it in his face right now was stupid. And ridiculous. And it *hurt.*

"From where I'm standing," he said, in a controlled and even voice, "my life experiences have prepared *me* for this moment. And it wasn't *my* ex who kidnapped me and brought me to an uninhabited island to suffer. It was *yours.* If it wasn't for you being so mean to me all the time, I wouldn't even be here, and you'd be by yourself. If Donny hadn't thought it was so funny to strand you with the 'biggest nerd in school,' you'd be alone right now.

"I'm the one who got us into this house. I'm the one who found the blankets and the food, what little there is. And I'm the one who held you all night to keep you from freezing to death, and who comforted you when you cried.

"I'm sorry if my being homeless at one point offends you, Ginger, but my mom did the best she could. She always made sure I had food before she did, and I know without a doubt if push came to shove, she would've confronted one of the violent and desperate druggies who were always prowling around looking for money so they could get their next fix.

"You've never experienced *any* kind of hardship—and I'm happy for you. But you shouldn't look down on those who are less fortunate, because as you found out yesterday, circumstances in life can change on a dime. One minute you're minding your own business, happy in your popular clique at school, and the next you're freezing, abandoned with the nerd you picked on all the time, and you have no idea when anyone will realize you're missing and come find you."

Kash was breathing hard by the time he finished speaking.

And he figured he'd better put some space between himself and Ginger, or he might say something he'd *really* regret.

"I'm gonna go check out the other houses. Stay here. Or don't. I don't care at the moment. I'll be back—it's not as if there's anywhere else to go. I'll bring back anything useful I might find for us to share . . . because as annoyed as I am with you right now, there's no way I'd leave you to fend for yourself."

He didn't add that she might actually starve to death if he did that, but he so wanted to.

Instead, he stomped back toward the door and wrenched it open.

Ginger didn't say a word behind him, and Kash wasn't sure if he was happy or sad about that. All he knew was that, right now, outside was much preferable to being inside with someone who judged him for things that weren't his fault. For surviving.

He'd like to see *her* live in a car in New York City. She wouldn't last a day. She thought peeing in the woods was bad? Try peeing in a bottle because it was too dangerous to leave the safety of the car at night because of the people wandering around outside.

He shut the door behind him and headed in the direction of the closest cabin he hadn't already checked out. Maybe he'd get lucky and find a fully stocked pantry and a generator with gas. He wasn't holding out much hope for that, but never say never.

~

Linc hummed while he puttered around the kitchen on Sunday morning. Last night had been . . . he had no words. He and Harper had connected on a level they hadn't before now. And it wasn't just about sex, although that was amazing.

In between bouts of making love—on the couch, the kitchen table, the counter, in his bedroom, hers, the shower, and even on top of the washing machine while it was on the spin cycle, because she said she'd always wanted to try it—they'd talked.

He'd told her more stories about growing up on Lobster Cove, and she'd opened up about losing her mom and how it seemed to change her dad. They'd even talked about high school and the bullying. It had been more painful for Linc to see how remorseful Harper was for the way she'd treated him than it had been remembering how he'd felt back then.

He'd told her funny stories about being in the military, as well as some somber ones about losing a couple of friends. About how scared he'd been on certain missions, and how exhilarating it was to fly at the speed of sound high above the earth.

She shared more about her time in New York. Not all of it was bad. She'd met some amazing women, and had done things she'd never thought she would, like posing for Wilhelmina Models. But there were also the hard times she'd endured that made his heart hurt. Giving birth to Kash alone, scared to death about what was to come. Being so hungry, she'd stolen food out of a dumpster behind a restaurant at three in the morning when no one was around. How hard living in her minivan had been, and how she'd felt as if she'd failed as a mother.

He felt closer to her as a result and cherished every minute they spent together.

He'd left Harper sleeping in his bed—he'd kept her up extremely late, because he hadn't been able to get enough of her. He'd lost count of how many times she'd orgasmed. Linc couldn't wait to get his vasectomy, because then he wouldn't have to worry about condoms and they could relax and not have to stress about an unwanted pregnancy.

As much as he loved spending one-on-one time with Harper, Linc was also very much looking forward to Kash getting home. He missed the little bugger. Missed his babbling about the solar system and black holes and nebulas. Missed teaching him things, the stuff his own father had taught *him*, like how to paint walls without leaving streaks, how to fix the vacuum cleaner's motor. Missed the time he spent with him in this very kitchen.

Kash was a sponge, and it felt awesome to see him soaking in the positive reinforcement Linc tried so hard to give him. The kid was going to be a force when he grew up. It was going to take a very patient partner to keep up with him. To stimulate his mind and to nurture him.

But on the flip side, Kash would make an *amazing* partner in return. He was very in tune to the feelings of others and had a protective streak that rivaled that of Linc and his brothers. He'd seen it in the way he spoke to and about Harper, and even when he interacted with Britt, Marit, Evelyn, and, to some extent, his grandfather.

Since he was thinking about Kash, he picked up his phone from where he'd left it on the counter when he'd started breakfast, shooting off a quick text. It was early, he didn't know the exact schedule of the competition, but he took a chance that Kash would already be awake. Excited about the day and the awards ceremony.

Linc: Hey, Bud, just checking in. How's everything going? You good?

It took ten minutes, but when Linc heard his phone vibrate, he smiled. He rinsed his hands after cutting veggies for the tater-tot-and-egg casserole he was making, along with a huge pan of cinnamon rolls, since they were Kash's favorite and he wanted them waiting for him when he got home later that afternoon. He reached for his phone.

Kash: I'm good.

Linc: Any idea what time you might be home today? I'm making your favorite . . . cinnamon rolls.

Kash: Yum. Not sure about the time though. I'll see if I can find out.

Linc: How's the competition going?

Kash: Fine.

Linc waited for Kash to say more, but when there were no dots on the screen indicating that he was still typing, he frowned.

Linc: Everything okay?

Kash: Yes.

Linc: Okay, Bud. Your mom and I miss you. We can't wait to have you home. The house has been too empty without you.

Kash: Yeah. I miss you guys too. Gotta go.

Linc: Okay. Good luck today. Can't wait to hear all about it.

Kash: Bye.

Linc stared down at his phone. Something niggled at the back of his brain. He remembered reassuring Harper when she'd had the same feeling, and now he felt bad for not asking more questions.

Because she was right. Something seemed *off.* He'd have thought Kash would be full of things to say about the competition. About spending a couple of nights in a fancy hotel. About Portland. About the robots.

He was still frowning at his phone, racking his brain about what could be going on with Kash, when Harper walked into the kitchen.

"Morning," she said in a husky voice.

Looking up, Linc's heart melted. She looked amazing. Her hair was mussed, she had small abrasions on her neck from his beard, where he'd nuzzled her all night, and under the big fluffy robe she had on, he could picture the hickeys he'd loved putting all over her body. She looked like a woman who'd been thoroughly ravished, and he'd been the man to do the ravishing. Just seeing her made his cock twitch.

"Morning," he returned, holding out an arm in invitation.

She didn't hesitate, just walked into his space and leaned into him. "Is that Kash?" she asked, nodding at the phone still in his hand. "Did he tell you what time he was getting back today? How much time we have to ourselves before we have to leave to go get him?"

The last part was said suggestively, but Linc couldn't tease back. Not when he still couldn't shake the feeling that something was wrong.

"He's not sure about the time . . . but you know how yesterday, you said you thought something was off about him?"

"Yeah?"

"Well, I agree. Here, look at our conversation, see what you think." Linc handed his phone to Harper, and she read the short texts they'd exchanged.

When she was done, she looked up at him. "I can't put my finger on what's different, but *something* is. Do you think maybe it's that they aren't doing as well as he'd hoped?"

"No. Kash would see that as a challenge. He'd be disappointed, but I don't think we'd be getting these weird vibes from him. It's something else."

"He's usually much more verbose," Harper suggested with a small frown, still looking down at Linc's phone.

He was staring at the screen as well when it hit him. He reached for his cell without a word and scrolled up. He read a few texts they'd shared from earlier in the week, and then last week.

"Holy *fuck*. Harper . . . I don't think this is Kash texting."

"What? But it's his number," she argued, straightening from where she'd been leaning against him.

"I know, but look—every other time he texts, he doesn't bother with punctuation, or uppercase letters, or anything. He abbreviates words where he can. Uses that text language kids like to use so they can type faster. But in this conversation, he's using apostrophes, periods, capitalizing each word at the beginning of a sentence."

Harper took the phone and scrolled back and forth between old texts and the conversation from minutes earlier.

When she lifted her head, Linc could see the panic dawning. "So who's got his phone? Who's pretending to be him, and why?"

"Take a deep breath, Harp. We don't know that anything's wrong yet."

"Yes, we *do*! You feel it just as much as I do. Don't minimize this."

She was right. Linc felt as if his skin was too tight, and all he wanted to do was jump in his SUV and go find Kash. Something was wrong. *Really* wrong. If someone had his phone, and was pretending to be him, this wasn't good.

Hadn't his family been through enough?

Was this Lucas Pearson, hiring someone from prison, retaliation for not succeeding in his plans for Marit? Or hell, had the *Calverts* paid off someone from prison, to continue harassing the Young family? They'd somehow made their share of enemies in the last year.

Of course, the *first* person who came to mind was the boy who'd been making Kash's life miserable at school . . . but he was just a kid. He might steal Kash's cell and pretend to be him, a relatively harmless prank. But if he had, Kash would have called his mom with someone else's phone way before now.

No . . . to actually make Kash *disappear*? That was a whole different level of bullying.

A ball of fire in Linc's gut was screaming that he needed to find out what was happening. Now.

"I'm not minimizing this. I won't. Go get dressed. We'll make some calls. To the school, to the hotel in Portland. See if we can't figure out some reasonable explanation. And if not, I'll call my brothers and the police."

"I'm scared," Harper whispered, looking up at Linc as if her world was crumbling.

"Me too," Linc admitted softly.

She closed her eyes for a moment, then took a deep breath. "Right, I'll start with trying to call Kash. See if he'll pick up. If not, I'll call the hotel in Portland."

"And I'll find the number of the robotics club adviser. I think his contact info was on the permission slip we had to sign. There's a copy of it around here somewhere."

Feeling a little better now that they had a plan, and hoping against hope that Kash would answer his mom's call, Linc did his best to stay calm, as he'd told Harper to do. It was easier said than done. His heart was beating a million miles an hour, and he felt just as panicked now as he had when he'd realized his plane was crashing in North Korea.

Without a word, Harper turned and rushed back toward the bedroom, where she'd left her phone. Linc stared at the text conversation that was still on his screen.

He had an urge to type out a message to whoever it was who had his son's phone—that he was coming for them, and if they hurt one hair on Kash's head, the person would spend the rest of their life regretting their fucking choices.

But he also didn't want to give whoever it was a clue that the jig was up.

Phones could be tracked. And while he didn't know anyone who could do that without going through proper channels, he had no doubt that his brothers might know someone. Between the four of them, they had a lot of military contacts. They had to know *someone* who could get them the intel they needed—yesterday.

Time was of the essence. If their suspicions were right, it had been two days since Kash had gone missing. Since Harper had gotten that first text that felt off. Which was *way* too long. The golden hour was ticking, and if they didn't find him, and soon, it might be too late.

Which wasn't acceptable.

Breakfast forgotten, Linc rushed over to the pile of papers on the edge of the counter. He'd gotten in the habit of stacking stuff there that he didn't want to throw away immediately, just in case, or things that he'd deal with filing later. He vaguely remembered putting the copy of the permission slip for the robotics competition in the pile. He just prayed he hadn't tossed it already.

He found it almost immediately, and relief filled him as he saw the contact info for the teacher who'd taken the kids to Portland, Mr. Simpson. Without caring that it was still early, Linc punched the number into his phone.

He wasn't going to wait to hear whether or not Harper had been able to get a hold of Kash. He had a feeling he knew what the outcome of her trying to call would be. He wasn't waiting another second for intel.

"Hello?"

The man who answered sounded as if he'd been awakened from a deep sleep. Linc didn't feel an ounce of remorse.

"This is Lincoln Young. Harper Bates is my girlfriend, and Kash is her son. Is he there?"

"Here?" the adviser asked, obviously still mostly asleep.

"In Portland. At the robotics competition," Linc clarified impatiently.

"Uh . . . no. He texted Brad, one of the other kids, and said he was sick and couldn't make it. We're really missing him. He's a smart cookie and has great ideas. Wait . . . why?"

Fuck. Fuck, fuck, *fuck*. "He's not here. He's not sick. We don't know where he is."

"Oh no."

Oh no, indeed. But Linc was done with this conversation. Kash wasn't in Portland. Had never been in Portland. And he doubted Kash had actually texted this Brad person and told him he was sick. He'd been looking forward to the competition for weeks. He wouldn't have ditched. Definitely didn't run away, as he was sure the cops might suggest. Not that he'd blame them. Teenagers ran away all the time, then usually showed up back at home.

But that wasn't what happened here. Something was wrong. Bad wrong.

"Thanks," Linc said.

He heard the adviser stuttering and asking him to wait, but he hung up. He felt a little bad, but if the man didn't have any intel, Linc was moving on.

"He didn't answer," Harper said.

Turning, Linc saw that she'd changed into jeans and a sweatshirt. Her hair hadn't been brushed, and she was just as disheveled as she had been when she'd entered the kitchen the first time. Except now she looked on the verge of a nervous breakdown.

Linc hated this. Wished he could take away her fear. Somehow reassure her. But he was just as freaked as she was.

Where the hell was Kash, and how were they going to find him?

Chapter Eighteen

Ginger hadn't gotten better with time. Even though Kash had managed to get into another cabin and brought back a couple of cans of Spam, canned chicken, and even a can of SpaghettiOs, she was still as sullen and full of drama as she'd been their first night and all Saturday.

It was taking every ounce of Kash's patience not to yell at her to shut the hell up.

Last night, they'd both slept on the couch again, and once more she'd huddled against him under the blankets. She'd cried herself to sleep, and while Kash was annoyed with her, he couldn't deny her the comfort she'd so desperately sought.

She'd been awful to him, like usual, said some terrible things, but she was still human. And at the moment, so out of her element it wasn't even funny. It was kind of hysterical that Kash, the boy who didn't like the outdoors all that much, except to look at the sky, was the more experienced one in this situation.

Late last night, he'd left Ginger in the house—crying like usual—while he went out to stare up at the sky. The stars were brighter than he'd ever seen them, and he could even see the Milky Way without his telescope. It was awe inspiring, and if he was in any other situation than the one he was in, he probably would've enjoyed it a lot more.

But he was stressed. Even though he was prepared to spend several days, a week, even a month waiting to be found, he was still scared. He wanted his mom. It wasn't a very cool thing to admit, but he wasn't ashamed of how he felt.

And he also wanted Linc. He felt safe around the larger-than-life man who'd come into his world, and he knew without a doubt if Linc was there, he'd know exactly what to do. What to say to Ginger to make her feel better. How to find more water than the dozen or so bottles someone had left in their cabin for the winter.

Linc would also be worried, and Kash couldn't help but wonder if they knew he was missing yet. That he hadn't texted Brad to tell him he was sick. That he didn't go to Portland.

There were cameras at the school, and eventually someone would think to look at them. They'd see him being led off the premises by Owen and Scott. Would maybe see Donny luring Ginger away. But would they make the connection? He wasn't sure about that part. Plenty of kids knew Owen and Scott were good friends with Donny. They'd figure it out *eventually*. But how fast?

Sighing, Kash disentangled his arms and legs from Ginger's and slipped out from under the blankets. He didn't bother waking her up and asking if she needed to pee. Yesterday, she'd finally given in and done what she'd needed to do, then complained about it for at least an hour afterward.

Every time.

He went outside, peed against a tree, then quickly returned to the cabin. He had no way of heating up the SpaghettiOs, and was afraid to start a fire—not that he had anything to start it with, because it wasn't as if he knew how to use sticks or whatever—so they'd have to eat the treat cold. But even thinking about the noodles in tomato sauce made Kash's stomach clench with hunger.

If he was a different kind of person, he would've eaten the entire can at the other house right when he'd found it. Not brought it back to show Ginger. Even though she hadn't been impressed, had wrinkled her nose at the mere thought of eating processed noodles, Kash wasn't sorry he'd brought them back to share.

For the first time, he had an inkling of what his mom had probably gone through. Being hungry herself, but doing everything in her power to let him eat first. It was a huge sacrifice he hadn't fully understood until now. Because everything in him was urging him to go out and find more food and keep it all to himself. Because Ginger sure wouldn't appreciate his efforts. But he wouldn't do that.

"I'm cold," Ginger whined from the couch.

Kash sighed. It was going to be a long day. Week. Month. Whatever. But his mood was actually a little better regardless—because today was Sunday. Today was the day his mom and Linc and everyone else would realize he and Ginger were missing.

Maybe Donny would come pick them up, laughing at the scare he'd given them, sure he'd taught them a lesson. What lesson, Kash didn't know, but at the moment he didn't care. He just wanted to go home.

"I have breakfast," he told Ginger, as he popped the top on the SpaghettiOs.

"I don't want anything."

For a split second, Kash's hopes rose. He could eat the entire can by himself. But then common sense kicked in. She needed to eat something. He'd have to convince her.

He took two spoons from the silverware drawer and headed back to the couch. He sat next to her and handed her a spoon. "You have to eat. It's not so bad, promise. Sit up and share with me?"

He was relieved when Ginger huffed out a breath but moved to sit upright. Her face was blotchy and dirty. Her hair a mess. She no longer looked like the put-together popular girl he'd gotten used to seeing at school. Kash kind of liked her better like this. Not miserable, of course . . . but more approachable? They were on a more even playing field out here. Both out of their element. Surviving together.

He handed her the spoon and held out the can, letting her have the first spoonful. She dipped the spoon into the tomato sauce and looked at it skeptically before opening her mouth.

Kash quickly took his own bite, and the flavor burst on his tongue. It tasted delicious, even cold.

"That wasn't bad," Ginger said with a tiny smile.

They shared the can of SpaghettiOs, taking turns scooping out the saucy noodles until it was empty, which was way too fast.

Kash sat back and put a hand on his belly. "I remember this feeling. Of knowing what you ate wasn't all that much, but feeling so full you thought you were going to pop."

"Yeah, it's weird that I'm so stuffed," Ginger agreed.

They sat in companionable silence, and Kash felt relaxed for the first time since they'd been stranded here.

"I'm sorry for how awful I've been to you. I don't really have an excuse. I just went along with Donny because . . . well . . . I don't know why."

"It's okay," Kash said. He wasn't the kind of kid to hold grudges. It didn't really help anything, and just made him feel more angry.

"It's not. I judged you badly. I won't lie, I was pretty upset when I realized what Donny had planned, that he'd picked *you* to be stranded out here with me. But I know now that I was stupid. I would probably be a popsicle down at the dock if you weren't here, telling me what to do, getting us into this house, keeping me warm at night. I appreciate it."

Kash was surprised. He honestly hadn't thought Ginger would actually apologize for the way she'd treated him. Or for thinking bad things about him.

"Thanks," he told her quietly.

"When we get back, things are going to change," she said firmly.

And Kash was thrilled she'd said *when*, not *if*. He was glad she wasn't so lost in her head anymore that she still thought they were going to die here.

"I've hated everything about this experience," she said with honesty. "But I haven't hated having you here with me. I'm going to be a better person at school. Stand up for the nerds."

Kash rolled his eyes. "Maybe start by not calling us 'the nerds,'" he suggested.

She chuckled. "Right. Sorry. I mean, I *am* dating a band geek now."

"How about calling him a musician instead? Words have power, you know."

She thought about that for a moment, then nodded. "Again, you're right. Sorry."

"It's okay. I just appreciate you making an effort. And I don't care if you ignore me at school. Kids suck. I know that better than most."

"I'm not going to pretend we didn't go through what we did together."

Together might be a stretch, as it wasn't as if she'd done much to help their situation, but Kash was too relieved that she wasn't crying or bitching at the moment to call her out on specifics.

"My daddy has some bigwig friends. I'm going to make sure Donny, Owen, and Scott pay for what they did. They *kidnapped* us. Maybe attempted murder? There's got to be some serious charge that will stick."

Kash hoped so, but he wasn't holding his breath. Donny and his friends were minors. That didn't mean they couldn't be charged with a whole bunch of stuff, though he wasn't sure how it all worked. But he hoped that maybe, just *maybe*, they'd get kicked out of school for what they did. That would make Kash's life so much better if he didn't have to deal with Donny and his jerk friends every day.

The alternative, that nothing happened to the three boys, was terrifying. There was no telling what they'd do next time if they got away with this.

"Do you think they know we're missing yet?" Ginger asked softly.

"Yes," Kash said firmly.

"I hope so."

"They'll find us. If your dad knows people, he'll stop at nothing to figure out where you are. And I know Linc and his brothers will do the same. We just have to hang on until they get here. Just think of the stories we'll have to tell our kids. Not *our* kids—you know, yours and mine together. But, you know, our kids in general."

She giggled. "I know what you meant."

"You aren't my type," Kash blurted.

"You aren't mine either. But that doesn't mean we can't be friends, right?"

Friends. Huh. Never in a million years would Kash have thought he'd hear one of the popular girls in school call *him* a friend. And mean it.

"Right," he agreed. "It doesn't feel quite as cold out this morning. Maybe we can sit by the dock for a while later, after the sun's fully up. Maybe we'll get lucky and see a boat or something."

"Sure," Ginger agreed. "But . . . first I gotta pee."

Kash grinned. "I'll take care of the dishes," he said, lifting the empty can with the two spoons inside.

"We're so domestic," Ginger joked.

Kash walked into the small kitchen and put the empty can into a trash bag he'd found under the sink. Then he used a paper towel to clean off the spoons as best he could. It wasn't completely sanitary, but he had no water to waste on dishes.

Ginger returned after a few minutes, and Kash asked, "Want to play a board game? I noticed there are quite a few to choose from."

She shrugged. "Might as well. I'm kind of sick of just sitting around crying."

Kash gave her a small smile.

"How about Trivial Pursuit? I haven't played that in ages," she suggested.

Kash didn't have the heart to remind her that he was a nerd through and through, and he'd likely wipe the floor with her. Trivia was his thing. He had more useless knowledge in his brain than the average human. Except in the entertainment category. He sucked at that one. But he didn't think there was a question in the science and nature category that he didn't know. In fact, his mom had found a set of the cards in a thrift store when they were in New York, and they used to go over the questions late at night for fun.

"Sounds good," he said, planning on purposely throwing the game so it would last longer, and so Ginger wouldn't have a fit when he won in six rounds.

Even though they were preparing to play a game he enjoyed, and even though he and Ginger were finally getting along better, he still missed his mom. Still wanted off this darn island.

Please let today be the day, he thought to himself, as he rolled the dice to see who would go first.

Chapter Nineteen

It was early afternoon on Monday, and Harper and Linc were no closer to finding Kash than they'd been when they first discovered he'd never made it to Portland. Except now they knew another kid was missing as well.

They'd spent most of Sunday talking to the police, searching the neighborhoods around the school, calling everyone Harper could think of to call, and generally being scared out of their minds.

Ginger, the mean girl who'd made such fun of Kash, was also nowhere to be found. And the police had to split their time talking to Ginger's parents and friends, trying to track her down as well and determine if there was any connection between the missing kids.

Of course, there *was*. The first person both she and Linc had thought of—Donny. Ginger's ex-boyfriend, and the kid who'd been bullying Kash all year. The police had gone to his house and questioned him. He'd claimed ignorance, swore that he didn't know anything about what had happened to "that nerdy little punk."

Without proof of any wrongdoing, the questioning stopped almost as soon as it had started. And the cops were doing their best to cover all their bases and interview anyone and everyone who might know something . . . but Harper was still convinced Donny was hiding something. Maybe even her son.

Which made no sense. Why would he *do* that? Kash was a good kid. Kind. What could he have possibly done to Donny or anyone else to make them hate him so much? To take bullying to such a crazy extreme?

The fact that Ginger was missing as well—and possibly with Kash, wherever he was—didn't make Harper feel any better. Her baby was most likely scared. Hungry. Cold. And she wanted him back in her arms. *Now.*

Harper couldn't stop thinking about how he'd spent three nights . . . somewhere. While she'd been enjoying her time with Linc, her son was probably suffering. She felt guilty and heartbroken. And angry. So damn *angry.*

She refused to think about the worst-case scenario. That he was gone. She'd feel it if he was dead. She knew that without a doubt. But that didn't make this any easier. Kash was out there, and she needed him home.

It was her turn to lose sleep. Linc had held and rocked her all night . . . well, for the three hours he'd convinced her to lie down. She'd spent every other hour pacing, alternating between exhilaration when it seemed as if they might have found something and disappointment when any information they'd learned hadn't immediately led them to her son.

And when she paced—back and forth, back and forth—everywhere she looked, she'd seen reminders of Kash. The kitchen, where he laughed as he made dinner with Linc. The half-painted wall in the laundry room, which he'd been working on by himself. His pile of clothes waiting to go into the washer. The telescope in the corner of the living room. His books on the end tables. It was enough to make her cry . . . and she quickly grew so sick of crying. Of feeling helpless.

Harper had no idea what she would've done without Linc and his family. They'd been her rocks, helping her and Linc every step of the way. And each time she began to spiral, to lose hope, they reassured her that they'd find Kash.

Britt, Chad, Marit, Zach, and Knox had come over a couple of hours ago, along with Evelyn, and even her dad. The house was bursting at the seams.

And today felt . . . different. She had more hope.

Yesterday, it felt as if they'd been spinning their wheels. Running around without much of a plan, talking to anyone and everyone and getting nowhere. But first thing this morning, Linc had gone to the high school to meet with the chief of police and their digital forensic officer. The guy who was best at interpreting and cleaning up digital video.

She'd wanted to go with him, but Linc convinced her to stay home, by the phone, and promised he'd call if they had any information. Harper had hope that today, they'd be able to find out what happened to Kash.

She'd resumed her pacing, the other women busying themselves in the kitchen, when Chad's phone rang. Harper stopped in her tracks and stared at him as he answered.

"Any news? Right . . . uh-huh . . . wow, okay. Now? Of course. On my way. See you soon."

Harper was at his side before he'd hung up. "That was Linc, right? Did they find him?"

"Yes, it was Linc, and no, they haven't found him or Ginger yet, but the footage at the school was huge. It took a while to scrub through it. Come on, we're meeting Linc there."

She was more than ready to go. To do something. *Anything.* Harper didn't even press Chad for more information. She could ask on the way to town. But if Linc wanted her there, she could only hope that meant they were close to finding Kash.

There was a flurry of activity as she and Chad prepared to head to the high school. Zach volunteered to stay back at the house with the women and her dad, while she, Chad, and Knox all headed out the door.

The ride to the high school was tense, and Chad was driving well above the speed limit. He told them that he didn't have a lot of information, just that Linc said the video surveillance at the high school was promising.

Harper frowned upon hearing that. What did that even mean? She trusted Linc, but she needed a lot more than "promising" right about now.

Chad didn't park right away, simply drove up as close to the entrance as he could and dropped off Harper and Knox, saying he'd park and be inside in a moment.

Harper jogged to the doors, and to her relief, Linc was right there waiting for her. She threw herself into his arms. "Did you find him?"

"Not yet, but we're getting close," he reassured her.

His arms warmed the cold, dead places inside her better than all the sweatshirts and fuzzy robes ever could. In his arms, she felt whole. But as much as she wanted to simply stand there and let him comfort her, she needed to let him go so they could get on with finding Kash.

"Come on, after watching the videos, the principal immediately acted. As a result, there's someone in his office we think has something to tell us."

Harper frowned as Linc took her hand and led the way. She didn't know who might be able to shed light on the situation, but she didn't care if it was the devil himself, as long as they got the information they needed to bring Kash home.

Chad caught up to them as they entered the main office. Linc didn't pause, striding past the secretary's desk to the principal's office.

Inside, Harper saw a boy she didn't know, and someone who she suspected was his father standing behind him with his arms crossed over his chest and a frown on his face. The boy was staring at the floor and didn't even look up when they entered the room.

The principal was also there, as were three police officers, one of them sitting behind the desk, doing something on the computer. The room was extremely crowded with the addition of Harper, Linc, Knox, and Chad, but no one seemed to care.

"Right. Miss Bates, if you'd please go stand over there," one of the officers said, pointing to a spot behind the desk that would allow her to see the computer screen.

She realized it was the police chief who'd spoken. She'd never met him, but now that she was paying attention, she saw the badge on his chest that indicated he was in charge of the department.

Linc kept himself between her and the kid in the chair, acting as a barrier. Harper assumed he was the reason they were there. That he knew where Kash was. She wanted to lash out, scream at him to tell them what he'd done, but she took a deep breath. Yelling wouldn't help the situation. She had to trust Linc and the officers.

She moved into position, and the officer at the computer turned his head and nodded at her before looking back at the screen.

"When we went over the videos from Friday, we got glimpses of both Kash and Ginger, the other teenager who's missing," the officer said. "It took a little while to track their movements, but here's what we found." He clicked on something, and a video began to play on the screen. It was a little grainy, but clear enough that it was easy to distinguish between the people walking the halls of the school.

The officer pointed out two people. "This is Ginger. And that's Donny."

Harper inhaled. *Donny.* She and Linc had suspected that kid from the beginning. Had told the police he was the connection between Ginger and Kash.

Deep down, she hadn't wanted to believe that a bully could do something so much worse than just pick on her son. But clearly she'd been wrong. And why not? Donny had bullied Kash relentlessly for months, Ginger right by his side for most of it. Though, Harper recalled Kash telling her that the two had broken up.

She watched the video as Donny walked next to Ginger. There was no sound, but it seemed clear that he was taunting her. He'd walk backward in front of her, then drop back to her side.

It almost happened too fast for her to make out, but since she was watching so intently, she saw the moment he reached out and snatched Ginger's phone from her back pocket.

The teenage girl reacted immediately, trying to grab it back. But Donny easily kept it out of her reach, teasing her with the phone.

Harper watched as Donny jogged away, turning around and waving the phone. Ginger followed quickly, looking pissed.

The pair walked out of frame, and the officer immediately clicked on another video. Harper saw the duo approaching a set of doors that led outside. Ginger followed Donny right out the door, probably still demanding he give the phone back the whole way.

The view switched to an outdoor camera, and her gaze followed the pair as they walked across the parking lot and off campus, toward a neighborhood.

"There's more," Linc said softly, nodding at the computer screen. He'd moved with her to the spot behind the desk, and now he put his arm around her waist, letting her lean on him. Which Harper appreciated. She was nearing the end of her rope. Adrenaline only lasted so long, and with little sleep, almost no food—how could *she* eat when she had no idea if her son had any food himself?—she was dead on her feet.

Another video was playing now, a shot of the cafeteria. She recognized Kash immediately. Her breath caught in her throat. He looked . . . fine. Normal. The cafeteria was pretty full, and she wondered about that, since Kash had told her recently he'd been getting there early and grabbing his lunch before heading to a safer place to eat, away from Donny and his friends.

She saw two other boys intercept Kash and take hold of his arms. If she hadn't been watching so closely, if she didn't know her son as well as she did, she might've thought it was just some friends palling around. But Kash looked tense, and he clearly tried to jerk his arms out of their hold.

He was turned around and led out of the cafeteria. She watched as the threesome walked down a hall and out a door. A second camera, and they were momentarily in a courtyard—and she saw Kash *really* begin to struggle. Then a third camera showed them crossing the same parking lot as Donny and Ginger in the previous video. They disappeared into the same neighborhood as well.

Harper looked up and pinned her gaze on Donny. He knew where Kash and Ginger were. She'd bet her life on it. He'd probably orchestrated everything.

"We have officers knocking on every door in that neighborhood, looking for surveillance cameras," the police chief said. "But it will go a lot better for you, Donny, if you simply tell us what happened. Where Ginger and Kash are. And no lies this time like yesterday when we talked to you."

"I don't know."

"Yes, you do!" Harper exclaimed. "You've made Kash's life a living *hell* at school! He avoids going to the cafeteria because he knows you and your friends will be there, waiting to torment him. You bully him *constantly*! What did you do? Where is my son?!"

"You need to start talking *now*!" his dad barked, making even Harper jump.

"Easy," Linc whispered, tightening his hold around her waist. She could feel how tense he was behind her, but she admired his restraint. She wanted to leap across the desk and beat the hell out of Donny. Get him to tell them everything. Linc had to feel the same way.

"I've had enough of your bullshit!" his dad continued. "Skipping school, smoking pot, back talking . . . you've been on the wrong path, Donny, and I wrote it off as teenager rebellion. But *this*? Bullying other kids? Luring Ginger out of school? Doing something to that boy? You've gone way too far. You've made your bed, and now you'll pay the consequences. I'm not bailing you out. Not anymore. Your best bet is to tell everyone what you did. And what part Owen and Scott had to play in this. Maybe a judge will be more lenient if you show the smallest hint of remorse."

A muscle in Donny's jaw ticked, but he stubbornly kept his gaze focused on his feet.

His dad shook his head. "I'm ashamed of you. Never thought I'd say that about my own kid . . . but that's the truth. I didn't raise you to be a bully. Didn't raise you to think it's okay to harass a girl just because she broke up with you. What's *wrong* with you? You have a chance to do the right thing, son."

Harper held her breath. Amazingly, she felt kind of bad for Donny. To hear your father say he was ashamed of you had to hurt. But would it make him talk? She hoped and prayed what his dad was saying would sink in. That the kid would realize whatever dangerous game he was playing was finished.

The silence in the room was almost painful as everyone waited for Donny to talk.

"We didn't hurt them," Donny finally muttered. "It was a *joke*. I was mad at Ginger, wanted her to suffer like I was. She picked a band geek over *me*! It's humiliating! She had to learn that what she did wasn't cool."

"What'd you do, son? Where are they?" his dad asked in a quieter tone.

"Owen borrowed the skiff his dad uses to get to the mooring where he keeps his boat in the summer, and we took them out to Ragged Island."

At Knox's shocked inhalation, Harper stiffened and immediately looked over at him.

"Jesus, Donny! Ragged Island? That's at least an hour off the coast," his dad exclaimed.

"No one lives there in the winter," Donny mumbled. "They'd be alone. I just wanted to scare them!" he insisted, finally looking at his dad. "I was gonna go get them tomorrow," he said defensively.

"And you have their phones? It was you who texted Ginger and Kash's friends and family?"

Donny mumbled, "They're in my locker."

For the first time, Donny looked like the kid he was. And he was frightened, that was plain to see. But Harper figured he was more worried about himself than what was going on with the two people he'd stranded on a deserted island.

Knox's fingers were flying over the screen of his phone, and he turned toward the door without looking up.

"Come on," Linc told Harper, pushing her around the far end of the desk, away from Donny, after Knox's retreating form.

"I'll stay and relay any other pertinent info," Chad said as they passed.

Linc nodded but didn't stop as he exited the small office.

Another officer continued to question Donny, while the police chief and the principal followed Harper, Linc, and Knox out the door.

"I can call the fire department and get them to bring a boat around to the Rockville dock," the chief told them.

"No need," Knox said, with a shake of his head. "I've contacted my boss at the Coast Guard. They already know my nephew's missing and have been on standby. They'll meet us at the dock in five minutes."

Harper stared at him in disbelief. *His nephew.* Tears sprang to her eyes. Not only had Linc claimed her and Kash, but his brothers had as well.

"I'm still sending an officer out there."

"Fine. But we aren't waiting," Linc told the man.

"I understand. Assuming you both know first aid . . . just in case."

Harper's blood turned to ice. She'd been so excited about finding out exactly where Kash was that she hadn't even stopped to think that he might be hurt . . . or worse. She closed her eyes for a short moment, praying that they hadn't found him only to find out that he hadn't survived three days in the freezing-cold Maine weather.

"We know first aid," Linc said, his voice quavering.

Knowing that he was just as affected by the police chief's words did nothing to make Harper feel better.

"Come on, they're on their way," Knox said firmly. "Let's go get Kash."

"Wait, is someone going to tell Ginger's family?" Harper asked, as they began walking toward the main doors. She didn't know the girl, but her family had to be just as frantic.

"They're on their way," the principal said. "I'll let them know what's happening."

They were probably going to be pissed that they didn't get to come with them to the island, because that's how Harper would've felt, but she wasn't willing to wait. They could catch a ride with the fire department. Nothing was going to keep her from getting to that island and her son.

They practically jogged back to the car, and before Harper even had her seat belt on, Knox was pulling out of the parking space.

Before she knew it, Harper was watching a Coast Guard boat come screaming into the harbor, ignoring the no-wake-zone signs. Since it was winter, there weren't many boats in the harbor anyway, so there was no damage done.

Then she was on board, Linc was putting a life jacket over her head, and the boat was already on the move back to open water.

Linc held on to a railing inside the small cabin with one hand and kept his other arm wrapped around Harper's waist. No one spoke, the only sound the radio crackling with intel going out about the emergency situation. Because Ragged Island was so far offshore, and it wasn't prime lobster season, there were no boats anywhere close to the area they were headed.

They would be the first boat to arrive, and Harper could only pray they weren't too late. That even with the odds against the two kids, they'd found a way to survive.

Feeling sick to her stomach, Harper held on to Linc and stared blankly out the front windshield as they zoomed across the water.

Chapter Twenty

They hadn't come.

Kash had been so sure that yesterday would be the day. Everyone would figure out that he and Ginger weren't where they were supposed to be, and they'd discover what happened and would come and get them. Or Donny would come back, laughing his ass off about how pathetic they were.

But no one came. The island was just as silent as it had been when they'd been left there on Friday afternoon.

It was disheartening, but Kash refused to get depressed. Yes, there was always the chance that they'd be there for weeks or more, but he knew his mom. She was like a dog with a bone, she wouldn't give up until she found him. That's just how she was.

He and Ginger had spent another night on the couch, huddling together for warmth. Both their bellies were growling because they'd eaten all the canned food they'd found in the house. Kash really didn't want to break into another cabin, but he would if no one showed up to rescue them by dinnertime.

"Kash?" Ginger asked.

"Yeah?" He was lying behind her, his arm around her waist, the other under his head as a pillow. He wasn't very comfortable, didn't really enjoy being all snuggled up to his ex-tormentor like this, but he wouldn't ever admit that to her. It wouldn't be nice.

"I'm scared."

It wasn't something Kash didn't know. She'd said that several times in the last three days. But he wasn't going to yell at her or tell her to shut up. He was just as scared, and even though Ginger was probably the last person he'd choose to be in this situation with, he was still glad he wasn't alone.

"I know. Me too," he said after a moment.

"And cold. And hungry."

He rolled his eyes. Yeah, he'd heard *those* complaints over and over from her too.

"Same."

"And I have to pee."

He chuckled at that. "Then get up and pee," he said reasonably.

"But I'm cold and hungry." She giggled.

Kash couldn't help but laugh with her. "Later this afternoon, I'll go check out the houses again. Maybe I missed some cans of food somewhere."

"Would you mind if I went with you? I'm going stir crazy in here."

"Of course I don't mind," he said honestly. He was glad she finally wanted to do more than sit and cry all day. He could understand being scared, but it seemed silly to him to cry all the time. That didn't solve anything, it just made your face puffy. Besides, they didn't have the water to spare in their bodies.

"Do you think they'll come today?" she whispered.

Kash sighed. He wasn't sure if it was better to say yes and raise her hopes, only to have her fall into a depression again when no one showed up. Or be a jerk and say no, that they'd probably be stuck on this island for weeks.

He finally settled on saying, "I don't know. I hope so."

"He wasn't always such a jerk," Ginger said softly. "Donny. When we first started dating, he was really nice. Buying me lunch, bringing me flowers, telling me I was pretty . . . you know, things like that."

Kash pressed his lips together. All those things were superficial. He thought about the things Linc did for his mom. Made her dinner so she could eat when she got home from work, invited her and Kash to live with him practically rent-free, looked after him so his mom didn't have to worry . . . those were things that mattered. Not flowers and compliments.

"Huh," he said after a moment, not knowing what else to say, but realizing Ginger was waiting for some sort of response.

"But then he started getting possessive. Didn't want me hanging out with my friends. Telling me I was stupid, then laughing and saying he was just kidding. I gave him my virginity, and he didn't even seem to care that he hurt me."

Now that was a topic Kash *really* didn't want to talk about. He knew about sex, but he wasn't interested. "That sucks," he told her.

She sighed. "I realized I deserved better. But he didn't like it when I broke up with him."

"Obviously," Kash blurted.

To his surprise, Ginger laughed again. "Yeah. Anyway, I wised up and still . . . here I am."

"This isn't your fault," Kash told her.

"Isn't it? You're here because of me. Because I was stupid and followed Donny because he wouldn't give my phone back. He picked *you* because he was mad that I'm seeing someone he sees as a nerd."

"First, this is on Donny, and *only* Donny. He made the choice to do this, planned it all out. Got Owen and Scott to agree to help him. It's not your fault. Second, you should probably stop calling your new boyfriend a nerd. I mean, I don't mind the label, because to me, *nerd* means smart. And I like being smart."

"Yeah, you kicked my butt good in Trivial Pursuit," Ginger said.

He had. And he'd even tried to throw the game, but it was hard not to answer the questions correctly.

"I have no right to ask you anything, because we're nothing to each other, but please don't ever go back to him. Donny."

"Never," Ginger breathed. "And . . . we're not nothing. We're friends now, remember?"

"Yeah. But again, you don't have to say hi to me at school, I understand it would make you look bad to your friends."

"Screw that," she said. "This experience has taught me that I've been a shallow bitch. Judging people for things that just don't matter. I don't care about your red hair, or that you're skinny, or that you're in the robotics club. You've been amazing out here, and I wouldn't have known what to do without you."

Okay, that wasn't exactly a compliment, but Kash knew what she meant. And was pleased about it. "And I don't care that you're rich and stuck up and care way too much about clothes and makeup. You're pretty okay yourself, Ginger."

She laughed. "I guess I deserved that, didn't I?" she asked. She sat up, allowing Kash to sit up as well. They rearranged the blankets so they each had one wrapped around their shoulders.

Looking Kash in the eye, she said, "All I'm trying to say is . . . I'm sorry."

"Apology accepted."

"Just like that?" she asked skeptically.

"Just like that," he said firmly.

"Okay."

"Okay."

"Now I really *do* have to pee," Ginger said.

"Me too." They shared a small smile before standing. "You go left and I'll go right?" Kash asked.

Ginger nodded.

The rest of the morning went by extremely slowly. They played another game of Trivial Pursuit, but it was hard to concentrate when their bellies were growling so loudly. The weather had warmed up a little, so that was a relief, but it wasn't warm by any stretch.

"Want to go for a walk?" Kash asked Ginger.

"No, but yes. Anything to get out of this cabin."

Kash had no destination in mind, but figured they could walk around and check out the island, since they hadn't been able to do so before now because of the cold. It really was a pretty place. He wasn't surprised there were people who built cabins out there. Even though it was so far from the mainland, he could see the appeal of the peace and quiet.

They were circling back around to the cabins, to see if they could get into one of the others that had been boarded up tight, when an out-of-the-ordinary noise registered.

He froze, and Ginger did the same.

They shared a look—then started running toward the dock at the same time.

A motor! There was a boat out there. Maybe they could signal it somehow. Make someone see them and come investigate.

His heart beating out of his chest, Kash burst from the tree line ahead of Ginger and stared in disbelief at what he saw. The boat they'd heard was coming straight for them! It wasn't puttering around in the water, wasn't a pleasure craft—it was coming for *them*!

Joy and relief filled his heart. They were rescued! The last three days felt like an eternity, but knowing he wouldn't have to be stuck here for weeks made him almost dizzy with gratitude.

"They're really coming for us, right?" Ginger asked.

"They are," Kash confirmed. He couldn't stop smiling. He couldn't see who was on the boat, but it didn't really matter.

As the craft got closer, Kash realized he was wrong. It *did* matter.

He could see both his mom and Linc standing at the side of the boat. They looked anxious and kind of freaked out, but just knowing the two people he loved most in the world were there, that they'd found him, broke through the stoic front he'd been putting on for Ginger.

He burst into tears, not ashamed in the least.

His mom had come. She'd found him.

Kash could've sworn Linc jumped out of the Coast Guard boat before it even stopped at the dinky little dock. Then he was in his arms. The embrace hurt, but Kash didn't care. Having Linc's arms around him was the best feeling he'd ever experienced.

Then his mom joined them, wrapping her arms around him from the back. He was sandwiched between them, and their warmth seeped into his soul. Strangely, no one said a word, they didn't need to. The love they had for each other, and the relief they all felt, was so large it didn't need to be expressed.

Eventually, Linc relaxed his grip and lowered Kash to his feet. He hadn't even realized he'd picked him up. He put his hands on Kash's shoulders and stared into his eyes. "You okay, Bud?"

"Yeah."

"Not hurt?"

"Not really. Hungry, cold, and tired, but okay," Kash said honestly.

He heard his mom sniff next to him but didn't take his gaze from Linc's. There were so many things he wanted to say, but the only thing he could get out was "I love you."

The change in Linc was immediate. Kash thought he might cry. "I love you too, Bud. So much. I'm so proud of you for staying strong."

Hearing this man say he was proud of him was one of the most amazing moments in Kash's life. For years, he'd felt . . . less than. He was the skinny nerd. The guy people liked to pick on. People always wanted him to be different from how he was . . . his grandfather, girls, teachers. And yet here Linc stood, a man who was larger than life in Kash's eyes, saying he was proud of him. Not even winning the crate race could top this moment.

"I love you, Kash. We were so worried!"

Kash turned to hug his mom, loving how soft she was against him. How she smelled. How tight she held him. She'd always been his safe space, and this moment was no different. He'd longed to feel one of her amazing hugs again, and his wishes had come true.

But as grateful as he was to be in his mother's arms, the confidence he also felt was overwhelming. If people had taken bets on whether he'd be able to survive being left on a deserted island for more than a day, they probably would've lost a lot of money for betting against him. Kash felt as if he understood Linc a little better now. Of course, their situations weren't even close to being the same, but he'd kept going one minute at a time, just as Linc had done when he'd been hiking across North Korea. Neither of them had given up.

Ginger sobbed loudly then, and turning, Kash saw Knox patting her on the back as she buried her head in his chest.

Kash's mom let go of him and pulled Ginger into her embrace, holding her the same way she had him. And Kash wasn't jealous or resentful. He felt bad that Ginger's parents weren't there, wondered why. But ultimately he was too overjoyed that he'd been able to be reunited with both Linc and his mom.

It was only a few minutes before they heard another motor. There were two more boats heading their way, just as fast as the Coast Guard boat had come in. They all backed up a little, onto the walkway leading to the tiny little pier, making room for the newcomers, and as Kash stood between his mom and Linc, he watched as Ginger was reunited with her parents.

She and her mom were crying hysterically, as her dad stood with his arms around them both. It was touching and a little dramatic. But Kash hadn't really expected anything different. After all, he'd just spent three days with Ginger and was well aware of how much of a drama queen she could be.

"We have a lot to talk about," Linc said quietly.

"It was Donny. And Owen and Scott," Kash blurted, needing them to know.

"We know. The police are talking with Donny now, and I'm sure they'll go pick up the other two as well. You and Ginger will need to tell your side of things. About what happened."

"Okay," Kash said, having no problem with that. He was eager to let everyone know exactly what Donny had done. What he'd said. What an asshole he *truly* was.

"But not today," his mom said firmly. "I need to get you home. Fed. Clean."

All those things sounded awesome. "I don't suppose there's any food on the boat? I could eat a cow right about now."

Linc chuckled, but his mom simply frowned. "I don't know. But we're about to find out. Come on. I don't know about you, but I want to get off this island."

Kash nodded. But after two steps toward the pier, he stopped. "Linc? Mom?"

"Yeah, baby?"

He didn't even protest the *baby* thing. It felt good to hear the familiar term of endearment. "I broke a window or two. And we used their stuff. I want to replace it."

Linc ruffled his hair. "I'll make sure it's done."

"I want to do it," Kash insisted. "I messed things up, and I want to make it right."

"You don't mind coming back out here?" Linc asked.

"Will you come with me?"

"Of course."

"Then I don't mind."

"We'll make it happen sooner rather than later. And if you want, I'll find out who owns the cabins out here and see if we can arrange to meet them."

"Oh yes!" Kash said with a smile. "I want to thank them. For the food, the blankets, and everything. We all know that I'm not much of an outdoor person, and without these cabins I don't know what would've happened."

"You would've figured it out," Linc said without hesitation. "You're the smartest person I know."

Once again, his praise made Kash's self-esteem rise by a few notches. "I'm not saying I want to become Paul Bunyan or hike the Appalachian Trail . . . but Mom, do you think Granddad would be willing to teach me some outdoor stuff? Survival things?"

"I bet he'd be thrilled."

Kash nodded. Then frowned. "Not that I don't want *you* to teach me stuff, Linc, but Granddad's always been wanting to, and I've always told him no."

"I understand, Bud. And I think that's a great idea. I think he'd love that," Linc said.

Kash never again wanted to feel as helpless as he did when he'd watched Donny and Owen driving off in that boat, leaving him and Ginger alone on the island. For a split second, he'd also thought they were going to die. Because he knew nothing about building shelters, fires, or finding food. He hadn't lied. If there hadn't been cabins on this island that he could get into, that had a few provisions, they might've frozen to death. Certainly would've been way worse off than they were.

"Come on, Bud. There are a lot of people waiting anxiously to see you," Linc said.

"Hospital first," his mom said.

"Mom," Kash whined. "I'm fine. I don't want to go to the hospital."

"No one *wants* to go to the hospital, but you're going and that's that. I need to make sure you're all right."

Kash frowned but nodded. He understood his mom had been worried, was *still* worrying. She had a death grip on Kash's hand and wouldn't take her gaze from him. It was comforting in a way, even if seeing a doctor would be annoying.

"Can we please stop and get a hamburger or something on the way? Maybe The Lobster Buoy's lobster and truffle oil mashed potatoes. Ooooh, or some Ruckus Donuts! No—pizza!"

Linc chuckled. "We'll get you something, but I have a feeling you aren't going to be able to eat nearly as much as you want to. Not at first."

Kash figured he would know, considering his own experiences with being hungry. He thought back to how full he was after eating the SpaghettiOs and realized Linc was right. "I love you guys. Thank you for finding me," he blurted.

"Nothing would've stopped us," Linc said.

"We left to come out here and get you the second Donny admitted what he did," his mom agreed.

Some kids had a ton of toys. Or clothes. Or money. But Kash thought he was the richest person in the world. He had a mom who loved him with everything she had in her. It was more than enough.

He stepped onto the Coast Guard boat and watched the island get smaller and smaller as they headed back to the mainland. He should probably hate the sight of it, but in actuality, he felt proud of himself. He'd been put in a horrible situation and came out mostly unharmed on the other side. He felt as if he was a different person . . . in a good way.

Turning back into his mom's embrace, he let her hold him steady as the boat flew over the waves. Linc was at his mom's back, keeping her upright. They were stronger together than they were apart, and Linc was the father he'd always wanted but never had.

Life had a strange way of throwing curveballs, but for once, Kash felt as if he'd managed to hit a home run.

Chapter Twenty-One

A week after Kash and Ginger had been found, Harper still wasn't sleeping. And Linc wasn't sure what to do. He finally understood her feelings of helplessness over his own insomnia.

She'd fall asleep in his arms quickly, but within two hours, she'd be awake and going upstairs to check on Kash. To make sure he was safe and sound in his bed. His disappearance had done a number on her psyche, and he shared the guilt she felt over what they'd been doing while Kash was suffering on that island.

Something had to give. They needed to deal with this and move on. Just as Kash had done.

To everyone's surprise, the boy was amazingly resilient. He'd bounced back with barely a blip. He was upset that he'd missed the robotics competition, but was happy that they'd placed third overall. He'd watched the tapes of the bouts and come up with ways to improve their next robot so they could maybe place higher.

It was his mom who was falling apart at the seams.

Today, they were having an unusually warm day. It was one week into April, and it actually felt springlike outside. So instead of staying inside and working on the house, Linc, Harper, and Kash were heading out to Lobster Cove, where an impromptu party was apparently happening. Chad and Britt were there, of course, and Marit and Zach were heading over, as was Knox.

Walt and Barry were also coming by, despite the fact it was their day off from the auto body shop; Jonah and Eliot, Marit's lobstermen coworkers, were going to be there; Harper's dad would probably make an appearance; Kash had invited his robotics club friends; and even Ginger was coming with her new boyfriend, Alistair.

It was going to be absolute chaos, and while Kash was excited about the get-together, Harper seemed reluctant.

"Talk to me," Linc ordered gently, as Kash was upstairs showering before they headed out. "What's bothering you about today?"

"I don't know."

"Sure you do. Let me help you," Linc pleaded. "I love you, and I want to help you through this, but I can't if you don't let me in."

Harper sighed. "I just . . . I could've lost him." The last bit was whispered, as if saying the words aloud was almost too much for her to bear.

"Kash is smart. Too smart for his own good sometimes. And he didn't panic. Even though he was completely out of his element, he got himself and Ginger to safety, found blankets, scavenged for food. He was able to do all that because of everything *you* taught him."

Harper shook her head. "I didn't teach him anything," she protested.

"The hell you didn't," Linc said a little too fiercely. He lowered his voice as he continued. "He knew to stay calm because that's what he'd seen *you* do in other stressful situations. He was kind to Ginger, the girl who bullied him, because you've taught him to always see the good in people. And he knew without a doubt that you would never give up looking for him. That allowed him to go with the flow and simply wait for you to show up.

"I won't lie to you and say that things couldn't have been a lot worse. If there weren't any cabins on that island, if Donny hadn't talked, if they didn't have any food, if it had been snowing . . . I could go on and on, but what's the point of thinking about the what-ifs?

"He's back with us, and he's healthy, both mentally and physically. If anything, this has taught me that I need to let go of what happened to *me* once and for all. For years, I've been thinking about all the things that *could've* happened, about everything I lost as a result of my injury . . . but life is funny sometimes. The worst thing can somehow eventually be the catalyst to the *best* thing.

"Because of my crash, and my injuries, I wasn't able to fly anymore. I was medically discharged and lost for a time. My dad's death sucked, but it led me to moving back here to Maine, to meeting you and Kash, to finding the missing piece of myself I've been searching for my entire life."

Linc could tell that Harper was taking his words seriously. She was staring at him with her heart in her eyes. "I thought moving in with my dad was the icing on the shit sandwich that was my life. Instead, I reconnected with you," she said after a long moment.

"Exactly."

"And Kash . . . how he was conceived, it was awful. But I wouldn't go back and change anything, because that would mean I wouldn't have him today."

Linc nodded again.

"So what's the good that came out of Kash being kidnapped and left on that island? Because I'm having a really hard time seeing it right now."

"The bullies are leaving me alone."

Linc's head whipped around, and he saw Kash coming down the stairs. He stiffened, wondering how much the kid had overheard. If he'd heard his mom talk about his conception or not. But Kash quickly put his fears to rest.

"Sorry, Mom. I heard what you asked Linc as I was coming down." Kash walked up to his mom and snuggled into her, wrapping his arms around her and putting his head on her chest. Before too long, he'd be too tall to be able to fit in her embrace the way he did now, but as with everything, it would change, but not necessarily in a bad way.

"I realized that Ginger doesn't have the perfect life she tries to portray at school. She has a lot of pressures that I don't. I wouldn't want to be in her friend group for anything. I like being a nerd, I'm not judged for things like what kind of clothes I'm wearing, and I'm not expected to be happy all the time. I don't have to worry about dating the 'right' person or being in all the 'right' clubs.

"And like I said, the bullies aren't bothering me anymore. A lot of kids stare at me, but I don't think it's because they think I'm a freak now. It's . . . nice. Another good thing that happened is that Granddad seems really happy he's going to be able to teach me outdoors stuff. He's already planning a camping trip up north for us this summer. He even said I could bring my telescope and show him some stuff about the stars, so *that's* awesome.

"Don't be upset, Mom. I don't like seeing you so stressed. What happened wasn't fun, but it wasn't horrible either. I knew you and Linc would find me, it was just a matter of waiting."

Linc was so proud of this kid, he was almost bursting with it.

"I'm sorry that I didn't realize it wasn't you texting me right away," Harper said in a low voice.

"It's okay."

"I should've known," she insisted.

Kash pulled back and said in an exaggerated, theatrical tone, "Oh my gosh, Mom, did you become clairvoyant while I was on that island? Cool! What grade am I going to get on my next math test?"

"Smart-ass," Harper said with a small smile. "And you're going to get a hundred, of course."

Kash grinned. "Of course I am. You don't have to be able to see the future to know that. But seriously, Mom, Donny had everything all planned out. If they didn't have those videos, you guys would've had someone track my phone eventually, and it would've led straight to Donny. *Everyone* knows that phone signals can be traced. He might've been smart enough to trick people for a couple of days, but he was never going to get away with it. Besides, he said he was gonna go back to the island and get us on Tuesday. I'm not sure I believe him, but it doesn't matter now. I heard that Owen and Scott are cooperating with the police. They're singing like canaries . . . wait . . . where did that idiom come from? I need to look that up."

Linc frowned. "How do you know about what Owen and Scott are doing?" he asked. He and Harper knew, because they were keeping in close contact with the police chief about the progress with the case.

"Duh. Everyone knows. It's all over school. They're gonna get a slap on the wrist because Donny was the instigator and because they're cooperating with the investigation. Donny's in juvie, and the DA is considering charging him as an adult because of how serious everything he did was. I'm guessing he might get a few years. But it's possible he could only get a few months, since we weren't hurt, and he swears he was going back out there to get us. Even though he can't prove it.

"Anyway . . . between the phones, my robotics trip ending, and all the school videos, he was always going to get caught. Ginger and I were never going to be on that island for weeks, like he probably wanted us to think. And the whole thing was stupid anyway. He was just trying to punish Ginger, which is ridiculous.

"My point is, there was *no way* you could have known he'd do something so crazy, or that it was Donny texting. And once you realized I wasn't where I was supposed to be, you got to me twenty-four hours later." Kash studied his mother. "Stop feeling guilty, Mom. Seriously. You need to let this go so you can sleep. You don't look good."

"Gee, thanks," Harper said sarcastically.

But Kash didn't even crack a smile. "I mean it."

"It's not that easy," she said. "Linc and I were . . . well, we were having fun while you were suffering."

"The world doesn't stop when bad things happen," Kash said simply. "And you didn't know. If you and Linc were partying it up while you *knew* I was missing, that would be different. But you weren't. I love you, Mom, and if you keep feeling guilty, then *I'll* start feeling guilty. I'll stop sleeping right along with you, and probably stop eating too. And we all know I can't afford to lose any weight. I'm a growing boy, I need my nutrients. I'll sink into a depression and drop out of school and have to live with you and Linc for the rest of my life . . . playing video games all day and eventually gaining eight hundred pounds."

"Dramatic much?" Harper muttered.

"Learned it from Ginger. That girl is the biggest drama queen *ever*. But seriously, you'll stop feeling bad about what happened, right? It wasn't your fault, you got to me as soon as you could. I'm not messed up in the head over it, and Linc is right, we have to look at the good things that have happened as a result of the bad."

"I'll try."

"Let Linc help you. He makes you happy."

"He does," Harper agreed. "And I'll do my best, as long as you promise to talk to me if you ever start to get depressed about what happened."

"Deal. But I'm not going to get depressed. I'm good. Can we go soon? I'm hungry, and Zach said he was making some good old-fashioned comfort food. Tacos."

Linc chuckled. He wasn't sure when tacos became comfort food, but if that's what Kash wanted, that's what he'd get. He grabbed his SUV keys off the counter and held them out to Kash. "Want to go start the car? Pull it around?"

"*Seriously?*" Kash asked, pulling out of his mom's arms. "I can drive your SUV?"

"You can pull the car around," Linc repeated. "That's not exactly driving, but yes, you can."

"Sa-weet!" Kash exclaimed, snatching the keys out of Linc's hand.

"Jacket!" Harper called out as he jogged toward the door.

"No need! It's hot out!" Kash hollered back.

After he was gone, she rolled her eyes. "It's warmer, yes. It's not *hot*. Why are kids so reluctant to wear coats?"

"Don't know. But does it really matter? Are you okay?" he asked, wanting to see where her head was at. Kash had made some very good points, and he hoped Harper really took what her son said to heart.

"I'm better," she admitted. "I still feel guilty that we were having wild monkey sex all over this house while my kid was suffering. But Kash is right. We didn't know. And . . ." She hesitated, then licked her lips as she looked at Linc. "I have to admit that last weekend was . . . amazing."

"It was," Linc agreed.

"I love you."

"I love you too. Are you ready for today? It's going to be crazy."

"I know. But I think we all need this. Need to be around the people we love the most."

"Agreed."

"And Zach and Marit are going to tell your mom that they're married. I wouldn't miss that for the world."

Linc laughed out loud. "Mom's gonna lose her mind. But she'll be fine with it in the end, because all she really wants is for us to be happy. And about twenty-three grandchildren."

Harper giggled. "You aren't wrong."

"What do you think? Should we do my brother a solid and distract her with our own news?"

"What news is that?" Harper asked.

"That we're engaged."

She frowned. "We are? Funny, I don't remember a proposal," she sassed.

"That's what I'm talking about. I have a ring in my pocket. I'd like to ask you to marry me today, while we're surrounded by our friends and family. I've already asked Kash's permission, and he granted it."

"Wait, you did?" Harper asked.

"Uh-huh. Told him that I loved him and his mom and couldn't see living the rest of my life without you guys. Said I'd eventually like to officially adopt him, but that would be up to him, and no matter what he decided, he'd always be a son to me."

Harper's eyes filled with tears. "Linc," she whispered.

"Will you marry me, Harper? Live in this wreck of a house that will one day, hopefully, be completely renovated? Will you be my sleep aid, my confidant, my best friend? Let me love you like you deserve to be loved? Support you and Kash, share everything I have with you, and treat you like the queen you've always been?"

The tears in her eyes spilled over. "Only if you'll let me do the same to you in return."

"Yes," Linc said without hesitation. "Since you asked so nicely, I'll marry you."

Harper giggled. "That's my line," she protested.

Linc raised a brow, waiting for her to say it.

"Yes, Lincoln Young. I'll marry you."

"Thank fuck," he breathed. It wasn't as if he'd thought she would say no, but things had moved quickly between them, and Kash going missing was a huge disruption in how well things had been going, so he thought she might want to wait.

"You said something about a ring?" she asked with a smile, wiping her tears away with her shoulder.

"I did," Linc confirmed. "You want it now, or do you want to use it as a way to distract my mom from Zach and Marit's news that they went off and got married without inviting her?"

"You're a good brother," Harper said. "Fine. I'll let us be the distraction. But tell me this—is the ring big?"

"Huge."

She smiled. "Emerald cut?"

"What else? That's your favorite."

"I love you, Linc."

"Love you too. One thing, though . . . I want the whole shebang. Chad did the family thing, Zach did the secret thing, I want the wedding ceremony with all the trimmings. Bridesmaids, groomsmen, Kash as my best man, flowers, you in a beautiful white designer dress, your dad walking you down the aisle, a weeklong honeymoon somewhere warm where I can drool over you in a bikini . . . all of it. You have any objections to that?"

Linc didn't know *why* he wanted or needed that, just that he did.

"No objections," she whispered, her eyes filling with tears again.

"Good. Because I've already reserved the Samoset Resort for a year and a half from now."

Harper's eyes widened. "You did?"

"Uh-huh. It's beautiful. We can get married on the coast overlooking Rockville Harbor, have the reception there as well, so no one has to drive from one venue to another. They can put up a huge tent, so if it's raining it'll still work out. And since it's right by the Rockville Breakwater Lighthouse, our guests can walk the mile or so out to see it if they get bored. What really convinced me though was this one picture I saw on their website of a couple standing on the grounds at night, with the stars and Milky Way behind them. I thought Kash would love that."

She was still staring at him, and Linc couldn't read the look on her face.

"What? Too soon? You don't want to get married there? It's fine, I can still get the deposit back, I just thought—"

"No! It's perfect. I love that place. I just . . . I'm so happy."

"I'm glad."

"Do you think your mom will want to help me plan things?"

"I think she'd *love* that," Linc said, thrilled beyond belief. "She's dreamed about planning our weddings almost as long as she's yearned for grandkids."

"And a year and a half is perfect. Thank you, Linc."

"I'd marry you tomorrow if I could, but I want to give you a fairy-tale wedding, and in order to do that, we need time."

Harper leaned forward and pressed her lips to his. For the first time in a week, Linc felt *his* Harper in the kiss. The one before Kash's ordeal. She wasn't simply going through the motions. He hoped that meant she was well and truly starting to heal from the trauma of her child being missing.

A loud honk sounded from outside, and Linc pulled back with a laugh. "Guess Kash is ready to go, huh?" he asked.

"Sounds like it. Thank you for including him in your proposal," Harper said.

"Of course. This is as much his decision as it is yours. I realize he'll only be here for another five-ish years before he heads off to college to live his life, but since we'll be together the rest of *our* lives, I wanted him to be okay with everything."

"He loves you. Thank you for stepping up. For loving us both."

"He's a part of you. I couldn't love you and *not* love him. Now, let's get going. Since Kash mentioned them, I have a hankering for Zach's tacos as well. He does something to the meat that's amazingly good. He refuses to say what seasoning he uses though. It's so annoying."

"Little brothers usually are," Harper said with a chuckle. "Wait, should we talk about how this is going to go down? How you're going to propose?"

"I already proposed," Linc corrected her. "And you and Kash both said yes."

"You know what I mean."

"I'm going to get down on one knee, you're going to cry, my mom is going to cry, probably the girls too, since they've got those pregnancy hormones going on, and you're going to say yes. That's how it's going to go."

Harper rolled her eyes again, and Linc couldn't help but think about how much he loved that glimpse of sass. She would keep him on his toes for sure.

"I meant, *when*."

"Whenever Zach breaks the news to Mom that he's already married."

"You're hopeless. Should we tell Zach what we're planning?"

"Nope. Let him sweat it. Serves him right for not letting Mom be there."

"You're mean."

"Big brothers usually are," Linc said, riffing off her earlier words.

The horn sounded again.

"Right, let's get going before Kash wakes the dead," Linc joked. He held Harper's jacket as she shrugged it on, then kissed her once more.

He'd never get tired of touching her, of seeing the joy in her eyes when he told her that he loved her.

This woman was his everything. He'd never thought he could be as happy as he was right this moment. His future looked brighter than ever, and he was excited to live every day with Harper and Kash at his side. They made him a better man, lover, friend, brother, son. He was determined to always be there for them both. He'd make mistakes, because he was human, but together they could get through anything. That had already been proved.

He was looking forward to today. To spending time with his family and friends. To sharing the news that he and Harper were getting married. To seeing the joy on his mom's face when she realized she'd get to finally plan the big wedding she'd always wanted.

He hoped Victor would be on his best behavior, especially since he wasn't thrilled about Linc marrying his daughter. But if not, he wasn't worried. Linc had plans for that grumpy bastard too.

Nothing big. Just being the best son-in-law in the whole damn world. Loving Victor's daughter and grandson unconditionally. And supplying the man with all the craft beer he could ever want.

It would take time, but Linc hoped the man would eventually realize he was the best thing that had ever happened to Harper.

That the rift between the two families could be healed once and for all.

No matter what Victor's mood, today was a good day. A *great* day. Kash was home, safe and healthy, his sisters-in-law were pregnant, he was engaged, and to top it off, the sun was shining, warming up their little slice of Maine.

Life had a tendency to be turbulent and unpredictable, but he'd learned that with the right person at your side, you could weather any storm, and come out smiling on the other side. Cheesy, but Linc knew it to be true. He was living proof.

~

Harper realized that for the first time since she'd figured out Kash was missing, she was happy. Truly happy. She was surrounded by people who didn't judge one another for their differences. They simply enjoyed good company and lived each day as it came.

Seeing Kash interact with Ginger made her heart soar. He reminded her of how she and Linc were now. The former bully with the bullied. Not that she thought Kash would end up with Ginger, but life had a funny way of doing the unexpected.

Ginger's boyfriend was cute. He was very polite, calling everyone *sir* and *ma'am*, and getting Ginger food or drinks when he wasn't glued to her side. He held her hand and couldn't seem to stop staring at her with stars in his eyes. He was besotted, and it wasn't hard to see why. She was a gorgeous girl. And as the day went on, she loosened up, seeming to fit in with the Young family as if she'd known them for years.

Kash was having the time of his life, showing his robotics friends everything Lobster Cove had to offer, from the lobster swing to Fort Bad Assery, and even giving them a tour of the auto body shop with Walt. They also played hide-and-go-seek among the boats in the storage yard.

Her dad came over for a couple of hours, and while he hadn't exactly seemed comfortable, he also hadn't frowned at everyone, sitting like a grump in the corner. But he'd left immediately after Linc had pulled him aside to talk, and Harper worried a little about that. She guessed Linc had told him about them being engaged, and assumed that, once again, her dad wasn't happy.

Linc confirmed her guess, then reassured her, promising that her dad would come around if they just gave him time.

Beyond that, the day was stress-free. And they'd all just finished stuffing themselves with seconds of Zach's amazing tacos when it happened.

Zach cleared his throat and said, "I'd like to make an announcement."

Harper turned to catch Linc's eye. Her heart started beating faster with excitement. It was all she could do throughout the day to keep the huge secret that Linc had proposed earlier, and she'd said yes. Especially when she, Britt, and Marit had stood on the back deck watching Kash and his friends run around on the rocky beach.

"Marit and I are married. We didn't want a huge thing, so we went and did a civil ceremony. Sorry, Mom, I know you probably wanted to be there, but we just wanted it to be done. To make things official before our baby was born."

Evelyn looked confused. Then surprised. Then sad. "You got married without your family there?"

"We did," he confirmed.

Evelyn opened her mouth to say something else, but she never got the chance.

"Um . . . I hate to interrupt . . . but I think someone needs to call nine-one-one. The baby's coming."

Everyone turned to stare at Britt in shock—then every person spoke at once.

"What?"

"It's too soon!"

"Has your water broken?"

Chad was on his feet, looking absolutely terrified and panicked.

"I'm sorry! I think I've been in labor all day. I'm pretty sure my water broke when I went to the bathroom earlier, but I didn't want to be a pain in the ass. This is Kash's party, and I didn't want to do anything to mess it up," Britt said between quick breaths. She had a hand on her belly and was hunched over on the couch.

"Britt, you want me to drive you to the hospital?" Knox asked, sounding calm but urgent.

"Uh . . . I don't think there's time. I think I feel the head."

"Holy shit," Linc muttered from next to Harper.

The next few minutes were chaotic. All the adults were on their feet, doing what they could to try to make Britt more comfortable. Zach called 9-1-1 and was reassured the ambulance was on the way. Chad was at Britt's side, encouraging her to breathe like the videos they'd watched had instructed. Kash and his friends had been shooed out to the deck, but they were all standing at the windows, watching what was going on inside with huge eyes.

Marit and Evelyn were rushing around, gathering blankets and towels and trying to be useful.

On the front deck, Harper looked at Linc in shock. They'd gone outside to meet the ambulance. It would take ten minutes or so for help to reach them, and that was even going over the speed limits with lights and sirens.

"So much for our distraction," Harper said under her breath.

Linc let out a huff of laughter. "I was about ready to drop to one knee in front of you when of course my little brother had to upstage me."

Harper hugged Linc. "First babies usually take a while to come," she said. "She'll be fine."

"Of course she will. How long were you in labor with Kash?"

"Twenty-seven hours, forty-two minutes, and thirty-one seconds," Harper said.

"Holy shit! That long?"

"Yeah."

"And you were by yourself."

"Uh-huh. It sucked. I'm glad Britt won't be alone. We're all going to the hospital with her, right?"

"Of course. I'm sorry you had to go through that alone, Harp. But you aren't alone anymore. No matter if you have a splinter in your finger or something more serious, you've got a whole tribe who will gather in the hospital, annoying everyone else, anxiously waiting to see if you're all right."

She hugged him and rested her head on his shoulder as they stood there waiting, until they finally heard sirens.

"Here they come," Linc said.

"I'll go in and let Britt know," Harper said.

Linc nodded. "I'll run out to the road and flag them down." He kissed Harper hard and fast before turning and jogging across the property.

When she got inside, Harper was surprised at how tense everyone seemed. Britt was lying on the kitchen floor now, with Chad at her back, holding her up. She was panting and looked scared to death.

"It's coming," Britt said to no one in particular.

"Don't push!" Evelyn ordered.

"The ambulance is almost here," Harper informed everyone.

"Hear that? Hold on for another minute, hon, the paramedics are almost here."

"Not . . . sure . . . I . . . can," Britt said between breaths.

The next few minutes were chaos as the paramedics arrived and ordered everyone to back away from the kitchen. They huddled together in the living room instead, staring at Britt with concern as a paramedic checked the progress of the baby's arrival.

"Stretcher!" she barked at the EMT who'd come inside with her.

Before Harper knew it, Britt had been transferred to the gurney and was being wheeled out of the house. She was put into the back of the ambulance, and Chad climbed in after her. The doors shut, and now everyone stood in the driveway, staring at the back of the emergency vehicle.

It didn't leave.

Everyone held their breath.

It only took another minute or two before they all heard the sound of a very pissed-off baby screaming.

"Holy shit!" Evelyn breathed.

For the woman who very rarely said a bad word, it was a huge deal.

"The newest Lobsterite sounds angry as hell," Walt said with a chuckle.

That seemed to break the ice, and everyone chuckled.

"Does that mean Britt had her baby?" Kash asked, coming up beside Harper and putting his arm around her waist, leaning into her.

"Sure does," she told her son.

"Is it okay?"

"Not sure, but by the sound of it, I'd say probably."

Another tense few minutes went by as everyone waited for news of how Britt and the baby were doing. Then the back door of the ambulance flew open, and the EMT exited with a huge grin on his face.

"Mom and baby are doing great. Baby is just a little premature and underweight and will probably spend a few nights in the hospital, but lungs sound okay, color is normal, and so far so good!"

A huge sigh of relief went through the entire family.

Harper hugged Kash to her side, and she felt Linc relax against her other side.

"Is it a boy or girl?" Evelyn asked, taking a step forward.

Chad's head popped out of the open door, and he was grinning from ear to ear. "It's a girl!" he announced. "Apparently she wanted to be born literally *on* Lobster Cove. We've named her Carleigh Evelyn Young."

Harper looked at Linc's mom. It took a moment for the name of her first granddaughter to sink in, but when it did, her lip trembled and she burst into tears.

Zach moved to her side and took her into his arms.

"These are happy tears," she said with a shaky smile.

"We couldn't think of a better namesake than you, Mom," Chad said. "You're the glue that holds all of us crazies together, and we knew if we had a girl, her middle name would be Evelyn."

"I love you!" Evelyn said. Knox and Linc had joined their brother around their mom, and the four of them remained in a huddle as they watched Chad wave, then disappear back into the ambulance.

"See you at the hospital!" Britt called out, just before the doors shut.

"Everyone divide yourselves up," Knox ordered. "Mom, you're with me. Brad and Chuck, do you want to come to the hospital, or should we drop you off at home?"

"Hospital!" both boys said without hesitation.

Harper smiled. Apparently, a birth was way more exciting than anything they could do at home.

"They'll come with us," Linc said.

Everyone else quickly got themselves sorted. Marit's coworkers, Ginger and Alistair, and Barry and Walt all offered their congrats—and their thanks for an exciting party—before heading home.

Minutes later, Harper was in Linc's SUV, and they were headed to the hospital in a mini caravan of cars.

"This is so exciting, isn't it, Mom?" Kash asked from the back seat.

"It is, indeed," she said.

Linc had a huge smile on his face as he drove. And without looking away from the road in front of him, held out his hand to Harper. She went to grab it . . . then saw something on his finger. Looking closer, she saw it was a ring.

An engagement ring, to be exact.

She gasped.

"Since we don't need to be a distraction now, I didn't want to wait any longer to see this on your finger."

Kash leaned forward so he could see the ring too. "Cool! I like how it sparkles. You said yes, Mom, right?"

"Of course I did," she said almost absently, not able to take her gaze from the ring. It certainly did sparkle. It was at least a carat. Maybe two. And it was flanked by two princess-cut diamonds on either side. It was absolutely beautiful . . . and Harper wanted to cry.

"Go on, Mom. Put it on!" Kash encouraged.

"Is your mom literally getting engaged right now?" Chuck asked.

"I want to see!" Brad grumbled from the third-row seat.

As if in a trance, Harper took the ring off Linc's finger and slid it down her own. It fit perfectly. She held her hand out and admired the way it sparkled in the sunlight.

"Oooh, it looks good!" Kash exclaimed.

"Pretty," Chuck agreed.

"Sa-weet!" Brad chimed in enthusiastically.

Then the three boys immediately lost interest and began talking about how, if they had a million-dollar budget, they'd use diamonds to power their robots.

"I love you, Harp."

"Love you too." Then she grabbed hold of his hand and held on tight as he drove to the hospital, so they could all meet the newest member of the Young family. The ring on her finger felt strange, but it was a tangible reminder of Linc's love, which made her heart even fuller than it already was.

Life with this family would never be dull, that was for sure.

Suddenly, something she'd overheard earlier in the day popped into her head. "What about Knox?"

"What about him?" Linc asked.

"He's the only one left. Do you think he's upset about that?"

"Not in the least. He's always said he's never getting married. That he likes being single."

"I heard him tell your mom that earlier tonight, but does he really mean it? He was so excited about Carleigh being born."

Linc shrugged. "Don't know. Out of all my brothers, Knox keeps to himself the most. Don't get me wrong, he's always there when we need him, and he's done his part in helping around Lobster Cove. It's just that he's always kept his private life . . . private. Moving home hasn't changed that."

"Well, I don't like it. I want him to find someone. To be as happy as we are."

"Some people don't need partners to be happy," Linc said diplomatically.

"I never knew how happy I could be until I found you," Harper said with a shrug.

Linc looked over at her and nodded. "Yeah, me too."

"Well, I'll keep my eye out for the perfect woman for him. He needs someone special. To break through those shields of his."

"I agree. But I'm not sure setting him up on blind dates is a good idea."

"Maybe, maybe not. But I'm going to at least keep an open mind."

Linc simply smiled. "You think you'll be able to sleep tonight?" he asked. "After all the excitement?"

"As long as you're there, yes," she said firmly, believing what she was saying was true. After her talk with Kash earlier, and being around the Young family all day, the terror she'd been carrying around with her for the last week had faded significantly. She was exhausted, and she had a feeling as soon as she closed her eyes, she'd be out.

"Besides, if I have nightmares, you'll make them go away."

"Damn straight," Linc told her.

They shared another look, and the desire that had seemed to temporarily dry up due to her concern about her son flashed back with full force. She couldn't say what she wanted at the moment, not with Kash and his friends in the back seat, but she could let her fiancé know in no uncertain terms how much she wanted him.

Licking her lips, and lowering her gaze to his crotch, then back up to his face, Harper smiled.

"Fucking hell," Linc said under his breath as he squirmed in his seat.

This time when she looked down, she saw the bulge in his pants.

Satisfied that she'd made her intentions known, Harper smiled and said, "I'm thinking I know another way to make me tired."

"Count on it," Linc told her in a husky voice.

"You can let us out and go park," Kash instructed, breaking the mood.

"Got it, Bud," Linc told him.

After they'd dropped off the boys and parked, Linc turned to her. "For the record, that was mean," he said.

Harper giggled. "Have to be creative with kids around."

"I can't wait to make love to my fiancée tonight," he said, as he leaned toward her.

"Same," she agreed.

Their kiss was long, deep, and it had Harper so primed and ready, she considered jumping him right there in the parking lot. But they had a niece to meet.

Harper smiled all the way into the hospital. The excitement and joy from everyone in the waiting area was contagious, and thankfully there wasn't anyone else in there who might be disturbed by all their happiness.

Today was a good day, and she had high hopes that life would continue along the same path. There would be bumps in the road, but she and Linc, and his family, would make it through whatever life sent their way . . . together.

Epilogue

Knox stood at the periphery of his family with a smile on his face. He loved them all like crazy, wouldn't have moved back to Maine if he didn't. But there were times, especially now, when he felt like an outsider.

He didn't have any big traumas in his background, like his brothers. He'd gotten out of the Coast Guard because he realized he could make more money pursuing basically the same career as a contractor. Thankfully, he'd been able to seamlessly transition from his job in Florida to one here, doing the same thing.

He lived in town, not far from Zach and Marit, in a two-bedroom, one-bath place in a house that had been remodeled to include several apartments. He worked hard, checked in on his mom, and went home. Now he had a niece to spoil. And an almost-teenage nephew as well. Soon, his other niece or nephew would be born.

It was a lot of new beginnings for the Young family . . . and Knox felt a little like he was being left behind.

Despite that, he had no desire to date anyone, himself. To marry or start a family. He was only thirty-three. He had lots of time for that kind of thing if he changed his mind, but right now, he enjoyed living a bachelor's life. TV, microwave dinners, and doing what he wanted, when he wanted, without having to check in with anyone. He made good money he didn't have to share and was investing like crazy, so he could one day buy his own waterfront home.

He had no time for a woman in his life.

When his phone rang after he'd been at the hospital for a couple of hours, and after he'd peeked in on Carleigh, his new niece, through the window of the nursery, where he'd oohed and aahed and said how beautiful she was—even though she was a tiny, wrinkled raisin at the moment and couldn't possibly be considered beautiful, or even pretty—he answered. Wondering vaguely who it could be, since pretty much everyone who called him regularly was with him at the moment.

"Young here."

"Knox?"

He frowned. Knox had no idea who was on the other end of the line. "Who is this?"

There was silence for a beat, then the woman began to speak quickly. "I'm so sorry to have called you like this. I didn't know who else to call. It's Jordan."

Knox racked his brain to try to place the name, without luck. "Jordan who?"

This time when the woman spoke, she sounded embarrassed, and for some reason knowing he'd made her feel that way, even inadvertently, didn't sit well with Knox.

"Jordan Ward. I work with you."

It hit Knox then who she was. She worked in the same building as he did. Was one of the admins in his department. He was employed as a contractor for the government in maritime inspection and port/dock security and inspection. Knox wasn't in the office much, but he still had contact with the admins for things like getting his assignments, scheduling, paperwork, and accounting. She was a fairly recent hire, within the last six months, if he remembered correctly.

Aware of the awkward silence, Knox said, "Of course. What's up?"

"Um . . . are you busy?"

"No." The lie came out without him even thinking about it. He was curious as to why this woman was calling him when he couldn't remember having any kind of meaningful interaction with her in the past. "What's up?"

"I need help. I've called everyone I know, which admittedly isn't a ton of people, but I can't get a hold of anyone. I didn't know who else to try, and I have your number because I put all the contractors' numbers in my phone so if any of you needed anything, your names would come up on my caller ID, and I'd be sure to answer because I'd know it wasn't a spam call or anything. I wouldn't have called but—"

"Breathe, Jordan. It's fine. What's wrong?" Knox interrupted.

"I hit a deer."

"What?"

"With my car. I hit a deer!"

Knox could hear her crying, and he hated the sound. He might not know this woman, but the distress in her voice was clear as day. He was on the move before he even knew where she was or if she was injured. Motioning to Linc that he was headed out, Knox headed for the door.

His brother lifted a brow, asking if everything was all right. Knox loved how he and his brothers could communicate nonverbally.

He nodded and gestured to the phone still up to his ear. Linc nodded, and, satisfied his brother would let everyone know he'd left, Knox turned his concentration back to the woman on the other end of the phone.

"Are you okay?" he asked, as he walked through the parking lot toward his truck.

"Yeah. But the deer isn't!"

"What?"

"The deer! It's hurt bad."

"It didn't run off?"

"No. It's lying just off the road and . . ." Her voice hitched. "It's bleeding. It's awful, and I don't know what to do!"

"Tell me where you are. I'm on my way."

"Really?"

She sounded surprised, which was weird, considering she'd called him for help. Did she actually think he was going to say he *wouldn't* help her?

"How long will it take for you to get here? I don't know what to do. It's breathing funny."

"Get back in your car, Jordan. It could hurt you, especially since it's probably in pain," Knox ordered.

"I feel awful! I tried to stop but it ran right in front of me. I think it might have babies too." She was full-on sobbing now.

Everything she said made Knox a little more alarmed. "Seriously, get back in your car *now*. A mama deer with babies nearby, and hurt, is unpredictable."

"But I want to do something to help it!"

The woman was exasperating. But Knox couldn't deny her tender heart was a welcome change from dealing with the assholes he usually came into contact with while doing his job. People who lied their asses off trying to get away with whatever illegal cargo they were hauling, or who came up with excuse after excuse for why their boats weren't legal in one way or another.

"What you can do is, get. In. Your. Car."

"Are you going to shoot it?" she whispered.

Knox sighed. "I don't know. Maybe. I'm gonna hang up and make some calls while I'm on my way to you. We need to contact a game warden, or at least the local sheriff's department. Can you tell me where you are?"

He heard a car door shutting, which was a huge relief. She didn't have an exact address, but she gave him directions to her general location.

"I'm probably about fifteen minutes away. If you need me, or if anything in your situation changes, call me back. Okay?"

"Okay. Thanks a lot, Knox. I know this is a pain and you were probably busy. I didn't know who else to try, and I didn't want to just leave the poor deer out here. I mean, I know I could've called nine-one-one, but I didn't want to bother them since it's not a *people* emergency . . . if you know what I mean."

Yeah, more proof that this woman was different from most. Knox was intrigued.

"How's your car?"

"Um . . . smooshed?"

"Are you hurt in any way?"

"No."

"Are you sure?" he asked.

"I'm sure. I had my seat belt on."

It had been a long time since Knox had met anyone who was more concerned about an animal than they were about their car or themselves.

"Okay, hang tight. Stay in your vehicle. I'll be there as soon as I can."

"Drive safe, don't need you hitting a deer too," Jordan said.

"See you soon."

"See you soon," she echoed.

As he sped toward Jordan's location, Knox tried to tell himself that he'd be driving as fast as he was right now no matter *who'd* called him. But he couldn't deny that he was moving with a bit more urgency than he might otherwise.

He wasn't interested in her as anything other than a coworker, but he *was* mildly curious about the woman. Probably because she kept to herself. Because he knew next to nothing about her. Seemed to be kind of a loner, like he was.

So that she'd called him for help? He instinctively knew it was a big deal. He had a feeling she didn't ask for much from *anyone*. She did her job, did it well, and didn't go out of her way to interact overmuch with the guardsmen she came into contact with, or the contractors like him.

She didn't bring any attention to herself, as if she was happy with fading into the woodwork.

He guessed Jordan was younger than him by just a few years, yet based on their call, she seemed . . . naïve. Granted, he hadn't had a ton of contact with her. He tried to pay careful attention to those around him, but he didn't beat himself up for not recognizing her voice when she called. They simply hadn't talked often enough.

But now she had his attention . . .

Maybe he was bored. Maybe seeing all his brothers suddenly so happy in their new relationships was getting to him, and he needed a distraction. He wasn't sure. But Knox could admit that part of him was pleased she saw him as someone she could turn to in a crisis, even if, at the same time, he understood she didn't know who else to call.

He was flattered she'd thought of him at all, considering their scant exchanges at work.

No, he wasn't looking for a relationship . . . but Jordan Ward intrigued him. Anyone who seemed more worried about an injured deer than their own personal property was someone he wanted to know. And it looked like he was going to get that chance.

RETURN TO ALPHA COVE IN

THE GUARDSMAN

From *New York Times* bestselling author Susan Stoker comes a pulse-pounding novel of romantic suspense, where a brooding Coast Guard vet offers the only safe harbor for a woman hunted by her past.

In this intensely emotional finale to the Alpha Cove series, a guarded young woman and a Coast Guard vet must defend against her deadly past while opening themselves up to the possibility of love.

Jordan Ward is cursed. Raised in a nightmare, now living on the run, she's not known peace since testifying at her violent brother's murder trial a decade earlier, unable to settle with his vow of revenge haunting her every step. She doesn't expect her stay in Rockville, Maine, to last any longer than all her other temporary homes . . . or be any less lonely . . . until a reluctant call for help to a man she barely knows changes her life.

Knox Young is blessed. The former Coast Guardsman has three of the best brothers anyone could ask for, and they only get closer after returning to their beloved home in coastal Maine to help their widowed mother. In fact, the family has expanded, with all of his brothers finding their perfect partners. Knox is thrilled for them all, but he has no plans to give up his freedom, *ever* . . . until a shy coworker catches his attention and changes his fate.

When he learns Jordan's secret, Knox's protective instincts surge, then swell when her brother's threats spill outside his prison walls. But Jordan is no damsel in distress, and in the end, it may be Knox who's saved . . . in every way possible.

CONNECT WITH SUSAN ONLINE

SUSAN'S FACEBOOK PROFILE AND PAGE

www.facebook.com/authorsstoker

www.facebook.com/authorsusanstoker

FOLLOW SUSAN ON INSTAGRAM

www.instagram.com/authorsusanstoker

FOLLOW SUSAN ON TIKTOK

www.tiktok.com/@susanstokerauthor

FIND SUSAN'S BOOKS ON GOODREADS

www.goodreads.com/susanstoker

EMAIL

susan@stokeraces.com

WEBSITE

www.stokeraces.com

ABOUT THE AUTHOR

Photo © 2015 A&C Photography

Susan Stoker is a *New York Times*, *USA Today*, and *Wall Street Journal* bestselling author whose series include Badge of Honor: Texas Heroes, SEAL of Protection, and Delta Force Heroes. Married to a retired Army noncommissioned officer, Stoker has lived all over the country—from Missouri and California to Colorado, Texas, and Tennessee—and currently lives in the beautiful wilds of Maine. A true believer in happily ever after, Stoker enjoys writing novels in which romance turns to love. To learn more about the author and her work, visit her website, www.stokeraces.com, or find her on Facebook at www.facebook.com/authorsusanstoker.